the
Daughter *of*
Union County

ALSO BY FRANCINE THOMAS HOWARD

Page from a Tennessee Journal

Paris Noire

The Sisterhood Hyphen

the
Daughter *of*
Union County

A Novel

FRANCINE
THOMAS HOWARD

LAKE UNION
PUBLISHING

Text copyright © 2016 Francine K. Howard

Published by Lake Union Publishing, Seattle

www.apub.com

Amazon, the Amazon logo, and Lake Union Publishing are trademarks of Amazon.com, Inc., or its affiliates.

ISBN-13: 9781503937321
ISBN-10: 1503937321

Cover design by Laura Klynstra

Printed in the United States of America

This one's for you, Fred.

AUTHOR'S NOTE

The Daughter of Union County is a work of fiction. While it contains some real-life historical facts and events, some liberties were taken for creative effect, some of the story comes from my family's oral history and anecdotal information passed down over the decades, and some facts have been replaced by elements of my creation. I have changed incidents to better fit what and where the fictional characters were leading me.

CHAPTER ONE

Even his beloved books couldn't hold him. Henry walked out of his library again and started across the great hall toward the kitchen and into the back room where Salome lay. If only the woman had cried out, given him some sign in all these ten hours since midnight that she and their babe still lived. Instead, all he could hear were the scurrying feet of servants as they moved in and out of the kitchen, opened and shut doors and cabinets, pushed open the door to the little room behind the kitchen, or rushed onto the back porch to pump fresh buckets of water. Through it all, there was no sound from her—from Salome. His Salome. When his nerves got the better of him, like now, Henry ventured as far as the kitchen door leading off the great hall, only to have Mattie Lou or one of the other colored servants shoot him a horrified look and aim her eyes toward his library. Birthing babies was women's work. Not even the farm owner was allowed in the birthing room. Mattie Lou was an adequate midwife who'd been on his plantation since the days of slavery—but this was no ordinary colored birthing. This was Salome.

Why hadn't his mistress screamed out her pain? Lady Bertha certainly had. Loud, keening wails. Shouts beseeching God. "Not again! Lord, spare me this disgrace!"

Henry approached the closed kitchen door and heard Mattie Lou shout out a series of commands. He touched his chest, shook his head, and padded across the thick-tufted carpet, turning back toward his walnut-paneled library. His books always calmed him. This couldn't be happening again. Not two dead babies within a month. He wasn't much of a praying man. What religion the Hardins felt, they'd kept to themselves these three hundred years. They'd learned the hard way. He kept his religion secret, along with his gold crucifix with the family crest affixed to the back. Henry strode across his ivory-and-gold carpet and moved beyond the library fireplace—flanked on both sides with floor-to-ceiling shelves housing his five-hundred-plus book collection—over to the far wall. He grabbed the ladder always parked there and climbed the two rungs to reach the third shelf. His fingers fell on the family Bible, bound in red tooled leather that still looked as it must have forty-four years ago in 1835 when his mother had presented it to him at his own christening. His hand brushed against the volume titled *Brook's Peerage*. There, next to it. He fumbled for the ledger—a family heirloom—*American Descendants of the Dukes of Norwalk* . He grabbed both books and climbed down the ladder, the family treasure in one hand. His fingers slid inside the front cover of the heirloom. The velvet pouch with its gold-thread stitching still felt firm, his crucifix inside.

"Lord Hardin, suh," Celeste, Bertha's personal maid, called out from the library entryway. Henry opened a drawer in his walnut-inlaid desk and slipped the books inside.

"Salome?" He heard his voice rise. "Is she . . . is the . . . ?"

"No, suh, this ain't 'bout no birthin', this 'bout Lady Hardin." Celeste, the white apron covering her dark blue uniform, looked askew. One end of her apron strings flapped longer than the other. "I done tried and tried, Lord Hardin, suh, but I just can't get her out of bed this mornin'."

Henry shook his head. Celeste never had been very bright. In fact, he would have consigned the middle-aged woman to light kitchen duties if he hadn't inherited her. She had been his wife's mammy since Bertha was born. Celeste had naturally accompanied her mistress when Bertha, the belle of Union County, married Henry, the descendant of British aristocracy, at the highlight of the 1874 Union County social season. Then, Celeste had celebrated along with Bertha's entire family, but not now.

"Suh? What's I to do?"

"Do?" He'd already forgotten Celeste stood before him with urgency stamped across her face. In fact, he'd all but forgotten Bertha's malaise in his worry over Salome. "Stand aside, I'll see to my wife. You check on Mattie Lou. The birthing. Let me know if there . . . are any problems."

He pushed the servant toward the kitchen as he turned up the grand staircase, the centerpiece of the great hall. Yes, the staircase was much too big for his house, and every time he climbed its broad steps, he berated himself. He'd fallen into his older brother's trap. No proper Hardin would ever own a house that was not grand—including the staircase. Right before his marriage to Bertha, he'd installed the silly thing. Oh, his new in-laws had oohed and aahed, declaring his the finest house in all Arkansas. Even then, his older brother, James, inheritor of the family's imaginary title, had looked down on Henry's efforts.

"Bertha, I want you up and dressed each and every day," he called out even before he pushed open the mahogany door to their bedroom. He'd think about his nearly bankrupt brother another time.

"Uhh." Caught between a groan and a *no*, Bertha's muffled response escaped from beneath the sheet she held over her face.

Henry sat on the bed beside her. "Darling, I know this is difficult, but I believe you will only heal if you go about your daily duties. Doc Henderson says you're fit enough."

The white sheet slammed down on the bed, revealing a face and arms even paler than the bed linens. "Fit enough? Fit enough?" Bertha's voice rose into its familiar screech. "I'm the disgrace of Union County!" The sound climbed higher. "Four babies? I've lost four babies." She covered her face with the sheet again. "How can you stand to look at me? I've failed you. I've failed the Hardin dynasty!"

He didn't love Bertha. Never really had. Oh, he wanted to bed her all right, and that had been the why of his marriage proposal. After the first two weeks of unrelenting marital lovemaking, during which she simply lay there, he discovered that nothing about his wife, other than her shapely body, appealed to him. The woman had no mind for knowledge. John Donne and Don Quixote might have been the same man in her unlearned head. Still, she was not a bad woman. Not a shrewish bone in her body. Some of her looks remained, though at twenty-four, the blushed cheeks that had given her ghostly white skin some much-needed color had faded. And after four miscarriages, her belly had turned to the feel of clabber pudding. Still, she was his wife, Lady Bertha Hardin.

"Sugar," he cajoled, using her native Arkansas tongue, though the Hardins looked down on adopting too many American colloquialisms, "when the time is right, God will bless us with a child." He didn't believe his own words.

For the longest time, he'd wondered if, somehow, his wife's failure to deliver a baby had been his fault. Bertha had never been able to carry beyond three months. But now there was Salome heavy with his Hardin child—albeit a black one—to the birthing bed.

Bertha squirmed against the bedpost, fiddling with the sheet. "Henry, promise me, you won't say nothin' to nobody 'bout this last baby?"

Henry took her hand as he fought to keep a slight trace of annoyance off his face. Why did Arkansas women end statements with a question mark? He'd never heard such a speech pattern back in his native Maryland.

"Honey"—he tried to mimic Bertha's father—"nobody knows anything about the last child we lost or . . . the one before that . . . or the one . . ."

She pulled the sheet to her chest. "Bless you, Henry. I couldn't bear it if eve'body in Union County knew I was as barren as an ole mule?"

He stroked her hand. "Sugar lump, we didn't even tell your mother about the last two babies. We'll let them know when we finally have our—"

"Lord Hardin, suh," Tessie, Mattie Lou's thirteen-year-old assistant-in-training, puffed as her running feet slid to a stop just outside the open bedroom door. She tapped on the doorjamb as she spoke. "I reckon"—she shot a glance toward Bertha—"Cook wantin' yo' say-so . . ." The girl's eyes darted between Henry and his wife.

Henry withdrew his hand from Bertha's. She grabbed his wrist. He turned to gaze into her hardened face. The pouty lips she'd puckered for him at eighteen now looked sunken into her mouth. The vivid eyes resembled blue ice.

"Get Celeste in here," she said. "I'll go down and take care of Cook myself." Not a question mark to be heard in Bertha's command.

That he had a colored wench as a mistress was certainly no surprise to his wife. Henry was no different from any other man of means in Union County. They all had colored mistresses. Many had more than one. Henry sighed the universal signal among their class—the sound of feigned understanding of his wife's discomfort. It was expected behavior from a gentleman dealing with his mate under such a circumstance. The woman was not required to condone the situation, but she knew she must signal back her silent acquiescence with a turn of the head, a tightening of the mouth, or a stare into space. Henry broke free of Bertha's grip and stood. "I'll send Celeste right up. Darling, I'm glad you're feeling better." He followed Tessie downstairs.

CHAPTER TWO

Henry waited while Tessie, her blue uniform too large on her thin frame, led the way into the kitchen. Mattie Lou, standing with her arms holding a basin filled with bloodied rags, blocked Henry's path toward the still-closed servants' room off the kitchen. He stared at the midwife.

The woman shook her head. "Lord Hardin, suh, it's liken she don't wanna push it out. She holdin' back. Liken she don't wanna——" Mattie Lou stopped short, her eyes widening, looking for all the world as though she'd just remembered to whom she was speaking.

"Let me in there. Let me see her." Henry approached the midwife.

Mattie Lou held up a beefy hand. "It ain't fittin', suh. I can't rightly say if she's gonna make it or not. Look to me like she's hopin' to die."

Henry shoved the stout woman aside. "Nonsense." He pushed open the door.

"Oh, Jesus, you ain't sposed to be in . . . I mean to say, Lord Hardin, this here's the birthin' room."

The gangly but strong Georgia, one of his field hands now doubling as a midwife's assistant, stood over the figure in the bed, a paper fan in her hand. Henry glanced at her and with a nod motioned her out.

"Lord Hardin, suh." Mattie Lou loomed behind him, her body casting a shadow even in the shade-drawn room. "She can't hold on much longer." Mattie Lou lowered her voice. "We gonna know one way t'other iffen . . . iffen they both make it or no."

"Out!" Henry shouted. "And close the door behind you."

Georgia dropped the fan on the birthing bed and scurried past him while Mattie Lou lumbered backward. He stared at the sheet-covered figure.

"Salome," he whispered.

"Uhh." She spoke between gritted teeth, her eyes closed, her face aimed toward the ceiling.

Henry peered down at her. He scanned her head and neck, the only parts not covered by the sweat-drenched sheet. Her skin was swamped in perspiration. Salome fluttered her eyelids open. Almost as quickly, she clamped them shut again. He heard only a slight groan, but the grimace on her face signaled great pain. She turned her head toward the wall, away from him.

He stared down at her, his eyes taking in her form. No, she couldn't die, not before birthing his babe. Not before giving him living proof of his manhood for all of Union County to see. He sat on the edge of the bed. Henry had never before come this close to fatherhood. He fumbled for Salome's hand.

"You hold on to me. We—you and me—we're going to get this baby out of you."

She turned to him, her mouth opening as another wave of pain ratcheted through her body. "Can't . . ." She shook her head.

"You can." He pushed the sheet aside, most of her body still covered by the birthing gown.

A fresh pain sent her slender frame rocketing across the bed. She bent her knees. "It . . . ain't . . . right." Salome grunted between each low-spoken word. "Me . . . havin' . . . a . . . baby . . . like . . ." The last sounds drowned in her throat.

Henry pulled the end of the linen off Salome's body and stuffed it behind her back. He lifted her head and shoulders and settled them on the bunched-up sheet. His hands pressed into her cheeks as he turned her to him. "Now you look at me, Salome. You are not your mama. Giving birth will not make you lose your mind." A wave of heat much too early for mid-April washed over him. "Didn't I promise I'd take care of you and the child—forever?"

How could she think he'd do anything else? He reached for a clean birthing cloth and wiped the sheen from Salome's forehead. She was the most unusual-looking girl-woman he'd ever seen. Salome was just eighteen, but her face carried the picture of timelessness. She was the perfect complement of her blue-eyed Irish father and her half-black/half-Creek mother, with skin the color of burnished bronze, slightly upturned, amber-colored eyes, and those kissable lips. He swiped the cloth down her neck and across the top of her chest. Salome, her mouth held tight and taking in not one breath, nearly writhed off the bed. Mattie Lou had been right. The mother-to-be was refusing to allow the child to leave her body alive.

"Salome, listen to me." He squeezed her cheeks. "This is 1879. The days of slavery are gone these past fourteen years. What happened to your mother . . . such a thing . . ." He loosened his grip and stroked his hands down her face as she grunted. "It's not likely . . ."

Salome's eyes, signaling her doubt, drilled into him. Henry cleared his throat. Life had changed so much under Yankee rule. The damn Northerners had even given coloreds the vote. Thank God Reconstruction had been over these two years.

"Yes, my overseer was your father, but I never, ever, gave him permission to take a house slave as his woman. Never mind beating her when she fought back." He nodded his head. "You know I had that man fired as soon as I learned the truth." He'd done more than that to Tyrone O'Brien for trifling with a comely house slave Henry had also set his eye on.

Salome's breathing came faster, almost in a pant, as she escaped his grasp. "But . . . he . . . that man . . . done . . . that . . . to her . . . most of three . . . months . . . before you . . . aahh." The sound rushed out even louder. Her head lolled side to side as she groaned. "Ain't . . . right . . . a . . . white . . . child . . . put . . . in . . . a . . . black . . . woman . . . against her . . . wantin' it . . . oh, Jesus!"

Henry reached for her hand. He laid his other hand on top of her birthing dress. He pulled the dress up to her waist and splayed his fingers across her mounded belly. He leaned toward her and pushed down. Salome screamed.

Mattie Lou burst into the room, her eyes taking inventory. She advanced on the bed. "Keep on doin' what you doin', suh. Get her to hollerin' and that baby bound to pop out."

Salome's eyes opened wide. "No. I . . . thinks . . . I wants it . . . to . . . di . . . uhhhnnh." The scream poured into the kitchen.

Henry slapped Salome's hand on her belly. With both of his hands over hers, he stroked down hard on her stomach. "You are going to give me this child. You do your dying after that." He forced her knees apart.

"Oh Je . . . sus!" The grunts came regularly now.

Mattie Lou bent over Salome, the woman's hands between the girl's legs. "I got me a head," she shouted.

"N . . . n . . ." Salome rolled her head back and forth against the makeshift pillow.

The thought flitted through Henry's head a split second before the back of his right hand plowed into Salome's cheek. Too late. He watched her nose, with its straight lines and provocatively flared nostrils, angle off kilter. He hoped he hadn't marred her beauty permanently, but the act had to be done.

Salome's cry came through her mouth, but it started elsewhere—someplace deep inside. The cry sent a chill through Henry's body, and judging by the looks of horror on Georgia's and Tessie's faces, the two servants felt the same.

"I gots me a baby!" Mattie Lou's hands busied themselves just out of Henry's line of sight.

He held his breath. Where was the child's cry? Weren't newborns supposed to . . . ?

"Waaaaaaaaah."

Even before Mattie Lou suspended the infant by the ankles, the baby's high-pitched tones bounced off the bedroom walls.

"Have mercy, suh, if this here ain't a little girl." Mattie Lou swung the child toward Henry.

He reached for the infant.

"No, suh, let me clean her up first." Mattie Lou looked at Salome, tears trickling down the new mother's face. "And the mama, too." She turned to Henry. "Lord Hardin, suh, would you care to step outta the room?"

"No. I'm stepping nowhere." He bent over Salome and patted the side of her face. "I had to get that baby out of you."

She grunted as she moved away from his touch. "I know . . . this ain't like the days of slavery, but, even so, this child belongs to you."

Women. Made no difference if they were colored or white, they delighted in befuddling a man. Henry looked down at his suddenly stubborn mistress. She'd been a real man-pleaser ever since he first took her to bed last year. Henry had taught Salome the moves that especially delighted him. Unlike Bertha, the girl complied without too much of a fuss. He never had to strike her. She offered no complaints, and he repaid her well, taking her out of her washhouse duties and putting her on the main floor cleaning detail with no more than six hours a day of work. When he discovered the seventeen-year-old pregnant with his child—and that pregnancy had moved into the fifth month without a problem—Henry had installed her in the room right behind the kitchen. She'd said nothing then about not wanting the child. He'd kept his own pride to himself, of course. After all, he was forty-three going on forty-four with nothing to show the world that his seed could produce a living child. As her belly grew, Henry outdid himself for his child mistress. He'd even given her four dollars a month. But now that she had done her duty and delivered him a living infant—despite herself—he wondered if he had been too generous. Too kind.

Tessie had the first look as she took the birthing remains from Mattie Lou. Georgia, peering over the midwife's shoulder, sneaked the second peek.

"Hand me that there warmin' cloth." Mattie Lou spoke to no one in particular. Georgia complied while Tessie stood transfixed. "Get on outta here, girl," Mattie finally called out, though Tessie showed no signs of moving. Mattie glanced up at Henry.

The midwife pasted a smile on her round face that clearly didn't belong there. "Lord Hardin, suh, best if you step on out to the kitchen. Salome here gots to put this chile to the tit."

"No!" Salome's voice boomed throughout the room, her eyes showing panic. "I ain't havin' nothin' to do with that."

"But . . ." Mattie Lou looked dumbfounded.

"My ma ain't had nothin' to do with me 'cause of how I come into this world, and I don't wants nothin' to do with this one neither," Salome muttered.

So that was it. Why hadn't she told him her complaints when Mattie Lou finally confirmed a baby was on the way? Was that the reason for all this female consternation? He had done his best by his young mistress and her mother, even though Eyota had been useless for any work after the Tyrone O'Brien affair. Salome's mother could sit eight to ten hours as still as any tree trunk on Henry's property. In all the eighteen years since Salome's birth, her half-breed mother refused to utter even one word. Henry never wondered at the why of Eyota's refusal to succor Salome or even recognize the Irishman's child. His former overseer had simply tortured the slave into losing her mind. But why would Salome harbor those same feelings against a child of his? Henry Hardin was no raping white man. He'd never taken Salome against her wishes.

"Hand me the girl." Henry stood. He'd waited these five minutes to get his first look at his daughter.

Mattie Lou, Georgia, and even Tessie shook their heads in unison.

"Naw, suh," Mattie Lou declared. "Uhh, I'm aimin' to say . . . to say . . ." Her eyes grew wide.

"No more twaddle." Henry walked to Mattie Lou and held out his arms.

The midwife stood there like stone. Henry laid his hand on the blue coverlet he'd ordered his weavers to make just for this child. Mattie Lou stepped back with the babe still in her arms.

She shook her head. "Suh, it's just that . . . that, the chile needs her mama's tit befo' . . . befo' . . ." Mattie Lou's face sank into a frown.

"Show me how to hold the baby," Henry commanded. "Salome will feed her, but not right now. Now give her to me."

Salome's sniffles floated off the bed as she rolled to her side. "I can't. I just can't feed her."

"Mattie Lou!" Women were bedeviling him again. He had to tolerate Bertha, but these others—these colored servants—never. "Hand over that baby."

"It's just that, suh, may be best if her ma first taken a look at her."

"Ooh?" The cry escaped from Salome as she rolled on her back, her face grimacing with each movement. "Is somethin' wrong with her?" She turned to Henry as she pushed up on her elbows.

Henry touched his chest where his crucifix would hang if he dared wear it. He'd wanted fatherhood so long he'd never even considered his wish could be granted with a deformed child. Had his child been born with a hunchback or one leg shorter than the other? Perhaps water on the brain? Henry pulled the warming wrap from his daughter's face and looked at the wriggling infant.

Mattie Lou stood there shaking her head. Now Salome looked worried. She rolled to her side and tried to slip her legs off the bed. Georgia held her back. The midwife turned to Salome.

"It ain't never good when they comes out this co . . . like this." Mattie Lou kept her eyes away from Henry.

Henry looked at the women. Why all this commotion? Now Salome appeared worried. He turned back to the screaming baby, who looked perfectly proportioned.

The baby girl's eyes opened and shut in a frenzy of flailing arms and legs. Her eyes—they were blue like his own and her immigrant grandfather's, Tyrone O'Brien. The baby's squalling brought out the redness in her skin, but underneath, Henry could see this child was as white as he.

Mattie Lou dared brush past him, still clutching the newborn, and bent down to the new mother. "Don't you fret none, Salome, honey. Most young'uns what comes out lookin' like this, they turns darker when they gets a little older." She laid the child on the cot next to Salome.

"Her hair! Her hair!" Salome's face reflected panic. "Seem to me like it's yella, but is it gonna turn nappy?" She pleaded with Mattie Lou. "Not the wrong color eyes and straight hair, too. Please, Lawd."

Hair? What was Salome going on about? She had tried her mightiest to deliver him a dead baby. Now she looked the picture of the concerned mother. "What of the baby's hair?" Henry peered at the light-colored fuzz atop his daughter's head. He turned back to Salome. Her own hair, caught between light chestnut and oak brown, swung in a long braid down her back. Henry loved the way Salome's hair waved between crinkles and curls, allowing his fingers to unravel each strand.

"Peek behind the ear," Georgia said, interrupting his reverie. "True color come out there."

Mattie Lou grunted as she flicked the baby's ear. "Un-uh," she groaned. "Same color."

Henry caught the midwife's glance at Salome. Mattie Lou looked as though the Devil had run a footrace with her and won. What was all this talk about hair and color?

"Does she have all her fingers and toes?" he demanded of the barely competent Mattie Lou.

"Ain't a thing wrong with this here girl's body, Lord Hardin, suh. It's jest that she . . . she . . . well, suh, she just don't look like no colored girl ought."

"What are you babbling about?" Henry's day had been much too long. His patience was in frazzles, but that wasn't it. Maybe Mattie Lou, at close to forty, was too old for this job. "Will this child be able to walk and talk like a normal person?" His voice was gruff. He knew it had been a mistake to end slavery and allow coloreds to say their mind with too few consequences.

Mattie Lou held out the infant to Salome. The new mother slid down in the bed, her arms clamped across the covering sheet.

"Mattie Lou." Henry turned his glare on the midwife and away from the cantankerous Salome. "Out with it, woman. Tell me what you're stuttering on about, or I'll dismiss you from the farm and make sure no other landowner in these parts hires you."

"No, Lord Hardin, suh. Ain't no need to be doin' all that." She turned from Henry to Salome. "I ain't keepin' nothin' from . . . that is to say . . ." She plucked the baby from the bed and held out the bundle to him.

Henry gathered the child into his arms. He struggled to keep the squirming blanket from slipping to the floor. This definitely was not like carrying a five-pound sack of rice. "Well?" He couldn't keep his eyes off his baby. "What is the problem?"

"She don't look colored 'nough." Salome raised her voice though she kept her eyes on the child. "A white-lookin' colored girl ain't gonna live no life 'cept one of misery."

Henry stared at the babe. "How white-looking will this child be?"

"Powerful, suh." The midwife ran a finger over the baby's hair. "It might curl up a mite by and by, but it ain't never gonna be real nappy." Mattie Lou looked as though she'd thrown the first fistful of dirt into a grave.

"Good." Without a glance at the baby's mother, Henry headed for the door leading into the kitchen, his daughter in his arms.

CHAPTER THREE

The baby quieted as Henry climbed the grand staircase to the second floor.

"Not so tight with those corset straps, Celeste, or I'll sure as spitfire put a belt to you. I'm just goin' to the kitchen, not hostin' a tea party." Bertha's voice, streaming from the bedroom, sounded close to her pre-malaise rancor.

Henry stood just outside the open door. "Celeste, let your mistress be. You get yourself on downstairs."

"Let me be?" Bertha barged through the doorway, the harried-looking Celeste right behind her. "It was you wantin' me to get out of be . . . What's that you carryin'?"

"Celeste, you better mind." Henry jerked his head toward the back stairs the servants were ordered to use. "Get on to your other duties."

The woman bobbed her bandana-tied head, scooted past Bertha, and headed toward the back hall.

"Well, I never?" Bertha, clad only in her corset, chemise, cotton stockings, and bloomers, slipped her hands to her hips. "First you tell me to get up and get my clothes on. Get over my melancholy over losin' my chile, then you tell . . ." Her lips stopped midquiver.

The baby wriggled and let out a cry. Henry turned to the bundle in his arms.

"Henry?" The sound struggled out of Bertha's mouth. "That's not . . . that can't be . . ." Her face flushed plum. "What in the name of God in Heaven are you doin' bringin' that . . . that thing upstairs . . . here . . . to me?" She recoiled as though he held a water moccasin.

"Get back inside and get your dress on." Henry pushed his shoulder against his wife. "You look a disgrace standing out here in the hallway in nothing but your underthings."

"Uh?" Bertha's chin wobbled as she retreated into the wallpapered bedroom. She reached for the yellow daydress Celeste had laid across the velvet-tufted chair. "Henry? Henry!" Bertha threw the garment to the floor, then kicked at it. "What you doin' bringin' . . . ?" Her raised finger, pointing at him, matched the upturn in her voice. "Get that thing outta here."

The baby's cries began in earnest.

Henry juggled the infant over to his left arm. With his free hand, he pushed Bertha backward and onto their four-poster bed. "I'll not have hysterics out of you. This, Bertha, is what we're going to do." The babe's cries grew louder. Henry bounced her on his arm. "I'm told she's hungry. I'll take care of that directly, but first you and I are coming to an understanding."

Bertha looked caught between anger and surprise, with anger eventually triumphing as she sat on the goose-down mattress. Henry was a Hardin and trained in the ways of an English aristocrat, though few of his family had set foot on English soil in over two centuries. Still, he had every right to expect his wife to reciprocate his lordly manners. But here she was, behaving like some dirt-underneath-the-fingernails frontierswoman. No wonder. Look at her rough-mannered, Alabama-born, white-trash grandfather, who lucked on a decent piece of timberland in Arkansas, put together a ramshackle sawmill, and made a fortune, only to lose it in the War Between the States. But for all her family's prewar income, wealth could not buy polish. Beneath Bertha's very thin layer of schooling and tea party manners, she remained as ignorant as any American washerwoman. He'd have to practice more patience with Bertha, but not today.

He caught her watching him and stared back. She broke their mutual glare first.

"Can't you get that . . . thing to shut up?" She spoke low. "If it's understandin' you want me to do, then you get Celeste back up here. I want to get downstairs, and I'll understand real good then." She looked up at him. "Runnin' this here household is my business." Her eyes sparked blue steel.

Henry took in a deep breath. In the five years of their marriage, he'd troubled Bertha little, recognizing the simplicity of her mind, and fortunately, she'd never given him cause to chastise her. Not before now.

"There's no need for Celeste. Not now." He stepped over the dress. "Bertha, if you listen carefully, I believe you will see the sense of my plan."

"Henry, I wish you'd quit treatin' me like a child?" She pushed off the bed.

Henry slammed his free hand into her chest and shoved her backward. She sank onto the mattress with a grunt. He laid his knee across the bed and leaned into her. "Bertha . . ." Best if he chose his words with care. "I have no intention of remaining childless. Now, I pray fervently that you will, one day, give me a living baby. But until that day arrives, this girl will do just fine."

His wife's red-brown hair, still done up in curling rags applied at least a day ago, swung in the air as she shook her head. "Henry, what is it you're talkin' about?"

He pulled the blanket from his squalling daughter. "Look at her."

Bertha turned her face to the white linen sheet on her unmade bed. "I'll do no such thing. I don't need to see me no colored ba—"

Henry's free hand, palm first, landed hard across Bertha's left cheek. Her head snapped to the side, but she remained upright. Her blue eyes, filled with shock, darted to his. He leaned in closer, the bundled baby brushing the arm she held to her face.

"Now, I've never struck you before, nor do I intend to make a habit of it, but, Bertha, this child is white-looking enough to be called our daughter. She—"

Bertha ducked under the crying baby and scooted away from Henry. She held herself up on one arm while the other rubbed at her cheek. She twisted her neck to stare anew at her husband. "Have you lost your senses? That colored baby can't be none of mine."

Henry inhaled as he straightened. He took one step to his left and planted himself in front of Bertha. "Celeste"—he raised his voice to thundering levels—"get on up here and bring Mattie Lou with you."

Bertha shook her head as her eyes climbed over his face. It was clear to see that she believed his mind had slipped.

He inched to the edge of the mattress and caught her knees between his spread legs as he towered over her. He squeezed tight.

Wordless, she stared up at him, wide-eyed.

"This is not a discussion, Bertha. Since you are my wife, I am giving you the courtesy of informing you of what will be before the rest of Union County learns of the successful delivery of our latest pregnancy. Our daughter has arrived."

"Our . . . what? Daughter? Henry, you know as well as me I'm not a swearin' woman, but such a thing sure as hell ain't never goin' to happen."

Henry finally felt comfortable holding his daughter in only one arm. In fact, despite all the infant's wriggling, the newborn felt quite light. He shifted his weight. There. He felt well balanced, his right arm free. He didn't put all his force into it, of course. After all, Lady Hardin was his wife, but she was also a stupid, silly girl who unfortunately had to be made to see reason the hard way. Henry heard the thwack as his balled-up fist made contact with his wife's chin. He nodded. Nothing broken. Not even her teeth, though he heard them rattle in her head. The blow had been much too soft for any of that. Still, Bertha slammed onto her back as though she'd been felled by lightning. Other than the soft rustle of feathers battling against one another, there was not a single sound. Bertha just lay there, arms askew, one breast, all but the nipple, popped over the top of the loosened corset. Henry released Bertha's imprisoned legs just as Celeste tapped on the door frame. Mattie Lou pushed the lady's maid through the doorway first as she lumbered in after her.

"Celeste. Get your mistress under the sheets." Henry held out the baby to Mattie Lou. "You. Get a wet nurse to feed this child."

Mattie Lou cocked her head while Celeste stood staring at the still-prostrate Bertha. "Wet nurse, suh? But she got a mama what can . . ."

Henry stared down at the round Mattie Lou. "This child's mother is not feeling well." He jerked his head to the scene on the bed. "Celeste here is making sure she gets more rest before she receives our . . . daughter."

Mattie Lou had never been a woman to hold a silent tongue, even when it was in her best interest. And though even now her mouth opened and her tongue waggled, this morning no words emerged. Henry watched the woman stare at him unblinking, the squirming, crying baby now in her arms.

"Don't just stand there as though each and every one of your senses has disappeared. Find me a wet nurse and tell the carpenter to make me a fitting cradle."

"Oh, Jesus, my ears done gone bad on me." Celeste now stood in the parade of those stuck staring at him.

"Get her back in that bed." Henry pointed to Bertha.

With a groan, she rolled to her side, knees drawn to her chest, one breast now fully free of its encasement.

"Celeste, Mattie Lou, all of you, I want you all to pay me close attention." Henry fought to keep his voice steady. They were all vexing him.

"Uhh," Bertha gurgled as Celeste tried to wrestle her to sitting.

"Get your mistress out of that corset and into her nightdress." Henry turned to Mattie Lou, whose eyes had jumped to life. "You're certain this child will look white all her life?"

"Lookin'"—Mattie Lou cleared her throat as she shook her head—"ain't bein'. Suh."

He was used to speaking slowly to servants. They were supposed to be simpleminded, and instructions often had to be repeated. "Tell Lady Hardin what you told me about the appearance of this baby." He turned to Bertha.

"You wantin' me to . . . ?" Mattie Lou peered around Henry and Celeste as she captured Bertha's eyes. "It's jest that this here child, she come out kinda pale-lookin'. Reckon that's reasonable 'cause the mama's half-white and the papa's . . ." Henry thought coloreds couldn't faint; but Mattie Lou seemed as though she were about to dive into a swoon.

"Tell her what this child will look like as she grows." Patience.

At last a look of understanding shaded Mattie Lou's face. "Yes, suh." She walked up to the bed and shook her head at the mess that was her mistress. "This here chile's most likely gonna keep her white skin and her blue eyes. Hair gonna be a little frizzy, though."

"But that's a colored baby!" The words coming from Bertha's mouth stopped as soon as she looked at her husband.

"Celeste, stop your dawdling. Get Lady Hardin to bed." Henry went to the bedroom door, peered into the hall, then shut the door. "Are we all clear here?"

"I ain't never been mo' cloudy in all my days," Celeste said as she maneuvered Bertha to the edge of the bed, climbed behind her, and began loosening the last of the corset straps.

"You all, pay close attention now." He pointed to the bundle still in Mattie Lou's arms. "This child is going to be raised a daughter of this household. Anyone saying anything different will have a very unpleasant surprise in store for them." He cocked one eye at Bertha just as Celeste positioned a nightdress over his wife's head. "I believe it's common knowledge in the county that Lady Hardin has suffered a number of miscarriages. Naturally, such grief has taken a terrible toll on my wife. So much so that she has been reluctant to inform even her parents of any further pregnancies—afraid to have them face yet another disappointment. She deliberately kept the news of this last expecting secret until she was sure of an actual live birth."

Celeste shoved the nightdress over Bertha's face, covering the woman's eyes. The servant's face folded into a scowl.

"I believe I can share with those in this room that my farm, unlike most in the neighborhood, has survived the war and that dreadful Reconstruction reasonably well. That my acres have been able to turn a profit in these dreary times, I credit to the loyalty and hard work of my employees." He answered Celeste's questioning eyes. "Didn't I hear you wanted that little house on the edge of my property for yourself? Hoped to buy it someday?"

"Suh." Celeste helped Bertha free her face as they both tugged the gown around Bertha's hips. The servant reached under the nightdress and pulled off the offending corset. "I was gettin' 'round to askin' Lady Hardin once I come up on 'nough money." Now she stared at the counterpane on the bed.

"And you, Mattie Lou." Henry turned to the midwife. "You've already got your piece of property. Will your son—the one who wants to go to that colored preacher college—come back to live with you after he graduates?"

"Gradgiate, suh? My boy can't go to no school, though he's a right good Christian. Ain't got 'nough money." Mattie Lou nodded her head in a slow rhythm. She worked a wad of spit in her mouth. "That's fine and good, Lord Hardin, suh—college and all fo' my boy—exceptin' fo' one thing. Salome."

Henry laid a hand on the doorknob. "You take care of my new daughter"—he turned to Bertha—"and her mother. I'll take care of Salome." Henry opened the door and walked down the hall toward the grand staircase.

CHAPTER FOUR

The smell of Delfine's cooking greeted his nose even before he set foot on the first-floor landing. What was dinner to be tonight? Okra, of course—a staple in the Creole woman's repertoire. And was that some sort of cassoulet she was preparing? Did he scent beans, carrots, the sweet smell of rabbit? Henry strode across his black-and-white marble foyer and into the kitchen.

"Delfine. I want a good wine this evening. One of my special ones—straight from France."

"The wine? You want the wine from *la belle France*?" Delfine harrumphed. "Never mind the wine. The dinner, she may be the late since I was kept out of the kitchen that is supposed to be all for *moi*." She shot Henry an accusing look. "Kept out of the kitchen *pour la naissance de bébé*."

Because of the baby? "Do your best." Henry would never tolerate such insolence from any of his former-slaves-turned-servants, but Delfine had been neither.

The freeborn daughter of a Frenchman and his mulatto mistress, Delfine—reputed to be New Orleans's second-best house cook—had only agreed to leave her native Louisiana and work for him after he had offered her the enormous salary of fifty cents a day. And full dispatch of two assistants. Experienced in French cuisine, the thirty-year-old cook was well worth whatever salary she commanded. Henry's dinner parties featuring Delfine's fine meals were legendary not only in Union County but as far away as Little Rock.

"Delfine." Henry stopped at the closed door of the back room. "How old is your boy now?"

His cook's only flaw hinged upon her taking up with Henry's half-blood coach driver. Not a bad sort but far too ambitious for a man with color to his skin.

"*Mon fils*, he is the one year and how you say . . . the two months?"

"Fourteen months. And do you still nurse him?"

"*Mais oui.*" She straightened up to her full height—considerable for a woman. "I am no the field hand. I take the time to feed *mon fils* when he desires." The slender woman bristled.

"Of course. Of course. Delfine, I believe I may have a new job for you."

The cook cocked her head. "*Monsieur* is not pleased with the cooking of Delfine? I do the best I can, but the no fish in the Arkansas make cooking the gumbo and the *ratatouille* almost no good."

Henry held up a hand. "No, not a new job away from here. A different job . . . on my farm. You and I will talk later. For now, ponder a doubling of your salary."

He opened the door to the small back room with its tiny window and stepped inside. Tessie held a broom and dustpan in her hands while Georgia sat talking to the still-in-bed Salome.

"Out!" Henry commanded.

Salome couldn't have missed his entrance into the room, yet she kept her face turned to the wall. He dusted off the chair Georgia had vacated and sat.

"You've made it quite clear that you have little interest in raising this child."

Other than her open eyes, Salome gave no indication she knew that another person sat beside her.

"You were not given up for dead when your mother abandoned you. I saw to it you were well cared for."

"My ma ain't 'bandoned me," Salome whispered to the wallpaper. "Her mind gone 'cause of what that overseer done to her."

"Could be, but that is not this child's story. Your mind is not gone, and I've certainly never mistreated you." He reached out for her shoulder, changed his mind, and clasped his hands instead. "This child will be raised in this household."

Salome thrashed around to face him, her eyes blinking. "Like you done me?" She raised up on one elbow. "Soon as I come to be of some size, you put me to work in the washhouse. Foldin' clothes was my first job, and I wasn't but fo' years old."

"I fed and clothed you those four years with you giving me nothing in return." Henry spread his fingers and laid a hand on the bed. "Salome, this is not a day for arguments. I'll always be grateful to you." He stroked the creases ironed into the cotton sheet. "I've decided how this child will be raised. And what will become of you."

She shook her head. "I know it ain't the chile's fault, her comin' without a proper pap . . ." Salome scooted up in bed, dislodging his hand, her head almost level with his. She prattled on as though he hadn't spoken. "I reckon I wanted this chile to have a right proper ma and pa. Didn't think I was the one. Georgia tells me there's a colored schoolteacher man over in Camden. His wife, like Lady Hardin, she can't have no chil'ren." Salome sucked in her lips, sending him a silent acknowledgment of her misspeaking. "Anyways, them folks can give her a good life. Get her some schoolin' and ever'thing. 'Sides which, Georgia says they both got bright skin. Lookin' like she do . . . other people won't take to questionin' why my chile look nigh 'bout white."

"I see, Salome. You have been thinking." Henry scanned the face of the girl-turned-woman who had just made him a father. "And here I thought less than an hour ago I heard you declare absolutely no interest in this baby." He watched her stare at the floor in that demure way that sent thrills down his spine. Her eyelashes swept her cheeks, hinting at her innate shyness. But was she just playing the coquette? "I will tell you this. That baby will not be living with a colored schoolteacher. Salome, I've taken care of both you and your mother all these years. I'll do the same for this child."

She pulled the sheet to her chin. "Oh, suh, I ain't doubtin' you gonna do what's best for this girl." Salome turned those golden eyes on him, her cherry-colored lips pulling back over even teeth and into a fleeting smile.

She was just eighteen years old. Yet he had every sense that Salome carried the womanly wisdom of a thirty-five-year-old harlot. She said all the things he wanted to hear and certainly performed everything he asked of her. But somewhere lingering in the back of his mind, Henry entertained the thought that Salome O'Brien might grow into a woman of intelligence. He had determined on the day he decided to bed her he would never let that happen. A smart colored was a dangerous colored, no matter how beautiful.

"That's settled, then. I'll see to it that you have a little house built. Hmm. Not at the top of the old slave row—too close to the main house—somewhere in the middle." He looked at her, expecting a smile of gratitude.

"Slave row?" She gave him a wide-eyed stare. "I know it'd be a bit of a walk—me gettin' up here to the main house ever' mornin' totin' Savannah—but I'm fancyin' a place next to Mattie Lou."

"Savannah?" His voice rose, making him sound almost like Bertha with her question-ending sentences. "Salome, who is Savannah?"

Her smile seemed genuine, as did the little giggle in her voice. "I knowed I shoulda talked to you first, but that name, Savannah, it jest come into my head." She fluttered her eyelashes. "Jest like it was the most perfect name for her—my daughter."

"Your daughter?" Henry shouted before he remembered that Delfine undoubtedly had her ear to the door. "I've told you I've made arrangements for this child, and none of them include the name Savannah." He rose to his feet.

Salome shook her head, her damp, heavy hair clumping over her forehead. Her face tumbled in confusion. "Suh? I reckon I didn't act my best when Savannah was a'comin' but I was hurtin' somethin' awful." She pushed the hair off her forehead as she tilted her head toward him. "I'm all better now. I knows her new mama and papa gonna call her somethin' different, but I fancies the name Savannah 'til I gets her weaned. Then her new folks can have her."

"That may well be." He sat down beside her again. Henry debated taking her hand. He did feel something for this girl-woman—something more than her satisfying the man in him. "Salome, this child will not be called Savannah." He watched her lips prepare a protest. "And she will not be living with you. In fact, from this hour forth, you are never, ever, to refer to her as your daughter again."

The eyelashes brushed her cheeks, but this time there was no hint of flirtation in them. "Suh? Don't never call her Savannah? But this here is my chile."

"No, she isn't."

Her intake of breath chilled Henry. "I . . . I jest done gave birth to her." Words bubbled out of her mouth. She scoured his face as though she were looking for telltale signs of madness. "I knows you ain't took serious my carryin' on when the pains laid into me like they done. Quite naturally, I want this chile. Leastwise, for the first few months."

"Salome, I do hold an affection for you. You please me a great deal. I should like to keep the situation the way it is, but"—Henry watched her jaw jut forward—"if you refer to this child as yours once more, I will see to it that you never lay eyes on her again."

"Not see Sava— Not see my own baby? How can that be?" She pushed the sheet to her waist.

"I'll say this just once, Salome, and I advise you to pay close attention. I will provide you with a house—you may have two rooms and a kitchen if that pleases you—next door to Mattie Lou. I will visit you there, and I may even bring . . ." He checked her face. She cocked her right ear toward him. ". . . my daughter for a visit every now and again. Do you understand?"

Tears welled in Salome's eyes. "But, suh, you can't be sayin' . . . is you sayin' . . . How's I'm sposed to do that? It ain't like I wants to keep her fo'ever, but she's lookin' so teeny-tiny right now. I reckon I owes it to Savannah to start her off right."

"That's just it, Salome, this baby is not yours. She belongs to me and her mother, Lady Hardin."

"Oh, Jesus in Heaven, no!" Salome shrieked.

"Is that your wish, Salome? To deny me the companionship of my only child? So be it. I'll make arrangements tonight to have you taken out of Union County." He watched the shock climb over her face. "No need for a lying-in for an ungrateful wench like you." Henry headed toward the door. "Make no mistake," he called over his shoulder, "I'll alert every sheriff's deputy in Union County to be on the lookout if you attempt to return to Hardin House. I can guarantee you will never see my daughter again."

He heard her feet plant on the squeaky floorboard as she pushed off the bed. Her unsteady legs took one step, then two. Henry heard her plunge to her knees with a hard thud.

"God and Jesus, Lord Hardin. Suh. No. I begs you to the angels that you won't keep me from . . . from yo' . . . chile. I'll do whatever you says. Whatever you wants." The sobs crowded her words. "It's jest that . . . that . . ."

Henry half turned and looked down at Salome on her knees, hands clasped in prayer. "I prefer to keep you here at Hardin House, but if you ever give me the slightest cause to doubt your willingness to obey my orders, you will be banished. Salome, do I have your word?"

She tried to climb to her feet, but stumbled. Her nightdress staining with red, she slumped back to her knees. "I swears to God, this chile is yours and I won't never tell her no different."

"And you will treat her as though she is your white mistress?"

"My mist— ? White? Me?" Salome's eyes resembled an owl's. "Yes, suh. Ever' time I lays eyes on her." Her words croaked and crackled out of her throat.

"And every time you mention her to anyone, you will remind them that she is without question the white daughter of this household?"

"Uh-aah." A sound like a mouthful of gravel fought its way between Salome's lips. She swallowed. "Yes . . . suh. I can do jest what you wants."

"I will give you an opportunity to prove that to me." He turned toward the door, his eyes fixed on its green panels. "If you ever give me cause to disbelieve you, I'll not only have you thrown out of Union County, I'll make sure at least six white men have a turn at you first— all in one night. The last one will be instructed to beat you without mercy so you will never bear another child." He opened the door to the kitchen, almost knocking Delfine in the head, Salome's gasp of shock flooding his ears.

"Delfine," Henry addressed the woman as she rubbed a spot over her right eyebrow. He closed the door. Mattie Lou stood across the kitchen, still carrying the squalling newborn. "Now I see why dinner will be late." He brushed past the cook. "Mattie Lou, good that you're here."

"Yas, suh." Mattie Lou didn't look at all like she believed anything was good at this moment, including Salome's overheard screeches. "I was just bringin' this here chile to her mama fo' her first feedin'."

"Mattie Lou, go find Delfine's two kitchen helpers. Surely the two of them are trained well enough to cook okra. They are to finish dinner."

"The helpers of me? Finish the dinner? Those two are fit for nothing but the rice washing and the kitchen sweeping." Delfine headed toward her oak worktable standing in the center of the kitchen and its rising mound of bread.

"Ain't that Delfine's job? Fetching them gals? I'm the midwife. I got to give this baby to her mama before this young'un throws herself outta my arms, she so mad."

Henry glanced out the kitchen window. Just a hair past noon, yet this day already felt twenty-four hours long. He was tired. Salome, Bertha, Delfine, and now Mattie Lou. He had more important matters to arrange than directing hard-of-hearing servants and a disobedient wife. He sighed. Best to pace his words. "Mattie Lou, hand the baby to Delfine, then go to Salome, get her dressed, and take her to your house within the hour. Delfine, you—"

"Suh?" came out of Mattie. "You wantin' me to take a lyin'-in woman out into the daylight sun not but an hour after the birthin'?"

"*Qu'as-tu dit?*" Delfine asked. "What do you say?"

Both women looked stupefied.

"Mattie Lou, that's exactly what I want you to do. Go to the back room and get Salome out of here. Now!"

Mattie Lou jumped.

Henry reached the midwife in five strides. He wrested the child from her. "Get." He pushed Mattie Lou toward the back room. "Unless you want me to pick up Salome and throw her into the chicken coop, bloody dress and all, I suggest you tend to her."

The calico on Mattie Lou's skirt rustled as she sidestepped Henry and rushed to the back room. She slammed the door. Henry walked to Delfine.

"I don't want Salome to see you feeding her." Henry held out the infant.

Delfine's gray-green eyes stared at him, arms clamped to her sides.

"Do the feeding in the pantry until Salome is out of here." He pushed the bundle into Delfine's chest. "Then you may use the back room. In fact, I will set up the space as your own. You may even bring your own child here when you're on duty."

Delfine lifted her arms as though her shoulders were pained with rheumatism and gathered in the baby. She adjusted the squirming bundle in her arms. She looked up at Henry. "Monsieur, I do not know the way of feeding the *fille* of another."

Henry reached for the middle button on her bodice and gave it an opening twist. "Would you like me to undress you and pull out your tit to show you how it should be sucked?"

A wave of shock played across the cook's face as she jumped out of Henry's reach. She backed toward the pantry, paused, and aimed a stunned face at him. "If I am the nurse of the breast, what is the *nom* I call this infant?"

"Name?" Red with fury, Henry glanced at his child. "I'll let you know." He headed out of the kitchen, across the foyer, and past the grand staircase. This child was his. Now, for a fitting name for a daughter of the noble House of Hardin.

Henry hurried into his library. He shut the door and turned the key. There it was—the book, *Brook's Peerage*—lying where he'd placed it in a drawer of his desk. He picked up the roster listing Britain's aristocratic families and turned to the section outlining the genealogical and historical background of the dukes of Britain.

There, listed first and foremost, was the House of Hardin, the dukes of Norwalk—dating from before the reign of William the Conqueror. The exact year in which the Hardins had entered the ranks of British nobility had been lost in time. They achieved their ducal status under the reign of Richard III. Henry stared at the pages—his copy of *Brook's Peerage*, relatively new and given to him by his mother on his twenty-first birthday. His older brother, James, held the two-hundred-year-old original. Henry sucked in his cheeks as he remembered his father's repeated lessons on the grandeur of the House of Hardin—their ranks numbering earls, dukes, and three queens of England. But all their

English glory had disappeared in a seventeenth-century family feud when his branch of the family fled England after their ancestral duke quite literally lost his head. The third duke of Norwalk—Frederick III—defied his powerful cousin Philip and fell to the swordsman's not-so-swift blow in 1629. The stories of terror, death, and flight that Henry heard as a child growing up in Maryland still gave him the occasional nightmare. Plots, palace intrigues, battles to the death between Catholics and Protestants, Hardin heads lopped off willy-nilly, all permeated his childhood nightmares. His ancestors scrambling aboard an America-bound ship in 1630, their jewels, money, and papers secreted in the women's clothing—the axman at their heels.

Henry grunted as he flipped two pages of *Brook's Peerage*, grateful that his family had not only been safely delivered, but had prospered in the new land. There, in print, were the names of Hardin women: *Catherine. Margaret. Agnes. Elizabeth.* The same names over and over again. A family pattern. His eyes scanned the page. His finger stroked a name. One woman had been a blue-eyed, light-haired beauty, according to the stories written about her. Lady Margaret. He leaned back into the soft contours of his chair. Yes. He opened the desk drawer and pulled out the leather-bound family album, *American Descendants of the Dukes of Norwalk*. He opened the book to the last page, where Grandfather Hardin had painstakingly written in his distinctive script the name of Henry's father, James Bertrand Hardin. Across the page, the man had also inked the name of Henry's mother, Nola Hayes. He listed the first son of this union: firstborn and heir, James. Here the handwriting changed to that of Nola Hayes Hardin, Henry's Mother Dear. In her flowing hand, she penned the name of James's wife, Elvera Walton. No children. Next to that, and on the same line, Mother Dear had written his own name and that of Bertha. Children of this union: none. Not until now. Henry dipped the pen in the inkwell, shook off the excess ink, and wrote in a flourish that would have made his tutor proud the name of his firstborn, Margaret Hardin, b. April 18, 1879.

CHAPTER FIVE

"Ugghh." Salome clutched at her stomach as she leaned over the yellow, flower-sprigged basin. The tumult in her body had been going on for almost an hour now. Worse, she'd awakened in her bedroom each and every morning these past two weeks with the same urgency to reach for the washbasin before she could even slip out of bed. She took one, two, three breaths. Lord, let this not be so. She fumbled for the washrag she'd been forced to keep handy on her bed table. Swiping the dampened cloth across her mouth, she slowly lifted her head out of the bowl. She squinted toward one of the four windows of her little house, peering through the yellow, ruffled curtains. The sun was up. Just. Even so, Salome knew she had to hurry. Today was big doings up at Hardin House. Mistress Margaret would be celebrating her third birthday and her real mama couldn't afford to be sick on this important day. Especially not this kind of sick.

Salome clutched her nightdress to her belly as she inched her way to the side of the bed. Last night's dinner thrust itself into her throat. She groaned as she heard footsteps crunching along the pebbled path leading to her front door. Mattie Lou coming to hurry her up. This whole thing was Mattie Lou's fault.

"Gal, now what's keepin' you?" Mattie Lou opened the front door without knocking, as usual.

Salome took one look at the midwife. "Mattie Lou, you tole me them herbs was surefire." She gave her neighbor the best hexing glare she could manage this morning.

"You musta took 'em wrong. Ain't failed you these three years, has they? Only knowed them to go wrong one other time." She slipped one meaty arm to her hip. "And that were twenty year back."

"I ain't the one done somethin' wrong. I used 'em jest like you tole me—push them leaves as high up as I kin befo' he come into me."

"Did you keep the jar stoppered tight 'til it was time to use 'em?" Mattie Lou wagged her head. "Did you douse 'em with that pepper sauce I made special for you?"

Salome nodded, forgetting that motion sent her head and belly warring against each other. A fresh retch spurted out of her mouth. She barely reached the basin in time. "Pepper sauce . . ." She gagged. "Fo' drops old cider vinegar. Put the whole mess out in the quarter-moon one hour after sunset. Ooh." She released another round of last night's dinner.

"He ain't caught you unawares no time, did he? Lord Hardin be wantin' what he be wantin' without waitin'. Gal, I tole you how to handle a man when he like that."

Salome leaned over the crate holding the now-full washbasin as she eased to her feet. She would have given Mattie Lou a good head shake if that movement didn't threaten a fresh round of throw-up. "Lord Hardin, he ain't like that." She cranked herself upright. "He like to think he ain't makin' me do what I don't want." She took a step toward the hanging hook and her work dress. "He give me plenty time to 'get in the mood.'" She slipped the dress over her head. Last night's turnip greens roiled. As she tied the apron strings over her blue work dress, she glared at Mattie Lou. "I gots me plenty time to pack in them leaves and he don't know the difference. It ain't me, it's yo' no-good medicine!"

"My medicine always work, lessen I gets a bad batch." Mattie Lou tapped at the knot of her head covering. "Sometimes when the rains ain't jest right, them herbs might not be powerful 'nough to fight off a potent man."

"Potent man?" Salome pushed her braided hair to the top of her head and tied on her own blue printed head scarf. "Lord Hardin ain't got but that one chile, my daught—"

Mattie Lou's big, ham-like fingers grabbed Salome by the shoulders so hard she winced. "Salome, gal, I'm tellin' you this again. Don't you never, ever, call that chile yours to nobody. Not even when you is talkin' jest to me. One slip, Salome, and that man will have you out of Union County—hell, gal, out of Arkansas—befo' you can say *thunderin' tarnation*." She loosened her grip and headed toward the door. "If you is expectin' again, I'll cook you up a batch of my for-sure-take-care-of-business cure in a day or two. But right now, me and you got to get to steppin' befo' Mistress Margaret's party. Ain't no tellin' what Lady Bertha gonna get up to."

Salome closed her front door behind her. Big doings all right; Henry's folks were here from Maryland—his ma, brother, and sister-in-law. First time they set eyes on Henry's girl. Salome walked behind the huffing Mattie Lou as the two approached the springhouse, wondering if Bertha Hardin would take this chance to tell her in-laws the God's truth—that their white granddaughter and niece was nothing but a colored girl in disguise.

CHAPTER SIX

Henry pushed open the door to the nursery, situated two doors down the hall from his and Bertha's bedroom, and stayed there at his wife's insistence to keep the child's cries as muted as possible. Back when the child was still a baby, Henry would often slip into the room he had ordered wallpapered with tiny pink and yellow primroses. He hadn't tarried, of course. Unmanly. But he had so enjoyed watching baby Margaret as she nestled in Delfine's arms, the newly appointed nursemaid rocking the baby to and fro in the white wicker rocker. Delfine had proven irreplaceable in the kitchen, so now the slow-witted Tessie was the fill-in when Delfine became too busy with her fine New Orleans cooking—like tonight.

"Girl, get a move on! That bow in Mistress Margaret's hair is lop-sided." Would that girl ever learn? Despite Celeste's best efforts at training, Tessie would never make a decent lady's maid—never mind a governess.

"She won't set still, suh. That's why—"

"Papa, I don't want Tessie combing my hair. She hurts. I want Delfine." Margaret turned those eyes on him—blue washed in green—eyes that made him want to lavish everything he possessed upon his only child.

"Sugar pie, let Papa have a try," Henry cajoled his daughter. "You know Delfine's busy with dinner." He watched the three-year-old's pouty, full lips waver as she shrugged.

Mattie Lou had been wrong. His child's hair was light colored, all right—blonde, in fact—but it carried a definite frizz that only Delfine seemed able to tame.

"Papa," Margaret giggled. "Papas can't fix hair. Only ladies. Delfine says so." The child pulled on one of her carefully constructed curls, the ends immediately flying into a crinkled frizz.

Henry started toward his daughter just as a shadow appeared in the doorway. He turned. "Mother Dear." He walked to his mother and planted a kiss on her cheek. "I see you've dressed for dinner already. Delfine declares the meal won't be on the table for another forty-five minutes, however."

The dowager Lady Nola Hayes Hardin—the title she bestowed upon herself—lifted the side of her black mourning gown and slipped the fabric behind her, careful not to disarrange the bustle. Papa had been dead almost twenty-five years, yet Henry's mother insisted upon wearing black well beyond the formal one-year mourning period. The black dress of night was only distinguished from the black dress of day by the addition of elbow-length gloves covering his mother's dress sleeves, and a sparse sprinkling of jewelry.

"That's precisely why I came to you. Send that girl on to her other duties." She nodded toward Henry. "I wish to speak to you."

"Of course, Mother Dear. Tessie can go as soon as she arranges Margaret's hair."

"Have her take the child with her."

Henry nodded his assent. Tessie, hairbrush in hand, grabbed Margaret's hand and headed toward the door.

"Wait!" Mother Dear commanded. "Bring the child to me first."

"Margaret, go to Grandmother. Be sure and give her a proper kiss on the cheek."

Margaret looked quizzically at him. "Papa, I already kissed the lady. Yesterday. When the big carriage bringed her to our house." The child pointed to her grandmother.

"*Brought*, my dear, and a second kiss is not necessary." Mother Dear turned her head.

Tessie, almost tiptoeing, led the child toward the dowager, who bent down to straighten Margaret's hair bow. She lifted the disarranged curl and pursed her lips. "There. Now you may leave with your nurse."

Tessie bobbed a quick attempt at a curtsy. Henry swallowed a groan. All his efforts at training the slow-witted girl had come to naught. He watched Tessie sweep Margaret out of the room, almost bumping the child into the doorjamb in her haste.

"Where does that girl get such curly hair? I declare, I can't remember a single curly head in the entire Hardin line. And Bertha's hair is as flat as a johnnycake."

"What is it you wish to speak to me about, Mother?" Surely his daughter's hair would straighten as she grew older. No need to discuss such a prickly subject with his mother.

"Your brother. More precisely, Castle Hardin."

Henry shook his head. Mother Dear was nearly seventy, but until now, she'd given every indication that her faculties were intact. "Castle Hardin? I assume James has made the necessary repairs. I haven't been back to Maryland in over ten years."

Lady Hardin walked to the bedroom door, her taffeta dress announcing every step. She peered both ways into the hall, then shut the door and motioned Henry to the far corner of the room. She pulled him within touching distance and said to him in a quiet voice, "I'm afraid that is just the problem."

"Mother Dear, problem? I'm afraid I really don't unders—"

"The war has been terribly hard on us." Her gloved fingers intertwined.

"Yes, Mother Dear. I'm aware. But the war has been over for seventeen years."

She ran a hand over her left glove from fingertip to elbow. "And you, Henry, have prospered despite those dire times of Reconstruction." Mother Dear crossed herself, presumably touching the jewel-encrusted crucifix she always wore underneath her buttoned-to-the-neck dress.

Lady Hardin turned toward the rose-pink drapes and slid a hand down the fabric. "Not so, your brother."

"James? He isn't doing well?" Not that Henry was surprised. "But he inherited everything." Henry fought back the bile that threatened to pool in his mouth whenever he thought of his wastrel brother. "Although there really is no law of primogeniture in America, you know." He tried to swallow back his words, but the bitterness lingered. What was done was done.

Mother Dear twisted her head, and her eyes widened in a mixture of surprise and annoyance. "James has no mind for figures, as you're very well aware."

He read his mother's face and saw surprise at his audacity. Henry knew better than to attack the heir to the Hardin dynasty, no matter how unsuited the man for the role of family patriarch. Sometimes, in these infrequent conversations with Mother Dear, thoughts Henry meant only for his own head erupted into words, as they did again now. "James certainly had a considerable number of figures with which to learn." He clamped his jaw shut. Such provocation only forced his mother to defend her wayward eldest all the more.

Mother Dear turned square to him, the swish of her taffeta dress an accusation. "Henry, you never really appreciated your heritage despite my best efforts to teach you. You speak of laws in the United States when you know full well our legacy goes back nine hundred years to England. That we are sojourners in this America is merely an unfortunate turn in history."

"Mother Dear, what is it you wish of me?" Would his mother forever persist in perpetuating this family fairy tale?

"Though you speak disparagingly of James's right to inherit your father's entire estate as called for by the right of primogeniture, I certainly saw to it that you weren't sent away a destitute second son as often happens in families like ours."

Henry bobbed his head. Mother Dear had succeeded magnificently in teaching him the manners of an aristocracy of a different time and place—manners that held no place in his world. "Of course, Mother Dear. I am forever grateful. Without your sacrifice I could not have made my way here to Arkansas and purchased land."

"And that sacrifice included the loss of my most magnificent pearl suite."

How many times had Henry heard of his mother's ultimate sacrifice for him? Her three-foot-long, flawless matched-pearl necklace, gone to give him seed money for a fresh start. The accompanying nine-strand bracelet and diamond-encircled pearl ring discreetly sold so that he might buy acreage in land-cheap Arkansas and build a suitable replica of Castle Hardin to uphold the family honor.

Mother Dear turned those brown eyes that reflected no light upon him. "Now you must repay the family."

He blinked, though it was his ears that seemed to have dimmed.

"Your brother has made a series of ill-advised investments, and none of them involved restoring Castle Hardin to its proper glory. Every room leaks with rainwater. There are buckets atop buckets. I'm forced to plan my entertainments only when I am certain the weather will not be inclement." She fingered the yellow onyx brooch affixed to the bodice of her dress. "The short of it is that James no longer has the necessary funds to maintain Castle Hardin."

Henry's hearing had returned, but his eyes couldn't stop their blinking. "Mother Dear, I'm afraid I'm still at a loss . . ."

Lady Hardin swished the skirts of her dress behind her—a habit she displayed whenever she was miffed. "You are at no loss, Henry. You understand me perfectly. We are down to a mere six house Negras and a dozen field hands. And even those few we must pay for their work, thanks to the Yankees." Her face screwed into a grimace.

The last glint of sun caught on the gold workings around the onyx stone. Were those mounts empty of the diamonds they once held?

Mother Dear watched his face as he scanned her bodice. She laid a hand over the stone. "If I sell this, my last piece of jewelry, I can pay the staff, but only for another six months." Her hand trembled.

"Last piece of jewelry? What of your cross? Those rubies alone are worth a fortune."

"Gone since February last." Mother Dear drew herself to her full height. "To maintain the Hardin position in Maryland, you, Henry, are the only one who can supply considerable sums of money."

"Mother," Henry gasped. "I had no idea times were as dire as that. I've known the old house . . . When was it built? In 1675, 1680? Ten years back, I saw the building was badly in need of repairs. I assumed . . ." He waited for his mother, but her face revealed nothing. "James inherited nearly a million dollars." The gall threatened to rise to Henry's throat again. "More than enough for the needed work."

Mother Dear gave her head a tiny shake as she gestured toward the door. "Your father passed on in '59." She slid her hand from the brooch. "Outrageous taxes imposed by the Yankees, poor investments, bad luck at the gentlemen's gambling tables"—she softened her voice—"wastrel women: they've all taken their toll." She looked up. "Henry, despite what you feel about the unfairness of primogeniture, it is the law."

"In England, Mother, not in Arkansas, nor in Maryland." He reached for her shoulders. "Of course, I will help, but keeping up this pretense . . . behaving . . . living like royalty in America—it's an absurdity."

The dowager stiffened under his grip.

"I will see that the repairs are made." He had to chance it. "But then I suggest the property be sold and you all move here—to Union County, Arkansas."

The gloved hand that smacked his left cheek caused little sound and minimal pain. Even if he'd seen the blow coming, he would not have dodged it. He had spoken sacrilege. About time someone did. "Mother Dear, I only meant that running a forty-room, nearly two-hundred-year-old house for three people—you, James, and Elvera—is a bit . . . a bit . . . extravagant."

"Are you not aware that this 'pretense,' as you call it, is all for your daughter?" The words hissed out of her mouth. "As of now, she is the only living heir to the Hardin legacy after you and James. Both you and your brother have made the unfortunate choice to take barren, rather stupid women as your wives."

Henry pressed his hands into his sides. Mother Dear was never going to change. Couldn't. "Thank you for your concern for Margaret, but I believe I can care for her adequately."

"Can you?" Mother walked around him as though she were circling prey. "Care for her adequately? Why was I not told of this child's impending birth?" She held up a gloved hand as Henry opened his mouth. "I'm afraid I find it difficult to believe you delayed the upcoming birth announcement for six months because you feared another miscarriage. Word certainly could have been sent at seven—or even eight—months into the pregnancy." She stopped as she faced him. "Then there is the issue of the girl's looks."

"Loo— Mother?" Henry clutched at the sudden thumping erupting through his shirt. "Whatever can you mean?"

"I've seen them, you know." Her face hardened. "Light-skinned Negras. Don't act as though you have no idea what I'm saying. You grew up with enough of them surrounding you back home at Castle Hardin." Mother Dear appeared as though she wanted to spit on Henry's Turkish rug. "The Potts family!"

His childhood raced before him. Of course Henry knew the Potts family. Slaves, all of them. Skin colored a light tan, but no darker than the sun-drenched poor whites forced to work their own puny fields. Hair the color and texture of Margaret's, but each had a broad nose and overly full lips like their brown-skinned mother. When Henry's father died, the late duke freed each and every one of the Pottses in his will—Henry's half siblings. But Mother Dear knew none of that, did she?

"I can read your face, Henry. There were six of them. All fathered by the same man who fathered you."

"Mother Dear, no."

The widowed duchess knew better. Such topics were never to be spoken of out loud by the aggrieved wife.

"Mother Dear, yes. Henry, I've reached the age where these games no longer interest me. I lived through the Potts family, and I know enough to question your Margaret. Bertha avoids that child at all costs. Margaret is brought into a room, and Bertha walks out. She speaks not one word to the girl who is supposed to be her daughter. I know the signs." She shook her head. "Bless Bertha. At least your father never tried to pass off his Negra bastards as his own white children." She trained her eyes on him. "But this is not about hurt feelings—mine or Bertha's. You've had a stroke of luck."

Henry didn't feel very lucky at that moment. He pointed to one of the two stuffed chairs flanking Margaret's play table. "Mother Dear, take a seat."

The dowager stood, unmoving. "Your Margaret does not present herself as an obvious Negra. Except for the hair. Oh, her nose is a shade too broad, and her lips a bit plump, but both are passable in a fulsome white girl. Now, Henry, I will put the matter to you simply. I do care for your father's legacy. Your father and you are direct descendants of the dukes of Norwalk—England's greatest aristocracy. May the Lord smite my tongue, but despite her mother's parentage, so is Margaret. I will keep your secret. I will even control Bertha for you. All you must do is preserve Margaret's legacy—preserve that which has been handed down to you. Position the Hardins so that, one day, we may regain our rightful place in England." The taffeta shimmered under her touch. "You will supply the funds to maintain Castle Hardin. In exchange, when the time comes, I will entertain Margaret in Maryland. I shall introduce her as my granddaughter—Bertha's daughter—due all the rights and respect suitable for a Hardin. Is that clear?"

"Mother Dear, are you blackmailing me?" She'd never been much of a mother, leaving both boys to be raised by slave mammies. Even during the brief daily audiences she granted her two young boys, her conversation had focused upon their shortcomings. That she would resort to blackmail was no surprise to Henry.

"This western frontier called Arkansas has dulled your wits. Ill-bred and ill-mannered louts have caused you to forget your birthright." The taffeta swished as she headed toward the nursery door. "I will not allow that to happen. And remember, Henry, I can control Bertha far better than you. Under my tutelage, your wife can be taught to show public affection for her only child—or she will not. The choice is yours."

Henry grunted as memories flickered. *The choice is yours.* Mother Dear's favorite phrase. Would you rather eat with the slaves or at the family dining table? The choice is yours. Would you rather ride in the fields with the overseer from sunup to sundown, or play with your toy soldiers? The choice is yours. He shook his head. "My banker will prepare the necessary documents for a twenty-thousand-dollar transfer in the morning." He watched his mother slip a gloved hand on the doorknob. "More will follow every six months."

"And James is not to know." She twisted the knob.

"Of course."

A faint smile dashed by Mother Dear's lips as she opened the door and stepped into the hall.

CHAPTER SEVEN

"I won't be stopped, Henry. Not this time." Bertha pulled down the top of her already low-cut evening dress, displaying even more of her white-powdered bosom.

Henry's wife, standing next to their four-poster bed with its gold-threaded quilt, ran her hands down the sides of her dress, emphasizing the new corset she'd made him order straight from New Orleans. She had whacked poor Celeste often enough until the servant finally got the hang of tightening the corset strings almost to the breaking point to narrow his wife's waist to twenty-two inches. Bertha, with her auburn hair arranged in billows about her face, looked handsome.

Here it was not yet four in the afternoon. Bertha had started wearing breast-baring dresses—suitable only for his most fashionable dinner parties—earlier and earlier in the day, and even for the most mundane of occasions. His mother had visited eight months earlier; had she had a hand in transforming his wife into some kind of seductress? It hadn't worked. Naturally, Henry still took his husbandly rights on a regular basis, but Bertha, with her decent-size breasts, still was no Salome. Of course, these last weeks, Salome hadn't been available to him. And now Bertha wanted to intrude into the birthing room.

"If I'm to be mother to another pickaninny, I want to see the thing right after it's pulled out of . . . that woman." The frown creeping over Bertha's face destroyed what little prettiness she possessed.

"The child has just been born. The doctor ordered me out of the room right after the birth."

Bertha lifted the skirt of her green velvet dress to peer at the matching slippers she'd had him order. "Doctor?" She looked up at him. "I declare, I don't know of anybody in all of Union County that has a white doctor tend the birthin' of a Negra baby?"

"Very well. If you insist upon seeing the child, come with me." He wanted no further discussion of doctors and Salome.

In most things Salome was compliant. She never cajoled, bargained, or demanded anything. Yes, he'd added a third room to her cabin and furnished the space in solid pine crafted from his own timber. It was where he bedded her three nights out of seven. He'd even assigned Salome to clean Margaret's room so she might catch a glimpse of the child before the governess whisked her off to the newly converted upstairs playroom. That Salome loved Margaret, Henry never doubted. So why had she tried to rid herself of his second child? Of course he'd been forced to call the Hardin family doctor—and paid Dr. Henderson a handsome fee for his silence—after Mattie Lou's last-resort botched abortion job almost killed Salome. Now Bertha was questioning him on the why.

"Well, are you coming?" He held the door open for his wife.

Bertha led the way down the grand staircase, through the back hall, and into the kitchen. Dr. Henderson stood at the new sink Henry had installed, his hands held out while Georgia poured warm, soapy water over them. Henderson started when he saw Bertha.

"Ber— Lady Hardin." The doctor's face reddened.

"I know it's not the usual thing, Doc Henderson, but thank you for lookin' in on my Negra staff. You may go now."

Dr. Henderson turned toward Henry, and Henry wondered if he read panic in the doctor's eyes?

"Is all well with mother and . . . with them both?" Henry stepped between Bertha and the doctor.

The man nodded. "The child is healthy, and your servant is doing fine. I will leave them in her hands." He pointed to Georgia holding out the drying towel.

"And me." Tessie, at seventeen, still hadn't proven herself to be much more than a helper.

"Very well." Henry walked to the backroom door and cracked it open. "Salome," he whispered, "Lady Hardin and I would like to take a look at the child."

In the shade-drawn room, Henry could barely make out the figure of his mistress. It was the white of the receiving blanket that drew his eyes toward the bundle in her arms. A quiet bundle. Henry turned back to the kitchen.

"Dr. Henderson"—Henry waited as the man put the last of his supplies into his medical bag—"the child is not making a sound. Are you sure . . . ?"

"Oh, your servant has delivered a healthy babe. With excellent lungs. Go on in. You'll soon hear for yourself."

Henry nodded as he strode into the room. He heard the soft swish of velvet behind him. Henry took the chair beside Salome. She looked frightened, her eyes focused on Bertha.

"Ain't no need to take this one," Salome whispered to Henry as she wrapped an arm tighter around the bundle.

A mewing sound erupted from within the blanket.

Bertha stood with her arms held snug around her waist as though she were holding an explosion inside.

Henry reached for the blanket. "I've not seen the child since it was pulled out of you. Let me take a look now that Georgia has done the cleaning."

Salome tried to scoot away from his touch, grimaced in pain, and fingered the cloth covering the infant's face. "See." She opened the top of the receiving blanket.

Henry bent closer, his eyes on the child. He sensed Bertha standing there, straight as any soldier in General Lee's army.

"It ain't gonna work?" Now Salome sounded like Bertha. "Looky here." She drew one finger down the side of the child's face.

The perfect little oval was covered by tan skin. Darker by a shade than the Potts children. Salome frowned as she stroked a strand of her child's hair. Straw-colored. And straight. Not a Margaret crinkle in it.

"The other thing . . ." Salome pointed to the infant's eyes. "They blue."

"That's too da— Unfortunate." The sound of Bertha startled Henry as she moved to stand next to him, that New Orleans perfume snaking into his nostrils.

Henry glanced up. Was that the beginnings of a smile on his wife's face? Yes, the baby had the skin color of a mixed-blood colored, and the light hair to go with it, but with uncommon blue eyes. What of the rest? Henry peered at the infant, now deeply asleep. The nose, the lips, the shape of the face. All his. All Hardin. Henry laid a hand over the white blanket. This couldn't be happening. He jumped from the chair, knocking Bertha off balance. Grabbing his wife by the shoulders, he ushered her out of the room and into the kitchen.

"This one I won't be claimin'!" Bertha shouted as he shoved her out of the kitchen, one heel catching in the hem of her gown. She stumbled.

"Tessie, get your mistress upstairs. Now!"

The girl-servant jumped and rushed to help Bertha regain her balance. Henry slammed the hall door on the pair and stood with his back against it.

"Georgia, where's Mattie Lou?"

"Mattie Lou? Suh, Lord Hardin, she ain't here."

"I can see that. But she's the only one who can tell me." Henry's hissed words came out louder than he intended.

"Tell you what, suh?"

Henry took a breath. He had to stay calm. He walked up to Georgia, who watched his approach with eyes growing bigger by the second. To her, he might have been the overseer with a whip in his hand. "The color. Will it change?"

Georgia let out a whistle as her eyes settled down. "Is that what you wantin' to know, suh? Will this here baby lighten up over the years?" She shook her head. "I already done looked behind the ear. Ain't gonna get no whiter. This here young'un gonna be light-brown skinned."

"And the hair?"

"Oh, it's straight as a stick, suh. Might get a bend or two in time but it's gonna be pretty much like it is." She swallowed. "The rest of this young'un ain't gonna change. Fact is, Lord Hardin, suh, that chile gonna be a little colored version of his dadd—" Georgia's hand slapped against her mouth so fast and hard, Henry marveled she hadn't knocked herself out.

"How can that be? Margaret is certainly not . . ." Henry's eyes bored into the woman.

Georgia straightened, a look of *I-know-more-than-you* playing across the servant's face. Henry waited.

"Ain't nothin' strange 'bout it, suh. Salome got a white daddy, folks say. Her ma had Injun in her. And African. Any baby Salome brings into this world gets to pick and choose what color skin, hair, or eyes they wants. That's why I looks behind the ear. That be where they real color stay . . . fo' life."

His feet felt like lead as he headed to Salome. He sat down beside her. She watched him. Fear covered her face.

"Pull off that blanket."

49

"Suh?"

Henry began unwrapping the child until the naked infant awakened, screaming. Henry inventoried the baby. Fingers and toes all accounted for. A face almost an exact replica of his own except for a shade too much color in the skin. How could the Lord be so cruel? At last, a male heir to the Hardin dynasty. A boy—but a son Henry could not claim.

"This one's yours, Salome. But I'll see to it that he's well educated, and I swear he'll want for nothing. Ever."

Salome's cheeks quivered. Her eyes puddled. "I wants to call him Waylon, if that be all right with you?"

Henry nodded. "Waylon Frederick. Frederick is a Hardin family name going back six hundred years." He stood. Despite everything, he'd write down the name of his son in his journal, *American Descendants of the Dukes of Norwalk*. Waylon Frederick Hardin, born November 3, 1882. Even if young Waylon couldn't be officially claimed as his own, this baby was a Hardin.

CHAPTER EIGHT

Waylon watched as Maxwell Joe drew the handsaw across the last of the pine boards, sawdust clouding the air. The boy frowned as he stood behind Jacob Slocum, Lord Hardin's farm manager—a term his mother still had a time over. Salome was used to *overseer*. Waylon waited to hear the verdict. Maxwell Joe, at well over forty years, was Hardin House's best sawyer—white or black. In fact, the man's furniture was the finest in all Union County. Maxwell Joe never made a miscut, but the way Mr. Slocum inspected the carpenter's angles, strangers would swear the brown-skinned man was an apprentice on trial for a job as cleanup boy. But Mr. Slocum was white, and in Union County—indeed, in all of Arkansas—a white man's word carried all the say-so over any colored's. If a man or woman didn't do the work according to the law of Jacob Slocum, he sent them packing off Hardin land. There were other jobs around the county, but none paid wages as good as those offered by Lord Hardin.

Waylon felt funny standing behind Slocum, and not because at fifteen, Waylon already topped the man's height by three inches. Everybody else around Hardin House walked a careful step around the farm manager—most trying to shy away from his angry judgments, a few putting on fake bows and overly toothy grins to curry favor—but not Waylon. Three years ago, on Waylon's twelfth birthday, Lord Hardin simply walked up to Salome's oldest son and told him to learn all he could about running the Hardin acres—running the sawmill, growing cotton, cutting miles of fine timber, tapping the maple trees, operating the two stores—all of it under the critical eye of Jacob Slocum. Lord Hardin never said the why of it. These were not jobs meant for coloreds. When Waylon asked his mama about his turn of fortune, she offered no answer. More than that, she hadn't acted surprised.

"Maxwell Joe." Slocum's voice wasn't a strong one, but in the hearing, it made a person feel like vinegar was pouring over an open sore. "You gonna have all them tables ready and set up for Margaret Hardin's eighteenth?"

Waylon brushed a strand of hair out of his eyes. For the time it took a fly to escape a swatter, he thought he read a look of disgust on Maxwell's face. But when Waylon blinked, he saw only Maxwell nodding.

"Yes, suh. I already done a dozen." Maxwell Joe nodded at the pine tables with their intricate, lathe-turned legs, laid out in the spacious carpenter shop behind the group. "Each one seats twelve folk. This here's the last of the lot, and the barbecue still two days off." Maxwell Joe shot a quick glance at Waylon before pasting on that fake smile his mama taught him to use in front of white folks. "I reckon we all gotta start callin' Mistress Margaret *Lady Margaret*, once she done had her comin'-out party."

"Hmm." Slocum worked a wad of tobacco from one cheek to the other. "That'll be the day." His low, raspy words were aimed at the ground.

"Iffen it please you, Mr. Slocum"—Maxwell Joe nodded at Waylon—"I'd be happy to give the boy a try at puttin' this here last table together. Workin' the lathe, and all."

"The lathe?" Slocum adjusted his suspenders as he mumbled through the tobacco juice filling his mouth. "That oughta be a job for a white man, anyways. 'Sides, ain't no time for learnin' no lathe. I've got to take this boy to both stores." His booted foot pawed the ground. "All this fuss over that darky woman's three bastards. Parties. Learnin' 'bout business," Slocum muttered between streams of tobacco juice. "In the end, ain't none of 'em nothin' but nig—" He turned to the sound of a buckboard approaching the carpenter shop.

Waylon watched the mule with its cart trot up the path with Jebediah, Jacob Slocum's son, at the reins.

"My boy's here to take the three of us over to Smackover." He spat a stream of tobacco juice on the ground. "What the hell a nigger boy's supposed to do at a white store, 'cept empty the slop jars, beats me."

Waylon groaned quietly. Did Jacob Slocum naturally assume all colored people were hard of hearing, and he could insult them at will? For all the years he'd been assigned to work under the man, Waylon endured Slocum forever talking ugly, supposedly under his breath. Jebediah, at twenty, and Slocum's only boy, had a mouth on him just as ugly as his pa's. Waylon didn't fancy spending the afternoon with either of these oafs.

"Mr. Slocum, sir . . ." The farm manager hated it when Waylon enunciated his *r*'s the way the Maryland-born tutor required of Mistress Margaret. Waylon's cheek muscles twitched as he struggled against the broad grin threatening to erupt over Slocum's discomfort. "Maybe . . . sir . . . we could ask Lord Hardin if it would be all right if I learned to work the lathe."

"Pa, you 'bout ready? I'm sposed to go over to Lizzie Mae's house this afternoon and . . ." Jebediah's quick flick of the reins signaled his impatience.

Grumbling, Slocum ignored Waylon and took a menacing step toward the buckboard. "Boy, you sassin' me? What the hell I care 'bout you sparkin' Lizzie Mae? You damn sure ain't the first with that one, and you sure as hell won't be the last."

"Pa." Jebediah's cheeks reddened. "Lizzie Mae was 'bout to marry, when Peter Paul up and died. They was as good as engaged!"

"Ain't takin' no engagement for Lizzie Mae to drop those drawers of hers. Am I gonna have to knock some sense into your head again?" The farm manager walked over to the buckboard, turned back, and glared at Waylon. "Suit yourself. Work that damn lathe all you want. One day this here cushy life all gonna be gone." He pushed his son aside as he swung onto the buckboard. Slocum took up the reins. "Always is for niggers what don't know their place."

"Get on in here, boy." Maxwell Joe, his voice light with merriment, moved into the shaded interior of the carpenter shop. Maxwell Joe walked behind the boy and closed the door. "Young'un, I suggests you watch yo' face a little bit mo' around that overseer. It ain't always the words that gets a colored man dead. It's what that white man see on the face. And he see plenty on your'n." He put a hand on Waylon's shoulder and moved him to the center of the shop. Maxwell ran his calloused fingers across the business end of his biggest saw. "But that white bastard, Slocum, he right, you know. Might come a day when Lord Hardin won't be around no mo'. I hear tell he well past sixty. Do you good to have a fallback trade."

"I think I might fancy carpentry." Waylon touched the smoothness of a just-sanded tabletop.

"Hmm." Maxwell Joe picked up a piece of timber and walked toward the lathe. "If Lord Hardin live long enough, you ain't gonna be no carpenter like me. But, jest in case . . ."

Waylon scratched the itch behind his right ear. "Lord Hardin? He's got me doing all sorts of things. I don't know why. A colored man can't work most of those jobs." He watched Maxwell Joe adjust the lathe spindle. "I know I'll never be as good a carpenter as you, Mr. Maxwell Joe, but I sure would like to learn all I can."

Maxwell attached the wood to the lathe. "Turn that there handle, boy," he called out as he picked up a trimming tool. "That ain't the stuff of it, boy. Seem like to me, somebody's got plans fo' you to go on up to that colored preachers' college over in Little Rock—Philander Smith College, ain't it?"

"Preachers' college?" Waylon squinted a close look at the older man. Maxwell Joe had always been extragood to him—as well as to his brother, Thomas, and especially to his mother. Now it looked as though the man was about to have a head stroke. No colored from Hardin House ever went to college. "Mr. Maxwell"—he slowed his words so that a person possibly in the middle of a seizure could understand—"my ma doesn't have the money to send me to college. Besides, I'm not sure how much store she sets in preachers. She tells me not one of them came to comfort her mother after . . ." He watched Maxwell closely. No spasms visible. Maybe they would come later. Waylon readied himself to catch the man if his falling body aimed toward one of the saws.

Maxwell Joe said nothing as he worked at shaping the table leg on the revolving lathe spindle. With the rough cuts finished, he eased himself upright, shook his shoulders free of tension, and half turned to Waylon. "Can you read and write?"

Waylon took the opportunity to rest his arm from the incessant crank-turning. "Yes."

"Can you figure yo' numbers?"

"Of course."

"You know how to study them stars with one of them telescope things?"

Waylon pushed down an impatient groan. "Yes, Mr. Maxwell, I can do all those things. I learned them when Lord Hardin assigned me to be the fetch-and-carry boy for Mistress Margaret's classroom tutor."

Maxwell Joe nodded for Waylon to resume the turning as he selected another tool. He bent over the rotating chair leg. "And you been doin' that since you was six years old?"

Of course he had. The fact that every inhabitant of Hardin House knew every little detail about one another was just one more thing in a long list of what-was-wrong-with-plantation-life that annoyed Waylon.

"Didn't you sit in that classroom 'longside Lady Margaret all these years, learnin' what she learned?"

"No. I told you, I was just the fetch-and-carry boy." What was Maxwell talking about? Margaret Hardin was three years older than him. Waylon tried to remember back to when he first entered the upstairs room at Hardin House where nine-year-old Mistress Margaret received her education. The memory was hazy, but did he recall the tutor—Mr. Warden—sitting with him and going over the letters of the alphabet while Margaret worked her numbers? "Tutor Warden only explained things to me so Lady Margaret could practice what she learned on me. If I got the lesson, then Mr. Warden was sure Mistress Margaret learned it, too." Waylon cocked an eye at Maxwell Joe. "Why are you asking?"

The carpenter made a final cut at the lower end of the new chair leg. "Boy, you is right. 'Tis best you learn all you can 'bout a good trade like carpentering. They might be aimin' to send you to that school, sho enough, but, if anythin' goes wrong . . ."

Waylon's hand dropped from the crank as he stared at Maxwell Joe. "Wrong?" Maxwell Joe sounded as though there was some plot afoot to plan his life—a plot of which he knew nothing.

Maxwell straightened and worked out the second round of kinks in his back. "You fifteen years old now. 'Bout time, I'm thinkin', you asked yo' ma what's what."

CHAPTER NINE

Even though it was barely quarter-moon, Salome sure-footed her way down the path she'd known all her life as she headed from the Big House to her own four-room cabin near the main road. Lights in three of her rooms blazed in the distance, while Mattie Lou, next door in her two-room house, only had her kitchen kerosene lamps lit. Salome peered at the one darkened room in the cabin: Waylon's. He hadn't made it home yet, though it had to be past eight. Must be helping Maxwell Joe set up the last of the outdoor tables for tomorrow's barbecue. Salome had just finished her own chores, putting the last stitch in Margaret's beribboned French-blue satin dress, making it perfect for the girl's debut dance party tomorrow night.

Salome squeezed her shoulder blades together. Imagine, Margaret now eighteen. How could the time have passed so fast? Why, Waylon was fifteen, and her last child, Thomas, had just turned thirteen. She'd only been eighteen herself when she had Margaret, her daught— Salome shook her head. She knew better than to keep a thought like that in her mind. Mistress Margaret was Lord and Lady Hardin's only child, and Henry Hardin had reminded her of that fact often since their daughter's birth. It had been a difficult thing to keep quiet, watching her girl take on the airs of whites. The daughter of her body treated Salome the same way she treated Delfine or Celeste or Tessie—as servants who held no right to covet Margaret's white world. Indeed, the only colored person the young woman seemed to tolerate was her childhood companion, Waylon. Of course, Margaret had no idea he was her full brother. Salome shuddered. Margaret could never hear the truth from Salome's lips, no matter how much the secret pained her.

Salome had kissed Henry Hardin for real when he announced on Waylon's sixth birthday that the child would be assigned as errand boy to Margaret's tutor. Henry secretly instructed the teacher to educate Waylon as well as Margaret. The memory of that night always brought on a smile. Not so, however, two years later when Salome asked the same of Lord Hardin for their third child and second son, Thomas—her Tom-Tom. Lord Hardin declared the five-year age difference between his first and last offspring too great to afford Tom-Tom such an open public education. Not so easy to explain away two errand boys in the schoolroom. Those were the words Henry used on Salome to explain the unexplainable, but Salome spent many sleepless nights fearing she understood the truth of Henry's reasoning.

With the lamps of her whitewashed house beckoning her closer, Salome conjured up her third child. Tom-Tom carried the fine features of the white Hardins, all right. His eyes, too, were a blue-green match to Margaret's and Waylon's, but not his skin tone. Each of her children had come out increasingly darker. Margaret carried white skin, Waylon a beautiful light honey, and Thomas favored amber. When Mattie Lou shook her head at Henry after her first look behind Tom-Tom's ear, Lord Hardin had hinted something about his recent hire, Maxwell Joe. Oh, he did it in a most roundabout way, but Salome got a good reading of her lover's face. The tilt of his head, the arch of that right eyebrow— Henry Hardin wondered about the who of Thomas's actual father.

It had taken Salome more than a month after Maxwell Joe's arrival at Hardin House fourteen years back to realize the new woodworker set an appreciative eye on her. She should have minded, but somehow she didn't. In those first few weeks, he tried to pay her court until everybody on the farm told him about her situation. Most of the women on the farm—indeed, most of colored Union County—disliked Salome because Lord Hardin loaded favor on her. Only the old ones, like Mattie Lou and Georgia, knew the price she paid to bear children for a man she did not love. So the old ones took pity on her. But in that quick courting time, as proper as those stumbled words, sly glances, and tiny little hand movements were, Salome felt the stirrings of a woman for the first time. When Henry pressed, right after Thomas emerged almost as dark-skinned as Salome, she'd sworn to the father of her child she'd never given Maxwell Joe cause to think he was anything more than another Hardin hired hand. Other than smiles she couldn't stop from forming or her fluttering heart whenever the carpenter came near and bored those dark-brown eyes into her, that was the truth. There'd been the occasional accidental brushing against each other, a one-time holding of hands for a few seconds, but nothing more. Though her heart and body longed to melt into his arms, she kept her feelings bottled inside. The price to uncap that bottle was too high.

Henry nodded his *all right* after she proclaimed her innocence, but underneath, he must have suspected something. Though he'd kept his promise about all three of his children, Lord Hardin had been just a little bit cooler toward his second son. Both boys received toys, clothing, and money from the master of Hardin House, but Waylon's share was always a shade nicer—because he was the eldest, or so Lord Hardin said. Then there was the schooling. Henry had kept to his word. Though he had not offered a teacher for Tom-Tom, he did supply books and paper to Salome's house. He added the fourth room to act as a schoolroom for Tom-Tom—all with Salome's promise never to reveal the true father of any of her children.

Salome stopped at her front door, her hand poised in midair. Bless Waylon. He'd done all he could to teach Tom-Tom the things he had been taught, and both her boys were as bright as brass buttons. She opened her front door.

"Maxwell! What you doin' standin' in my front room?" Salome's heart thundered in her chest as she stared at the tall, well-muscled man. "You can't be in here." Her eyes went on a frantic search. Who else was in her house? She eyed the kitchen and the open door of her bedroom. No one. What to do? Push the carpenter through the door, or . . . "Where's . . . where's . . ."

"Shut the do', Salome. Me and you gotta have us a talk."

Salome stood there in the doorway. She felt the cold of the April breeze brush her backside. Maxwell walked over to her, the lamp lighting his even-featured face. Grabbing her arm, he pulled her inside.

Salome stumbled across the threshold of her own house. Maxwell Joe reached around and closed the door.

"Good God Almighty." Breath wheezed out of her. "You can't be in here. Waylon. Tom-Tom. Lord Hardin, he comin' to visit toni—"

"I sent yo' Thomas up to the Big House to help Waylon finish settin' up the tables in the breezeway. Lord Hardin"—Maxwell's nose crinkled like he'd sniffed a skunk—"he busy lookin' over each and ever' one of my tables—fo' mistakes. Jacob Slocum at his side like a lapdog."

Salome hurried to her windows. Should she draw the curtains? If she did, and Mattie Lou had seen Maxwell come into her house, what would the woman say? Would the old midwife spread tales? If she didn't, then anybody passing the main road might peek into her cabin and find a colored man instead of the lordly Henry Hardin. Salome clutched at her blue uniform.

"Don't take on so, Salome. I done spoke to Miz Mattie Lou. She the one let me in yo' do'. She know I'm here jest to send Tom-Tom on his way and nail up that loose board you got in yo' kitchen."

"What loose board?"

"This ain't 'bout no board, Salome. This here 'bout yo' boy, Waylon."

"Waylon?" Salome smoothed down the front of her dress, fumbling with each button. Her heart threatened to explode. She walked to the window and drew the first set of curtains.

"I reckon it ain't rightly my business, but yo' Waylon don't know nothin' 'bout nothin'. What gonna come of him? He thinkin' he got a right to talk proper and use all them hifalutin words in front of white folks." Maxwell Joe shook his head. "I fears that boy gonna come to harm lessen he learn the truth 'bout hisself."

"Harm? The truth?" Salome shook her head. She knew she sounded like a polly parrot repeating everything Maxwell Joe said, but she couldn't help it. Her mind felt stuck. "You right 'bout what it is you ramblin' on 'bout, Maxwell Joe. It ain't none of yo' business." Salome pulled closed the second set of curtains. She walked into her kitchen. "Iffen you don't get outta this here cabin right now, all of us is gonna come to some harm. And that is the truth."

Maxwell lowered his voice. "Salome, 'tis my business to see no mo' colored men and boys get killed by the night riders. Killed 'cause they thinkin' theyselves above any white man—even the lowest-class drunk in the street."

If she had had her say, Maxwell Joe would have been the man she gave her *I-love-yous* to, but she had no say. Her hands raked her throat as she turned to face him. "Stirrin' up trouble bring nothin' but pain to all my chil—" Her throat was scratchy. "And to you."

"This ain't 'bout me. This 'bout Waylon, Thomas, and . . . If that oldest boy of your'n don't know what's real 'bout hisself, bad gonna come of it. You think on it, Salome. There's mo' than one white folk around this place. Ain't but one of them wish you and your'n well. When that white man move on to Glory or to Hell—whichever—that gonna leave you and your'n in a fine pickle. Time Waylon start actin' like a colored man in Union County. Stop goin' to that white store over in Smackover, actin' like he know mo' than all them white workers. That boy ain't gonna be runnin' no Hardin House. No matter how hard he trainin', he can't be the next Lord Hardin." Maxwell Joe worked his mouth. "The next Lord Hardin runnin' this place gonna be the white man that marries Lady Margaret." Shadows from the kerosene lamp played across Maxwell's face. "Salome, fo' yo' sake and all yo' chil'rens, I hopes to God nobody tell that white man no different."

April weather turned quicker than a crow could flap its wings. A shiver that felt straight out of January shoved itself into the marrow of Salome's bones. She wrapped her arms tight around her waist. But it wasn't her own arms she wanted around her, holding her fast. A strong chest to melt her body into—arms that held her upright when she wanted to sink to her knees—that's what she needed to steady her battle with the truth. "Lord Hardin"—her voice squeaked—"he ain't wantin' Waylon to know nothin' 'bout . . ."

Maxwell Joe took a step toward her and lifted his hands, his arms spread wide—welcoming—then dropped them back to his sides as his hands fisted. "More'n Waylon be in trouble if he ain't tole the true facts. Ain't time for Thomas jest yet, but somebody got to stand beside you if things don't go all that good fo' . . ." Maxwell's mouth set in a hard line. "Lady Margaret—I hopes that's what she gonna be all her days, Lord willin'." Maxwell opened the kitchen door. A drifting cloud fought and won its race against the quarter-moon. "Salome." The name whispered off his lips sounded like spring rain. "You needs somebody to stand beside you if ever'thing don't go jest right. I reckon fo' right now, Waylon is best fo' the job." Maxwell stepped into the April night. "But Waylon don't never need to do the job by hisself." He closed the door.

Heart pounding, Salome rushed to draw the last of her front room curtains shut.

Salome pulled the quilt up around her chin. The moon signaling her it was two hours past midnight burned through the bedroom window. Her sleep had come only in fits and starts and never lasted long enough to cover even one dream. Henry was supposed to visit her last night for a private celebration of their daughter's eighteenth birthday. He hadn't come. Had he been on his way to her cabin when he caught sight of Maxwell Joe sneaking out her kitchen door? Oh, Lord. Sweat drenched her, forehead to chest, on this cool night. What was Maxwell Joe thinking? He'd risked them all, and for what? Were Waylon and Tom-Tom really in danger? Salome shivered under the cover. She knew not to trust a white man. Especially Henry. She'd heard too many tales of women just like her, covered with promises from their white lovers for years, only to be stripped bare in the end.

What to do? Did she trust her life and the lives of her children in Maxwell Joe's hands, no matter how right the man? She turned her head from side to side against the feather pillow that tickled her cheeks. No matter what the carpenter promised, she couldn't let the truth be known—especially to Margaret.

CHAPTER TEN

"Boy, what are you doin' in here? Where's Delfine?" Lady Bertha swooped into the Hardin House kitchen laden with platters and bowls of food and drink just as Waylon poured the last drop of champagne into a cut-crystal glass.

Careful not to waste a drop of the precious wine, Waylon took his time looking up at his mistress. He pushed back all the words he wanted to ask the woman, such as *Why aren't you in the ballroom with your daughter on her big night?* The strains of a Virginia reel drifted from the converted ballroom—usually the second parlor right off the dining room. Tonight, the space had been turned into a dance floor for thirty or so of Union County's finest families. Waylon flipped the bottle upside down as he watched annoyance spread across Lady Bertha's face. When it came to him, the mistress always looked angry.

"Well?" She snapped the fan in her hand closed and flicked it across her wrist as Celeste hobbled up behind her.

"Ma'am, Lady Hardin"—Waylon pulled up the respectful voice Mama had taught him—"Delfine went to fetch the key to the cellar to bring up more wine for the toasting." He righted the empty bottle. "We're all out."

"Why didn't that stupid cook send you to the cellar?" Lady Hardin fumbled with a button on her long white glove. "Celeste, you've misbuttoned this thing." She slapped her fan across Celeste's lined face.

The servant winced but said nothing.

Waylon controlled the grimace he felt coming, but the twitch in his lips must have given him away. Lady Bertha stepped full into the kitchen, her purple taffeta gown sweeping across the clean kitchen floor.

"You loathsome creature." She stopped in front of him. "What makes you think you qualify to pour champagne?" She spread the fan just as Celeste limped forward, her rheumatism-ravaged knees buckling at every step. "You get yourself down to the cellar and help Delfine with that champagne." Her fan jabbed into Waylon's chest. "On second thought, I don't really give a dandelion's fuzz if there's enough champagne or not."

As she turned to leave the kitchen, her fan brushed against one of the champagne flutes. The crystal fell to the wooden kitchen floor, shattering and sloshing liquid on the bottom of Lady Bertha's dress.

"Thunderin' balls of fire!" Lady Hardin shouted as she shook her formal gown.

"Bertha! Whatever are you doing in here?" Lord Hardin rushed into the kitchen. "I've looked all over for you." He paused and looked around. "What is that mess on the floor?"

Lady Hardin reddened as she lifted the hem of her dress. "Him." She pointed at Waylon. "That dreadful boy has ruined my dress? He dropped one of the glasses?"

"Ma'am?" Waylon's head began to shake no. He caught himself as quickly as he could. "I mean . . . I'm sorry. I didn't . . ."

Lady Bertha spun around, her dress scattering shards of glass. "You are a clumsy boy who has no business in the kitchen of a fine house.

You should be in the fields hoeing cotton!" She faced her husband. "I've told Lord Hardin that very same thing many times."

The muscles in Lord Hardin's cheeks twitched twice before they settled into a hard line. "It's almost time for the presentation. Come along."

"No." Lady Hardin lifted her chin.

Waylon's eyes darted between Lord and Lady Hardin. The lady of the house looked as though she were readying herself for combat in one of those new pugilist contests he'd read about. Lord Hardin's eyes narrowed as he slowly held out a hand to his wife.

"I . . . mean to say . . . ," Lady Hardin said haltingly, "I can't go in there for the comin'-out 'cause my dress is ruined?"

"Celeste, wipe off your mistress's gown." Lord Hardin turned to Waylon. "Get Celeste a wet cloth."

Waylon hurried to comply. Celeste eased herself to her knees, her moans soft behind her clamped jaws. Waylon was sure he heard more than one pop as the old woman busied herself soaking up the champagne stain.

"I still can't go," Lady Hardin announced as Waylon bent over to help Celeste to her feet. "That creature"—she pointed to Celeste—"has lost a button to my glove." She held one hand over her gloved arm.

Lord Hardin reached his wife in one stride. He grabbed her elbow, almost knocking Celeste back to the kitchen floor. "Our daughter is being presented to society in ten minutes. Her parents—both of them—will be there, smiling and wishing her well. Bertha, do you understand me?" He started toward the kitchen door, dragging Lady Hardin behind him, then stopped short as Salome, carrying her sewing kit, walked through the doorway and into the room.

"Her parents?" Lady Hardin pulled against her husband's grip. Her face looked like one of those gnomes the gardener set in the backyard. "I reckon you meanin' all three of us."

Waylon watched his mistress's mouth twist into a puckered grimace. Perhaps that explained her garbled words. His mother must have noticed, too, because Salome's eyes carried a startled look.

Lord Hardin jerked his wife through the door and brushed past Salome. "Waylon," he called over one shoulder, "bring the tray into the ballroom, but save the serving until I give you the signal."

He stopped and turned to Salome. "You may stand in the hallway in case Lady Margaret needs a dress repair." He glanced at Lady Bertha. "But stay out of sight."

Did Waylon see his mother's lips open into the beginnings of a smile before she clamped them tight as though refusing a dose of cod-liver oil? As the Hardins moved toward the music and the animated laughter, Waylon reached for the full tray, lifted it, and under the guidance of his mother carried the silver platter through the hallway, past the grand staircase festooned with blue-and-gold garlands, and into the ballroom. The music swelled with every step he took. Waylon glided to the ten-foot-long sideboard and set the tray directly underneath one of the three smaller chandeliers sparkling their gaslight along the length of the room. Mrs. Morse, wife of Union County's premier judge, approached, with a wobbly Lord James, the master's brother, on her heels. The visitor from Maryland reached for a glass on the tray. Waylon held up a hand as he aimed his eyes below the man's chin.

"Sorry, Your Grace." Waylon was proud that he'd remembered two of Salome's most important lessons in dealing with Lord Hardin's brother: Look no higher than the collar of an aristocratic white man and always address him by the name reserved for dukes—Your Grace. "Lord Hardin says this champagne is to be served only for the toast to Lady Margaret."

"Why, you insolent . . ." His Grace snatched a crystal glass from the silver tray.

Mrs. Morse flushed as she fluttered her fan. She quickly clicked open the blue-spangled, lacy confection and covered her face. "You see,

Your Grace," she said, her voice muffled behind the fan, "toastin' and all. That is to say . . . we all do know our manners out here in Arkansas?" The music swelled as couples twirled on the ballroom floor.

Waylon kept his eyes downcast as he searched the room for Lord Hardin, hoping the man would retrieve his bothersome brother. This drunken fool couldn't be the subject of all those lessons Waylon absorbed in Lady Margaret's schoolroom, could he? Waylon had paid particular attention to the studies of Hardin genealogy. Tutor Warden hadn't taught those classes, of course. But Margaret's father had taken particular care in doling out information about which Hardin descended from what duke. He emphasized the seventeenth-century beheading of the reigning duke by the king during the Catholic-Protestant wars in England. Waylon recalled the shiver that raced down his back at the telling. Lord Hardin always paused in detailing the surviving family's scramble to board a ship bound for the Americas in 1630. The master always waited, his eyes boring first into Margaret then Waylon, until they nodded understanding of how the Hardins were considered American nobility. Lord Hardin had made both him and Margaret learn the names and dates of the Hardin ancestors all the way back to the tenth century and a noble named Haredan. Waylon could recite from memory all the dukes, even the so-called American ones, way before Margaret could—and she was three years older. Waylon found himself torn between the ridiculousness of an American aristocracy—the duke of Maryland, indeed—and his pride at his mastery of the subject. He almost always gave the correct answer before Lady Margaret. Waylon looked at this first-time visitor to Arkansas—and current holder of the American title—with disbelief. Lord Hardin had said nothing about foul-mouthed drunks being elevated to dukedom. Nor had he said anything about wives of dukes who almost never left the confines of their bedrooms. Lady Elvera complained to her husband that this evening's headache was especially severe.

"You speak of gentility?" His Grace's voice could have chilled two bottles of champagne all by itself as he addressed Mrs. Morse. "On the contrary, madame, you are all bumpkins here. You can't even properly train a lowly servant." The American duke turned to the dance floor, where a dozen couples in their taffetas, brocaded waistcoats, and satins, twirled across the polished-to-perfection parquet floor. Eight or ten other couples, equally bedecked and bejeweled, stepped and pirouetted in the adjoining, similarly reconfigured parlor. "Though with a farce such as this, it makes little difference how poorly trained the staff." His Grace, Lord James Hardin, slammed the glass onto the sideboard, leaving a ring on the polished mahogany. He reached toward the serving tray and picked up a second glass.

A flush covered Mrs. Morse's forehead and spread down to her puckered, spotted chest. "I declare . . . suh . . . I'm sure I don't rightly know what you mean." She pointed her fan at the dance floor. "Won't be long now before Margaret makes her bow?" The portly woman's voice wavered between shock and feigned lightness.

His Grace twisted his head around to face Union County's second-most prominent woman. "And who is the poor fool who will escort the so-called Lady Margaret?"

"Fool? So-called?" Mrs. Morse's watery eyes blinked over and over. "I . . . my . . . I . . ."

The breeze stirred up by her fan brushed Waylon's cheek. He couldn't tell which was worse: the lines on Mrs. Morse's forehead clumped together in one giant furrow, or the beet-red color that turned her already-unpretty face into a fright that mimicked the Devil. The woman beat her fan at her chest as though she feared her heart might quit on the spot.

"Madame Morse, you can be no sorrier than I. My brother's a desperate man, you see." His Grace drained the second glass. "We have not—either of us—been blessed with children. Damnable bad luck to strike both Hardin brothers, wouldn't you say?"

Bad luck? No children? Now Waylon blinked in time with the frazzled Mrs. Morse. He'd have to ask his mother—better yet, Maxwell Joe—about the ramblings of drunks.

"Suh, I'm sure I don't quite . . . that is to say . . . it is my son who has the incredible honor of escortin' Lady Margaret?" Mrs. Morse laid a steadying hand on the sideboard. "I mean to say . . . I declare, I am sorry about your wife. No children and all . . . I mean your brother . . ." Her mouth gaped midsentence. She looked as though she had run out of air.

"Madame, you needn't keep repeating yourself." His Grace picked up a third glass. "Your son, you say?" His Grace snorted a laugh. "If he is the one escorting my brother's so-called daughter, then I am the one who is sorry. For you." A look akin to pity passed over the man's face as he sighed. "I suppose in the spirit of Christian charity, I should tell you what I know to be the god-awful truth."

Waylon held out a hand for the empty glass. He took inventory of the remaining containers. Where was Delfine with those bottles?

"Why are you still standing here?" James Hardin spun toward him. "I thought I told you to . . . Say, you look familiar."

Lord James grabbed Waylon by the shoulders, pushed Mrs. Morse aside, and planted Waylon underneath the chandelier. His blue eyes bored into Waylon's own. "I should have known. More treachery on my brother's part." He pushed Waylon aside. "That damnable brother of mine. Determined to steal the title from me with his black bastards."

Waylon stumbled backward. Bastards? Title? He shook his shoulders, struggling to rid himself of the painful handprints he was certain had dug into his skin. What could he do to escape this idiot without disgracing his employer?

"You go get Lord Hardin, nigger boy, and you go get him now! I've had enough of this foolishness!" The man advanced on Waylon. The fiddle player stopped midnote, along with the pianist. His Grace stumbled against the sideboard in the sudden quiet, spilling not one drop from the crystal glass.

Waylon backed to the doorway only to bump into someone. Salome clamped an iron hand to his back.

"Hold yo' tongue, and watch yo' face," his mother hissed in his ear. She inclined her head toward His Grace. "Pay you no mind to that white man. Master's 'bout to speak."

With Lady Bertha in tow, Lord Hardin worked his way through the crowd of partygoers offering their congratulations. He strode to the center of the room, his hand firmly around his wife's wrist. He stationed them under the fifty-flame gaslight chandelier above the center of the room, his arm tight around Lady Hardin's waist as he pulled her to his side. Her grunt reached Waylon's ear in the doorway. Lady Bertha looked stricken, as though the gas fueling every chandelier in the room had suddenly been extinguished.

"My dear friends, this is a special day for my family." Lord Hardin nodded to the waiters stationed around the room. "I would like you all to raise a glass of champagne . . ." He frowned as he looked at the sideboard Waylon had vacated.

Salome pulled Waylon out of the doorway and into the great hall, out of Lord Hardin's line of sight. She stayed behind him, her hands tugging at the back of his jacket to prevent him from returning to the ballroom. Waiters circulated the room offering flutes of champagne to the guests. His Grace poured his fourth glass down his throat. He twirled the crystal in his hand.

"To my esteemed younger brother."

Lord Hardin narrowed his eyes against the glare sparkling off the center chandelier. His gaze roamed the room and finally landed on Waylon, almost out of sight in the foyer. "Boy," Lord Hardin called out, "escort our guest and my brother, the Honorable Duke of Maryland, to me." The smile on Lord Hardin's face looked as though it hurt.

Waylon broke free of his mother's grip. He thought he heard her gasp as he walked toward Lord James. The duke stiffened as Waylon approached. He reached for another flute. Turning his back on Waylon, he whirled to face Lord and Lady Hardin.

"Now, brother of mine, I can salute you with both hands." His Grace took a sip from the full glass. He stuck his tongue into the empty flute in his other hand. "For your cleverness." He bobbed toward Mrs. Morse, who eased herself away from the sideboard, a crooked grin marking her face. Lord James reached for the woman's arm, missed, and spilled half the contents of the fresh glass down her low-cut dress. He fell back against the wall, waving both glasses in the air. "This good but simple woman tells me that it is her son who is to escort the so-called Lady Margaret in this, her debut into polite—that is to say, white— society." He put one of the cut crystal glasses to his lips, sucked in a gulp, and swished the liquid between his teeth before he swallowed. "I had no idea that ni—"

Waylon felt the bump before he discovered it was his mother who had propelled him toward the duke.

Waylon collided with the man. "Suh . . . I . . . ?" Waylon backed away as fast as his feet would carry him, barely missing Salome. His face flushed as Lord Hardin dropped his grip on Lady Bertha and hurried across the floor.

"James, you are ill." Henry Hardin raised his voice as he grabbed his brother. "I believe Dr. Henderson is in the other room." Lord Henry, a look of panic on his face, wrestled his brother toward the doorway. "Salome, hurry and find the good doctor." Henry Hardin turned to face his guests. "Just a temporary diversion, my good friends. My brother is prone to sudden attacks of the . . . the melancholy. I'm sure he'll be fine as soon as Dr. . . . In the meantime, enjoy more of my fine champagne."

His Grace broke free, his feet nearly entangling him in a fall. "Yes, yes, brother, do go on with the festivities. My melancholy, as you call it, will pass far quicker than this charade you're planning for your dark daughter."

Was that a cry Waylon heard from his mother? The sound drowned in the gasps, moans, and shouts erupting throughout the room—sounds riding a wave from low to high.

Lord Hardin latched one hand on the back of the duke's neck and pulled his brother's face into his dinner jacket. His Grace flung an arm around Henry's shoulders, spilling the last drops of champagne.

"Oops." The man's muffled voice reached Waylon. "But I am not the one who has made the misstep." His Grace pushed his arms against Lord Hardin's shoulders and broke free. On shaky legs, he spun to face the guests. "Ladies and gentlemen of Union County," he slurred, "a mockery, a tragedy, a terrible mistake is about to be committed against you good citizens of Ark—"

"James!" Lord Hardin used the full weight of his body to muscle his brother through the doorway and toward the grand staircase.

Gurgles escaped from the mouth of the American duke as right foot tripped over left. He swallowed as he steadied himself. "Good people of Arkansas, ask Lady Bertha if you don't believe me. She knows all about the so-called Lady Margaret. A lady, indeed. Underneath that white powder and that pulled straight hair, she's as bl—"

At the foot of the staircase, Lord Hardin's hand caught his brother across his Adam's apple. Dr. Henderson puffed into the foyer.

"Help me get him upstairs. My brother suffers from melancholy. We've tried all the best doctors but . . . Waylon, summon some of the bigger men to help carry him upstairs to his room." The fear coming off Salome reached Waylon before he felt her iron grip on his arm. He tried to pull away, to rush off to do Lord Hardin's bidding. The look on his mother's face stopped him midflight. Salome looked as though both her sons had been taken by the night riders, but it was not Waylon who drew her fright. Her eyes bored into Lord Hardin. With a strength Waylon didn't know the slender woman possessed, his mother pulled him into the kitchen. She slammed the door behind them and stood with her back against it.

"I want you to go . . ."—her voice shook—"to Maxwell Joe's. Don't go to the house. They'll find you there. Tell Maxwell to go get Thomas. All three of y'all, hide out. I'll get word to you."

"Mama?" His mother wasn't a drinking woman as far as Waylon knew, yet she sounded as addled as His Grace. What was happening?

"Get! Now!" She pushed him out the kitchen door. "Run through the woods. Don't let nobody see you." She slammed the door behind him.

CHAPTER ELEVEN

Henry shoved his knee against James's backside as Dr. Henderson wrestled his brother to the leather settee in Henry's upstairs guest room.

"James, I'll thank you to keep your mouth shut." Henry shot a glance toward the physician as he kneed his brother's face deeper into the leather. "I know, brother dear, you are not responsible for the ramblings of your tongue when you are in the throes of your melancholy, but you do talk out of your head."

"Has your brother—er—His Grace, long been troubled by the melancholy?" Dr. Henderson stood at the end of the settee clasping his hands.

"Melancholy, my ass!" James twisted his face free. "You, good doctor, must be aware of the truth. What is my brother paying for your silence?"

"A damp cloth, man!" Henry laid a frantic hand on Dr. Henderson's sleeve. It was not the time for the truth about Margaret. What was the truth, anyway? Margaret was the daughter of his body. "My brother is feverish."

"I'm afraid I don't see . . ." Dr. Henderson's face wrinkled into contortions worthy of a carnival performer.

"To the kitchen!" Fear even greater than he had felt at the Yankee invasion of Castle Hardin iced through Henry. "Fetch a cloth and a basin of warm water." Time, that's what he needed. "Wait for the water to heat."

"Water to heat? But you said a fever," Dr. Henderson said, his forehead crinkling as he leaned toward James. "Lord Hardin, let me examine His Grace."

Henry shoved an arm against the doctor's chest. "No, no. I've dealt with this often. You get to the kitchen."

"Doctor, he . . ." James struggled to sit.

Henry clamped a hand over his brother's mouth and nose. James, one hand trapped at his side, used his free arm to paw at Henry's wrist.

"There's no more time, Henderson. Can't you see the man's getting worse and threatening a seizure?"

"A seizure?"

Henry drew up his most menacing look.

"Well, no. I don't see any signs of . . ." Dr. Henderson straightened, his flushed face moving from James to Henry to the library door and back again.

"Go!"

The physician slid a hand from his forehead to his chin, then backed away from the settee and turned toward the door. His feet flicked across the carpet as he hurried into the corridor and flung open the door. Henry's heart thumped as he glimpsed the blue-outfitted form of Salome standing just outside.

"Shut the door behind you, Henderson. And clear the hallway!"

James broke Henry's grasp as he faced the open door. "Might as well let the wench hear her fill." He slurred, "I'm sure your black woman will be ever so grateful to hear the precise time of her daughter's downfall."

"The door, Henderson!" Henry laid a knee against his brother's face. The brass lock clicked its closing. Even as he glared at James, Henry strained his ears but did not hear Salome's tread across the carpet-covered hallway.

He bent close to his brother. "James, I know you're drunk, but I suggest you pull up every ounce of whatever sobriety you may have once possessed to listen to the precise time of your own downfall." He pulled his brother to sitting.

James rubbed at his neck. "Do not presume, brother, that because Mother Dear has gone to her reward, you can insert black blood into our noble lineage."

Henry grabbed his brother's face hard. "Blue blood, black blood, or no blood, what is your choice?" Henry's nose inched closer to James's. "You and I are the last of the blue bloods," he added, inserting as much venom as he could muster into his hissed whisper. "Is it your preference to have our branch of the Hardin line die out after two hundred and fifty years? To have no more American dukes?"

James's bloodshot eyes—one always lazy—struggled to focus. "Umm."

"Do better than that, brother dear." Henry pushed James against the back of the settee. "Do not pretend abject ignorance with me. Mother Dear knew the truth, and yet she was well prepared to present Margaret to Maryland society."

"You and Mother Dear. Quite the pair." James belched. "Pour us both a stiffener if you must persist in this lie. And take your hands off me. We're alone now, unless your woman in the corridor cares to join us."

Henry turned toward the paneled door. No time to fret over Salome. "A stiffener? I think you've drunk this party nearly dry as it is. You could never hold your liquor as a gentleman should." Henry caught his breath as he eased off his brother. "If truth be told, you are the most ill-suited man to ever assume the coat of arms of the duke of

Maryla—" Henry caught his breath. Margaret. He needed this derelict to protect her.

James tugged at his waistcoat as he squirmed himself upright. "Oh, don't hold your tongue on my account, brother." He cocked his head as he rubbed at the light stubble on his cheek. "It's about time we spoke truth to one another. I knew from the day you gained your lessons quicker than I in the nursery that Father wished you had been the first-born. As for Mother Dear—a woman who could put a Chinese empress to shame in the dragon department—she, too, wished it."

"How dare you speak such evil of our mother? She's not two years in her grave."

"Has your inability to face the truth covered everything in your life? Not just your dusky daughter?" James ran a hand through his gray-speckled hair.

"I accept the truth far better than you, my brother. When Father died, Mother Dear paraded you in front of all Maryland, determined to present you as the greatest duke since the first Hardin set foot on American soil."

"But you so conveniently forget"—James patted his pomaded hair back in place—"as duke of Maryland, I was entitled to everything our family accumulated over those two-hundred-plus years. The entire Hardin estate belonged to me alone. The least Mother Dear could do was to accept my coronation, though it nearly killed the woman to do so."

That smirk James never bothered to conceal took Henry back to their days in the nursery when the heir had successfully purloined all Henry's toys under the acquiescing gaze of Mammy Potts.

"And believe me, it was the most our mother ever did for me." James struggled to focus.

Henry moved to his feet and tugged at his own waistcoat, his mind filled with the dozen or more jewelry boxes where Mother Dear had stored her most precious gems. All gone. Would the memory of her sacrifice for this worthless heir ever leave him?

"Hurry with that bourbon, brother dear. I am becoming much too parched to continue this senseless conversation with you. Of course, I'll make a final effort to save my voice . . . so I may speak once again to that charming, if quite dowdy, judge's wife. You see, she seems eager to hear the truth about my nappy-headed niece." James waved a hand toward Henry's liquor cabinet. "Make mine a large."

The Kentucky bourbon Henry poured for himself filled almost the entire glass. Henry splashed the bottom of a second piece of cut crystal with a mere trickle of the dark liquid. Henry's hand shook as he brought the full glass to his lips. "You know quite well that I was banished from Maryland. Unlike you, I inherited nothing." He took in a bigger gulp than he intended.

"Banished? I should say not. Not only were you needed in Maryland, you were the one trained to run the business end of our estates—a task quite unsuitable for the heir." James pointed a finger at Henry. "Yet you abandoned your obligation to me in favor of pursuing your own selfish needs."

Henry's hand clutched his bourbon glass. Yes, he needed all the strength he could muster to tame James, but not like this. "I did what was prudent for us both. In Maryland, I had no chance for a fortune of my own. You were ensconced in the ducal chair. I was left with nothing."

"Precisely. You were left with nothing other than what I chose to give you. But you and Mother Dear conspired against me, completely ignoring a second son's responsibility to support his elder brother's position." James rose to his feet and reached for a glass.

The annoying, rapid blinking of his brother's eyes, complete with his spreading smirk, felt like a vise wrapped around Henry's chest. James had convinced himself that Henry was the culprit in the downfall of Castle Hardin. So like him. Henry stroked the bourbon glass. His shoulders ached to lift the crystal to his lips, but he shook his head. Gathering courage was one thing, but it was much more important to maintain a clear mind. Neither one of them needed more drink. Henry held out the barely dampened glass to his brother.

James reached around the offering arm and plucked the full crystal from Henry's hand. "As a younger brother, you were subordinate to me. Your only job was to secure the family's continuing success by devoting yourself, heart and soul, to me." He glowered at Henry. "You and Mother thought I did not grasp my duty. Oh, I know you both considered me a flibbertigibbet—all puffed-up air with no substance. You both were wrong." He hoisted his glass but did not take a sip. "I hold honor as sacred as any of my predecessors. I know my duty, and you should have known yours." He ran the glass over his bottom lip. "In return for your loyalty, I was prepared to give you a substantial allow-ance. More than most second sons. But instead of following centuries-old protocol, you and Mother Dear hatched up your own little scheme. She'd sell off her jewels, sneak thousands of dollars to you against all custom, and you would hie yourself off to Arkansas to build your own selfish fortune." James swirled the liquid in the glass, sloshing some across Henry's Aubusson carpet.

A breeze raked Henry's shoulders. He thought he'd ordered the bedroom windows closed against the variable April weather. Still, the crispness of the air filled his lungs.

How could his brother be so deluded? "Is that what ails you, James? Yes, I accepted the pittance—not quite three thousand dollars—that Mother Dear gave me. Money she'd gotten by selling a strand of pearls. Gems, I might add, which she brought into the marriage. Mother Dear had every right to do what she did."

"And you had every responsibility to share your frontier fortune with me—the rightful duke. You were honor-bound to save Castle Hardin."

A second breeze filled Henry with far more strength than a swallow of Kentucky bourbon. He waited until James's eyes met his own. "Castle Hardin is but brick and mortar. I'm about something far more important, brother dear. I aim to save the Hardin line." Yes, he'd promised Mother Dear to keep his contributions to Castle Hardin secret, but first and foremost he was a father.

James brought his glass to his mouth. Henry swiped it aside. More than half the contents splashed across the cherished Aubusson.

"With your black bastard?"

The knot in Henry's belly doubled back upon itself as he tried to steady his breathing. "You speak of your role in the Hardin dynasty—a lineage you assume will go on forever." He snatched the glass from James's hand and slammed it on the desk. "You were handed a fortune . . . and you squandered it all. Now you have the audacity to complain to me because I parlayed what little investiture I received into . . . into this."

"Hardin House." James lifted his bourbon-soaked right hand in a slow arc and wiped it across Henry's sleeve. "I know what I shall do."

"You know what you shall do? And I suppose you will use the same knowledge you employed to squander away the Hardin legacy on your new scheme?" He grabbed James's wrist as he glared at his brother. All the lost fights over tin soldiers, miniature steam engines, and full-blooded ponies surged within him. Henry blinked first. "No. I'll not argue. Brother, this is not the time for us to engage in dispute. In the end, both you and I are aiming for the same purpose—to save the Hardin line. Though you may doubt me, I even want you to remain duke. There is only one way to do that."

James shook off Henry's grip. "You are asking too much, brother dear. Our family name means everything to me."

"And to me. Would you like to see our line die out as you slip into a poverty that everyone will witness?"

"Don't be absurd."

"Understand, brother dear, my own family's downfall will not be the only one brought about if you choose betrayal."

"Betrayal? My betrayal?" He inclined his head toward Henry. "I think you have that quite backward, brother dear."

Another cooling breath of air soothed the room. Each word must convince. "I am aware that Castle Hardin is mortgaged beyond redemption." Henry ordered his voice to emerge only in measured tones. "I also know it was Mother Dear who sustained you, Elvera, and Castle Hardin these last twenty years. Mother Dear did what she thought best. The past is past. What is important now is to save the Hardin line."

James took a turn around the floor before facing Henry. "The price you must pay is the salvation of Castle Hardin."

Henry shook his head as his gaze caught his brother's eye. "No. Castle Hardin is beyond redemption." He doled out his words carefully. "Even I do not have that kind of capital. But I can save our line. Think, James." He hurried on. "With that rock pile in Maryland and its enormous drain on all our purses gone, you and Elvera can move here to Union County. I am prepared to keep you both in a style befitting your social standing. Don't fret, you'll be fawned over here even more than back home." The breaths came hard as Henry scanned his brother head to foot. Had the fool understood?

"And?" A quizzical look streaked through the anger on James's face.

"There is more. You and Elvera will live here with me during most of the year, but when you do visit Maryland, I will see to it you travel with all the trappings expected of the American duke."

"Hmm." James lifted his chin. "And if I don't want such trappings . . . and all that goes with them?"

"The answer is quite simple, brother. The Hardin name will die out."

"My silence—isn't that what this is all about?"

Henry held himself still. If Margaret were to be saved, this was the moment. "A silence that will save us all. Without you holding your tongue, that myth, that dream, that story drilled into us both during our twice-weekly visits at Father's footstool—that story will die." Henry nodded his certainty. "That forlorn hope that one day, one of us—an American Hardin—will be welcomed back into England and celebrated as the rightful holder of England's most ancient and aristocratic title— Duke of Norwalk—that dream, dear James, will disappear. But it will not die under its own absurdity." He shook his head. "No, that fairy tale will collapse because you, James, will have killed it."

James cocked his head, one eyebrow arched. During their nursery days, Mammy Potts had punished Henry for James's infractions. James had learned to read his brother's face to see if Henry was going to take the fall for him or not . . . and also to see how Henry felt about doing so. Indeed, James' survival depended upon it. Tonight, the tiniest hint of doubt would leap out of those empty eyes. James grunted, but he kept Henry's face in sight.

"Have you considered who will be the greater loser if you persist in this slander?" Henry had to chance it. "No matter what tales circulate about my family here in Union County, I see very few business reper-cussions to my estate. To my social position, yes. Bertha and I will be social outcasts. Not just Margaret. But my ability to make money will be little affected. This frontier, as you call it, is much more forgiving of those who generate wealth."

"Frontier enough to accept a black child as a member of the aris-tocracy?" James snapped.

"Never . . . if one were to believe your tale. I will insist to the end, and so will Bertha, that our darling daughter's reputation has been besmirched beyond repair by the vindictive nature of my wastrel of a brother. No wonder I've cut him off without a penny, and he has fallen into the life of a pauper."

A smile creased Henry's face as he spoke, words pouring from his mouth. "James, all may not be lost, after all." Henry read his broth-er's face. "If you speak your lies, my daughter is ruined. After such a debacle, I will not be inclined to be so generous. Do you suppose you might make your own existence through riverboat gambling? Perhaps Elvera could show a bit of those stumpy legs of hers as she slides into her new role as a dance-hall girl." His chuckle came out low.

"Your humor has always suffered, Henry, under the odious serious-ness of your basic nature. Am I to understand you will continue my lifestyle, even here in Union County, in exchange for . . ." James glanced at the closed door. "Is that what you've just offered?"

"You are the American duke, lord of all the Hardins. As long as our line exists, I shall not forget that fact." Did Henry read reluctant acquiescence in his brother's face? Best to act quickly. "Now, shall we go downstairs and complete your niece's introduction into Union County society? You may have the second dance after I've twirled her across the floor." He willed his hands away from a heart that threatened to break through his shirt studs.

James walked to the sideboard, removed the stopper from the bour-bon, and poured himself half a glass. Henry threw open the library door only to spot Dr. Henderson huffing up the grand staircase, Delfine behind him. The swish of Salome's blue uniform blurred before him as she headed for the back stairs.

CHAPTER TWELVE

How long could it take, this last dance of Lady Margaret's coming-out party? Salome felt fresh perspiration soak into her already-wet uniform. How could one woman sweat so? *Please, Jesus, let Waylon make his way safely to Maxwell Joe.* His Grace held Margaret at arm's length, like she was a rattlesnake—as he waltzed her around the floor. But that look on the man's face—what was it? Neither a yes nor a no. The strings of the violin all sounded harsh and piercing. The new gaslight chandeliers flickered in her eyes, making her dizzy. *What, oh Jesus, was Lord Hardin's brother going to do?*

Salome had scurried into position right ahead of Lord Hardin as she ran from the sound of Doc Henderson's plodding feet climbing the stairs. Salome arrived at her post inside the ballroom doorway in time to catch buzzing talk bouncing around the party room. Salome strained to read guests' faces. Did that dried-up biddy who lived two farms down the road pass Margaret's name between her skinny lips in a gossipy way? What about Margaret's escort, the pimply-chinned but well-muscled judge's son, Sylvester Morse? The man Margaret hoped to marry someday. He didn't look too happy. Then Lord Hardin had appeared, Margaret on his arm.

The presentation had gone all right, and Salome sent up prayers of thanks that she could breathe again. All the low talk in the room had stopped. Lady Bertha stood during the entire presentation like a stone statue. As she surveyed the guests, Salome tried to blend into Lady Bertha's silk wallpaper. But His Grace's face kept pulling her eyes toward him as Lord Hardin got on with the formalities. Salome studied every tilt of his head, arch of his eyebrow, and twitch of the ducal lip, but His Grace gave away nothing as he stumbled Margaret across the floor for the required two minutes. Then sixty more anxious minutes as Salome held her place next to the wall before the music finally stopped.

"This show's 'bout over. Why don't you get on with your other duties?" Lady Hardin, her face purple enough to complement her lavender dress, startled Salome. The woman swept through the ballroom archway and into the foyer. "Go fetch Celeste from wherever that lazy wench is hidin' and send her up to my bedroom. I've got myself a frightful headache."

"Yes'm." Salome managed the little bow that all Hardin House servants were trained to use. Rarely did Lady Bertha Hardin speak to her in tones either good or bad, and Salome took special care to keep a goodly distance between herself and Lord Henry Hardin's wife.

"What do they call you, wench?"

Salome, on her way to fetch Celeste, hadn't heard His Grace walk up behind her.

"Whatever it is, you've lived to see another day." The alcohol-drenched breath of His Grace burned her left ear. "Well, what's it to be?"

His Grace's hand squeezed her backside through her blue uniform, getting in a quick rub. Salome's shoulders shuddered. *Do not turn around.* She took a step toward the kitchen and away from the duke.

His Grace moved forward as servants bustled about handing out wraps and hats to the departing guests. "Tell your lover that one night's victory does not a winning war make." He stationed himself in front of her, holding an empty glass. "I plan on examining every bit of what it is my brother sees in you under that blue outfit." He shoved the glass into her hands. "I'll come to your cabin, wench. You be ready for me. And if you value your Lady Margaret"—his face pinched—"I suggest you keep our trysts secret from my brother." His Grace looked around the room. No eyes were trained on them. He stepped past Salome and into the hallway, his arm brushing across her breast as he left the room.

"You get on outta here," Celeste mouthed as she walked out of the crowd and stood beside her. "I'll see to Lady Margaret."

"No. That ain't gonna work. I needs to see Lord Hardin."

"Not now you don't. Get on outta here befo' things goes from bad to worse." Celeste nodded toward the kitchen.

Salome started across the great hall when she spotted Henry Hardin with Margaret beaming on his arm. "Uh, suh, Lord Hardin, is there anythin' I can do fo' Lady Mar . . . ?"

Henry Hardin walked past Salome as though she were part of the blue peony wallpaper. "Get on upstairs, sugar," he said to Margaret. "Papa's going to have a word with your uncle James." He turned toward the front door and the last of the departing guests. His eyes swept past Salome, not one signal in them.

No help from Henry. Waylon. She had to see to her son. Salome rushed to the kitchen, grabbed her cloak, and stepped into the chilly April night. A cloud covered the quarter-moon, making her path almost unseeable in the darkness. No matter. She could take this walkway with three woolen blindfolds stretched across her eyes even if she picked up her pace.

"Woman, you headin' off lickety-split to meet up with Maxwell Joe?"

Salome stopped short as Jacob Slocum strode out of the brush on the side of the gravel-strewn roadway.

"Pardon, suh?" The only reason this fool of a man was troubling her was because of his dislike for Waylon. "Is there somethin' I can do fo' you, Mr. Slocum, suh?"

"Yeah. Judging from what the folks waitin' 'round for their carriages is hintin' at, you and yours can get to packin'. Be off this place by week's end." He smirked as he stood within touching distance of Salome. "Course, me or mine might want a taste of that girl of yours first." The man's laugh sounded more like a guffaw.

"Yes, suh. I'll take that message straight where it ought to go." She stepped around Slocum, her heart pounding. There had been talk about Margaret—talk that had drifted to the likes of Jacob Slocum.

The farm manager grabbed her arm and squeezed. "Don't you get smart with me, gal. Sass me, and I'll show you what's what."

She dropped her head. She'd say anything to get to Waylon. "No, suh, you's right to discipline me, though I didn't mean no sassin'."

He released her arm. Salome tightened the cloak about her and bobbed her sorrys. She began a slow saunter down the path. Between the sound of her own footfalls, she listened for Jacob Slocum. She sighed. Halfway home. No, he hadn't followed her, but he hadn't moved from his patch of ground either. She kept stepping through the darkness until she spotted the two lit windows of her own cabin. Waylon or Tom-Tom? What about Maxwell Joe? Jacob Slocum had already figured out that Waylon might be at the carpenter's dwelling. What did that man have planned? With her own house just thirty yards distant, Salome stepped off the path and scurried through the brush, traveling the quarter mile to Maxwell Joe's two-room cabin.

She picked up a clump of April mud and threw it against the side of the house. "Waylon, you in there?" She raised her voice just above a whisper. Nothing. She stepped closer, this time clutching a handful of pebbles. She flung them against a window. No sound other than the creak of the shed door opening behind her.

"In here, Miss Salome," Maxwell Joe called from the direction of the shed.

Salome surveyed as far as her eyes could see on this almost-moonless night. No Jacob Slocum. Not yet. She backed her way into the shed. Maxwell Joe's arm reached in front of her and closed the door. He slid a plank across the opening, locking them in. Salome started. She couldn't be this close to Maxwell. What would Lord Hardin say?

"Waylon?" She raised her voice. "Is you in here?"

"Yes, Mama, I'm here, but for the life of me I don't know why I've got to hide out like a scared rabbit. That duke fellow doesn't frighten me."

"Y'all needs to talk." Maxwell Joe laid a hand on Salome's arm as he led her deeper into the shed, her eyes adjusting to the gloom. "I'll step outside and hold guard on the do'. Waylon, you slip that there plank in place after I leaves."

"Yes, sir. Now, Mama, tell me what this is all about?" He hoisted the locking board across the narrow door.

The moment had come. But how would she do it? How would she tell her son about himself? He would most surely never love her again. He would hate her. Even in the gloom of the shed, the light from the small window let her see into the blue depths of her son's trusting eyes.

"Way . . . ," her voice croaked. "Waylon, I wants to . . . that is to say, I has somethin' to . . . ." Salome put her hands to her face and shook her head. This was too hard. *Father in Heaven, there must be another way.*

"Mama, what is it?" Waylon's voice climbed in alarm.

"You ain't never gonna fo'give me. Not in this life." She grabbed at his wrists. "But, promise me, when you gets to Heaven, you won't think all bad of me." The tears coursed down her cheeks. If she could take everything back she would. Taken baby Margaret and run away to

New Orleans. Make her way as a streetwalking woman if need be. But then, she wouldn't have had Waylon.

Her son broke her grip only to plant both hands on her shoulders. He gave her a shake, as if she were hysterical. "Mama, what are you talking about? Forgive you in Heaven? Forgive you for what?"

"You . . ." The tears running down her cheeks puddled on her upper lip. "You used to ask me 'bout . . . 'bout yo' pa. Wanted to know what become of him."

Waylon dropped his hands. "You said you couldn't talk about him. The very thought of the man made you remember the day he'd run off, leaving you, me, and Tom-Tom to make our way alone on this farm."

Salome bobbed her head as she clamped her stinging eyes shut. "That . . . ain't . . . the . . . straight of it."

Her son took a step backward. "What do you mean that's not the straight of it? Mama, don't take on so. I know more than you think I do. I figured . . ."

"What?" Salome stared at the outline of her son. "What you think you figured?"

"My pa, my father, was he a . . . a white man?" Waylon sucked in his lips.

Salome's mouth opened and closed like a river fish's. No sound came.

"Mama, I can see it. So can Tom-Tom. Your eyes aren't blue. Mine are close enough. Your hair's frizzy. Mine's straight. And my skin's three or four shades lighter than yours." He gathered her into a hug. "Mama, tell me who he was, and I'll kill the bas . . . kill him for what he did to you."

Oh, God, no! She broke away. "No! I mean to say, Waylon, that ain't it. I mean to say that is it. But not rightly all of it."

Salome watched as Waylon shook his head in confusion.

"Promise me, Waylon, you won't up and kill nobody if I tells you what you got a right to know."

"Mama, if a man has wronged you, then I've got no choice but to—"

"Waylon, you ain't but fifteen. Not time yet fo' you to be seekin' vengeance."

Waylon's lips set in a thin line. "Who was he?"

"Lord Hardin." There. After eighteen years of being scared of the truth every morning and every night, Salome finally blurted out her secret.

"Lord Hardin? What's he got to do with this?" Waylon towered over Salome by almost half a head. Now he bent down to look straight into her eyes.

Salome bit down on her lip. The words in her head could not get themselves in order. "Lord Hardin . . . he the one." The moonlight was brighter now so she could see her son almost as clear as if a kerosene lantern hung from Maxwell Joe's shed rafter.

"The one? Lord Hardin is the one?" The blue of his eyes glowed bright. "The one for what?" He cocked his head. "Mama, you're not trying to tell me . . . trying to say . . . that Lord Hardin is my father?"

Salome knew she was supposed to nod, but her neck muscles wouldn't allow it. She understood she was to fall to her knees and beg Waylon's forgiveness but her legs refused to budge. All she could do was stand, frozen in place.

Waylon took a step backward, his probing eyes scanning her up and down. Judging her. "The schooling." His voice dipped into a hoarse whisper. "Teaching me to speak proper English. Training me for jobs that coloreds could never have. He . . . you . . ." Waylon clutched at his belly right before he doubled over. Supper spewed between his fingers.

Something that felt like a bullet shot through Salome's body. She was at her son's side without knowing how she got there. "It wasn't like I . . ." No, she couldn't tell her boy she went unwilling to Henry Hardin's bed. Waylon was but fifteen. He'd do something more than foolish. "He took a likin' to me. The way some white mens do fo' their colored workers. He promised to take care of all y'all. He even 'lowed you to go to school with your si—" A pitchfork worked its way inside Salome's gut. What had she almost said? She had to tell the whole story to save all her children, but how?

Waylon pushed her away as he rushed to the front of the shed and the plank.

"No," Salome shouted, "I can't let you outta here 'til you hears the rest of it." Her breathing slowed itself. He had damned her to Hell. So be it, but she had to help Waylon. "You 'most a man now. Maxwell Joe tells me so."

Waylon whipped around. "Maxwell Joe? He knows the truth, too? About you and Henry Hardin?"

"Don't nobody know the truth fo' sho but seven people. Plenty others think they know, but they just guessin'. Now, you gotta hear the whole story. This here ain't 'bout me. This here 'bout you and Tom-Tom and . . . and . . ."

Waylon turned from the plank, his eyes searching his mother. "Tom-Tom. Who's his pa?"

Salome heard her son's breath come out heavy and leaden. "Listen to me good, boy. I'm gonna tell you 'bout the papa of all three of my chil'ren, and you . . ."

"Three?" His voice exploded in the shed so loudly that Maxwell Joe rapped on the outside wall for quiet.

Salome put a finger to her lips. "People's lives is at stake here. You gotta pay me close mind."

Waylon stared at her like he didn't know what to believe.

"I was a young gal when Lord Hardin spotted me. I reckon he did have a little mo' care for me 'cause of what his overseer done to my mama—yo' grandma—that got me born and made Henry Hardin feel kind of bad. But not bad 'nough not to take me to his bed when I got up to some size."

Waylon turned his head. "I don't need to hear this."

Salome stopped herself from gathering her boy into her arms. "You young, yes, but you got to be a man now 'cause this is so important."

He turned back to face her. "You let a man use you. A white man."

"I didn't want my firstborn. Tried to stop that child from bein' born, but Mattie Lou and Delfine, they wouldn't have it my way."

"Mattie Lou? Delfine? What do they have to do with this?"

"I was shamed, you see. Shamed 'cause my mama had been beaten and mistreated so bad in bed by that white overseer, she went crazy. She didn't want me, and, like her, I didn't want no chile that didn't come out of love, and I ain't never loved Henry Hardin."

"Mama." At least his condemning voice lightened up.

"I needs you to hear me out. Soon as that baby was pulled out of me, I knowed I was glad she'd been a'born. I would have . . ."

Waylon tilted his head. "She?" Confusion spilled out of his eyes. "You mean *me*. You were glad *I'd* been born."

"Weren't none of you."

"Not me?" He stared at her as though the strain of talking about his father had addled his mother's mind. "Mama, I'm your firstborn. Your son."

"No. You ain't."

"Huh?"

"You wasn't none of my firstborn. And she was a daughter, not a son."

Waylon stood there, in the dark and damp of Maxwell Joe's shed, blinking his eyes at her. She could read her boy's gaze. Disappointment faded, replaced by worry. If he could, Waylon would certify her insane, and if Union County had a home for the colored crazy, he'd lock her up.

"Mama." Her son's voice came out soft. He must have told himself that to raise his voice would throw his mother into some kind of a fit from which she'd never return. "Your firstborn was a girl? And she died? How old was she?"

"She ain't dead."

"Yes, Mama, I know it must feel to you like she's still alive, but you don't have a living daughter." Waylon held his open palms toward her as if reaching to bring her back from the brink. Her boy had always been old for his years.

"She's livin', and she's right here at Hardin House."

Waylon frowned. Was he trying to identify all the light-skinned colored girls about the place? That list would be quite short—and none were lighter-skinned than her elder son. He shook his head.

Salome took in as big a breath as she could muster. She closed her eyes. "Lady . . . Margaret." She opened her eyes. "She's my daughter . . . and your sister."

Waylon's face, his entire body, lit up in Maxwell Joe's shed as sure as if every flame in every chandelier in the Hardin House ballroom aimed itself right at him.

"Sister? Lady Marg . . . ?" Both eyebrows arched almost to the shock of straight hair that fell across his forehead. "Mama . . ." Waylon pointed to the front door, where Maxwell Joe stood guard. He mouthed the words: "Lady Margaret is a white girl. She can't be your daughter."

"You ain't never taken a peek into her eyes? You ain't never seen they was the same color as yours?"

Waylon's mouth twitched as his eyes roamed Salome's face.

"You ain't seen that you and her look just like brother and sister? Her skin come out white, while your'n is yellow. If you'd been born with white skin, it woulda been you that was Lord Hardin's rightful heir. You'da been the next duke of Union County."

Salome watched Waylon take a wobbly step backward. He put a hand against the shed wall to steady himself.

He looked about to cry. "Mama, you're telling . . . are you telling me that . . . that Lady Margaret and me . . . we've got the same father?"

"And Tom-Tom, too."

"Tom-Tom?" Waylon answered Salome as though she'd been speaking one of those foreign tongues he'd learned up at the Hardin House schoolroom.

"He come out the darkest of all." Salome glanced at the door. Maxwell Joe stood outside. She knew why her thirdborn had been the least favored of all three of Henry Hardin's children, but she couldn't let on to Waylon that Lord Hardin suspected her of an affair with the carpenter. "Yo' father promised me he would see to it that you and Tom-Tom was always taken care of as long as I keep my counsel to myself. As long as I didn't make no claim on Mar . . . my daughter."

Waylon stiffened. "A claim? What about Lady Hardin?" He shook his head. "No, Mama, you must be wrong. Lady Bertha would never go along with such a thing."

"Oh, don't fret none. Lady Hardin ain't never had a kind word to say to or about your sister. You and everybody else in Union County know that for the God's truth. But whatever misery she feels, she ain't tellin' nothin'. I don't know what he said or did, but Lord Hardin done took care of Lady Bertha."

Waylon furrowed his brow. "You said seven people knew the truth for sure. You, Lord Hardin, Lady Bertha and . . . ?"

"Mattie Lou, Delfine, Georgia, and Tessie. They pulled all three of y'all chil'ren outta me."

Waylon walked up to her. "What about Lady . . . Margaret? Does she know?"

Salome clutched her son's arm. She caught his eye. Was he ready to hear the full truth? "I know yo' sister acts uppity sometimes. It's 'cause that's the way she's been trained—to act like a rich white woman. It ain't none of her fault." She tried to read the thoughts forming inside her son's head.

Waylon pounded his chin with a fisted hand. "Mama! You're trying to tell me Margaret doesn't know she's . . . she's colored? Oh, Jesus Lord!"

"You see why I needs you, son. His Grace seems like he done guessed the truth. If they is even one little chance that Lord Hardin can save yo' sister, I knows he will. But if everything goes wrong, you gotta be ready to get outta Union County and take Margaret and Tom-Tom with you." Salome's heart beat so loud she could barely hear her own words. "You all right to do that?"

Waylon's face showed only shock. "All right to do that? Lady . . . Margaret thinking she's something she's not. Why should she get all the privileges just because Tom-Tom and I are two or three shades more brown than her?"

Salome waited patiently. She knew this had to come. Waylon's tirade. No, it wasn't fair, but for now, it was the way of the world. "'Cause that's the way colored folk do this thing. Margaret ain't the first colored person to step into the white world—a place where she's got a chance to live free with the right to say yes and no to a thing—includin' men." Salome clutched Waylon's arm. "I wish to God ever' one of His creatures—you and Tom-Tom, too—had the same chance as Margaret. The Good Lord ain't seen fit to make that happen jest yet. But, I swears I'll go to my grave protectin' any colored person who gets a chance like this. Jest 'cause most of us suffers, don't mean ever' one of us got to."

Waylon kept his distance. "You want me to protect Margaret despite everything?"

"You almost a man."

Waylon nodded. "I'll protect you all. You, Tom-Tom, and Lad . . . and Margaret."

Salome laid a hand on the plank holding the door shut as she sent up a quick prayer to the Lord. Pushing up the board, she opened the door. Maxwell Joe, his face heavier with worry than she'd ever seen it, looked back at her.

CHAPTER THIRTEEN

"Tom-Tom, you in here?" Salome stepped through her back door and into the kitchen. She could barely turn the knob to close her door, her hands shook so. Walking over to the sideboard, she grabbed the water pitcher, her enamel drinking cup beside it. She spilled more on the wood sideboard than she got into the blue cup. It took both hands to get the enamel vessel to her lips. She downed the contents in four big gulps. She leaned back against the sideboard and eyed the four kitchen chairs surrounding her table. She could think better if she could make her way to one of those slat-backed oak chairs and sit for a spell, but she couldn't trust her legs to carry her. She'd barely made it into the house. Thank the Good Lord she'd convinced Maxwell Joe to stay with Waylon in the shed, though the man had just about insisted on walking Salome back to her house.

She'd done the only thing she could to save her children, but it had taken everything out of her to do it. She'd just lifted the water pitcher again when a thump and a quick burst of cold air forced her eyes to her kitchen door—now standing wide-open. Oh, Jesus, Mary Magdalene, and God Almighty! The pitcher clattered to the wood floor. His Grace!

The figure stepped across her threshold and closed the door behind him. James Hardin moved to the far window, snapping her calicos together. He slipped over to her. "Wench, where's the bedroom? Let's get to it." He pressed her body against the sideboard.

"Ah, suh, Lord James. Yo' Grace . . . I . . . my boy . . . he a'comin' here any minute." Salome tried to work her arms between the man's body and her breasts.

"That scalawag? If he knows what's good for him, he'll shut up and watch." His Grace gobbled at her neck as he bent her almost backward over the sideboard.

Salome squirmed against him, but he held her fast. She worked a knee between his legs. Her kitchen walls bounced in and out of her vision. She struggled to force her knee into his manhood but she couldn't lift her leg high enough. "Lord . . . Grace." She gasped for air as the man squeezed her around the chest and swung her away from the sideboard. "This here ain't gonna work."

He took a step back. "I'll tell you what's not going to work—you defying me. Now I asked you, where's the bedroom?"

The shaking in her knees traveled to her throat. "Suh, I ain't defyin' you. Jest . . . jest let's figure out a better place . . . a better time . . ."

The black of His Grace's dinner coat sleeve blurred across her eyes a split second before she felt his fingers grab the top of her blue uniform. Salome sucked in a breath as the ripping sound blasted her ears. She blinked when two buttons struck her cheek and forehead. When she opened her mouth to let more air into her body, James Hardin's hands yanked the carefully stitched uniform off both shoulders. She wore no chemise. She watched a lopsided leer cross the man's reddening face as he stared at her naked breasts.

"No!" The sound came from somewhere deep inside. Salome took the last of her breath to give her the strength to pound her hands against the man's chest. She had to get away.

James dropped his arms, took a step backward, and laughed. "If this is how you wish it, I'm delighted to play."

When the blow from his fist landed on her chin, Salome felt her knees buckle. She was on the floor, the taste of blood on her lips. His Grace jerked her upright and gathered her into his arms. Her head lolled as Lord James carried her and stalked through her kitchen. The whitewash of her ceiling flickered in and out of her sight as he carried her into the next room—Waylon and Tom-Tom's kerosene-lit bedroom. He dropped her hard on the feather mattress and knelt beside her, his hands tearing open more of her uniform.

"Naw, suh." Paring knives shredded her chest with each sound that stumbled out of her mouth. "Not this here room. Please, suh. Let's go to my room. Not here."

He yanked the dress over her feet and tossed the ripped garment to the floor. Salome wore the store-bought bloomers Lord Henry had given her. She grabbed at the tying strings holding them tight around her waist. Lord James pounded on her knuckles.

"Ahh, Jesus!" She flailed at the duke as he wrestled the drawers off her.

James Hardin climbed on the bed and straddled her. He drove his pant-covered knees between her legs.

"Suh, I begs you to Jesus. Take me in my room, please. Not here. This here's my boys' . . ."

His Grace unbuttoned his trousers and pulled out his manhood— was it even two inches long? "Wench, you'd better cooperate. With you, I bet I can get a rise. But if you don't want to . . ." He scooted back onto her belly, knocking even more air out of her. "Margaret, isn't it? In fact, I'm feeling I need me a young one, anyway. Unused." That laugh that sounded like it came straight from the Devil blew across her face.

Salome eased her head around to look up at Lord James. She struggled to lie still.

"That's more like it, wench." He eased away from her while he took off his jacket and shirt. His pants slipped to the floor, then he hoisted himself back onto her and spread her legs farther than they ought to go.

"Mama! Mama, what is it?" Waylon's voice flung itself from the kitchen door and into her bedroom.

"No, boy." It was Maxwell Joe. "You stay in here."

"No. Something's wrong with my mother."

"I'm tellin' you, you stays right here."

"No."

His Grace started to pull away when he heard the voices. Salome took in a breath. She heard the smack, the cry, and then the thud. Footsteps marching to the closed bedroom door pounded in her ears. Lord, please not Waylon. She heard the door open. Salome couldn't see through the blocking body of James Hardin, but she heard the startled voice. Maxwell Joe.

"Uh, suh?" The surprise in the man's voice melted into caution. "Sorry, suh, ain't realized it was . . . thought Salome . . . she might be needin' . . . her boy. He here. Wanna come see his mama."

"Get out of here, nigger. This is none of your business. You take that yellow bastard on back to wherever it is you two came from." His Grace twisted his body just enough to allow Salome a peek at Maxwell Joe.

Please, Lord, let the man know to keep Waylon safe. Never mind her. James Hardin wasn't the first white man to enter her. She let her son's name form on her swelling lips. Please let the carpenter read her face. She put pleading into her eyes.

"Yas, suh. Mighty sorry, suh. I'll be goin' now." But Maxwell Joe didn't move.

He kept his eyes trained on His Grace. She gave little shakes to her head. *Please, oh please, don't do nothin' foolish.*

"Well, get, then." His Grace still held his body twisted toward Maxwell Joe.

"Yas, suh. It's jest that Waylon come down from the Big House with a message from Lord Hardin." Maxwell Joe kept his arms in front of him, down near his waist, going through the motions of rolling a cap in his hands. He looked the picture of perfect obedience.

His Grace turned back to Salome; his manhood, never fully engaged, was now dead limp. He scowled at her. "What's this nigger's name? You'd better get rid of him."

"Maxwell . . ." Where was the breath she needed to get out his name? "Maxwell . . . Joe. I knows what Lord Hardin be wantin'. You can tell him I'll fetch Lady Margaret's shawl to her in the morning." She'd borrowed air from tomorrow.

"Master say you's to put the shawl in that rosewood box I made for Lady Margaret's comin'-out party. Say's you's to fetch it to her right away. Yo' Grace, suh, I can waits in the kitchen, or outside the do' if you likes, but Master tell Waylon, he wants that shawl right away."

"Get the hell out of here, nigger, and close the door behind you."

"Yas, suh." Maxwell shut the door, but Salome did not hear the clicking of the catch.

Lord James shifted his body over Salome's. "You're a good-looking wench, all right. I see what my brother wants with you." He licked the blood off her lip. "That nigger's ruined it for tonight, but the next time I come to see you, you're going to be more cooperative. Agreed? And if you say one word to my brother about this, not only will I tell the world about Lady Margaret, I will personally take every stitch of clothing off that girl. Teach her a few things." He backed off Salome and reached for his clothes. "Make her yellow brother watch."

"But, suh, that would be against the Bible. She . . . Margaret, she yo' blood niece."

"All the more fun for me." His Grace buttoned his trousers and walked out the door.

The tears caught in Salome's throat loosened themselves and made their way to her eyes. She shifted her hips, struggled to roll to her side, winced, and fell back onto the feather bed. Her boy might rush in at any moment. She had to cover herself. Tightening her belly, she eased one leg over the other as she rolled to her side. The effort ravaged her insides. Groaning, she drew her legs to her chest as she heard a commotion in the kitchen.

"Mr. Max . . . ughh . . . why did you hit me?" Waylon sounded groggy.

"'Cause you wasn't payin' me no mind."

Salome spotted her torn dress on the floor. She knew she had to grab the garment and, at the least, throw it over herself for cover, but her arms refused to stop clutching her knees. She couldn't move as she listened to Waylon staggering to his feet.

"Mama? My mama." The boy's voice rose. "I heard her calling out."

"I done took care of all that. Now you get on over to Miss Mattie Lou and Tom-Tom. Y'all stay the night."

"Stay the night?" Waylon sounded like sense was coming back to him. "What's happened to my mother?"

"Ain't nothin' happened to her, and I aims to keep it that way. Now you git."

"Mr. Maxwell Joe, I'm not going anywhere. Please move. I want to see what's wrong with my mother."

"Not now. Yo' mama's had to deal with Lord Hardin's brother, and he ain't no easy man to converse with."

"Converse with His Grace?" Now Waylon sounded alarmed. "He was here? In this house?" Waylon's voice climbed even higher. "With my mother?"

"He threatened, all right. Come to talk 'bout Lady Margaret. Don't rightly know 'bout what, but he come to make sho Salome keep her mouth shut 'bout somethin'. I come in, and they was arguin'. I knowed you'd misunderstand. That's why I had to make sho you stayed put."

Salome licked the salty tears off her lips. In all her troubles, the Lord had sent her a good man to help. Praise Jesus for Maxwell Joe and his lies.

"She's all right, then?" Waylon sounded hesitant.

"No, she ain't all right. What you think I'm tellin' you? Yo' mama's upset. A white man done come into her house and tole her she'd better keep her mouth shut or he gonna give her a good whuppin'."

"If that so-called duke of anything ever lays a hand on my mother, I'll—"

"You enough to worry yo' mama into her grave. That man ain't laid a hand on her, but he scared her plenty. Now, she wants you to run on over to Mattie Lou's and look after Tom-Tom. I don't reckon nothin's gonna happen tonight, but I'm gonna keep an eye out fo' an hour or two, then I'll head on back home. Yo' mama be good and asleep by that time. Now, you git."

Salome, still on her side, shivered as she heard Waylon take his leave. Maxwell Joe headed toward the bedroom. She heard the tap-tap on the doorjamb. Why couldn't she reach for that dress?

"Miss Salome, I gots to come in. Sees you all right."

"Uhh." Salome drew her bare legs even tighter to her chest. She fixed her eyes on the far wall as Maxwell Joe's footsteps crossed her wooden floor. She caught the scent of the man approaching her. She spotted his sleeve-covered arm as he bent down to scoop up what was left of her blue uniform. Maxwell Joe threw it over her without even a glance at her naked body.

"Miss Salome, I don't wants you to fret none. Both yo' boys is gonna be kept out of this here. It gonna look like an accident. Ever'body you loves gonna be okay."

She turned to him. Maxwell Joe stood looking her in the eyes. Grimness etched itself across his brow. Her heart, that thing that had tried to stop its beating, blasted to life again.

"No. Maxwell Joe." She clutched at the scraps of uniform covering her. "Ain't no need to do none of that." She eased her knees away from her chest. "He hit me, all right, and he ain't had no good intentions towards me, but he ain't had time to do nothin' mo'." She slipped one arm out from the covering uniform. She held out a hand. "You got here jest in time." The tears came out in big aching sobs. "You the best man I ever knowed. Ain't none on God's earth no better."

Maxwell Joe knelt beside her, his face muscles twitching as he folded her arm across the covering uniform. "You ain't jest tellin' me you all right, is you, Salome? If that man done anythin' to you, it won't mean nothin' to me to see that he dead. I got me a way to make that happen without nobody bein' the wiser."

"He wanted his way with me, I ain't denyin' that"—she worked her mouth to stop the trembling—"but you came jest in time. He ain't . . . he didn't . . . I's all right."

"You ain't all right. A blind man can see that, but if you says . . ."

"I'm good 'nough all right, thanks to you, Maxwell Joe." She wiped at her eyes. "Oh, Lord in Heaven. If only this world was different, then you and me . . ."

"Salome, I . . ." He reached for her uncovered arm but stopped himself.

Salome looked into his eyes. Not one time did this man look down at her body. She bit her lip, but the words came out anyway. "I jest wishes I was a woman decent 'nough fo' you. I'd give jest 'bout anythin' if . . ."

"Miss Salome, you the most decent woman I've ever knowed. I'd do anythin' fo'—"

Bam. The kitchen door slammed open.

"Maxwell Joe, Mama, somebody coming up the path. I think it's Lord Hardin. I spotted him when I was almost over to Mattie Lou's. I ran all the way here." Sure enough, Waylon sounded out of breath.

Salome scooted up in bed, still covering herself as best she could with the ripped garment. "Waylon, if you ever thought you loved yo' mama, get outta here now."

"Mama, are you sure?" The voice came from closer to the bedroom door.

Maxwell Joe turned and disappeared from Salome's view. She heard struggling as two pairs of feet moved through her back door.

"I'm gonna be right outside this do', Miss Salome. Waylon here gonna do what he's told." The kitchen door closed quietly.

"Salome, are you in there?" The whispered voice of Henry Hardin called out from her front porch.

Salome leaned her back straight against the headboard as the never-locked front door opened. She heard Lord Hardin step across her front room. Jesus, what was she going to tell the man? He couldn't hear the full truth. He'd start up a fuss that could bring bad to all her children. Thank the good Lord Waylon had finally heeded her words.

"Salome? Salome? Where the hell are you?" His footsteps clattered into the kitchen. "Salome! Answer me."

"Here." Her voice cracked as she sent up her prayer: *Let Waylon and Maxwell Joe be long gone.* "In the boys' room." She sounded louder this time.

"What are you doing in . . . ?" Henry Hardin trod across the floorboards. He stopped short in the doorway, his eyes searching her out. "What in the name of . . ." He rushed to her side and with one hand jerked away the scrap of blue uniform. "Oh, my God." He dropped onto the mattress beside her.

Salome closed her eyes as Henry held her close. A shudder raked her body. Henry Hardin had struck her more than once, but he'd never beaten her, nor had he hurt her in bed. Tonight he was at his best. She understood that he wanted to comfort her. But neither her body nor her head wanted either Hardin man anywhere near her. Henry released her. His eyes scanned her face and body. Laying a gentle finger across the cut on her lip, he shook his head.

"Once I got Margaret settled I decided to come see you." His voice sounded heavy. "To talk to you about our girl. That's when I spotted him on the path."

Was that a bruise on his left cheek? And that eye sure appeared black and blue. "Yes, suh?"

"James. I knew he'd come to torment you. We had a tussle. He swore to me he hadn't . . . he hadn't hurt you. Is that true?" Lord Hardin peered into her eyes.

"Yes, suh. Oh, he hit me good. Says I was to stay away from Lady Margaret . . ." The words soared out of her mouth.

Lord Hardin shook his head. "No use lying to me, Salome. This will go better if you give me the truth. Did my brother force you?"

She shook her head no.

"How did your dress . . ." He held the rag up to her face. "How did this happen?"

The trembling swept through her limbs so hard, her teeth chattered. "He done it," she whispered. "Tore off my dress, but he ain't gone no further 'cause . . . 'cause Waylon, he come in. Even so, don't reckon he could do much anyway." She watched Henry's face drop into a scowl. "No, no. I don't mean to say Waylon saw anything. He ain't. But the sound of him, it scared off His Grace."

Henry examined his hands. Salome spotted bloodied and bruised knuckles.

"My brother declared he came in and found you with . . . with Maxwell Joe. That's when he hit you . . . for being untrue to me." He placed both hands on her face. "Was Maxwell Joe here?"

The whitewashed walls of her boys' room bulged. Henry's hands gently squeezed her cheeks. Her head felt light.

"Salome, Salome. You need a stiff drink." Henry Hardin sounded frantic as he hovered over her.

"Him . . . and . . . Waylon . . . they saved me. Lord James . . . he was on top of me. He—" The sobs welled up from somewhere deep inside. She knew she had to tell Lord Hardin bits of the truth—to keep Maxwell Joe safe—but she couldn't find the words.

Henry tapped at his wounded cheek before he looked back at Salome. "What was Maxwell Joe doing here?"

Her voice gurgled. She reached for the water pitcher next to the kerosene lamp. There was no cup. Henry held the pitcher for her to take a swallow.

"Bringin' Waylon home," she managed. "I had to tell him . . ." Oh, Lord, with all the other troubles, her daughter's plight had slipped from the front of her mind. "I had to tell him 'bout Lady Margaret. He got upset and run off to Maxwell Joe." She gestured for more water.

Henry tipped the pitcher to her lips again. "Go on."

"Ain't neither one of them seen . . . seen what His Grace was tryin' to do to me. His Grace, he rolled off of me befo' . . . befo' . . ."

Henry set the pitcher on the wooden cabinet. "I know my brother. I know very well when he's lying. I am grateful to Maxwell Joe for coming when he did. I can handle James. For now, I've got to keep both you and Margaret safe."

Salome crossed a hand over her naked chest. "Henry, suh, please tell me Lady Margaret don't know they's been talk."

"She does not know and I will keep it that way, but you've told Waylon." He put down the pitcher. "I didn't want that."

"Yas, suh. I knowed it was wrong of me, but he got suspicious with all the talk tonight." Her head hurt so, she prayed she could keep the lie straight. "He was 'bout to guess." She spread her hands open on the coverlet. "Suh, if all this talk did get to Lady Margaret, you reckon it's time to tell her the truth 'bout herself?"

Henry jerked his head up. "I absolutely forbid it. My daughter is, and will be treated as, a white woman. Better. I'm determined she will receive all the courtesies due a woman of her position." He waited for

Salome to give the nod of the head she didn't feel. "All of us will go on as before except for one thing."

Lord Hardin couldn't be more wrong, but how to tell him that, she didn't know. "What that one thing, suh?"

"James. I'll keep a close eye on my brother."

"Won't he be goin' back to Maryland soon, suh?"

"I'm keeping him right here at Hardin House. And you, too."

Salome shook her head. "Me, too? Me too what, suh?"

"We've both got to protect Margaret—you and I. And I've got to protect you. I can't do that with you living almost a mile from the main house. I'm moving you."

"Movin' me? Where, suh?" *Lord have mercy.* Salome had heard the old slavery stories about colored mistresses being sold south when their white lovers tired of them. She shivered.

"Hardin House." Henry nodded as though his words made the most sense of any spoken tonight. "You're going to share a room with Delfine. Oh, you can keep this little cabin for the boys, and of course, you and I can still spend our nights here."

Salome's voice was full force. "Hardin House? Suh, you jest said His Grace gonna be stayin' there." A shudder made her jump. "If I goes to the Big House, I won't have no need fo' this cabin. Lord James, he have me ever' night up at Hardin House, Delfine or no."

Henry wrapped his arms around her. "That's exactly what won't happen. I'll keep all three of you under my watchful eye. You, Margaret, and James. If my brother even says a harsh word to you, I'll know. After my discussion with James on the path a few minutes back, he understands his role very well. He'll not bother you—not if he wants food in his belly, rain off his head, and all the fixings of a duke." Henry stood and reached out a hand. "Let's get you cleaned up and into your own bed. I think I'll spend the night."

What did this man think of her? If Henry Hardin had any feelings at all for her, he would never expect her to sleep with him or any man after what almost happened. Not for some time. But here he was. As always, Lord Hardin's wants were not to be denied. She nodded as she took Henry's arm and eased herself out of bed. He did have feelings for her, Salome was certain, the same kinds of feelings he had for his favorite hunting hound or his best riding horse. Henry, knowing what she'd gone through, was going to bed her tonight while Maxwell Joe had never sneaked even one glance at her nakedness.

Lord Hardin helped her into bed. He poured water from a basin and handed her a washrag, then he peeled off his own clothes. Salome dabbed at her sore spots. She was a colored woman, and everybody knew colored women would never have an easy time in this life. Like many women before her, she'd have to wait 'til Heaven time. Putting the rag in the basin, she settled herself on her back. She lay still while the duke of Union County climbed on top of her bruised body. She closed her eyes. She'd do what she had to for Waylon, Tom-Tom, and Margaret.

CHAPTER FOURTEEN

"Lady Margaret, best if you have yo' shawl at the ready fo' the fireworks tonight." Salome folded up the woven, blue-striped length of cloth and dropped it into the straw basket she'd prepared for her charge's outing. "This here's gonna be the biggest doin's Union County ever seen—this bein' the first Fourth of July in a brand-new century. My, my, sure seems funny talkin' 'bout a new number. Nineteen hundred."

Margaret stood in front of her oval floor-standing looking glass, hands stretched around her waist, trying to make her fingers meet. She frowned as she twisted her body, first right, then left. "Salome, can't you pull my corset tighter? I look as big around as Mattie Lou!"

"If I do, Lady Margaret, them strings is gonna bust faster than—"

"Lady Bertha's right. Salome, you do chatter on." Without taking her eyes off her reflection, she called over her shoulder, "I think I want Tessie to be my chaperone tonight."

Salome stared over her daughter's back and into the mirror. Her girl favored her father in more ways than looks. Sorry to say she wasn't a natural beauty, not even to a mother's eyes. Now that Salome was a lady's maid, she worked extrahard at pulling and twisting her daughter's frizzy hair into that Gibson-girl piled-on-top-of-the-head pouf that made Margaret look passable. Funny how the world worked. Waylon, eighteen now, was the one with all the good looks, down to his straight nose, just-right lips, blue-green eyes, and straight hair. Only his golden skin gave him away. But Margaret's face wasn't the only thing that put Salome in mind of Henry Hardin. His daughter carried those same airs as did he—expecting folks to fall all over themselves, with never a kind word when they did. It wasn't a pretty picture in the father, but Henry Hardin was a rich white man. Margaret was a secret colored girl. What would happen to Salome's baby if folks said out loud what too many already thought in the quiet of their heads?

"Yes'm." Salome pushed the thought out of her mind as she snapped the straw basket closed. These three years close-up with Margaret hadn't been easy. The girl had bridled when Lord Henry replaced Tessie with her. Salome knew the why of it. Tessie had never been much of a lady's maid, and Margaret's tantrums always won the day—sometimes annoying even Henry. Tessie never did have the nerve to correct the girl. "Lady Margaret, I don't mind at all watchin' over you at this evenin's fireworks."

"Mama's right, you know. You do take on airs that are too uppity for a servant. I'll decide who's to chaperone me."

"Of course, Lady Margaret." Salome stood aside as Margaret flounced out of her bedroom and into the upstairs hallway, almost bumping into Celeste.

"Has Lady Bertha gone downstairs yet?" Margaret snapped at the elderly woman.

"Yes'm. She 'bout ready to step outside to the barbecue doin's. Lord Hardin, he already out there."

"Hmm. I'll just go down and speak to Lady Bertha." Margaret headed toward the grand staircase. She called out as Salome and the limping Celeste moved toward the back hallway, "Tell Tessie to meet me in the foyer after I've had a word with Lady Bertha."

"Reckon she ever gonna stop callin' that woman Lady Bertha?" Celeste, her arms around an even larger straw basket, waited until Salome reached the top of the back stairs. "That girl ain't never called that woman Mama in all her life."

Salome turned toward Celeste. Lady Bertha's maid knew better than to say such a thing, especially to her. "Celeste, can you go fetch Tessie? I'll tote yo' basket fo' you."

Celeste, her plaited gray hair tied up in a red-white-and-blue bandana, nodded as she handed over her basket. She rubbed at her always-painful hip. "Why Lady Margaret pretendin' she gonna get anythin' outta Lady Bertha other than a hard time, I swears to Jesus I don't know."

"Celeste!"

"Keep yo' drawers on, Salome. I'll fetch Tessie so you can get an earful of what's goin' on downstairs. If you was to ask me, I'd tell you that Tessie ain't much good, lookin' after Lady Margaret. Lord Hardin's girl too full of herself."

Salome juggled the second basket in her arms as she made her way downstairs, through the hall, near the wood-paneled study. She shivered. Another worry. Celeste wasn't the only one who noticed Lord Hardin's wife never permitted her so-called daughter to call her anything but Lady Bertha.

"Have they arrived yet?" Excitement poured out of Margaret's voice as she stepped into the room with its heavy, ruby-red drapes and marble fireplace that comforted in the winter.

Salome halted outside the open door, out of sight of the two women. Even though she lived under the same roof as Henry's wife, Salome prided herself on keeping their face-to-face meetings few and far between. Neither one of them wanted to look the other in the eye.

"If you meanin' Judge Morse and his family, I believe the answer is yes." Bertha, in her gray flannel dress dolloped with a touch of dark green at the bodice, looked anything but festive. "That's why I'm about to go out to this here dreadful event. Used to enjoy barbecues, but now with everybody in the neighborhood whisperin' and pointin' fingers . . . tryin' to guess which one of my servants . . ." Bertha Hardin stood with her arms folded across her chest as she talked at the window. "Where is that Celeste with my basket?" She turned toward the open study door, her eyes sweeping past Margaret.

Salome took just enough of a step backward to keep the two women in sight.

"She's coming." Margaret always looked pained when she was in the presence of her supposed mother. "Lady Bertha . . . do you think I should go out to greet him, or wait for him to come to the door looking for me? We've not had doings this big since my coming-out party."

Lady Bertha turned from the window, a frown of annoyance streaking her forehead. "Greet him? Which him? Oh, you're prattlin' on 'bout Judge Morse's boy, Sylvester. Margaret, what is it you think you want with him? Yes, his chin could do with a little cleanup, but he's a big, strapping boy. He's goin' to make a fine lawyer one day. Graduated two years back from the University of Arkansas law school and already has him a practice over in Little Rock. His family will be wantin' him to marry into high society. I hear tell they're preenin' him to be governor of Arkansas." She turned back to the window.

Salome heard the swish of Margaret's cotton daydress as she took a step toward Bertha, stopped, and clapped her hands. "I think that would be glorious. The two of us—me and Sylvester—in Little Rock. Me, a governor's wife."

Lady Bertha spun around so hard her flannel skirt cracked the air. "You? You believe you'll be a governor's wife one day?" She tilted her head. A smile that looked like it hurt worked its way over the woman's lips. "You came out to society three years ago. Haven't you had yourself the slightest bit of wonder why there haven't been all that many proper young gentlemen beatin' a path to this door? You, the daughter of the duke of Union County?"

"This here's yo' basket, Lady Hardin." Salome stepped into the room, feeling suddenly light-headed. "Celeste went to fetch Tessie fo' Lady Margaret."

"Tessie? I thought you were the one accompanyin' Margaret tonight?" Lady Bertha sent a glare Salome's way as she turned back to face the window, the smell of sizzling pork ribs, chicken, and goat floating across the Hardin acres straight into the study. "Margaret, I wouldn't fret about which one of y'all meets up with the other first. Why don't you get yourself on outside and see what happens? Your uncle James is standing on the porch all by his lonesome. Seems Elvera's not feeling sprightly today."

"I want Tessie to chaperone me at the fireworks tonight." Margaret brushed past Salome before Bertha could nod her approval.

"Suit yourself." Lady Bertha kept her back to the room, her whispered words barely making it to Salome's ears. "Won't make no never mind in the long run, anyhow." She turned sideways to Salome, her eyes fixed on a painting of the first American duke. "You stand with Margaret 'til Tessie comes, otherwise I'll never hear the end of it from Henry."

Salome laid Bertha's basket on the mahogany table. "Yes'm." She backed out of the room with the required bow.

"Uncle James." Margaret, steps ahead of Salome, walked onto the veranda and over to the duke of Maryland sitting in his favorite rattan chair, a drink in his hand. And this just past one in the afternoon. "Lady Bertha . . . I mean, Sylvester Morse . . ." Her voice trailed off as James looked around the girl, spotting Salome. "Never mind. I'll ask Papa."

Even Margaret must have guessed by now that James Hardin was no friend of hers.

Salome, holding Margaret's carrying basket, stared at her daughter's back. She refused to let her eyes drift over to His Grace, and she wished the man would keep his own eyes to himself. She shivered. She could feel him sneaking peeks at her. But Henry had made good on his word.

Except for moments like this when James aimed his secret leer at her, the duke who'd lost his crown said nothing more to her than *Fetch this* and *Carry that.*

Even so, Salome could sense that James was holding that I'm-gonna-have-you-one-day look on his face long enough to make Salome want to turn back to the house. He released her from his gaze as he finally cocked an eye at Margaret. "What are you babbling about, girl? What did Lady Bertha say to you?"

Margaret advanced toward the front step of the veranda. She looked out at the gathering partygoers, the strains of John Philip Sousa played by the four-piece band filtering across the lawn. "Nothing, Uncle James. It's just that beaux . . . even my mother thinks I should have more." She whirled back to the duke. "I don't think it's how many beaux a lady has that counts. Pearlie Esther Simmons has six or seven, and everybody says she's fast." Margaret scanned the crowd gathering around her father's barbecue fires as a barbershop quartet harmonized from the platform of the white-latticed gazebo Henry had ordered Maxwell Joe to build for the occasion. "I think it's the quality of the gentlemen callers that's more important than how many a lady has." She turned back to James. "Don't you agree, Uncle?"

The sound coming out of James's mouth—something between a hmmph and a laugh—landed in Salome's ears. "Your 'mother' said so, eh?" Over Margaret's shoulder, he sneaked another peek at Salome. "You believe she wants you to have more beaux? Do you have any? Oh, I see young men come to escort you here and there—at my brother's insistence—but then these fellows, including Sylvester Morse . . ." He stood from the rattan chair. "They don't often come back after they've fulfilled their obligations to Henry, do they?"

Salome dug her fingernails into the straw of the basket. James Hardin must have been born with a hornet in his heart and the Devil riding his back. She watched her daughter's shoulders sag.

"Salome," Margaret's voice called out in disappointment. "You come with me until that lazy Tessie gets out here." Margaret ran down the stairs, almost tripping over the last step.

Salome started after her daughter, but James Hardin stepped across her path and planted himself in front of her. His broad back blocking Salome, he looked out at the guests assembling on the Hardin front acres. Carriages and a few fancy buckboards traveled the private road dropping off guests. Salome sucked in a breath. There were the Browns, the second-biggest landowners in Union County, her twirling a parasol over her winter-pale skin. Over there by the table holding Delfine's collard greens, candied yams, and succotash were the Appleberrys. That woman was the worst gossip from Smackover clean to Lisbon. Let her keep her mouth shut today.

"I can feel it in the air, can't you?" James's hissed words didn't match the friendly nods he gave arriving guests. "My brother's scheme is going to come crashing down on his head one day very soon. And when it does, I'm coming for you first thing." He tipped his head to a newly arrived couple. The gentleman answered with a hand to the brim of his bowler hat. "I have big plans for you and your family. Would you care to hear?"

"Lady Margaret be needin' me, suh." Her throat always hurt when she had to pull up words aimed at James Hardin.

"It's you who'll be needing me, Salome." Henry nodded to Dr. Henderson and his wife as they climbed out of their buggy. "Needing me to stop what I have planned for your children—all three of them. In fact, to stop my plans, you won't be able to get your clothes off fast enough. You'll beg me to take you to my bed. Plead with me to teach you increasingly naughty ways to satisfy me. To keep me happy." He turned sideways as he lifted a hand to the Lisbon town banker. "I've got quite a few new tricks in mind for you."

The smell of barbecuing pork slammed into Salome's nose and riled her stomach. One more sound from the duke of Maryland and she'd lose her breakfast. Salome bumped the man aside as she hurried down the stairs after Margaret.

"Papa, don't you find Uncle James just a little bit hateful sometimes?" Margaret wove her way between the neighbors as she approached Henry.

Salome held back. She spotted Delfine arranging her pecan pies and peach cobblers on the table not fifteen yards from where Lord Hardin stood talking to the mayor of El Dorado and Doc Henderson. Lord Hardin frowned at Margaret's approach.

"Sugar, come and say your hellos to Mayor Montgomery." Lord Hardin slipped an arm around Margaret's shoulders. "Has your uncle James denied you a second helping of Delfine's fine pound cake?" Even from where Salome stood, Henry's laugh sounded made up.

"Lady Margaret." The mayor touched his hand to an imaginary hat. "I trust your father will allow you to come to the fireworks tonight in El Dorado?"

"I'll be bringing her myself." Henry acted more relaxed. "Though I still say the fireworks should have been held right here at Hardin House."

"Well"—the mayor puffed out his chest—"Lord Hardin, your place sure is fancy enough, all right, but with El Dorado being the county seat of all Union County, it just seemed fittin' to hold the fireworks there."

From what Salome could see, Lord Henry didn't look at all convinced.

"If I could vote, it would be for El Dorado. In fact, Papa, I thought I'd go with . . . with . . ." Margaret was too distant for Salome to see if her daughter blushed. "Where is Sylvester, anyway?" She turned to the mayor.

That girl had her heart set on trundling off to El Dorado with Sylvester Morse. Henry hadn't told her, and Salome prayed it wasn't so, but she suspected that the young men who came to call on Margaret these three years after her coming-out party did so because Henry called in his markers with their fathers. All that buzzing talk started by His Grace's ugly mouth still hummed throughout Union County.

"If your ears choose to hear the words of others"—Delfine pointed to a small crate set on the end of her dessert table—"then tend to my pies so no one will know you do the eavesdrop."

Salome gave a quick nod as she busied herself arranging Delfine's foodstuffs.

"Mr. Mayor, time you stopped botherin' the good Lord Hardin." The mayor's beanstalk of a wife walked up to the group. "Come along with me, Lloyd, and let the duke get to greetin' his other guests."

Salome snapped a tiny piece of crust off a pecan pie as she strained to hear what was going on at the next table.

"Madam Mayor"—Margaret must have remembered that the mayor and his wife liked to be addressed by their titles and not their names—"have you seen Sylvester? He's to eat barbecue with me this afternoon."

Salome slapped a cobbler too close to a pound cake, spilling cobbler juice over the cake plate as she took a step away from the table.

"Is he, now?" The woman's face looked like it was fighting a mighty struggle to be polite to the duke's daughter. "I believe I saw him sittin' over there with Saidie Belle Brown. Come on now, Lloyd." She tugged on the mayor's arm.

Salome snatched up the straw basket and made her way closer to her daughter. Margaret watched her approach.

"Papa, Dr. Henderson, please excuse me, I'd like to greet our guests. Salome can stroll with me."

Henry shook his head. "I'm about to have the dinner gong rung to begin the formalities. You and Salome come with me to the gazebo." He winked. "Then you and your young man can enjoy a barbecue dinner together."

"But, Papa, I want to find Sylvester right now."

"I'll hear of no such thing. You listen for the gong."

Salome watched him scan the guests. Henry's face showed satisfaction when he spotted Judge and Mrs. Morse. "Now, excuse me. Salome, see to it that Lady Margaret gets to the gazebo."

Margaret scowled as she shaded her eyes with her hand. "Where can he be?" She spoke to herself more than to Salome.

Three unfamiliar-looking women, two of them young, and all too dressed up for a barbecue, neared Margaret. The older one's eyes, looking out from under a bonnet that wasn't even in style twenty years ago, darted around the front yard. As they approached, clouds of hoochie-coochie perfume spread in front of them.

Margaret shuddered. "I declare, Salome, I don't know why Papa had to invite everybody in Union County to our house. I don't even know half these people." She turned away from the trio as they closed in.

"Reckon it would please Lord Hardin if you make they acquaintance," Salome whispered in Lady Margaret's ear.

"She's got her mammy with her." One of the young women must not have realized her words carried beyond the hand she held to her face. "Must be somebody important. Let's meet up with her."

Margaret sighed as she turned in their direction. "So glad you all could come." Her words sounded hollow and untrue. "I'm the duke's daughter, Lad—"

"Oh, my Lord, so glad to meet you." The other young woman, whose face had seen too much sun, stuck out a gloved hand only to have the older woman snatch it back. "Mama?" The girl turned to the older woman, her face redder than before.

"You ain't . . . you're not . . ." The older woman fidgeted. "I mean to say, pleased to meet you. I hear tell the duke of Union County only got the one daughter. That's not you, is it?" The wide-eyed woman looked as though she expected either a rattler or a diamond ring to pop out of the grass, and she wasn't sure which.

"Of course I'm Lady Margaret." Salome's daughter had never felt the need to hide her annoyance toward those she considered beneath her, and that was just about everybody on God's green earth. Margaret turned to walk away but not before the older woman clamped a hand to her mouth.

"Oh, my Lord Jesus." The mother grabbed each daughter by the arm and backed away, almost tripping over her too-long gown. "We can't . . . she can't . . ."

With the daughters now yards distant, Salome caught the last words from the woman: "Don't you know what they're sayin' 'bout that one? I hear tell she's really a nig . . ."

Margaret stopped and stared at the fast-retreating trio. "Who are those people? They look like cotton farmers to me. No wonder they had no better sense than to wear gloves to a barbecue."

Salome dug her work shoes into the soft grass. Had everybody in every nook and cranny of Union County heard the story of Margaret, Henry, and his colored mistress? "Lady Margaret, there go the dinner gong. You'd best get yo'self on up to that gazebo." If only she could grab her daughter's hand and pull her away from anyone who would do her harm.

The dinner gong rang out a second time as Lord Henry mounted the steps to the gazebo platform. Maxwell Joe had set up scattered tables around the white lattice structure with its copper dome. Salome took four paces toward the structure and spotted James standing near his brother. His eyes drifting in her direction, His Grace lifted a glass in salute to Salome before he took a sizable gulp. Henry, a step in front of James, stared across the lawn as Lady Bertha, followed by Celeste, walked toward him. Salome hurried Margaret to the steps as Lady Hardin made her way to Henry's side. Salome spotted Celeste standing on a patch of grass just below the gazebo platform. She sidled behind the woman and turned her body to block as much of herself from James as she could manage.

"Friends and family"—Henry made a quick bow to His Grace—"it is with the greatest pleasure that my brother, His Grace, the duke of Maryland, and I welcome you, not only to Hardin House, but to a brand-new century!" Henry grabbed James and raised both their arms as the band struck up a rendition of "Maid of the Meadow." Henry slipped his other arm around Lady Bertha's waist, and she winced.

Guests all around Salome clapped, hooted, and sang to the music. Not Margaret. Instead, Salome's daughter scanned the crowd, no doubt looking for the judge's boy.

As the music simmered down, Henry released Lady Bertha. "After our great struggles of these past forty years—and your many lost loved ones—the Good Lord has blessed us. It is with the greatest delight that I share this bounty with you, my neighbors. I know that parties of this magnitude at Hardin House have been few and far between, but today is so special. Not since the coming-out of my lovely daughter have we gathered like this to honor our glorious country and Union County. Let's all salute this little piece of paradise, our country, and, most of all, a brand-new century!"

"Glory to Dixie Land!" a man deep in the crowd shouted. The band and Lord Hardin's great find, a barbershop quartet straight from Little Rock, rolled out two choruses of the rebel song that always gave Salome a pain in the belly.

Lord Hardin waved a hand in the air as the final "Look away! Look away! Dixie Land" rang through the crowd. "My dear friends, please find your places at the tables. I've got the finest cook in all Union County, and my servants will see that you are better than well fed."

"Hallelujah!" came out of more than one mouth in the crowd.

Salome turned to look for Delfine. Too many heads blocked her view.

"Let the festivities begin," Henry declared and kissed Margaret's cheek.

The noise from the moving crowd swarmed up as Henry pointed to the gazebo steps. "Salome," he said with a raised voice, "take Lady Margaret to the weeping willow tree. I've had a special place set up there for her."

"Yes, suh."

The trip over the lawn was full of stops and starts as Margaret scanned the crowd, no doubt searching for the tall Sylvester Morse.

"There! There he is." Margaret clapped as she spun around to Salome.

Thank the Lord. The weeping willow tree stood fewer than ten yards distant. Salome looked at the setup. Starched white linen covered the café table. Bowls of waxy white magnolia blossoms marched down the center. Sprigs of forget-me-nots lined the table's edge. Salome shook her head. It looked more like a setting for a debutante tea than a barbecue. A worry she couldn't quite find reason for welled in Salome's chest.

"It's Sylvester. Sylvester Morse. I don't know why that hateful woman said he was sitting with Saidie Belle." Margaret's face was wreathed in smiles. "He's coming straight for me."

"Yes'm." Even if she'd been white, Salome never would have picked the pimply-faced judge's son as her idea of any kind of a lover. She watched him as he walked his brawny frame over to the weeping willow. As soon as he spotted Margaret, still clapping her hands, Sylvester Morse laid on a smile that seemed about as natural on him as on a rooster.

"Lady Margaret." He stood in front of her. "Thank you for doin' me the honor of eatin' barbecue with me." He took her arm and seated her in one of the armchairs Maxwell Joe had made just for the family and a few of Lord Hardin's favorite guests. Sylvester Morse pulled up a second chair next to Margaret. He glanced up at Salome. "On with you, then. Fill up our plates." He turned his fake smile back to Margaret.

Salome kept her *Yes, suh* to herself as she picked up the two plates. Didn't this bone-ugly boy with the close-set eyes know it was not his place to give orders to any of Lord Hardin's servants? She carried the plates to the meat table manned by Maxwell Joe and watched him heap chicken thighs and wings, three pork ribs, and a thick slice of goat meat onto one plate. He looked up at Salome as she took the full plate from him, then handed him the second.

"This one here fo' Lady Margaret. She don't be needin' much."

Maxwell Joe nodded. He understood that Margaret had to pretend to be a light eater no matter how hungry she was. Gentlemen callers did not appreciate a woman who ate like it was her last meal. As he handed the plate back to her, Maxwell Joe brushed Salome's hand. "I got the best cuts saved under this here cloth."

Peering over the table, Salome spotted a crate covered with a blue towel.

"They's fo' you when it come servants' time to eat." He gave her a quick wink just as Judge Morse walked up to the table.

Salome spotted Mattie Lou, assigned to the vegetable table. She hurried over. Best not to spend too much time away from Margaret and Sylvester, not with the looks being thrown her daughter's way. With both plates loaded far more than she cared, Salome picked her way around the crowded eating tables and servants breaking their necks to meet the demands of the white folks. As she made her way down the little knoll, the top of a weeping willow caught her eye.

"My Lord!" Sylvester's plate tipped in Salome's wobbling hand. A chicken leg slid to the grass, joined by a good dollop of Mattie Lou's fatback-flavored greens. "Where did they get to that fast?" Salome stared at the empty armchairs. Even the straw basket had disappeared.

CHAPTER FIFTEEN

With the sun just beginning its slide down her back, Margaret clung to the iron side rails as the buggy swayed on the road leading to El Dorado. "Sylvester, don't you reckon you should slow down just a bit? My hair might come undone." With the July humidity, her unpinned mane would frizz all the more. Margaret checked the pins holding her hair in place. She turned an annoyed glare at Tessie wedged between the rear seat and the back of the buggy. Margaret's straw basket lay cattywampus across Tessie's right hip. Maybe it hadn't been such a good idea to sneak off from Salome so soon after Tessie showed up at the weeping willow.

"Lady Margaret, we don't want to spend our time around a bunch of old fogies, now, do we?" Sylvester flicked the reins. "'Sides, we agreed we'd have much more fun at a secret picnic, just the two of us."

"Well . . ." Margaret tilted her head the way her old governess said she should to catch a beau. "But Papa had the table laid out so pretty." She leaned in to Sylvester as the first strand of hair escaped the strongly pinned confinement Salome had arranged. She pushed the hairpin back into place.

"There's a likely spot." Sylvester aimed the horse off the road and onto a path that looked little better than a cow trail.

Margaret clamped down tighter on the side rails as the buggy bumped its way down the path, up a little hill, around three trees, and down a steep slope to a little creek.

"Oh my Jesus, Lady Margaret, I'm 'bout to lose my breakfast." Tessie, her right leg caught under her at an odd angle, called out from the floorboards.

"Oh, hush up. We're almost there." Margaret turned to Sylvester. "Is this the place for our picnic?"

"This'll do just fine." Sylvester pulled on the reins.

The horse neighed his protest but halted. Sylvester jumped down and tied the animal to a tree.

"Lady Margaret," Tessie moaned, "could y'all move so's I can unwrap myself from this here flo'?"

Without looking at the servant, Margaret hissed at the woman, "When I get you back home, I'm going to give you a good hiding. I can't just jump off this wagon, my skirts flying willy-nilly. It's unladylike. I've got to wait for Sylvester."

"Uhh." Tessie sounded like she was about to die.

So be it. Margaret had no time to worry over a stupid serving girl. Sylvester had asked her to sneak away with him to somewhere private. Why would he do such a thing, knowing full well both sets of parents would be furious? She glanced at her fill-in maid, still grunting and groaning over nothing. Margaret lifted a hand so Sylvester could not see her smile. There could only be one answer. Sylvester Morse, future governor of Arkansas, was about to propose marriage to her that very afternoon.

"Lady Margaret." Sylvester pulled out a handkerchief and wiped his hands before offering to help her down from the buggy. "Now, would you do me the real honor of picnicking here in this beautiful place? You'll find it so much cooler."

Margaret lifted the skirt of her new iris-print muslin dress and placed her handmade, lavender-blue, high-button shoes with their brass buckles on the buggy step. She took Sylvester's hand and alighted.

"Uhh, Lady Margaret, my legs done gone to sleep. I cain't get up."

"I'll get you out." Sylvester reached up and grabbed Tessie around the waist. He dragged her over the buggy's side.

"Ooww." The woman howled as Sylvester dropped her to the ground. "I think I done broke somethin'."

"I'll break you if you don't stop that infernal noise." He reached inside the buggy for the picnic basket. "Now get us set up." He tossed the straw container at Tessie.

Margaret looked out at the little creek. The water couldn't have been more than waist high. The thick trees leading down from the road to the water's edge crossed their branches against one another as though forming a wedding arch. The faces of red, purple, pink, and yellow flowers, blooming in the full strength of summer, dotted the deep green carpet of grass. Birds chirped as they flitted from branch to branch. Margaret smiled as she gazed around her. This secluded spot would make the perfect setting for a romantic proposal of marriage. Maybe this was the day she'd become engaged at last. After all, she was already twenty-one with oldmaidhood just around the corner.

She turned toward Sylvester, her face reddening.

Was she being too forward thinking such things? Could Sylvester read her thoughts? "How did you know about this hideaway? You're not a country boy. You're from Lisbon. I've never even been here, and this spot is not three miles from my home."

He walked over to stand next to her, close enough that she could feel his breath on her cheek. "This will do nicely for us, Lady Margaret."

Though no breeze stirred the air, the place—encased in green—felt degrees cooler on her body. But for some strange reason, Margaret sensed heat coming off Sylvester. "Tessie, fetch my shawl."

Tessie grunted as she fished the cloth out of the basket. "Where's it you want me to put the shawl, Lady Margaret? If y'all wantin' a picnic, I gots to put yo' wrap on the bare ground."

"Of course, you must," Sylvester said, grabbing the length of blue-striped fabric. He spread it over a flat spot ten yards from the creek.

Margaret slapped both hands to her mouth. "Oh, my Lord. A picnic." She turned a face full of panic to Sylvester. "I've just remembered. We have no food. You sent Salome to fill our plates, but as soon as she was out of sight, you said we should leave to go have our own private meal."

"And you told me it wouldn't be proper to go off without a chaperone." Somehow, Sylvester sounded scolding.

"But I did come with you as soon as Tessie showed up?" Why did she choose now to sound like Lady Bertha? And why was she defending herself? Society girls of marriageable age always went about with chaperones. Margaret moved her hands down the muslin half sleeves of her dress. She was nervous, but what young lady wouldn't be on the occasion of a marriage proposal? "Because we left so soon, I forgot to tell Tessie to bring our barbecue."

Sylvester shrugged. A funny little smile crossed his face. "Not to worry, my lovely. Let's just send Tessie back for our dinners."

My lovely? Had Sylvester Morse just called her, Margaret Hardin, his lovely? Her smile came before she could stop it. She'd been instructed always to act coy around a man. But now, her tooth-baring grin threatened to disqualify her from getting into any charm school. She put a hand over her mouth.

"Off you go, Tessie. Load up our plates." Sylvester pointed to the straw basket.

"Plates? Suh?" Tessie looked wild-eyed at Margaret. "Ladyship, it most three mile back to the barbecue. I don't rightly know how to drive a buggy. 'Sides, I ain't supposed to leave you by yo'self."

"Uhh." Margaret turned from Sylvester to Tessie and back again. Tessie was right. If the maid left, Margaret would be alone with Sylvester. What would Papa say? She sent a pleading look to her soon-to-be fiancé. Margaret knew very well what her father, Lady Bertha, and—if the truth be told—all of Union County would say if she were found unchaperoned with an unrelated young man. "Sylvester, that's a long walk for Tessie in this heat. Why don't we just head out for El Dorado? We'll be early for the fireworks for sure, but we can dawdle over our meal in the town square." She stopped herself from adding *And enjoy one another in a proper, chaperoned setting.*

Sylvester approached her and took her hands in his. "I'll hear none of it. Margaret, I need this time alone with you." He stared at the toes of her leather shoes. "To ask you something . . . something quite personal."

Oh, my Lord, she was right! Margaret Hardin would not only be a bride, but in time, she'd be First Lady of Arkansas. "Tessie, hurry along." She turned to the servant, who appeared rooted to the spot. "And you'd better be back here well before four. Now, get!"

Grumbling, Tessie gathered the straw basket, turned, and began her climb up the hill toward the road and out of sight.

"Come sit beside me, Margaret." Sylvester dropped down to her blue shawl, propping himself up on one elbow. "I've something to say to you."

All those mean-hearted comments Lady Bertha and Uncle James had made—that she'd never have a beau—smashed together in her head. How wrong they were. What color wedding dress should she have made? She'd heard white was quite popular these days. Margaret smiled down at Sylvester as he patted the shawl. She shook her head. Much more romantic to have him kneel down at her feet when he finally gathered his courage to utter the words.

She spotted a tree at creek's edge, part of its trunk curved into a natural bench. She walked over to the limb, admiring the deep green of the leaves festooning its branches. The perfect place for the perfect proposal. "I'd like to take a closer look at the creek. Care to join me?" She turned sideways.

"Oh no, my dear. I don't want a muddy riverbank and the sound of croaking frogs spoiling what I have to say to you." He sat up. "Do please sit beside me. What I want to tell you is important. To us both." He licked his upper lip.

Still standing, Margaret took another look at the paradise surrounding her, then turned to Sylvester, sitting on ground that might still be a bit mushy with the rains of two days ago. She shrugged. A proposal was a proposal. She made her way over to the shawl, and Sylvester helped her down. She arranged her muslin skirt around her and clasped her hands in her lap. Keeping her head down, she hoped she could look the picture of surprise when Sylvester finally got around to his speech.

Mr. Morse held his hands folded around his bent knees. "Margaret, I know you may not be aware, but your father has spoken to mine. Your father believes that you and I might have some interest in one another."

"Interest?" She lowered her head, one leg laid demurely across the other as she sat on her shawl. "What sort of interest?"

"That we—you and I—might find one another . . . attractive."

Her plan to act the demure young lady flew out of her head. "Attractive?"

Sylvester grabbed her around the shoulders. "That's how I find you. Most attractive. In fact, I don't think I can go another minute without knowing that you feel something for me, too. Do you?"

Oh, Lord. She'd answer the man if only she could get her lips to stop their trembling. Should she nod a lot or a little? Her head wobbled betwixt the two.

"Is that a yes?" Sylvester gathered her into his arms. "Margaret, you and I could be so beautiful together." He kissed her neck.

A kiss? She startled. No man, other than her father, had ever kissed her anywhere. So this was how proposals began. She held her body still. What was she to say? Why hadn't Lady Bertha trained her more in the art of accepting a proposal of marriage? One lesson, from Salome, not Lady Bertha, poured into her mind. Salome taught that she remain demure around men. Sit like a lady—knees together even under her skirts, hands folded in her lap, palms up, eyes downcast, but always a little smile on her lips. Over Sylvester's shoulder, she watched the horse nibble at the grass. She held herself as still as she could while she waited.

He planted three more kisses running from her neck to her ear. She tried holding her breath but the scent of full-bodied, wild roses caused her to gasp. One more kiss, then another. How many were required to loosen a suitor's tongue before he gave his speech?

Sylvester kissed the tip of her chin before moving back to her neck. Margaret jerked as the wetness of his tongue slithered down the underside of her chin.

"Ooh!" She caught her breath. "Sylvester, what are you do . . . ?" She locked and unlocked her fingers. "I mean to say . . . is there something you want to say to me?"

"Of course." Sylvester ducked his head under her chin and sucked at her neck.

Margaret trembled. This was more than kissing. "Sylvester." Her voice slid thin out of her mouth. "No, I mean . . . What about . . . ? Do you want to ask . . . ? Engaged?" Her heart pounded as her words fumbled.

"Engaged? Oh, you mean the two of us?" He glanced up at her for the wisp of a second. "Yes, yes, if you wish to think it so." He ran his hand down her back.

Did she feel him poking and prodding at her corset? She angled her body away from him. Margaret caught a glimpse of heavy blue sky through two high branches that did not quite meet. "Are you saying . . . we are . . . the two of us . . . we may be considered . . . engaged?"

"So you want an engagement?" His words were muffled as his hands twisted her body back to him. He buried his face in her neck, nipping at her throat down to the top of her muslin dress. "Uhh-uhh." He reached for the top button.

Margaret pushed him away before her mind could gather itself. "Sir . . . Sylvester, aren't you supposed to . . . I mean . . . shouldn't you ask me formally to . . . ?" She lowered her eyes as her cheeks flushed.

Sylvester pawed at the top button with one hand while the other grabbed a tuft of her hair. He pulled her head back. "This is my engagement." His voice sounded hoarse as he licked the hollow of her throat.

"Oooh." Her arched neck strained. A hairpin dislodged itself. Strands of hair poufed about her face. She shook free. "Sylvester! Our engagement . . . to be official, it must be announced." Another hairpin loosened. She rubbed the back of her neck. "I don't believe it's quite proper to behave this way until after our engagement has taken place. Perhaps . . . our wedding?"

"Engagement? Wedding?" He slid his hands to her shoulders as he tilted his head. "Of course. But, my darling, you know our mothers. An engagement and a wedding will take ever so long to plan. You can't expect me to wait as long as that. I pine for you. Every day and each night I think of nothing but you." He stroked her arms as a funny look stamped itself onto his face.

"And I have . . . feelings for you, too." She tried to push her pouf of hair back in place as her head trembled in confusion. "I'm convinced we'll be the perfect couple. I'll make you a wonderful wife when you become governor." She knew she was prattling on, but how could she stop herself? "Together, we shall dazzle all of Little Rock, but shouldn't you first say . . . isn't there something you wish to ask of me . . . ?"

"Oh, you wish me to ask you to marry me?"

"Oh, Lord, yes!" Margaret tilted her head upward to the filtered sun. "Oh, Sylvester, absolutely, yes!" She reached for his hands. "Does this mean we are . . . engaged?" Her cheeks hurt from smiling. "Papa, Lady Bertha. I can hardly wait to get back to Hardin House and tell them the news. You can speak to Papa and make it all quite official."

"Of course I'll speak to your father, but right now, you and I must take this time to make plans for our future." He shook off her hands and reached for her top button again.

She twisted away, her joy suddenly clouded. "Sylvester . . . if we are . . . that is to say . . . if we are engaged, shouldn't we get back to Hardin House before Papa heads out for the fireworks in El Dorado? Lady Bertha . . . my mother . . . will be dizzy with excitement at our news." Why did she feel what Salome called the jitters?

Sylvester squeezed her cheeks between his hands. "We'll see about your mother." He bent closer to her face, his lips parted. He drew her lower lip into his mouth.

"Ooh? Sylvester?" She broke away. "Why . . . what . . . ?"

"Margaret"—he released her—"if it is an engagement you want, so be it. But you must understand it is perfectly proper for engaged couples to show their commitment to one another."

So she was engaged. She sighed her relief as she managed a coquettish smile. "I do understand, Sylvester, really I do. I am committed to you. I can barely wait to show you my devotion." Rounds of engagement parties with throngs of envious neighbor girls marched through her mind. What was all this uncommon kissing about? "Once our engagement is announced we'll have to wait the proper year before we marry, of course. But I'm sure Lady Bertha can help your parents plan our engagement party by October." She reached for his hands. "Think of it. We'll be married by October nineteen hundred and one." She squeezed. "Doesn't that sound exciting? Nineteen aught one." Margaret gathered her skirts about her as she started to move to her feet. "Let's not waste another minute. I'm so anxious for you to speak to Papa."

Sylvester threw his head back. "Marriage? October of next year? Oh, my God, Margaret, I cannot wait that long to be settled. A married man." He sat back on the shawl. "There is something you're entitled to know. My father has an understanding with Saidie Belle Brown's father.

That the two of us would wed one day." He grabbed both Margaret's hands and pulled her back to the shawl. "My feelings for you are so strong, I will defy my father. But I cannot hold him off for a year from this coming fall."

Margaret frowned as she settled on the shawl. What was Sylvester saying? All proper weddings followed the same protocol. After the formal engagement party hosted by the groom's family, the wedding took a year in the planning. Why, the parties alone—spaced a proper six weeks apart—would take up a year, what with all the best families vying to host the bride to be. That was how her own parents married, though Bertha's family had been several social notches below the duke's. She read the disappointment in Sylvester's face. "This is July." She studied her fingers. "I know Mother will find it unseemly, but if I beg and plead with my father, I'm sure Lady Bertha can arrange our engagement announcement by next month." She looked up. "I believe August will still be considered suitable?" She brightened. "Maybe we can marry by the middle of next August. That's just a little over a year from now."

Sylvester shook his head. "Margaret, it is torture you propose for me." He traced a hand down the row of buttons adorning the front of her dress. "Saidie Belle's family is not as prestigious as yours. They will not require such formalities. She will be ready for marrying by this coming September." He played with the top button of her dress. "I don't want Saidie Belle. I want you. It will be a torment, but perhaps I can wait for a December ceremony this year if only you would share just a bit of yourself with me now. To seal the engagement." He fumbled open the button.

She clamped both hands over the top of her dress. A bit of herself? Did he want her deepest thoughts? No. Lady Bertha had made one thing clear to her daughter: husbands gave not one whit what their wives thought. "Seal our engagement? Sylvester, isn't that what engagement parties are for?"

"A quick glance at your loveliness is all I request. That will sustain me until the announcement and let me know what I may expect on our wedding night. Every man is entitled to that."

"Wedding night?" Margaret flushed. "A glance at what?"

"You mustn't be such a child. You're almost a woman now—an engaged woman." He narrowed his eyes. "Women who are engaged to be married are required to share something of themselves with their future husbands. I must say, Margaret, I'm surprised Lady Bertha has not explained all this to you."

"Lady Bertha?" She lowered her head. Her mother had spoken nothing to her about the ways of husbands or fiancés. It had been Tessie who had dropped more than one broad hint—keep your knees together, cover your elbows except in the evenings, do not allow beaux even a glimpse of your ankles. But no one—neither Lady Bertha nor Tessie—had ever outlined the ways a maiden should move from receiving gentlemen callers to accepting a fiancé.

Sylvester stared at her as his hand went to her second button. Without shifting his eyes from her face, he slipped the button through the buttonhole. "Do not deny me a glimpse of the beauty you've tempted me with all these years. Since your coming-out party."

The trees rustled a symphony of July sounds. A slight stirring of air slid across the top of her chest. Margaret shook her head. She managed a weak smile as she laid a hand against his and tried to slide him away with as much daintiness as she could muster. He clamped down hard on her wrists and pushed her hands aside.

"Ooh." Her eyes widened.

Before she could protest, his fingers undid buttons three, four, and five.

"Sylvester?" She grabbed at the edges of her flung-open bodice. Salome popped into her head. Her new lady's maid had been right. Margaret's already-tight corset could barely contain her breasts as she struggled to take in more air. "A glimpse of me? What . . . sort of . . . ?"

She tried to scoot away from Sylvester's nimble fingers. "To seal our engagement?"

He climbed to his knees, tugged at the little belt Salome had fastened around her waist this morning, and unbuckled the thin strip of cloth.

"Sylvester!" Margaret called out his name in a strangled voice. "How much of a glance is required?"

The only other sounds she could pass through her throat sounded like the mewing of a newborn kitten. Her mouth turned to dust when Sylvester yanked the bodice edges from her hands and pushed the garment off her shoulders. Oh, God's help in ages past. Her ankles wobbled as he pulled her to her feet and slithered the dress to the top of her blue leather shoes.

"Sylvester!" The sound of her own voice bobbled in her throat. "Nooo!" She crossed her hands over the top of the corset. "My . . . dress . . . please . . . on."

He shook his head as a vein in his forehead bulged. "Stop carrying on so. I'm only asking you to do what is required of a woman about to be married."

"Married?" The trembling in her voice matched the shaking that captured her entire body. "You want to see my underthings?"

"I've driven myself close to crazy wondering how beautiful you are underneath all your crinolines. Yet I see very little under that corset." He grabbed her shoulders and turned her around, her back to him.

"Oww." Sharp pains ravaged her shoulders. Hammers beat at cross-purposes in her head. An image of home reared up in her mind. She had to get to Tessie—better yet, Salome. Her older servant would tell her the truth of this engagement ritual. "Sylv . . ." She struggled to break away from him, step off the blue shawl, and run with all her strength to the top of the hill—to the road, to a passerby, to Hardin House.

He held her fast by her corset strings—as he tugged them loose.

"Sylvester! No."

"Hush, girl. I just want to drink in your beauty." He pulled at the stiff whaleboning and yanked the corset past her bloomers. "You're a temptress, and you know what the Bible says about temptresses."

The garment skimmed down her legs to the ground.

The trees jumped and swayed in front of Margaret as Sylvester pulled her around to face him. Her head wobbled as treetop and tree trunk traded places. Words from the Bible—of Samson and Delilah—danced before her eyes. She pressed the straps of her chemise tight against her body. Sylvester shoved her hands away. His free hand moved to the hem of her chemise. Her throat wanted to scream *stop* but there was no air behind the effort.

"Oooh," she keened as Sylvester shoved the embroidered garment Tessie had stitched for her over her head and arms. Open her eyes, close her eyes—which was better, which was worse?

The most god-awful, off-center grin crossed her fiancé's reddening face. She crossed her arms over her bare chest only to have Sylvester grab her wrists and force her arms high over her head. Sylvester gave a slow, approving nod. Her knees buckled. Her head lolled to one side. Sylvester lowered her hands and dug his own into her sides to keep her upright.

"Nooo!" The word screamed out of her mouth.

"I only want to see what I'm entitled to enjoy forevermore. It's my right." With one hand squeezing her throat, the other pulled the drawstring on her bloomers. Her drawers slid on top of the discarded corset and dress. He shoved her cotton stockings to the tops of her shoes.

God in Heaven. Did Sylvester have a right to see her naked before their marriage? Margaret's head pounded so, she couldn't get her brain to work. Lady Bertha. What had her mother said? The only grudging compliment her mother had ever given her was on the size of her breasts. Shapely and big, Lady Bertha had declared. "Just like a colored woman's. At least you'll have that to offer some poor man." Was that why Sylvester was behaving in this horrid manner?

"Oh, God. Sylvester. No more." Margaret steadied one hand against her thigh as she bent over. Her free hand reached down to retrieve her bloomers.

The soothing sound of the creek suddenly turned into the bubbling of a boiling cauldron. The trees blurred with the spinning sky. Her feet slipped out from under her. Sylvester slammed her to the ground, her legs flailing in the air. She lay flat on her back as her fiancé tore off his shirt and worked on removing his trousers. She couldn't breathe properly. She dug her shoes into the shawl as she struggled to turn to her side and reach for her dress. No good. Before she could move, Sylvester slid one bare leg across her chest and pinned her on her back.

"Syl . . . please . . . no . . . let me . . ." She pushed at the offending leg with all her might.

"Quiet, wench. You wanted to be engaged. Well, this is what engaged people do. You mustn't fuss so." He discarded his pants.

"Sylvester. My clothes . . . back on." Her heart and head pounded against each another. She arched her back to buck him off her.

A look of utmost pleasure washed over his face. Sylvester's breathing came out in heavy spurts as though on a cloud of steam. "Margaret, you simply don't understand. Your mother hasn't had the chance to tell you." He puffed out more air. "But this is what couples do to seal their engagement. It means that they have to marry."

"Oh, my Lord!" Margaret swung her head from side to side. *Stop!* Her scream echoed only in her own ears.

Sylvester bore down on her and stretched her legs apart. What was he about to do?

"No. No." She clawed at his back as he ground into her. Margaret scraped her shoes against the back of his legs. She twisted her foot so the brass buckle would dig into his skin. To stop him. No good. She pushed against the man's shoulders. No good. The more she fought, the harder Sylvester dug himself inside her. More tearing. More pain. *Oh, Lord Jesus. Papa, come help!*

"Ugghhh." Sylvester shouted in her ear: "God! God!" He shouted to the ground right before he collapsed that trunk of a body across hers.

Margaret's throat and eyes felt like they were exploding. Her tears washed both their faces. Every part of her body and soul ached. But he was quiet. She had to free herself. Get away from this man. She pushed at his shoulders. Sylvester lay sprawled on top of her, something wet running down her legs. Her sobs racked her body.

With a grunt Sylvester rolled off her and lay on his back.

He slammed one hairy arm across her breasts, pinning her down. "Uhh." Sylvester opened his eyes and stared up at the canopy of leaves over their heads. "You've got a pretty good pussy. Fresh."

"Wha . . ." The thumping in her ears not only matched the misery throughout her body, it made her almost deaf.

He rubbed the back of his outstretched arms across her chest. "You've got damn nice tits, too."

She was in the presence of a madman. "I . . ."—her voice trembled—"want my clothes." She had to make him let her go.

Sylvester let out a little laugh as he turned to his side, planting his forearm between her breasts to right himself. "Clothes? Not quite yet. Give me a few minutes, and we can have another go-round."

Margaret squirmed to the edge of the shawl. She struggled against the misery in her body to sit up. Pulling her back down, he loomed over her.

"Sylv . . . engaged people . . . no. My clothes . . . I want them. I want to go back to Hardin House."

"Not yet. Too many things to explore." He leaned over, sucked her nipple into his mouth, and pulled.

"Ahh." Margaret pounded a hand across the top of his head. "No!" She dug the brass buckle of her shoe into his leg a second time. "Stop this!"

He let her go. "You don't really want to play rough with me, Margaret." He touched his injured leg.

She reached for her dress as she scrambled to her hands and knees.

"I can play rough, too." He pulled her back to the shawl and shook a finger in her face. "You will do what I say, when I say it. Is that clear?" He grabbed her shoulders and slammed her to the ground, the dress tumbling to the grass.

"Sylvester. I'm . . . I'm hurting. Our engagement, I'm not sure . . ."

He drew slow circles across her stomach before he looked her in the face. "Are you actually this stupid, Margaret? There can be no marriage between the two of us." His mouth twisted into that off-center smirk again. "But you and I will always have this."

A skinny ray of afternoon sun filtered through the canopy of leaves and caught in Margaret's eyes. "I don't want to marry you, you beastly man." The words rocketed out of her mouth. "But after this . . . after what you've done—what you're doing—our engagement is sealed."

"Oh, for God's sake, Margaret." He looked down at her. "Can it be you really don't know? Half of Union County's been talkin' 'bout you for three years now. Even if I wanted to marry you—and believe me, if not for your father's money and position, I wouldn't even consider it—the law won't permit us to wed."

Words, the chirps of robins, the hint of a breeze rustling through the trees, swarmed in her ears. She could make some sense out of what this monster was saying, but what? "Talk? Union County? What sort of talk?"

"Margaret. Margaret. I did have a good time with you just now. Wouldn't mind coming back for more. I'll even help your father keep up the pretense"—he leaned down to nuzzle her neck—"if you're extra-special good to me whenever I need it. I don't think Saidie Belle can deliver nearly as much as you. You being a col—"

Margaret jerked her head away as he lowered his body over hers. Her undone hair stood out around her face. "Get off me, Sylvester Morse, or I shall scream my head off. Tessie's due back about now. She'll get my father, and he'll have you horsewhipped if not outright strung up on . . ." She aimed a finger at a nearby stout tree. "On that."

Sylvester straddled her, rocking over her body. "It's you who'll be horsewhipped or better still, strung out like this, buck naked and ready for any white man who cares to trouble himself. You, trying to pass yourself off as a white girl, when all the county knows you're as black as any colored around here."

She arched her body to shake the man off. He clung to her. "You've lost your mind, Sylvester Morse. My father will kill you. I'm no more colored than you are. Now get off me!"

"Oh, you're colored, all right. Look at that nap you call hair." He pulled a clump of her hair. "Just like a colored. If you don't believe me, ask your uncle James. He said as much to my mother at your coming-out party. It's your father's money that's kept the secret going this long. The only problem is, we don't know which of his black wenches is your mother."

"Lady . . . Bertha . . . is my mother!" She pushed against his chest, trying to work her hands between their bodies when she heard the first voice.

"Salome, I know it's someplace 'round here." Tessie! "See that there little trail and them buggy wheels? It's jest up this here hill and down a spell to the creek."

Thank God and all the saints!

Sylvester grunted as he jumped off Margaret. "Get your clothes on, you colored wench." He threw her dress at her while he scrambled into his trousers.

Margaret stuffed her corset under the crumpled blue shawl. Were those specks of blood she spotted? From the pain in her bathroom place, she was not surprised. She jammed her dress over her head. No time for the chemise or bloomers.

"There they is!" Tessie stood at the top of the hill. "I told you this was the right place." She carried the straw basket.

"Lady Mar . . ." Salome crested the hill then stood still, staring.

Margaret, her dress askew, stretched out her arms toward the women. She'd had just time enough to fasten the top button. "Salome, oh God, Salome, help me."

"Lady Margaret's fallen." Sylvester fastened the last of his shirt buttons. "Injured herself, I'm afraid. I had to take rather strong measures to bring her back around."

Margaret ached her way to her knees. Tears flooded from her eyes. "Salome. In the name of God, get down here."

Salome jerked to life. She pushed past Tessie, who stood like a statue, and scrambled down the hillside, skidding twice. Her breath came hard and heavy when she reached down to help Margaret to her feet.

"Oh, Lord, my girl." Salome's eyes trained on the unbuttoned dress.

Margaret reached for her buttons. Her trembling fingers could not fasten the rest of them.

"I told you she was injured." Sylvester walked over to the wagon and his still-grazing horse. "I don't have room for all of you in the buggy. I'll go alone for help."

"He gonna leave us here to walk on back to the house one mo' time?" Tessie, still standing at the top of the hill, called out.

Margaret watched Salome turn toward Sylvester. What was that look on her face?

"You do what you reckon best . . . suh." Her words came out low and slow as though she were challenging a rattler.

Sylvester took one step forward, the reins in his hands, then stopped. "Are you the one?" He looked Salome up and down.

Salome returned his stare without a blink. "Suh . . . I be the one who'll get Lady Margaret back to her father. I be the one tellin' him 'bout . . . how she got hurt."

Margaret had never seen such a thing. It was almost as though a colored woman was condemning a white man. Why would Salome risk a good beating?

"Anythin' else, suh, you care to let Lord Hardin know 'bout how his daughter got herself in this here state?"

Sylvester led the horse slowly past Margaret and Salome before he climbed into the buggy. "It's Salome, isn't it? So you are the one . . . who'll take Margaret home."

"I am the one to tell Lord Hardin all he need to know 'bout his daughter. And you."

Sylvester leaned forward, an elbow on one knee. "Salome, none of us wants to worry his lordship. Yes, I'm mighty sorry that my horse got away from me and Margaret was tossed to the ground."

"Ain't no hoss got away from nobody." Tessie picked her way two steps closer. "Lady Margaret, she ain't fell to no ground, neither."

"Thank you, Tessie. You don't need to say no mo'." Salome reached down and picked up the blue shawl.

Margaret's bloomers and chemise lay crumpled underneath.

Sylvester straightened on the buggy bench. "Salome, Margaret's injury was a mite embarrassing. She was having trouble breathing. I'm afraid I had to loosen her corset to keep her alive."

"And her bloomers, too?" Salome stood unmoving, looking up at Sylvester Morse. "You had to take them off to keep her alive?"

"It's probably best if as few people as possible know about these little details." He kept his eyes on Salome. "If one thing can be kept private, so can others, don't you agree?"

"It's Lord Hardin you'll be needin' to agree, thank you, suh. You can be on yo' way now. We'll get back to Hardin House on our own."

Sylvester nodded. He flicked the reins, turned the animal, and made his way through an opening in the trees.

As the clopping of the horse faded, Margaret flung her arms around Salome. Thank God the woman had come. Margaret couldn't let go.

How long did the servant pat and comfort her before she quieted her cries long enough to get out words?

"Salome, oh, Salome. He did . . . What he did to me! Oh, my Lord. I'm ruined. I'm sure of it! I hate him! I hate him!"

Her servant rocked Margaret in her arms, cooing soft sounds into her ear. "I knows, baby girl . . . Lady Margaret." Salome stroked her face and worked at smoothing her hair. "You're not to fret. Ain't no such thing as 'ruined.'" She looked into Margaret's face. "This here, it gonna pass. Befo' you know it, you gonna be jest fine." She looked over her shoulder. "I'm sendin' Tessie on back to the house. A wagon be here to fetch you in no time."

"Me? You wants me to walk 'nother three mile back to the house? And it hotter'n Hades out there?" Tessie grumbled.

"On yo' way. And hurry, lessen you wants Lord Hardin to know you tarried while his daughter . . ."

"If these po' legs can carry me, I'm on my way." Tessie huffed up the hill.

Salome watched until Tessie was out of sight. "Come on, Lady Margaret. Let me help you over here to the creek."

Even with Salome supporting her, each step across the grass made Margaret feel every inflamed spot Sylvester had touched.

Salome settled her on the tree trunk bench. "Let's get you cleaned up from them 'injuries' Mr. Morse talkin' 'bout."

Fresh tears splashed her cheeks. "He did . . . the most awful things to me. He . . ." A thought slammed into her head. "Oh, my Lord. Lady Bertha! Salome, Salome, I can't tell her. She'll swear I led him on."

"We don't need to talk 'bout none of that right now, Lady Margaret. You rest yo'self a spell, then you and me can talk if you have a mind to."

Margaret nodded, but the pain in her body matched the sharp stabbings in her head. "You know what he said to me? Why he did what he did to me?" The memory of Sylvester's words confused her. "He said he couldn't marry me, but he could do what he did because . . . because . . ."

"Yes'm?" Salome dipped an end of the blue shawl into the creek water, wrung it out, and walked back to Margaret. "Lift up yo' skirt. We gonna wash you up good."

At least Salome understood. Margaret wanted to sink into the woman's arms, close her eyes, and drift into nothingness. And she would do just that if only she could sort out the why of Sylvester. What was that monster talking about? She spoke out to her servant as Salome soothed her bruised and bloody sore spots.

"Salome, he . . . Sylvester said what he did was just fine because I was just a . . . a colored girl. He said everybody in Union County knew I was . . . black. Why would he say such a hateful, impossible thing?"

Could coloreds go pale underneath their brown skins? Salome looked as though all the blood had drained from her face.

CHAPTER SIXTEEN

Henry stood with his back to the locked cabinet in his library, the cabinet where he kept his father's prized weapon: the walnut-handled LeMat revolver. His fingers clenched on the cabinet key as he tried to loosen his tightened jaw. "And you didn't see fit to come straight to El Dorado to tell me this at once?" He glared at Salome standing just two steps inside the room. The entire house was quiet this close to midnight, and Henry had turned the gaslights low.

Salome swiveled her eyes between the closed door and Henry. "The thing most on my mind was gettin' Lady Margaret home safe befo' they was mo' trouble. I brung her straight here."

Bile rose in his throat as tears threatened his eyes. He laid a hand across his brow. "Of course." Henry ran a hand from his forehead to his mouth. "Oh, my Lord, Salome. How is she? How is my baby?"

Anger and concern had ridden in the buggy with him all the way from tonight's Fourth of July El Dorado fireworks to Hardin House. All evening he had fretted over his Margaret's whereabouts. Yes, he understood his daughter sometimes behaved like a spoiled child, but she had never defied him. As darkness neared, where was she? Sparklers and firecrackers dotted the El Dorado sky while Henry searched quietly for his daughter. He had not alerted either Bertha or the stumbling-drunk James that the girl was not to be found anywhere in the crowd of awestruck celebrants. He could not let on that Margaret was not at the festivities, lest the talk about his daughter grow even greater.

Henry had been perfectly clear this afternoon when he told Margaret he would be the one to escort her to El Dorado. But he hadn't told her back at the barbecue that he needed a few more minutes to firm up his understanding with Judge Morse. Once the judge grasped the magnitude of Henry's generous offer—the Hardins were well prepared to heap upwards of twenty thousand dollars upon the judge's son to propel that young man's political career—he'd sought out Margaret. But by then, his daughter had gone off with Sylvester Morse. According to Salome, Tessie must have been the chaperone. Henry had berated his mistress. Tessie was no kind of a chaperone. How could Salome permit such a thing?

"Lord Henry, suh." Salome now waited for Henry to focus on her. "I was mighty grateful that none of y'all was here at the house when I brung her inside. Lady Margaret was frettin' so, but . . . ."

"My God!" The horror of what had befallen his daughter slammed fresh into Henry. He whirled to the cabinet and slipped the key into the lock. He heard Salome step across the carpet.

"Suh, don't you think that this here is a good thing to keep out of people's business?" He heard her stop in the center of the room. "I mean, when I got Lady Margaret to the house wasn't nobody here but a few hands and Tessie."

His hand on the key, Henry turned to Salome. "I gave the others leave to go to the fireworks. Tell me again what happened." He steeled himself. Had she told him the all of it? Salome took a step closer, turned to check the shut door behind her, and walked up next to him.

"He . . . ain't treated her right, that's fo' sho. But I taken care of her." She kept her voice low. "I had Tessie draw Lady Margaret a good hot bath. I put some of that sweet-smelling oil you gave her fo' her last birthday in the water." Salome studied the pattern of the carpet before she looked up at Henry. "She cried most of the time she was in that tub. Kept orderin' me to scrub her over and over. She'd holler. I'd scrub. She'd holler and cry all the mo'. I scrubbed some mo'." Salome's voice carried a tremor.

Henry's jaws ached from holding them so tight. "Did you put her to bed?" By the time he'd arrived back at the house, Henry had already decided to demand the engagement be announced as soon as possible. News that Lord Hardin's daughter had taken a long buggy ride with her gentleman caller—a ride that lasted well past ten o'clock—would provoke nothing but scandal. More talk that would ruin his girl unless there was a quick engagement. Furious that she'd disobeyed, he had stormed into the house, calling for Margaret. Bertha, her face alight at his daughter's looming disgrace, smirked her way up the stairs and to bed. Salome, hiding under the grand staircase, had caught Henry just as he began his own climb to the second floor. When she told him that story of horror, Henry's ears hadn't been able to take it all in.

"Is . . . is she asleep?"

"Oh, I doubts that, suh. But I did fix her up a tea and loaded it with a double dose of chamomile. I'm hopin' you don't mind, but I sent Maxwell Joe down to Mattie Lou's house. She got some good sleepin' drafts. She should be here any minute. I tole Tessie to be on the lookout fo' her."

"Maxwell Joe? What was he doing here? Oh yes. I had him stay to take down the tables." A pain gnawed at Henry's insides. He stumbled over to his desk chair. "Salome. Salome. I've got to make this right." He held out his arms to her.

She stood there next to him, shaking her head.

"And you are absolutely certain that . . . that fool of a boy has hurt our girl?"

Salome took a step back, her eyes working to hold her tears. "Most of her clothes was off and on the ground. She was cryin' that kind of cry that only comes when a woman's been took against her will." Salome moved toward him and lowered her voice. "And he was lyin'."

"Spare me." The gaslights, as low as they were, usually gave off a yellow glow. Now, they blazed red. Henry whirled around and turned the key in the cabinet. He flung open the door and pulled out the walnut case. He headed to his desk.

Salome stood trembling. "Lady Margaret—she's frettin' over who to talk to. Scared to say anythin' to . . . to Lady Bertha. Afraid folks might say she led that boy on. That she was too fast. That she was scared 'cause she 'bout to be an old maid at twenty-one, so she got desperate. Throwed herself at Mr. Morse."

Henry jerked open the walnut case. There it lay—the late duke of Maryland's nine-chambered, .42-caliber LeMat revolver. He laid his hand over the smooth walnut handle and eased the weapon out of its satin lining. He made a slow turn to Salome. "Let's just see how fast Sylvester Morse can run from this." He sighted the gun at the library door.

"Oh, Lord. No, suh!" Salome dropped her voice back to a whisper. "Suh, you can't . . . I means to say, you wouldn't do no shootin', would you?"

"With a pleasure so great I can't find the words to describe it." He turned back to the gun case, spotted the brass box, and pulled out the hand-cast bullets made especially for Papa's LeMat.

"Lord Hardin, suh, I ain't never asked much of you fo' myself, but please, suh, Lady Margaret, she got to come first in this here business."

He lowered his arm and stared at Salome. Her eyes were wet. It was true; unlike all his other women, including his wife, she had asked no special favors other than that he provide for Tom-Tom. That was why she'd lasted the longest. He nodded his head. "My daughter is my first business."

"Yes, suh. You always done made that right clear. And it's Lady Margaret you gots to think 'bout now."

He pushed the cylinder open.

"Please think on it, suh. The way I got it fixed, don't nobody know fo' sure what happened to Lady Margaret 'ceptin' her, you, me, Tessie, and . . ."

"Maxwell Joe? He knows." Henry slipped in two, three, five, nine bullets.

"No, suh." Salome shook her head. "When Tessie went to fetch him, she jest told him there'd been an accident and to bring the wagon. Mr. Morse wasn't there when Maxwell Joe drove up."

Henry glanced sidelong at his lover and wondered anew. That Salome might have been unfaithful to him with the carpenter had worried Henry even before Tom-Tom came out so brown. He couldn't bear the thought of sharing this good-looking woman with anyone. Was she now trying to cover up for the man? He slammed the gun closed and put the brass box with its extra bullets into his pocket.

Salome grabbed his gun arm. "Suh, iffen you do this here thing—kills Mr. Sylvester—folks will want to know the why of it." Her breathing came so hard he could see the rise and fall of her chest.

"What choice do I have? You're not suggesting I force my daughter into a marriage with a fiend, are you?" He shook her off.

Salome stared at the flower pattern on the library carpet. "Lady Margaret for sho don't be wantin' that." She looked up at him, her eyes boring into his. "But, suh, fact is, peoples already talkin' 'bout her."

"Talking about her? How dare you. My daughter has been raised with the utmost respectability. She—"

Salome shook her head. "I knows all that. I ain't talkin' 'bout her being a maiden woman befo' this done happened. I'm talkin' 'bout the reason Mr. Sylvester done what he done." She scanned his face as though waiting for a gaslight to turn itself to full power inside his head.

"Salome?" He tilted his chin. When she first broke the awful news to him, all he could think of was revenge of the most painful kind. A horsewhipping would be much too lenient, hanging too quick. "What sort of reason?"

Salome worked her lips. "I reckon you knows, suh." She stopped long enough to consider that he most likely did not actually know. "It's yo' brother—His Grace—when he was drinkin' at the comin'-out party."

Henry frowned. "That's foolishness. James has promised to keep his mouth closed."

"Oh, I ain't sayin' Mr. Morse come outright with the words, but that is what he tole Lady Margaret when he was doin' what he was doin' to her."

"What do you mean? Sylvester Morse told Margaret what?"

"First he tole her it was all right fo' him to . . . take liberties 'cause they was engaged. When she kept tellin' him to quit it, he tole her he could take as many liberties as he pleased 'cause she was just a pretend white girl . . . She was really colored underneath it all."

Henry squeezed the handle of the LeMat. He shook his head. First, he would shoot off Morse's manhood. Let him suffer for a day or two, stake him out on the ground for another two days. Invite every field hand to come take a look. Once they and the crows had their fill, shoot him in the head. Henry felt his whole body tremble. "Salome, have Maxwell Joe hitch up the wagon . . . the wagon, not the buggy. I'll need a place to lay that miserable son of a bitch's body." He tried to brush past Salome. She pushed against him.

"I reckon I knows what you feelin', Henry. I'm feelin' it, too. But this here's our baby. Our firstborn. A child God wants us to protect. It can't be this way." She laid her hand on the barrel of the LeMat.

He stared at her. She knew better in so many ways. "I've got to kill this man," he whispered.

"Then you kills Margaret. A white girl bein' ruined is one thing. Folks will talk and expect a marryin'. But if they 'spects a white man done had his way with a colored girl, that's a whole different tellin'." She pushed the gun farther away. "Folks in Union County already thinkin' Margaret might be a colored girl. You ups and kills the judge's son, and that there talk gonna get all the worse. Yo' daughter's a strong girl, but even a woman as strong as an oak can't take that kinda talk."

Henry jerked the gun from her. He held it sideways against his chest. His head throbbed. He had always had a clear head, but not tonight. "There is only one other option. They'll have to marry."

"She gonna have to marry, all right. 'Specially if . . ." The first tear traced down Salome's cheek. "I'm gonna beat Mattie Lou into gettin' nothin' but the best herbs jest in case Margaret is . . . oh, God, deliver us." Salome shoved both hands to her face. The sobs racked her body.

Henry gathered her in his arms, the gun still in his right hand. "Salome, don't even think such a thing. God would not be so cruel as to let our daughter be preg . . ." He pushed her away enough to look into her face. "I cannot permit that monster to marry my daughter."

Salome's face was wet with tears. Her words came out between sobs. "It won't be none of Judge Morse's boy what gonna marry Margaret. I don't reckon it's gonna be any one of them society fellas. But if Lady Margaret finds herself in the family way—oh, Lord—Henry, you gonna have to find her some kind of a white husband if we is to save our girl."

Henry dropped the gun on the desk and turned back to Salome. He pulled out his handkerchief and wiped at her tears.

CHAPTER SEVENTEEN

Henry stood on the path, facing his orchard. He looked up at the black apple trees he had nurtured these last fifteen years. Were the skins just a dark red or had they turned that perfect shade of burgundy? Lifting a hand to screen his eyes from the rising sun singling out his orchard, he turned to Jacob Slocum.

"Well, are they ready for the picking?" Henry didn't trust his farm manager with the final decision, but he did want his opinion.

Slocum walked in front of four of the first trees in the line, glancing at the top of each. He grunted, but Henry couldn't tell if that was a yes or a no.

"Ain't easy to say this early in September." Slocum pointed to the tree in front of him. "These here in the front look close to pickin', but I ain't so sure 'bout them in the back."

"Hmm." Henry waved a thumb at Waylon standing a few feet behind him. "Did you send the boy out to the midtwenty, as I asked?"

Slocum squinted an eye at Henry. "I had him workin' on the barrels we gonna put the crop in. But it took him ever so long to get that job done, I ain't seen the bother." He wrinkled his nose as he turned his back on Waylon. "I sent my son to check on them apples instead."

"And what did Jebediah have to say?" Henry wondered again why he kept Jacob Slocum on the job. Though he'd been farm manager for five years, he'd yet to bring in a bumper crop of anything.

"Lord Hardin," Waylon called out. "I heard you ask Mr. Slocum to send me to the midorchard. After Maxwell Joe and I cooped a hundred of the barrels, I went out to check on the crop."

Frowning, his forehead deeply furrowed, Slocum turned around to Waylon. He shook his head. "You tellin' me after you cooped them one hundred barrels, you went out to the orchard midtwenty? Musta been damn dark. How'd you see good 'nough to tell if any of them apples was ready for the pickin'?"

"I took a lantern." Waylon kept his head slightly bowed as he addressed Jacob Slocum. "An extrabright one Maxwell Joe fixed up special for me. It gave off enough light for me to see that some of the Arkansas black apples had a bit of green on them."

Slocum spit on the ground. "Last night was dark as tar; you ain't seen nothin'."

Henry turned to Waylon, dismissing Slocum's usual contrary self. "Green could mean they've had too little sun. Come over here. Take a look at that tree—the one in the second row and to the right from where we're standing. Is it ready for the picking?"

Waylon walked to the tree, reached up, and plucked an apple. He turned it over and over in his hands. "Mr. Slocum is better at this than I am." He looked first at Jacob Slocum then at Henry. "I'd only be guessing."

"And what would your best guess be?" Henry waited.

"Colored ain't no good at guessin'." Slocum's under-his-breath voice carried to Henry's ears.

Waylon, who acted as though he hadn't heard the manager, kept his eyes on Henry and slipped the apple to his mouth. He took a bite. "A bit too tart, sir."

"What the hell that boy know 'bout tart?" Slocum spat out. "Them apples in the front is just right for eatin'—crispy-like. It's them in back I ain't so sure 'bout."

"Of course, Mr. Slocum." Henry walked over to Waylon, took the apple from him, and bit down. "Hmm. Too close to call." He turned to Slocum. "For either of you. Now, Jacob, you realize these apples bring a pretty penny on the open market when they're picked at the peak of perfection." He took a second bite. "Problem is, none of us is quite sure when that peak is reached." He handed the apple over to Waylon and walked back to the path. "Don't you agree, Mr. Slocum?"

Jacob shook his head. "Lord Hardin, them kind of apples ain't all that common 'round these parts, sure 'nough. But it won't take me but another season or two to get the hang of it. I'll bring you in more'n a pretty penny then."

Henry stroked his chin. "A year or two?" He turned to Waylon. "Isn't that college of yours a four-year program?"

Waylon nodded as his eyes brightened. "It is, Lord Hardin, but I know I can learn to spot the right time to harvest black apples in less than two."

Jacob Slocum, that furrow digging deeper into his forehead, looked from man to man. "What kinda college, Lord Hardin?"

"Oh, I suppose I've forgotten to tell you, Slocum. I'm tired of these guessing games with my crops. I need to know precisely when a thing is ripe for the harvest or my timber ready for the cutting. There's a school over in Alabama that specializes in teaching agriculture. I'm sending Waylon there. He can learn what a blush of green means on a black apple."

"Waylon?" Jacob Slocum's mouth hung open. "A college?" He shook his head. "Lord Hardin, ain't no college school gonna take no colored lessen it's a nig . . . colored preacher school." He looked at Henry as though his employer had slipped a cog.

Henry grunted. There was something most unlikable about Jacob Slocum. "Tuskegee is a colored college specializing in agriculture. Waylon will do just fine."

Jacob Slocum worked his mouth as though chewing on a wad of tobacco. "Waylon, if it's all right with Lord Hardin, I need you to start bringin' over them barrels you cooped."

Henry shrugged. Waylon turned without a word. Slocum waited until the man reached the road leading out of the orchard.

"Forgivin' me, Lord Hardin, but I don't think that boy's cut out for no agri . . . college even if it is a colored one." Jacob pulled out his kerchief and wiped his forehead. "You want somebody what can tell green blush from ain't ripe. I'm trainin' my boy, Jebediah, all 'bout them things. He'll be ready to help you with everythin' you need in a year or two."

"That's good news, Slocum. I'm glad your boy's getting on so well. For a while there, he seemed a little work-shy."

Slocum shot a quick glare at Henry but got his face back into the proper expression of respect almost before Henry noticed the transgression.

"Waylon will be home summers. The two can compare notes." Henry turned toward the road leading back to Hardin House.

"Compare notes?" Slocum's raised voice rang out in Henry's ear. "Jebediah don't need to be comparin' notes with no colored even if folks say he is your s—" Slocum's voice clipped quiet just as Henry stopped and turned to the man.

"Mr. Slocum." Henry held his voice even. All Union County would pitch a fit, but Henry was determined to replace Jacob Slocum and his lazy-to-the-bone son, Jebediah, with Waylon as soon as the boy graduated from Tuskegee. "Why don't you go back to your office and get me those receipts for the cooping supplies?"

Slocum wore no hat but the way he fidgeted with his hands, rolling an imaginary brim, brought a quick smile to Henry's face. Jacob Slocum had best not forget his place again or he would be out way before four years. Henry turned back to the road. Let Jacob and Jebediah Slocum work out their own fates. He had more important things to deal with. Margaret.

It had taken his daughter two days after the horror to allow her own father into her bedroom. When he had finally coaxed his way in, he found Margaret swathed in a mound of blankets pulled to her chin despite the blistering July heat. She made Henry sit in a chair across the room while she clutched Salome's hand. After Margaret told him as much as she was able, she begged him not to tell Bertha. Henry kept his agreement—for the most part. He parsed his words, of course, but he let his wife know, in no uncertain terms, that Sylvester Morse was worse than a scoundrel. Neither he nor his parents were to be received at Hardin House again. Bertha, in her usual obtuse way, protested, but eventually came around. She left Henry with but one offhand comment: "James said this was bound to happen."

Was that Mattie Lou that Henry spotted as he padded up the path to the front door of Hardin House after his set-to with Jacob Slocum? He'd caught a quick glimpse of the woman hobbling across the south lawn cascading from the house and down the road to the help's quarters. Henry shrugged as he mounted the mansion's broad steps and opened the front door. How was his daughter this morning? He had checked on her every day since that devil, Sylvester Morse, forced himself on her. The sound of the man's name, even in his own head, sickened Henry.

Henry headed toward the grand staircase, still not certain Salome had been right. Sylvester Morse needed killing and the LeMat was the perfect tool for the deed. These last two months, Margaret had lived in almost complete darkness in her bedroom. It had taken all Salome had to get the girl out of the bed where she'd lain curled in a ball those awful first three weeks. Another two weeks to get her out of her nightclothes and dressed for the day. The battle between Salome and Margaret over the window blinds still raged. Salome pulled them up to bathe the room in healing sunshine. Margaret demanded they be down, determined to hide her shame from the world. So far, Margaret was winning. Her room was draped in dimness around the clock. Henry laid a hand on the banister of the staircase. What words could he come up with today to ease his little girl's pain?

"Lord Hardin?" Salome's voice came as a hiss.

He leaned over the banister. The door to the room he'd built under the grand staircase to house Salome—and himself many nights—was a quarter open. Salome's head peeked out.

"We needs to talk." She leaned out and scanned the foyer.

Henry followed her glances. The two were alone. He stepped off the stair and hurried into the off-limits-to-everyone-else room. He closed the door behind him and slipped the bolt into its lock. Although he'd assigned this private room to Salome years ago, it was his sanctuary as much as it was her space. The double-size bed, the two Tennessee-crafted bureaus, the two chintz-covered chairs, and the hanging rack for Salome's clothes had all been selected by him. The only thing the room lacked was gaslight. Even at half past eight in the morning, two kerosene lamps were the only light flickering in the hideaway.

"What is it?" Henry searched Salome's face and found only disaster.

She stood there swaying from foot to foot, her eyes wet, her lips trembling. Salome squeezed her hands over and over. "Mattie Lou."

Henry's heart thumped. "Mattie Lou?"

"She jest left."

Henry nodded. "What did she want?" Somewhere deep in his gut, he already had his answer.

Salome's tears came. No, they flooded. Henry took a step closer to his lover. He laid his hands on her shoulder. "What did Mattie Lou say?"

Salome managed a nod before she buried her face in Henry's shoulder. He held her tight.

"She's gone, all right 'nough. Margaret . . . Mattie Lou say . . . she 'bout two months gone." Her voice lost itself in the river of her sobs.

Two months. Sylvester Morse. Henry kept his arms tight and rocked Salome to and fro as he forced the pounding in his head to quiet. He laid his face against her braided hair. "Could Mattie Lou be wrong?" While Mattie Lou's herbs had never worked as far as Henry could tell, the woman had not been wrong about confirming a pregnancy. "Oh, my God" escaped out of his mouth. He tried to swallow his words back. "Don't you worry. I'll fix this."

Salome pulled away. "No, not no gun. Please, suh." A fresh wave of tears tore at her body. "No weddin' neither. Not to the likes of that one." She was lost again in a river of sobs.

He held her close as his brain whirred. His daughter needed a husband—a white one—and right away. He rubbed Salome's back. "Does Margaret know that she . . . she's in a family way?"

Salome shook her head as her trembling ratcheted up.

Henry kissed the top of her head, the scent of hair pomade tickling his nose. "I've got to go out for a spell. I'll be back in a bit. You stay in here. I don't want anyone seeing you until I return." He led her to the green chintz chair and sat her down. "You understand?"

"That's the only thing I can understand about somethin' as awful as this. I'll stay here 'til you says different." She looked up at Henry and grabbed his hand. "I knows you gonna fix this here mess the right way."

He nodded as he walked to the door. "Bolt this after I leave."

Henry sat back in the oak armchair, one hand on his chin. He was determined to look the picture of matter-of-factness as he faced down Jacob Slocum. Jacob, on the other side of the oak-plank desk in his little office, stared at Henry as though he were certain Lord Hardin, the duke of Union County, had gone addlepated.

"Let me get this straight, Lord Hardin." Slocum looked as though it might take twenty more tellings before he got even the most elementary details of Henry's orders straight. "You wantin' me to step up Jebediah's trainin'. You thinkin' 'bout makin' him farm manager after my time is up?" Slocum's eyes glazed over for the fourth time in as many retellings of Henry's request.

"That's right." That one bite of apple Henry sampled this morning threatened to wreak havoc on his insides right here in front of the jumped-up, little-better-than-a-dirt-farmer Jacob Slocum. But Henry had no other options. "I disagree with you about Waylon. I believe he will become quite competent after his schooling, but . . ."

"Compet . . . ?" Slocum's hairline dipped down almost to his eyebrows as he squinted his confusion at Henry.

"I believe he can do the job. But things being what they are, I think young Jebediah should be the one to wear the hat, don't you?"

"Hat?" Slocum fidgeted as though he were about to pee all over himself.

Henry couldn't stop a sigh from escaping his lips. He was pleased the sound had been so soft Jacob Slocum took no notice of it. Henry held his breath for a second. For the fifth time, he would outline what he wanted of the Slocums, knowing full well he would have to repeat himself ten minutes later.

"Yes. Hat. When the time comes, I'd like young Jebediah to be the official farm manager of Hardin House and all its acres."

"All its acres?"

Henry dropped his hand to the armrest. He hoped Slocum couldn't see him grip the thing like a drowning man finally clutching a rescuing rope. "The orchards, the timber, the sawmill, the maple trees, the—"

"Everythin'? You wantin' Jebediah to be in charge of everythin' after . . . after . . ." Slocum scratched his head again.

He'd done that so many times in the last fifteen minutes, Henry wondered how even one strand of the man's sparse graying hair remained on his head.

Slocum poked his tongue from cheek to cheek. "That's the part that ain't comin' in clear." He leaned across the table and lowered his voice. "You sayin' you gonna give Jebediah permission to marry . . ." Slocum shook his head and fell back into his chair as though he'd been struck.

Henry had to help the man. "That's right. I've noticed that your son"—Henry wasn't usually a praying man, but he sent a prayer up to God just in case—"and my daughter may have some interest in one another."

"Lady Margaret?" Just as it had done the last four tellings, Slocum's voice rose shrill in the office. "I gotta say, I ain't never seen Jebediah with nothin' lookin' like a quality girl. Ain't never thought . . ." Slocum calmed down enough to look straight at Henry. "You sure? Far's I know that boy don't have no decent lady friends. One time, he mighta been tryin' to spark a town girl, but mostly, he hangs around with farm girls. They don't have no worldly ways. Give 'em a box of chocolates or a hair ribbon and they're ever so thankful for the attention. Throw in some perfume and it's not unheard of for them to raise their skirts to say thank you to a man, if you know what I mean."

Henry struggled to hide his grimace. What an unsavory lout, but he had to save Margaret. He gave his head a slow nod like he understood. "They've both been most discreet, I must say. Their attraction to one another almost escaped my attention, but there was something in the way your Jebediah looked at my . . . Well, I'll say no more. Only that I believe it's best they wed before this goes any further." Henry tried to read Slocum's face. Had any more details registered in this, the fifth telling of the same tale?

"And you say Jebediah would move into the Big House—Hardin House? Live there with . . . with . . ."

"His wife." The words clogged Henry's throat.

A scowl slowly dawned on Slocum's face as his eyes narrowed. "So about this wantin' my boy to marry your daughter . . ." He worked his cheeks. "Ain't there been some talk . . . well, some folks say that Lady Margaret . . . that she could really be a col . . . That is to say, she might not be whi . . ."

Henry willed away the glare he felt climbing into his eyes. Instead he shook his head in mock disgust. "Since you and I are about to become relatives of a sort, I'm quite certain any kin of mine will not pay attention to vicious and untrue gossip. I know my farm manager, with so many added responsibilities and the subsequent increase in salary, would never stoop so low."

Slocum leaned toward Henry, then back in his chair and forward again.

Henry could almost see the slow wheels struggling to gear themselves up in the man's brain.

"Responsibilities? More salary?" Slocum scratched his head. Was that a louse jumping from one strand to another? "Did I hear you say you'd give me two thousand dollars a year just so's I could speed up my boy's trainin' if he was to marry up with your girl?"

"Did I say two? I meant three thousand a year for you and another three thousand for Jebediah." Henry leaned across the desk. "Now you go talk to your son. I'll arrange a wedding in New Orleans for next week."

"Next week?" Slocum sat up in the chair.

"We wouldn't want to keep those two apart, now would we? I know you'd like to come to the ceremony, but there's so much work around here with harvest right around the corner. Why don't you use this five hundred dollars here at home?" Henry pulled out his money purse and doled out five hundred-dollar bills that he had removed earlier from his library safe. He kept one hand on the bills as he laid them on the table. "Now you go speak to Jebediah. You explain I've granted my permission for a wedding. I'm sure he will be thankful that I did not put up too much of a fuss. I understand he's anxious to marry a girl as lovely as my daughter. Don't you agree?"

Slocum slid his dirty fingernails toward the bills. Without looking at Henry, he nodded. "If it's what you're wantin', Lord Hardin. My Jebediah marryin' your daughter . . . no matter what folks might be guessin' 'bout her . . ." He tapped the bills. "Four thousand dollars each and ever' year comin' my way for the rest of my life will work just fine for me."

CHAPTER EIGHTEEN

Henry closed the door behind him and glanced at the teakwood table holding the day's mail before heading to the little room underneath the grand staircase. He heard the distinctive sound of her footsteps before he spotted Celeste limping toward the kitchen from the back stairway.

"Celeste, has your mistress returned?" He looked at the grandfather clock in the foyer. Eleven forty-five. The nasty business with Jacob Slocum had taken over two hours. "I understood she was going to a tea over in Lisbon. With Judge Morse's wife." He shuddered. Henry blamed the mother almost as much as the son. How could anyone raise such a monster?

"Oh, Lord Hardin." Celeste looked up as she spotted him. "Yes, suh, Lady Hardin done come home early." Celeste turned toward the kitchen door.

"I thought she was staying for lunch."

The grimace sweeping Celeste's face made Henry curious.

"Well?" He needed to get to Salome, but something was amiss. "Did your mistress take ill?"

"Uhh." Celeste inched her way backward toward the kitchen. "Not zactly, suh. That is to say she ain't sick in the body." Something akin to panic rode her face.

Henry frowned. What had Bertha done now? He'd forbidden the entire Morse clan from visiting Hardin House these last two months, though there had been no occasion for festivities anyway. But Henry had relented and allowed Bertha to travel to Lisbon to visit her cronies. "Celeste. What ails Lady Bertha?"

The servant wiped her hands down her uniform. "Lady Bertha ain't told me, suh, but I suspects it might be her shoes. They was a mite too tight."

"My wife left a tea with her lady friends because her feet hurt?"

Celeste bobbed her departure to Henry. "Beggin' pardon, suh, but Lady Bertha sent me down here to fetch her lunch from Delfine since she wasn't up to eatin' at the Morses'." Celeste scurried through the kitchen door.

Strange. But Henry had no time to fret over Bertha. He had to get to Salome. With the foyer clear, he tapped on the door. He heard the bolt slide back with a sound like a grunt. Salome opened the creaking door, and Henry hurried inside.

Salome, her braided hair coming undone at the ends, stood there, sucking in her lips. Only one of the kerosene lamps remained lit. The bed was rumpled. A candle, emitting the scent of lavender, flickered low. Henry led her to the center of the narrow space and closer to the lamp. Salome's eyes were red, her face soaked with tears.

"One week from today our daughter will be safe." He looked into Salome's disbelieving eyes. "A respectable married woman." He stroked her arms.

"You ain't shot nobody?" Salome's voice betrayed the strain of a throat raw from weeping. "Married woman? It ain't none of . . . him, is it?"

"Jebediah Slocum." Henry licked his lips. "Jebediah Slocum will be Margaret's husband."

Salome's body slumped as though she'd been struck by a two-by-four. "Jebedi . . . Mr. Slocum? He's . . . he can't . . ." She shook her head. "He ain't no kind of husband fo' Margaret," she said pleadingly.

"You said it yourself: no gentleman in Union County will have her as his wife because of the talk."

Salome shook her head over and over. Henry grabbed her shoulders.

"I know what the Slocums are. Not two steps above white trash, but they will accept her into their white family as a legal wife."

"But that kinda man don't know nothin' 'bout how to treat a lady. And you trained Margaret to be a lady. He bound to be mighty rough on her." Fresh tears. "I can't bear to think 'bout that."

He gathered her in his arms. "I will never permit anyone to abuse our daughter."

Salome lifted her head from his chest. "The baby. Do he know 'bout the comin' chile?"

Henry gave his head a slow shake. "Margaret's only two months along. I'll arrange the wedding for next week in New Orleans. That way, people won't know the child was conceived before the marriage."

"Maybe not most folks in Union County, but I reckon even Mr. Jebediah can count."

"We'll tell that fool the baby came early." Henry released Salome, walked over to the water pitcher, and dampened a facecloth. "Let's clean you up. Margaret can't see you crying." He dabbed at her face. "You and I are going upstairs to tell our daughter two truths: that she's getting married and that she's pregnant."

Salome followed him up the last step of the grand staircase. Henry headed for Margaret's room, his hand poised to knock.

"I knew from the beginnin' this was goin' to end in nothin' but disaster." Bertha's voice boomed through the closed door.

Henry frowned as he turned to shush Salome.

"Do you have any idea how humiliatin' it was for me to sit there this mornin' while all those women signified 'bout you? Sipped their tea and signified 'bout your loose ways?"

Henry's jaw went slack. He sensed Salome shaking with fury behind him.

"Lady Bertha . . . no . . . I . . ." Margaret's weak voice broke down.

"Oh, stop your cryin', girl. It's me who should be doin' the weepin' and the gnashin' of teeth. Every woman at Sophie Morse's tea knows what you done."

"That's just it. I didn't do anything. He . . . Syl . . ." Sobs filtered through the door.

Salome tried to move past Henry. He held her back.

"For your information, missy, Sylvester Morse is gettin' engaged to Saidie Belle Brown in October." The sound of Bertha's feet stalking around the room crept through the door. "There I was. Mortified above all mortifications. Sylvester was supposed to marry you. Everybody in the county knew you'd set your cap for the man 'cause he's gonna be governor of Arkansas one of these days. Though both me and your uncle James knew that wasn't gonna work." Bertha's groan carried into the hallway. "He was supposed to marry you, but after you disgraced yourself with the man, he knew you weren't fit to be no gentleman's wife, let alone a governor's First Lady." Bertha gurgled out a cry. "Oh, Lord help me. Every one of them women looked at me like you bein' a hussy was my fault."

"How . . . why?" Margaret's voice came out strangled. "How did they . . . the ladies . . . know what happened?"

"How do you think? Sylvester must have told his father what an easy piece you were."

"Lady Bertha." Margaret's words came out on a cry. "No. Please . . . it was him . . . Sylvester, who did awful things to me."

"I reckon he did plenty of things to you after you lifted your skirts and dropped your drawers. That's what I reckon he told Judge Morse. And what was young Sylvester supposed to do when you threw yourself on the ground, gapped your knees wide open, and waved your legs in the air? You beggin' him to come in and help himself?"

Salome pushed against Henry as she reached for the doorknob. He grabbed her to his chest with one arm while he slipped a hand over her mouth.

"And now this!" Bertha's lament rose again. "How in God's good graces am I expected to hold my head up with your belly fixin' to swell any minute? Oh, Jesus, spare me the disgrace!"

"Belly? Lady Bertha, what do you mean?"

"Anybody with half a good eye can see you're in a family way. Expectin' a child with not a husband in sight. You lowdown slut!"

"Mama! No!" What sounded like a death rattle croaked out of Margaret's mouth.

"Don't you *Mama* me, you nigger whore. Don't you know no white man's ever gonna marry you? It's a sin against God."

The door crashed open after Henry put his shoulder to it. He hadn't meant to, but he slammed Salome against the hallway wall in the commotion. Henry grabbed Bertha by the arm, pushed her around the slumping Salome, and rushed his wife through the hallway and into their bedroom. He slammed the door behind him, grabbed an armchair, and shoved it against the door.

"What is it you think you're doin', Henry Hardin?" Bertha stood near their highboy, hands on her hips. "Haulin' me off like that. Tryin' to show off for your black wench, were you? Well, I think that day has just 'bout come to an end. The whole county's gonna know the truth. Your bastard is a nigger hussy tart."

The room went peach, then orange, and finally red but not from the almost-noon sun. Henry had to still his racing heart. He felt every muscle in his body jump and jerk.

"Bertha"—he didn't recognize the sound of his own voice as he stood inches from her—"if I ever, in this life or the next, hear you speak another ill word against my daughter, you will more than rue the day."

"Rue the day, is it?" She pointed a finger at him. "I'm thinkin' it's you who's 'bout to rue the day, the month, and the whole damn year! It's fittin' punishment after the disgrace you brought down on me!"

Henry grabbed her right arm. Had he twisted it as he pulled her to their four-poster? He heard her sharp intake of breath as she stumbled against the bed.

"What on earth do you think you're doin'? Turn me loose." Bertha struggled to shake free. "You, takin' that dusky slut to bed every other night. Right in my own house!" She stopped fighting him as she narrowed her eyes. "I never know when I come down those stairs what I'm gonna hear floatin' from the first floor. If I have to hear you and that colored trollop gruntin' and ruttin' around like two hogs in slop right beneath my feet one more day, I swear I'll take out a newspaper advertisement in the *Arkansas Gazette* and tell the world 'bout my so-called daughter!" She tried to pull away.

He held her fast.

"You get your hands off me, Henry Hardin." Spit flew from her lips. "You need a good thrashin' for what you done to me. I just wish James was up to the job." She winced and leaned into him. "You gave that blackamoor three pickaninnies. You parade them around the neighborhood like they was almost as good as white folks. And Jesus knows I'm not the one tryin' to pass off a yella bastard as a God-fearin' white girl." Her voice climbed. "But I am the one who has to pay for your sinnin' ways. All Union County whisperin', snickerin', laughin' at me. Well, God is ready to exact vengeance on you, your whore, and your bastard! And when all three of y'all burn in hell, I'm gonna do the Little Rock jig for joy!"

Henry surveyed the room. He spotted a small square of drying linen lying on the nightstand next to the washbasin. He snatched up the cloth and shoved the balled-up scrap in Bertha's mouth.

"Ughh." She swung at his arms with her free hand as she brought her foot down on his boot. Her eyes sparked fire and brimstone worse than the Devil. Bertha reached for the cloth.

Henry slapped her arm away, grabbed her shoulders, spun her around, and shoved her facedown into the feather mattress. Bertha landed with a squish as the mattress mounded up on both sides. She clawed a handhold on the sheets, ripping them off the mattress.

"Ahhh" gurgled out of her mouth as she tried to hunch herself upright.

Henry yanked back the bed coverlet, fumbled for the pillow, and pushed the goose-down lump over her head.

She struggled to get out what sounded like his name as her hands fought against the smothering pillow.

Killing's too good for her. Henry adjusted the pillow just enough to let her catch a bit of air. He reached back, grabbed handfuls of her gray dress, and shoved the skirt to the top of her corset. "Did I just hear you tell my daughter she couldn't wait to lift her skirts for Sylvester Morse?" Bertha's fingers stabbed at folds of fabric as she tried to push her dress back in place. Henry spotted the offending fingers, and bent one, then two, backward.

Bertha screeched. He bore down on the pillow. She sent up gasping noises as her arms stilled.

"That she willingly lifted her skirts just like you're lifting yours now? And, my darling wife, did I just hear you say to my girl that it was her idea to drop her drawers for Sylvester Morse?" He eased up on the pillow while he yanked Bertha's bloomers to her knees. "Just like it's your idea to drop yours now?"

Henry looked at the pale, dimpled, wobbling mass thrashing against his mattress, loosening feathers from the ticking. His face puckered. He hadn't willingly looked at that sight in years, and he wished he didn't have to look now. He took his time as he loosened his belt from its silver buckle. He laid a knee across Bertha's back as he slid his belt from the holding loops.

"Bertha, in all her life, you've never said a kind word to Margaret." He lifted the pillow and looked into the one eye she managed to free. "Not only have you not been any kind of a mother to my daughter, you've been her tormentor. I want you to remember each and every evil thing you've ever said to that girl—a child who's not to blame for her circumstance."

Bertha shook her yes as her hand reached for the cloth in her mouth. Henry dug into her wrists and stretched her arms over her head. He heard her left shoulder pop as he pulled.

A muffled *Uh-huh* came out of Bertha.

Henry, his leg still across her back, looked at his belt. He rolled the leather in one hand until no more than eight inches showed. "Bertha, can you remember all the evil things you've done to my child through the years?"

"Nnnn?"

"Allow me to help you. Remember when she was three and she wet the bed? You made her walk around the house wearing only a diaper, even in front of your ladies' sewing circle. Do you recall that?" Where had all the throbbing in his body gone? Now he felt as cool as spring rain. He raised his arm just enough to flick Bertha's bare bottom with the leather belt. "One, two, three. A lick for each of her years when you did that."

"Oww." More feathers came free under Bertha's thrashing.

"And when she was six, and you declared her too stupid to learn to read in front of your entire literary guild." Henry raised his arm higher. "Four, five, six."

Bertha's legs writhed on the feather bed up and down.

He dropped the strap across

"And at twelve. Do you recall what you said to her on that birthday? Most likely not. Let me refresh your memory." He let out another two inches of the leather coiled in his swinging arm. He didn't want to draw blood, but he certainly wanted to raise welts. "'Her breasts are growing too big for a respectable lady. She looks more like a colored serving wench.' Your words, not mine." He lifted his arm higher. "Seven, eight, nine." He dropped the strap across Bertha with a little more force. "Ten, eleven, twelve."

Yelps, or perhaps screams, came from somewhere deep within the feathers.

"Then Margaret turned eighteen. You must remember her coming-out party? When talk started, how you did nothing to quiet it? Recall that?" He uncurled a good foot of leather and lashed into her. "Thirteen, fourteen, fifteen."

Bertha's cries sounded like a fox with one paw caught in a trap. Each time the strap landed across her bare behind, Bertha jumped as though she were in the throes of a Saint Vitus's dance.

"Sixteen, seventeen, eighteen." The leather thudded harder. Clouds of feathers swirled around her.

"And now my daughter is twenty-one." His breathing came easy despite his efforts. He unfurled three more inches of strap. Henry lifted the pillow as he leaned his face close to hers.

Bertha, the color of an orchard grape, looked up at him, fear riding every inch of her face.

"You accuse Margaret of hurting herself. Of wanting a man—no, begging a man—to level God's greatest sin against a woman at her."

Bertha batted her eyes as she tried to muffle what sounded like *no*. Henry dangled fifteen inches of leather belt back and forth slowly in front of her face.

"Unh, unh. Plooos!" Bertha blinked her eyes.

"You stupid, stupid woman. My daughter was raped. Do you understand the word? Raped! She wanted nothing of Sylvester Morse other than a proper proposal of marriage. Instead, that louse ravaged her, and you . . . silly fool of a woman . . . blamed my child. To her face." He slammed the pillow back over Bertha's pleading eyes. "My daughter was an innocent."

Henry lifted the belt over his shoulder and snapped it through the air. "Nineteen." It landed with a thwack. A handful of feathers studded Bertha's backside. Henry set his jaw as he lifted his arm again. The belt whizzed, landing square on her bottom. "Twenty."

Bertha's body slammed into the mattress then bounced up as a shrill shriek careened from somewhere deep within the feathers. Henry let out the full length of belt, raised his hand above his head, and let the leather sing through the air. The strap crashed against the raised blue-red mess that was her behind. "Twenty-one." He dropped the strap on the coverlet, removed the pillow, and flipped a panting Bertha on her back.

"Aghh. Ahh." She twisted side to side, one hand reaching for the choking gag, the other struggling to soothe her behind.

"Be still, woman. I'm not through with you."

Her hands froze midmotion. Her face, streaked with snot, stared at him. Bertha sucked in a breath and lay as still as a statue.

"That's better." Henry pulled the linen cloth, wet with spit, out of her mouth. Her dress was crumpled around her waist and her bloomers dangled around her ankles. Henry rested his hands on both sides of her, pressing down on the feathers. "I've just whipped your ass. If ever there is a next time, I'll stripe your back, too." He glared down at her. "Do you understand me?"

Bertha lifted both hands to her throat. "Yeh," she croaked out.

"If you don't want me to put you in nothing but a diaper and parade you around in front of the servants—even the field hands if you rile me enough—you will do exactly as I say." He waited. "This is what you're going to do." He glared into weak eyes that threatened to jump out of their sockets.

Bertha, her chest rising in great heaves, nodded.

"You will go to your sewing circle, quilting group, ladies' literary guild, and every other damn thing you society biddies do, and you will tell each and every one of those god-awful women—including Sophie Morse—that you recall each and every birth pang you ever felt when you gave birth to your only child. You will lament how sad you feel that you cannot plan your beloved daughter's engagement and wedding parties because she has chosen to elope with a man she loves deeply. You will lie through your teeth to those puffed-up women. You will tell them without a doubt in your voice that Jebediah Slocum may not be quality folk, but that he has great potential. That you are proud to have him as a son-in-law." Henry ran out of breath. He moved away from her, reached over, and picked up the leather belt. "Now, Bertha, repeat what I just said. Forget one word and . . ."

Bertha's jaw jiggled and wobbled as though it had forgotten how to work. She nodded her head up and down as though she were a puppet. Her hands pulled at the deflated mattress. "Jeb . . . ?"

Henry fingered the belt.

Every vein in her neck stood out. "Henry . . . I tell ladies . . . Sophie Morse . . . Margaret my . . . daughter. I recall the birthin' . . . like yesterday. I . . . ." Her eyes sparked in terror as she stared at the belt in Henry's hand.

"And Jeb Slocum? What will you tell your lady friends about your soon-to-be son-in-law?"

Bertha flicked a quick glance at him. He ran his hand down the full length of the belt.

"Yes! Yes! Son-in-law. Proud." Her eyes were stuck on the strip of leather. "I'll say it. Every word." Her shaking body loosened more feathers.

Henry stood and slipped the belt back into its loops. "Then you'd better get to it, hadn't you? I expect you and your sore ass to ride back to Lisbon this very afternoon. Engage Sophie Morse and tell that prune-faced witch your news."

Bertha whimpered as she lay shivering on the bed. He headed toward the door.

"Oh, don't look so tragic. I've never beaten you like this before. Don't disobey me, and it will never happen again. Besides, nobody's going to see your beat-up backside, and I'll increase your dress allowance. You can even order that smelly perfume from New Orleans you favor." He dragged the chair holding the door into the center of the room. He laid a hand on the doorknob before he turned to her. "One last thing."

"I'll do it."

"Clean yourself up, put on some talcum, and for God's sake, pull up your drawers. I wouldn't want to trouble Celeste with such a disgusting sight." Henry pointed to the bed. "Use the pillow to cushion yourself in the buggy." He walked into the hallway, closing the door quietly behind him.

"My, my, did I stumble upon a contretemps in paradise?" James, looking his usual bleary-eyed self, stood just ten feet from Henry's bedroom door.

"Quite the contrary, brother dear." He walked up close to James. "The little chastisement I was forced to deliver to Bertha was but a gentle reminder of loyalties. You, above all, understand loyalty, don't you, James, duke of Maryland?"

"Return me to Maryland, and I most certainly will."

The taste of justice felt good on Henry's soul. "Your days in Maryland are over." He now stood within six inches of his brother, staring at his drink-ravaged face. "As are your days as duke of anything. I'm well aware, my dear, dear brother, that you understand loyalty cannot be bought. I would never demean you by suggesting the thousand dollars I deposit in your account each and every month is a reward for your continuing loyalty. Honor is its own reward, don't you agree?" He stepped back. "But sometimes my memory fails me. To save my soul, I can't recall what cash I'm supposed to dispense when, and to whom."

James raised an imaginary glass to Henry. "Touché. Your message is well received, brother dear." He walked toward the grand staircase.

"Oh, don't hurry. As I did for Bertha, I will do for you. A consolation prize. Once my wife has fulfilled her duties this afternoon, please feel free to have at her."

James stopped, turned, and tilted his head. "Have at her? Bertha?"

"Take all you want. Whenever you want. It hasn't escaped me that you delight in setting your eyes on women who belong to me."

"You do me a great wrong, Henry. As are you, I am a married man."

"So you are. Sad to say, Elvera has the constitution of a milksop. She spends weeks at a time complaining of nothing but her ill health." Henry took a step away. "I doubt she can perform much in the way of wifely duty." That twitch working the corners of his mouth felt good. "But all is not lost, dear James. I have noticed you and Bertha—workhorse that she is—seem to delight in making moon eyes at one another." Henry walked to Margaret's door and laid a hand on the knob. He sensed Salome standing on the other side. "My wife does not seem to grasp the concept of rape. James, she may protest your attentions for propriety's sake. Ignore that. I have a suspicion Bertha will more than welcome you into her arms." He twisted the knob, opened the door, and stepped into his daughter's room.

CHAPTER NINETEEN

Margaret stared at her reflection in the ornate, filigreed mirror—just like New Orleans. Except for the peeling Napoleon-blue wallpaper and the scarred, French-style bed, bureau, and dresser, she might have been in some seen-better-days hotel in Little Rock. The mirror was the only standout in the room—and her worst enemy.

Could that piece of glass, undoubtedly crafted in Paris, tell who she really was? She looked at her reflection in the just-cleaned mirror. Not a streak or speck of dirt to hide even one inch of her face and hair. Her hair. She lifted a hand to her head. She put a light finger against the tresses Salome had laid straight with a newfangled hot comb. Something her maid found two doors down from their French Quarter hotel. Margaret protested when Salome first heated the metal contraption in the flame from the gas-fueled lamp, but Salome assured her that the French comb had been used for a long time both in New Orleans and France by women with extracurly hair. Sure enough, Salome's efforts had rendered Margaret's hair shiny and kink-free. The maid coaxed waves out of Margaret's new locks, pinned them into alluring swags about her face, and studded the top with fresh pink rosebuds.

Margaret stared at her reflection. If beauty still existed in this world, she would declare her hair beautiful. She turned her head first to the right, then the left. Her hair was more than presentable, but what of her face? What color was she, really?

A bell—from one of those New Orleans streetcars, the ones with funny names—dinged on the street below her. Bourbon Street, was it? She kept her eyes on her reflection. Back home in Union County, she hadn't dared look at herself. Her gilt-framed mirror might reveal much too much. Would she find something in her own eyes or the way her mouth drew back to show her teeth, or would she discover some other little thing that had given Sylvester Morse leave to . . . ? Margaret bit down on her lip. Sometimes, when memories of that afternoon by the creek overwhelmed her, the twitching started in her eyelids, then spread to an uncontrollable wobble of her neck, and moved to her hands—her fingers shaking so much she couldn't hold a comb to her hair. Which was worse? The shaking or the tears? And she never knew which was coming when. She'd been teary eyed last week when Papa and Salome entered her room. Margaret wanted to tell her father about the dreadful, awful names Lady Bertha had called her—slut, hussy, whore, nig . . . But Papa looked so serious. Even Salome did, too. The two of them said the most god-awful thing to her, the same thing as Lady Bertha: that she could be—was—expecting. But worry and concern had filled their words, not hatred. Yet all three had pronounced her with child. If her laughter hadn't died last Fourth of July, she would have giggled at their sorrowing faces. How could she, Margaret Hardin, be with child? She wasn't married.

"Lady Margaret," Salome now called through the door of the hotel room.

Margaret couldn't take her eyes from the mirror.

"I brung yo' dress. All ready fo' you to put on."

Dress? Oh, her wedding dress. The quivering moved down to her shoulder blades, which kept scrunching themselves together. "Go away!" Margaret squeezed her fingernails hard into her palms. "I mean, please tell Papa I need another few minutes."

"Can I help you with somethin', Lady Margaret?" As usual, Salome sounded worried.

Funny. Ever since that day when the world ended, it had been Salome who fretted over her. Not Bertha. But why would that be? No need to dwell on that now.

"Lady Margaret." Salome tapped on the door, louder this time. "I'm gonna go get yo' father. You ain't got but an hour to get down to the marryin' place."

"Yes. Go get Papa." Marrying place? Was it just nine weeks ago when she expected a marriage proposal from Syl . . . ?

She leaned forward in her vanity chair. Margaret ran a finger down the side of her face. She dug in hard enough to leave a mark. Red. She squinted her eyes. Except for the blotch she'd just inflicted on herself, her skin was white. Well, creamy. Like the color of fresh-churned milk about to go to butter. Margaret Hardin was white. How on God's green earth could anyone think otherwise? Sylvester Morse. Oh, she understood Sylvester and his ridiculous claim. He would, and did, say anything that gave him permission to carry out his foul deed. But Lady Bertha? What had her mother meant? A nigger whore? Where had that come from?

Tessie had let the word *whore* slip once when she'd whispered to Celeste about some poor white-trash woman down by the railway station. When Margaret threatened the maid with a whack of her hairbrush, Tessie disclosed all. A whore was a woman who acted like a wife when she really wasn't one. Well, that certainly wasn't Margaret. Lady Bertha's anger clearly came from the disgrace of a ruined daughter, not because her girl had fast ways. Sometimes, Margaret understood her mother's outburst, but at others . . . What had Lady Bertha meant by her outrageous charge?

Margaret twisted her body in the vanity chair. She absolutely was not a colored girl. Her skin was white; at least, white enough. Her natural hair, of course, was a tangled mess. Salome claimed it was a throwback to some English great-grandmother on her father's side. Then there was her nose. A little broad at the tip. Could that be the culprit?

"All right, sugar." *Papa.* "Open the door. We've got to get you ready for your wedding."

Margaret pushed back from the dressing table. Wedding. As she rose, a new wave of stomach sickness overtook her. She laid a hand across her belly. No matter what they all said, she knew the real reason she retched several times each and every day. And it was not because she carried the Devil's child. That was impossible, no matter how Salome explained the way babies were made. Margaret was ill because Sylvester had shoved some awful, hurting thing inside her—something so sticky and terrible it had made her sick these past five weeks. But that thing was most certainly not a baby. Babies only came from love between married people. When Margaret was thirteen, she caught Celeste whispering almost the same words to a new, younger-than-Margaret assistant cook caught with one of the older groomsmen: *Keep your skirts down until you find the man who loves you no matter what. Then you can have all the babies you want.*

Her mother's maid had been right. No matter what Salome said about men and women coming together, no baby could come from such a disgusting act if there was no love. And there never, ever, could be love between her and . . .

"Margaret." Her father raised his voice.

She made her way across the faded blue carpet and opened the door. A wave of something sweet, probably from the market, roiled her belly even more. Salome, holding a sheet-covered dress in her arms and unfazed by the smell of sugary French doughnuts, stepped inside the room right after her father. The maid took off the covering from the dress, dropping it on the bed, then shook out the white confection festooned with blue ribbons at the blousy sleeves.

"Soon as I get these here buttons undone, we can get this on you." Salome's fingers fumbled with the back of the dress.

"I'll step out, sugar, while you get your dress on," Papa said. "But first I want to say a few words to you." He looked nervous.

One week. That was the extent of the engagement—if that's what this charade could be called—her father had allowed. After he and Salome delivered their ridiculous pronouncement about a baby, the two informed her she would be married. In New Orleans, in one week's time. In these past seven days, she'd never laid eyes on her chosen groom—Jebediah Slocum. Thank God.

"Umm." Oh, Lord. Another wave of stomach sickness grabbed at her as Henry closed the bedroom door.

"Sweetness, there are some things you must know before . . . before the wedding." He squeezed her shoulders.

Margaret swallowed once, twice, and the bile started its way back to her stomach. "I already know, Papa."

He ran his hands down the arms of her flowered robe. "I know Salome has explained certain things to you, but husbands . . . some husbands . . ." Papa cleared his throat. "Some men have certain needs. If ever these . . . these needs are of a hurting nature, you are to tell Salome all about them. Understand?"

Understand? How could she understand anything of this nightmare? "No."

Papa turned a frantic face to Salome, who held up the white dress with its two tiers of flounce at the bottom. "Salome?"

"Lord Hardin, suh, please turn yo' back so's I can get this dress on Lady Margaret."

"No," Margaret said. She watched her father aim a deeply frowning face back to her.

He stroked her cheek. "This is not what I wished for you, my wonderful girl. But I will do all in my power to make this right." He moved to gather her into his arms.

"No." Margaret broke his hold. "I know I must be married because . . . because I've been . . ." The trembling started again. "But why Jebediah Slocum?" Her shoulders twitched.

Henry turned to Salome but not before Margaret caught the second glimpse of panic on his face.

"Lady Margaret, ma'am, you been done a terrible wrong, ain't no doubt 'bout that." Salome reached for the sash to Margaret's robe. "And you feelin' like they ain't no justice in this here world. Forgivin' my words, but you right. Mr. Jebediah Slocum ain't worth the dirt 'neath yo' shoe, but this here is the way it's gotta be. Now, yo' papa is tryin' to tell you how he's fixed things so's you gonna be all right."

Margaret slapped Salome's hand from her sash. "'All right'?" She heard her voice rise. "How can I be all right when I'm married to the son of a farm overseer? He's not much better than a dirt farmer."

Now it was Salome who sent a frantic look toward Henry. Margaret watched his face turn from a pitying softness to one set in the concrete of determination. He looked at the bureau clock.

"Margaret, we've got less than forty-five minutes to get you to the parish courthouse." His head gave little affirmative shakes. "And there is still much to tell you." He shot a quick glance toward Salome. "Get that dress on her."

"No, for the third time." No matter what, she—Lady Margaret Hardin, descendant of an English duke—was not going to marry a common laborer like Jebediah Slocum. The man could not even speak proper English. How could she possibly go to parties with a thing like that in tow? "I refuse to marry a man I cannot respect."

Papa reached out a hand and yanked open her robe. He turned her around. "Salome. The dress!"

"Papa, no, I don't . . . I can't . . . I won't marry . . ." She wrapped her arms around her body.

"Oh yes you will. Margaret, you have no choice."

Salome stepped behind her and slid the wrapper off her shoulders. Margaret stood in her new bloomers, corset, and chemise. Before she could protest, yards of organza and ruffled skirt spiraled on the floor in front of her. Salome held the neck opening wide. Papa, behind her, pushed first her left, then her right leg, into the opening. Papa and Salome grabbed handfuls of dress, pulled the fluttery material past her hips, and slipped her arms into the sleeves. Margaret gagged as Salome tugged the neck tight while Henry fumbled with her buttons.

"Why are you making me do this?" She raised her voice as Henry did up the first button. "I know I've been ruined. The best gentlemen in the county will not have me as a wife. I realize I must have a husband. But why can't he be someone, anyone, other than Jebediah Slocum?" Margaret grimaced at the thought of the uncouth man. "How about the banker's son in Little Rock? I know he's shorter than me and only twenty years old, but maybe he will grow. If not him, how about Mr. Brock? He's a widower and almost fifty, and he has a belly that sticks out a foot from the rest of him. I'll even settle for him. Or . . ." She wriggled away from Salome, who'd pushed Henry aside from the buttoning business.

"None of them will have you, Margaret. I know you don't understand, but you must marry Jebediah Slocum. You're pregnant."

Margaret shoved Salome away as she backed against the vanity. So that was it. "As I've told you both over and over, I am not expecting. That's impossible. I don't care what Mama says. I did not agree to what Syl . . . that man did to me. I hate him." She bit her upper lip. "I know more than you think I do. I know there has to be love before a baby can come. There's no great rush to marry. You have time to find me a suitable husband."

Henry shook his head. His face hardened. "Margaret, I love you." His words slowed to the ticking of the clock. "I've loved you since the day you were born. You are my daughter. My white daughter. I will die defending you, but there is talk in Union County."

Her trembling stopped. Talk? Not the same kind of talk Lady Bertha and Sylvester mouthed. "Of course I'm your white daughter." Something acted up in her belly. Not the stomach sickness given her by that man, but something much more awful. Dread. Not only had her father's face hardened to stone, but Salome's softened into dust. Her lady's maid looked as though her entire self would crumble at any moment.

"There's something you must know. Something I've kept from you." The words came out of Papa though his frozen lips barely moved.

"Suh." The maid's voice filtered into Margaret's ears. "Please, suh, I'm beggin' you. Give me a minute or two mo'. I can get her ready in time. I knows I can."

"I am your father." Henry ignored Salome, who appeared on the verge of dropping to the floor in a dead faint.

"I know you're my father. And Lady Bertha is my mother." Margaret studied the markings on the carpet. "I've disappointed you both." She looked up as her father's head turned in little arcs, to the right, to the left, then back again.

"I am your father, but . . . Bertha is not your mother. She is not the woman who gave birth to you."

"Not my mother?" Margaret fumbled for the top of the vanity chair. Her knees wobbled and she collapsed into the chair. The Napoleon-blue wallpaper jumped to life.

Henry reached out to her.

So it was true. That awful woman was not her real mother. "But . . . if not Lady Bertha, then who?"

"You have a mother. A woman who loves you every bit as much as I do. A woman who made a tremendous sacrifice for you. A woman who wanted you to have nothing but the best in life even if it meant she had to remain secret from you. A woman who . . ."

Margaret's mind raced through all of Union County. Lisbon. Smackover. El Dorado. She saw their faces. Quality women—those invited to each and every one of the soirees at Hardin House. Not one face fit. She shook her head. Perhaps women not so grand. The daughters of shopkeepers, lawyers, bankers marched before her. Even Dr. Henderson's wife when she was young—could she be a possibility? Names and faces of any white woman who had less than straight hair flared up in Margaret's mind. But there was no one. Not one woman in all of Union County matched Margaret's looks. Fire and ice fought it out in her chest. Her eyes refused to focus. She felt Salome, on her knees, tug the wedding shoes onto Margaret's feet. She couldn't tell what color they were, or whether they had buttons or straps. She shook her head so hard a rosebud threatened to fall out. Who was her true mother?

"Set still, Lady Margaret." Salome pulled something across Margaret's left foot.

Perhaps her mother had come from a less-than-respectable family—a governess or a laundress or a New Orleans seamstress or . . . The muscles between Margaret's eyes knotted in pain. No family other than her own had ever employed a white governess, and all the washerwomen were colored. Who, then?

"Papa," she said, sandpaper scratching her throat, "tell me. Lady Bertha is not my mother and for that, Lord forgive me, I'm glad. But tell me, Papa, my mother . . . do I know her? Was she a great love of yours from Maryland? A woman beneath your status whom Grandmother forbade you to marry?" How could a heart beat that strong in her chest without cracking through rib bones?

Henry's arm moved with the speed of a snail. She wanted to, but Margaret could not shift her eyes away from her father and the woman who stood beside him—her lady's maid. His arm wrapped itself around the servant's shoulders.

"Your mother—your true mother—is standing right here beside me." He squeezed the woman's shoulders. "Salome."

To Margaret, her own voice sounded like the whistle of a steam train. But there were no trains here on Bourbon Street, just streetcars. She lifted a hand to her throat, which vibrated with its scream.

Her father fell to his knees in front of her. He clenched both her hands tight in his. "Salome is your mother."

"Oh, God in heaven, no." Margaret struggled to focus her eyes as the walls reached out and pulled Salome into them. "That can't be. Salome's colored. I'm a white girl."

"Of course you are, sugar. On my side, you are of the most aristocratic lineage in all of England. You must always remember that. You are even more regal than that German woman who sits on the English throne today."

The train whistle died in her throat. Margaret looked beyond her father to tan-skinned Salome, who slumped to the edge of the bed gasping for breath. "But, her side . . ." Margaret lifted an arm that felt like iron and pointed. "She . . . Salome . . . oh, Papa, she's . . . she's . . . How could you?"

"How could I?" Henry dropped her hands back to her lap as he rose to his feet. "Because I was married to Bertha, that's how. Married to a woman with absolutely no graces. A flibbertigibbet of a woman who could love no one other than herself, and even that not well. A woman who could give me no children."

"No children?" Margaret stared at this man who stood in the spot her father had just vacated.

"Bertha had five miscarriages. I needed an heir." Henry looked down at her. "You are that heiress." His voice turned stern. "Now get up and get to the church. Nothing is going to change. Do what I say, be relatively pleasant to that fool who's agreed to marry you for a sizable chunk of my money, and our secret is safe." He reached down and pulled her to her feet. "Union County may talk, but they have no proof.

Hold your head high. I'm white. Your mother's father was white. You are a white woman."

Who was this man speaking gibberish to her? "No. No. No. Even a little bit of colored blood . . . everybody knows that one drop and . . . God in Heaven help me . . . I am col . . ." Her chest stopped taking in air. "Tell . . . me . . . one thing." She whispered the words.

He kept his arms on her shoulders. "I will tell you that Salome will continue to act as your maid. If even one of the Slocums mistreats you or dares speak out of turn, she'll let me know."

"Babies only come out of love." She brushed this man's hands away. "Did you love . . ." Margaret looked over at Salome, who struggled to get a breath either in or out. "Do you love her?"

"Salome gave me three babies. I'd say that was an act of love."

Margaret shook her head. That steam-whistle scream had damaged her ears. "Three? Did you say three babies?"

Henry Hardin turned a spoke-out-of-turn face to Salome. "Waylon and Tom-Tom. They're your full brothers."

Margaret's legs gave way at last. Her eyes clamped shut as her knee brushed the once-gold-threaded fleur-de-lis of the carpet. Strong arms swept her up. Her body thumped against a man's chest as he moved her through the doorway and into a darkened hall. Her newly slippered feet dangled as the man carried her along.

"Is the carriage ready downstairs, Salome? We've got thirty minutes to get to the courthouse and get this damn wedding over with."

Margaret's already-dead world turned its last spin and threatened to fall out of the universe.

"We gonna make it in time, Henry. Got to."

Margaret's head lolled into the chest of Henry Hardin. Salome, her mother. Her childhood servant-companion, her brother—Waylon Hardin.

CHAPTER TWENTY

Salome closed the door to the just-finished half room—a nursery once again. What was twenty-two years back had come once more. She kept her hand on the doorknob, letting the past creep into her mind. Right after Henry had taken the newborn Margaret from her and made Lady Bertha claim Salome's body child, Lord Hardin ordered one of the six upstairs bedrooms converted to a baby's room. When Margaret got up to some size, Henry turned the nursery into a schoolroom. This was where Lady Margaret and Waylon had received their learning.

Ten years ago, Henry discovered indoor plumbing, though Salome never did see the sense of doing your business inside a house instead of outdoors where such doings belonged. When their daughter came up expecting, Henry pondered where to put the new young'un. What with the last four bedrooms all taken up—Margaret in the second grandest, His Grace across the corridor and near the staircase, Countess Elvera in a third, and Jebediah (oh, Lord, Jebediah) taking up the fourth and smallest bedroom at the end of the hall and down the corridor from Margaret—Henry had little choice. That fancy bathroom of his had to be chopped in two.

Salome let her fingers slip from the knob and moved toward the room where her daughter had just started her lying-in. The door to Margaret's room swung open, and Georgia—Mattie Lou's replacement—eased her way into the hallway, pulling the door almost closed as she grinned at Salome.

The new midwife nodded, looking for all the world like she couldn't wait to deliver the verdict on the color of Salome's new grandchild. Salome had brought up her worry only the one time to Henry about what color the Good Lord might decide to lay over Margaret's baby. But when she reminded Lord Hardin his own three children had come out with skin color that ran from cream to golden brown he gave her a funny look. She read that look—Maxwell Joe—and clamped her mouth closed.

"Ah, come in, Salome," Henry, sitting in the catbird seat next to Margaret's bed, called out through the nearly shut door.

"Salome," Jebediah, just barely in view, sitting as he was in a stiff-backed chair across from Henry but at the foot of the bed, said with a raised voice. "My ma and pa here yet?"

Only now had Jebediah been allowed inside the room where Margaret birthed the babe that was supposed to be his.

"Celeste say she just saw the wagon pull up." Salome moved into the bedroom, leaving the door half-open. "If it's pleasin' to you, Lady Margaret"—she gave a quick nod to Jebediah—"and you, suh, I'm right anxious to get a peek at y'all's brand-new baby boy."

"Umm." Jebediah scowled. "My ma and pa ought to have the look before you."

"Nonsense." Henry waved Salome closer.

"Yes, quite." Doc Henderson closed his black medical bag, straightened, and turned to Henry. "Congratulations, Lord Hardin. I can see you've got everything in order for your new grandson. The baby nurse from Little Rock should be arriving by week's end. And your new midwife, Georgia, performed admirably."

Henry nodded. "She was trained by Mattie Lou."

"Too bad about your old servant's stroke. I hear she's gone to live with her preacher son in Hot Springs." Doc Henderson walked to the doorway.

"With a handsome pension, I might add." Henry nodded, but Salome's eyes strayed to Margaret.

Margaret, her hair frizzed all over the pillow from the sweat of childbirth, lay wordless with her eyes closed. Georgia had bundled the baby and placed him on the bed next to his mother. Margaret laid not a hand on the sleeping infant. Salome shivered. She prayed for Margaret not to take out her unhappiness on this child just because she didn't fancy how that baby got put in her. She prayed for Margaret not to repeat and feel what Salome felt when Mattie Lou first pulled Margaret out of her. Salome bit down on her lip. That her daughter didn't want any truck with Sylvester Morse's seed was understandable. That would pass, but was there more to Margaret's turned-away face and clenched-shut eyes? Did this boy look more like his mama, or more like his uncles, Waylon and Tom-Tom?

Salome scanned Henry. He beamed. Salome let out a breath. Still, she had to see for herself. She reached down to tidy the stretched-taut coverlet, her eyes on the blue bundle lying on the other side of the bed. The sound of clunky-soled shoes coming up the staircase made her jump back before she got a good look at the newborn. Jebediah jumped to his feet.

"My brand-new grandson in here?" Jacob Slocum stormed into the room—a lady's bedroom—like he was running hogs into a slop pen.

"Where's Ma?" Jebediah sounded hopeful.

"You know she don't come out in polite company," Jacob said, grumbling.

"I thought, maybe, because of the baby and all, you might let her out."

Henry sent a funny look toward Jebediah. Jacob Slocum seemed to catch it instead of his son.

"Well, your ma's thinkin' like me that we had us a good two, nigh three more months, before this young'un got popped out." Slocum walked around the foot of the bed, shoved Jebediah aside, and peered down at the bundle.

Margaret opened her eyes and turned her head toward the commotion.

Without a by-your-leave to the new mother, Jacob Slocum whipped back the blanket from the sleeping infant's face. Salome eased herself on tiptoes to catch as much of a look as she could. Underneath that mark of struggling to get born, her grandson, though red-faced, showed white skin. The sigh jumped out of her mouth before she could swallow it back. By now, Georgia had made her way down the stairs, but there was no need to trouble the new midwife. Salome could see this child passed the ear test.

"Hey, Doc." Jacob Slocum waved an arm toward the open bedroom door and Dr. Henderson. The physician had already walked into the hallway and now stood at the top of the grand staircase.

"Why'd this baby come so early? Me, Jebediah, and the missus, we all thinkin' we had close to three more months."

Even from where she stood, Salome heard Doc Henderson clear his throat. He grunted a time or two, started to speak, then swallowed it. For a man who'd graduated from doctor school, Henderson was a slow-thinking man.

"Early? Yes, of course." Henderson sputtered twice more as he took his first step off the landing. "A honeymoon baby, no doubt."

"Honeymoon?" Jacob Slocum slapped Jebediah on the shoulder. "Speak up, you idiot. You told me and your ma that you and"—he finally glanced down at Margaret, who carried a scared-of-the-Devil look stamped on her face—"this one here ain't give you no kind of a honeymoon. Barely give you more than three, four pokes." Slocum had the sense to touch his hand to his forehead. "Beggin' yo' pardon."

Jebediah reached around his father and pulled off a bit more of the blanket. The little boy whimpered in his sleep. "This one's seemin' big and healthy." The supposed new father sounded confused.

"My ma's last baby came out two months before his time." Jacob Slocum jerked his head toward Margaret. "Two months early, my pa said. A boy. Baby no bigger'n my hand. Ain't lasted but a couple hours. By my countin', this one here should carry the look of an undercooked young'un. Instead, he's lookin' stronger'n an ox. Her layin' in this here bed . . . her and my boy been married just a hair over six months. How'd she come up with a big, strappin' baby so soon?"

Salome dug her fingers into her palms so hard she feared she'd draw blood. They had come so close—she, Henry, and Margaret. She didn't dare turn to Henry, but if what folks said about the Good Lord was true, she knew what to do—send every prayer ever uttered since God created man straight up to Heaven, hoping the Almighty would lay the right answer straight on Lord Hardin.

Henry rose to his feet. "Mr. Slocum, as you can plainly see, my daughter is exhausted after a very long and difficult delivery that surprised us all." He peered toward the grand staircase. "Dr. Henderson got here in the nick of time. With such an early birth, we might otherwise have lost both mother and child." Henry walked over and laid a hand on Jacob Slocum's shoulder. "It is only through the grace of God a living babe has been delivered to us." His fingers knuckled white as he squeezed. "You could have lost a grandson, and Jebediah here could have lost his wife. Now, forgive me. Margaret must get her rest." He turned to his son-in-law. "I think it best if you and your father come back tomorrow afternoon after the special nurse arrives."

"Special nurse?" Jacob Slocum said with a sneer.

"To care for both mother and child after such an ordeal." Henry carried impatience in his voice.

"Uh-huh. You wantin' me to get out of here before Jebediah done named his son?" Jacob Slocum seemed rooted to the spot.

"A name? I've yet to decide." Henry waved a hand, dismissing Mr. Slocum the same way he dismissed his house servants.

"*You've* yet to decide?" Slocum shook his head. "Baby namin's a right what belongs to the daddy and his family." He turned to Jebediah. "You're tellin' me this here's the daddy."

"Me and Margaret . . . well, we ain't . . ." Jebediah stumbled.

"I am much too tired to discuss names right now, Mr. Slocum." Margaret, sure enough, did sound worn-out. "In a day or two, I will . . . Jebediah and I will let you know."

Mr. Slocum folded his arms across his chest, looking for all the world like Union County's meanest overseer. "Is that so, missy?"

Henry dug his fingers into Jacob's shoulder. "Time to leave, Mr. Slocum."

The man winced as he shook free of Henry's grip. "I ain't got me no trouble leavin'—once I help give y'all this one's name." He pointed to the baby.

Henry dropped his arm and sighed. "What name do you propose, Slocum?"

"I ain't right good on the spellin' but the name's gonna be . . ." The man grinned like the greatest joke of all time had just planted itself in his head. "Morris."

Salome couldn't help it. She reached for the bedpost closest to her.

Henry sounded strangled when he said, "Morris? Why ever . . ." He stared at Mr. Slocum.

"Why ever? I reckon you know the why of it. That's the name I'm favorin'. If you don't want it, that's all right with me. Course, I'll have to tell folks all about the why of that name. You lays that name on this here baby and family business stays family business."

"Pa, what are you talkin' about?" Jebediah shook his head.

"Boy, you about as dumb as that worthless mother of yours. Come on, let's get out of here."

Henry waited until the last of the hard-soled boots made their way down the staircase, before shutting the bedroom door. Henry twisted closed the lock Margaret had him install right after she returned from New Orleans with her unwelcome new husband.

"Margaret, I don't want you fretting over a thing. Just rest and regain your strength." Henry looked like he was the one who needed his strength. All this plotting, planning, and worrying must have drained the man.

Salome rushed around the bed. "Lady Margaret, it would please me greatly iffen you'd allow me to hold this here chile."

At that, Margaret's tears came. Not little trickles down the cheeks—more like the great flood of Noah. Henry was by his girl's side in a minute. Salome scooped the baby into her arms and sat on the bed unbidden.

"Morris? Papa, no. This baby can't be named after . . . after . . ." Margaret's chest heaved. "They know. Jacob Slocum. Jebediah. They know this baby is Sylvester's." Her voice started to screech up the scale.

"My precious girl." He bent down and gathered Margaret in his arms. Henry pressed her face to his shoulder, and her cries quieted.

Salome had noticed through the years that Lord Hardin always knew what to do when it came to soothing his wounded daughter.

"Margaret, there is only one thing I want you to remember." Henry reached for a towel on the nightstand. He dabbed at Margaret's wet face. "It's God's truth this child is not a Slocum—a fact of which I'm not yet convinced Jebediah is aware. But paternity lags in importance to what really counts. In any event, your husband and his father are being well paid to keep their suspicions to themselves."

"Not important? Papa, how can you say that? You know nothing but scandal will fall on my head if Union County thinks Sylvester is . . .

is . . ." Margaret's voice edged close to a tremble. "Everyone will want to know what I did to get myself in such a fix."

"Nonsense." Henry shook his head. "They'll think no such thing." He turned to Salome. "Well, how does my new grandson look to you?"

Salome unwrapped the bundle in her arms. She scanned the little face as the babe grunted in his sleep. His skin was white, but what about the rest of him? Her eyes went first to the hair. A light brown, and not a frizz or a kink in it. Straight as a stick. His eyes were now closed, but she thought about how they looked. Blue like Sylvester's, sure enough, but that was no worry. Margaret's and Henry's eyes were blue, too. Salome traced a finger around the newborn's nose and lips. The lips felt full. Salome took a second, third, and fourth look while Henry soothed his daughter. Except for lips that only a colored person with a good eye for such things could spot, this child looked white. If he'd been born in Louisiana instead of Arkansas, folks would call him an octoroon—what with Salome being a mulatto herself.

"Name of Morris a nasty thing, sure 'nough. Look like to me Mr. Slocum tryin' to show all y'all who's the boss." Salome held out the baby to her daughter. "But, Lady Margaret, Mr. Jacob Slocum can't be nobody's boss if you don't let him. What Union County busybodies is gonna be lookin' fo' most in this child is his color. Color far mo' important to folks than who the daddy."

Was that a note of hope creeping into Margaret?

And was that Henry nodding encouragement to Salome?

"No, ma'am. Folks gonna be lookin' fo' to see if they can spot any colored in this young'un. Once they get they minds satisfied that they don't see nothin' but white, they ain't gonna care much about which white man the daddy. As long as this boy looks white." She laid a hand on the receiving blanket.

Margaret stared at Salome, then looked down at the bundle beside her. She inspected her son. "You really think so, Salome?"

Henry spoke first. "Margaret, I know this has been a difficult and very unfair time for you, but you have just made me a very proud grandfather."

A smile played on Margaret's face. "Papa?"

"Salome's correct. It's unimportant who fathered the child of a married woman—it's presumed to be the husband's. What counts is you—the mother—and your bloodline. A bloodline that will now be carried into the future." He sent a quick sideways glance to Salome. "A white future."

A shiver settled over her shoulders.

Margaret reached for her son. "Bloodline?"

"Margaret, my darling daughter, I want you to always remember who you are: the direct descendant of the most famous duchy in English recorded history, the dukes of Norwalk—a family line that goes back nine hundred years. This child carries that distinction with him because of you." Henry first laid a kiss on Margaret, then on the baby. "This child may have Morris written on his birth papers—we must concede that point to the Slocums to ensure the boy's future—but I will enter his real name in our family book."

"His real name? 'Scusin' myself, suh. That be the book you showed Waylon?"

Henry nodded. "*American Descendants of the Dukes of Norwalk*. I'm adding my grandson's name."

"What will you call him, Papa?"

"A name associated with our line . . . Bertrand."

Margaret clasped her hands. "Wasn't that your father's name?"

Henry patted the bundle now in Margaret's arms, then got to his feet. "I'm off to my study to write in the name. Salome, please stay with our . . . Lady Margaret . . . until I can summon Tessie."

Salome laid a hand against the door frame after Henry left. She stood with her back to Margaret. *Too many doin's today already. Still, one more thing left.*

"Salome," Margaret whispered, "I know this baby, little Bertrand, is not just Papa's grandchild—he's yours, too."

Her breath caught in her throat as Salome turned around. She leaned against the door. "Yes'm, that's the truth of it."

"But, Salome." Margaret's face scrunched into a look of pain. "I can't. I just can't bring myself to say it out loud. To call you my . . . my moth . . . Out loud. Even if it is only between the two of us. I know you are, but I just can't get that whole word out of my mouth every time I address you." Her bottom lip quivered. "You must think I'm awful. Hate me, even. Denying my own . . . the woman who gave birth to me." Margaret sucked in her cheeks. "I can't help it. Though the woman has been so awful to me, it's Lady Bertha I still think of as Mama."

Salome shook her head as her back flattened even deeper against the door. "I don't take you fo' awful. And ain't no hatin' in me. Not fo' you, Lad . . . Margaret." She straightened her body. "Ain't nothin' but natural that you thinks of Lady Hardin as yo' mother." Salome bit down on her tongue. "You was trained that way." Salome's girl might still think of Henry's wife as Mama, but the woman never, ever, allowed Margaret to call her that.

Margaret reached out her free hand. "Please don't think I'm being hateful. It's just so hard." More tears. "Most days I forget I'm not white."

Little Morris-Bertrand stirred. Salome crossed the floor at a run. She grabbed her daughter's hand. "This ain't no easy thing to settle in the mind of a girl who's been brought up white all these years." Salome shook her head as she lowered herself to the bed. "I ain't never told you direct about my side of the family."

Margaret blinked, but she didn't look away.

"Yo' kinfolk on my side been through some hard times. It does me good to see you don't have to suffer like my mama, her mama, and all our colored mamas back to the beginnin'."

"Suffer? The beginning?" Lady Margaret looked like she was hoping to hear a different set of words come out of Salome's mouth.

"Sufferin'—that's what I'm callin' what she done gone through, that first colored woman made to pick cotton whilst the sun cooked her body, ordered to scrub her fingers raw washin' Mistress's clothes, beat half to death if she didn't lift her skirts when Master said."

What little color there was in her girl's face seemed like it up and left. Margaret shook her head and turned to baby Bertrand. "I know I never met your mother, but I overheard snatches of stories about her." She lifted her eyes to Salome. "Papa's old overseer may have mistreated her?"

Salome licked lips that had gone dry. "When two womens get taken by two men against either woman wantin' it, it ain't right to compare which one hurt the most. But I'm thinkin' if you and my mama ever met up, she'd know just how you feel about Mr. Sylvester, and about how hard it is to love a little one put in you by an evil man."

Margaret's cheeks twitched. "I'm sorry."

Salome patted the sheet beside Margaret. "I knows you ain't been raised with givin' much mind to how coloreds feels 'bout such things."

Her daughter's eyes sparkled, like the idea of coloreds having feelings had never before entered her head.

"Margaret, we feel hurt and joy and pain and happy just like white folks. We wants what you been raised to think is yo' right from God—shelter to warm us in the winter and cool us in the summer, food enough so's all our chil'ren can get a bite of chicken, and . . ." She kept her eyes on Margaret.

Her daughter busied herself with the newborn.

"And most of all, a say in how we do our own livin'." Salome had gone too far to turn back now. "The same say 'bout how we handle ourselves as white folks."

"The same say? Like white people? But, Salome"—Margaret looked at her mother, a frown creasing the new mama's forehead—"coloreds can't have a say. I mean, they could have a say if they knew what was best for them." She shook her head hard. "No, that's not what I mean. It's just that colored folks . . . Well, Lady Bertha has always said we mustn't be too harsh on our coloreds because they're more like children, really. They aren't clever like us . . . uh . . . like white people." She let out a sigh. "I'm saying it all wrong. It's just that coloreds need help to take care of themselves. Everyone knows it's the responsibility of a good master to take care of his colored." Her face pinked.

"Margaret, now that you a grown woman, is you able to sort out yo' own life or do you need a man to tell you what you can and can't do?"

"A man? Like a husband? Absolutely not. I'm quite capable of making my own choices."

"That's what it feels like fo' colored—like we capable of makin' up our own heads. Like we don't need no husband—no man, no woman, colored or white—to tell us what they believe's best fo' us."

Margaret's head sent out little shakes like she wasn't quite sure she'd heard Salome's words right. "You, Waylon, and Tom-Tom can fend for yourselves I'm sure, but, Salome, not all coloreds are as smart as you three." She gave her head a strong shake. "And then there's the Bible."

"What 'bout the Lord's word?"

"Salome, you can't deny what the Bible says about black people. Cursed and condemned to slavery."

"I reckon I knows the Good Book as well as most."

"Then you know black people are destined to be slaves and servants because Ham cursed God." She nodded like she'd just spoken the final word. "I'm sorry about that now that I know about you, Waylon, and Tom-Tom."

Salome looked at her daughter. The girl couldn't help it. Margaret simply parroted the same old reason Salome had heard all her life. That slavery and Jim Crow were God's will. But Salome was ready for her firstborn.

"Ain't Jesus come here after them twelve tribes—Jacob, Ham, and all them—moved on to the next world? Wasn't it Jesus who brought forth the New Covenant? I believe that's what the preacher man tole me. Said it was Jesus who taught folks *treat yo' neighbor like yo'self*—even folks that come down from Ham's black seed."

Little twitches crossed the girl's face, as if her mind was about to burst with all these new ideas swarming her ears.

"Maybe that's why He took it into His head to allow you to come out of me with white skin." Salome swallowed. "Instead of brown like yo' brothers."

"White skin?" Margaret's eyes popped. "Mine? It never entered my head . . ."

"Margaret, you can call me Salome instead of Mama all the rest of yo' natural days, if that be pleasin' to you. I only wants you to understand one thing: in this world of Union County, you been blessed."

Margaret stared at Salome from eyes to lips, her head shaking in little circles.

If her daughter wanted to use the Bible, so be it. "You think on it. Wasn't nothin' but the grace of God that let you come out of me lookin' white. All three of Lord Henry Hardin's chil'ren got the same colored mama. Me. You lookin' white, that weren't no accident. That was God's will."

The girl shuddered.

"Margaret, I ain't tellin' you none of this to scare you, but colored done had dark times fo' quite a bit now. Yes, it's so, Lord Henry's a fair 'nough boss, far as white mens go, but ever'body ain't Lord Hardin. And even him can't last fo'ever."

"Salome!" Margaret squirmed herself upright in bed. "I'll not have you talk . . ." Her face crumpled as she remembered. "Sorry." The whispered word barely rose above the fresh white sheets.

"When them dark times come, and yo' papa ain't around to beat back that darkness, I needs to remind you the Good Lord wants somethin' of you in return fo' His blessin'."

Those blue-green eyes stared back at Salome. "What?"

"Yo' level best to look out fo' yo' blood kin."

Margaret's hand grabbed at the top of her nightgown.

"Deliver what the Good Lord wants of you."

"Oh?" Margaret looked scared.

"One of these days, God Almighty gonna fix what ain't right 'bout Union County, but 'til that day come, He wants you, Margaret Hardin, to look out fo' your tan-skinned brothers." Salome held her breath.

Margaret laid out a finger. Baby Bertrand-Morris grabbed on while the new mother shook her head. "God's plan? I know Waylon and Tom-Tom are my natural brothers, but how can I look out for them if I can't claim them in public?"

"I ain't askin' you to claim nobody. I'm askin' you to do what God wants of you. Waylon and Tom-Tom—they gonna believe they can fix whatever's bedevilin' them all by theyselves." Salome grunted. "As long as it's a white man's world, they can't. Not alone. That's when they gonna need you. Oh, they ain't gonna come right out and ask you fo' no help. They're menfolk. Too proud. That's why I'm askin' you to follow the Lord's will."

"Um."

"Margaret, why do you think yo' papa took you from me to give to Lady Bertha to raise? He could have left you with me to be brought up jest like any other light-skinned colored girl. Plenty of white mens roamin' around Union County who pay their white-skinned colored chil'ren no mind whatsoever. But the Good Lord seen fit to give you a different life by movin' yo' papa's heart."

Margaret's eyebrows scrunched together. "The thought never entered my head. Salome, I would help if I could. I don't know how."

"Yes, you do. After Henry's gone, it falls on you to carry both sides of yo' family into tomorra. Fo' him, you gonna make sure this duke thing goes on fo'ever with white-lookin' children like little Bertrand. Fo' me—I wants nothin' but the same. Waylon and Tom-Tom carries the same duke blood inside them as you. The Good Lord wants them to go forth and multiply, too." Salome's hands clutched into fists just out of

Margaret's sight. "Colored mens and womens way back to the beginnin' laid out their bodies in hot cotton fields, and even hotter kitchens, hopin' and prayin' they families would have a better life in the sweet by-and-by." Salome tried to read Margaret's eyes.

The girl's head wobbled.

Salome leaned in close to her daughter. She laid a hand to the side of her face and whispered into the girl's ear. "That's why He anointed you—to put the power to help both white and colored into one body." She'd said more than enough to her daughter, but had Margaret heard?

Margaret shook her head, that hair crinkling and frizzing as a fresh wave of sweat soaked her body. "Oh, Salome. I . . . I . . ."

"Margaret."

"Yes." She nodded. "Salome, I'll do what I can for Waylon and Tom-Tom—for my brothers."

CHAPTER
TWENTY-ONE

Waylon tapped the trunk of the loblolly. He ran a hand down the scaly side. Solid and ready for harvest. He took the wooden sign Maxwell Joe had carved for him and nailed it low on the trunk. "Loblolly. Harvested June 1904. Hardin Acres." A tract of land six miles long and one mile deep. Thick with the finest timber in all Arkansas. Orchards growing rare fruits. Wild game roaming the place. Waylon knew the impossibility of the thought. That's why it rarely surfaced in his head. Lord Henry believed in the law of primogeniture, or so Margaret said. Well, Waylon was the firstborn son. This—all of it—the fifteen-room brick mansion with its colonnaded two-story porches, broad marble steps, and wraparound veranda should all be his by right of birth. But it was not to be. Whoever married his sister would be the true master of all that was Hardin Acres. A red-shouldered hawk, perhaps sweeping across the sky from one of the many ponds dotting the acres, caught his eye. Something else lodged in his ear. In his concentration, he hadn't heard the sound of approaching footsteps moving across the soft summer grass.

"What you think you're doin', boy?" Jeb Slocum seemed to take delight in sneaking up on Waylon.

Tap. Tap. Waylon laid gentle strokes of the hammer against the nail as he drilled into the tree trunk. Tap. Tap. Two taps were all that was necessary to affix the sign, but he needed time to arrange his face into the proper look of Arkansas subservience. In his four years at Tuskegee College, he'd not had daily reminders that he was only a "colored boy." On the Alabama campus, he'd been treated as an equal, a scholar, and a man.

"Staking out trees ready for the cutting." He kept his voice matter-of-fact.

"Ain't none of these." The usual contrary words from Jeb Slocum, who held little idea of the differences between a loblolly and a shortleaf pine.

Waylon gave the already deep-sunk nail one more light tap before he pasted a smile across his face and turned to the inept farm manager.

"Mr. Slocum." Waylon prided himself on years of practice. In his time at Tuskegee, he'd learned from his instructors how to walk that tightrope between dignity and servility—a way to tell white folks what a colored man really thought of them while remaining alive. "This stand of trees is close to fifty feet. I think the timber might be ripe for harvest."

Jebediah Slocum folded his arms across his chest as he spit a wad of tobacco to the ground. "That what they taught you in that nigger college over in Alabama, is it?"

"I'm sure it was your father who taught me most of what I know, Mr. Jebediah." It was much too easy to jerk around this man with a mind not even a squirrel would envy.

The arms dropped to Slocum's side. "Well, my pa says they's got to grow to a hundred feet before they're ready."

Control was what Waylon needed to keep himself from bursting out laughing. "Mr. Jebediah, could it be that Mr. Slocum was thinking about the shortleaf pine? It grows that tall."

"You tryin' to say my pa is wrong?" Jebediah bounced on his toes, stretching his five-foot-eight-inch frame maybe a quarter inch taller.

"Almost everything I've learned—what to do and what not—I've learned from your father. Before I went off to school, it was Mr. Jacob Slocum who taught me lessons about timber. Which tree was which, when to cut, when not. I followed his lessons closely, and because of him, I understand exactly what to do." Waylon bit down on his tongue to keep from laughing out loud as he watched Jebediah struggle to figure out if his father had been complimented or insulted. One was a lie, the other a hanging offense.

The man shrugged. "Get on with your work, then. I'm heading over to the Smackover acres." He moved six paces from Waylon. "That's where my pa said the loblolly grows."

"Uh, that would be here, Mr. Jebediah. The stand of shortleaf is over by Smackover."

"Hmm." Jebediah Slocum stalked away.

Waylon waited until the man was out of sight before he let out a chuckle. Enough of Jebediah Slocum—an even worse manager than his newly well-to-do father. The sun had passed noon an hour ago. Time for the midday meal. He gathered his tools and climbed aboard the horse Lord Hardin gave him as a graduation present.

He nudged the red-coated animal into action. Once the Thoroughbred cleared the last stand of tree growth and trotted into the grassy clearing, Waylon spotted the framing going up on his mother's house a half mile distant. Maxwell Joe was doing his usual great job adding the two extra ground-floor rooms along with an entire second story. Even from here Waylon heard the steady slam of hammers as the carpenter and his assistant, Danny-boy, worked on putting up walls. Mama was even to have an indoor bathroom just like in the Big House. Ever since the rape and pregnancy disaster with Margaret, Lord Hardin had been quite generous with Salome, allowing her to spend most of her nights in her own home. Waylon slowed the horse to a trot. Lady Margaret and Jebediah Slocum. Never in his wildest dreams would he ever have imagined such a pairing. Before he knew that Lord Hardin's daughter was his sister, he'd disliked the girl's haughtiness. But after the shock of Salome's revelation, Waylon's heart ached for Margaret even though she had yet to acknowledge their relationship.

"Whoa." Waylon dismounted and tied the horse to the hitching post in Mama's front yard, the smell of Salome's dessert biscuits sifting through the open kitchen window. He shaded his eyes as he looked up at the roof. "Hey, Maxwell Joe. You've just about got that back wall up, I see."

"Afternoon, Waylon." Maxwell Joe, atop the old roof, pointed the hammer downward. He lowered his voice. "Yo' mama, she gots company. Why don't I come down and set a spell with you?" He made his way to the ground. "Danny-boy here can keep on workin'."

Uh-oh. What was it Maxwell Joe wanted to tell him, or what was it the man didn't want Waylon to hear from his mother?

Maxwell Joe pulled out his kerchief and swiped the sweat off his face and arms. "Ain't often Lady Margaret come here to see yo' ma. Let's me and you set a spell under yonder tree."

The weeping willow Waylon had climbed in his childhood play stood twenty yards from the house. Too far to overhear any soft-spoken conversation.

"I still find it hard to believe." Waylon settled himself on the grass in the mildness of late June, the grass still smelling sweet. "Lady Margaret and . . . Jebediah Slocum." Even though he'd witnessed the couple with his own eyes during his infrequent visits home, he remained stunned at the turn of events.

"Hmm." Maxwell Joe cocked an eye at him, looking for all the world as though he were trying to figure out just how much Waylon knew, and about what.

Waylon pulled up a tuft of grass; two dandelions stuck out of the dirt in his hand. His mother, with her limited writing abilities, had outlined the events of that Fourth of July in letters to him while he was away at college—but not until his sister had married Jebediah Slocum that September, four years prior. How much of the story had she shared with Maxwell Joe? That the man had had eyes for his mother ever since the carpenter set foot on Hardin land had not been lost on Salome's eldest son even in childhood, but what had she told him about her other two children by the Lord of Hardin Acres? "Did Lady Margaret bring her boys with her?"

"I ain't seen no chil'ren. Most days she don't take neither one of 'em out."

"Mama said the oldest one is four and the youngest, three. I hear tell the Slocums named the baby after Jebediah."

Maxwell Joe nodded. "Calls the little one Junior. The big'un, the Slocums named him, too. Goes by the name of Morris."

Waylon played with the dandelions in his hands. He knew that much of his sister's story. Morse. Morris. And so must the Slocums. Their way of jabbing it to Lord Hardin and lording it over his sister. Waylon turned to Maxwell Joe. "Margaret. Lady Margaret. Tell me about her. Mama says she's fine, but how could she be?"

"Yo' mama tell you what she want you to know, I reckon."

"My mother worries, Maxwell Joe. Mama wrote me while I was at Tuskegee, of course, but her writing's not the best. I didn't know until I got home how worried she really was." He turned square to the carpenter. "Mama's getting old before her time, worrying about Margaret. Tell me what you know, and I'll figure out a way to help them both."

Maxwell Joe laid a hand on Waylon's bare arm. "No. Yo' mama ain't wantin' you to get yo'self involved in nothin'. That's part of her worries."

"Look, Maxwell Joe, you know I'm not going to let this go. Margaret must be miserable with a fool like Jebediah Slocum. You've got to deal with him every day, as do I. If we can't tolerate the man, how can my sis—Lady Margaret—be expected to survive being married to the clown?"

Now it was Maxwell Joe's turn to run a hand across blades of grass. "She ain't takin' to them chil'ren like Salome want." He spoke to the dandelions peeking out of the grass. "Most ever' day, she orders Tessie to take 'em over to Jacob Slocum's place while Lady Margaret just sits around the house."

"And what does Mama say about Margaret?"

Maxwell Joe looked up at Waylon. "Yo' mama don't tell no tales outta school, but I'm thinkin' like you. It frets on her. Lady Margaret jest ain't takin' to motherin' them boys."

"And her husband? How's he treating my sister?"

"When I goes up to the Big House, I don't see no marks on her. Wouldn't 'spect to with Lord Hardin right there. But it sure is plain to see that Jebediah Slocum ain't feelin' comfortable livin' in Hardin House. Don't nobody, includin' Lady Bertha, ever say mor'n good mo'ning and good evenin' to the man."

"Hmm. What does . . ." Waylon looked up as the sound of crashing and thrashing feet running along the path from the Big House reached his ears. "Who . . . ?" He jumped up.

Maxwell Joe headed toward the house and the path. The front door opened, and out stepped Mama. Waylon watched her pull the door half-shut. He caught a quick glimpse of Margaret, holding a jam-covered biscuit, before she moved back into his mother's front room.

"Salome! Salome! You come fast!" Delfine called out as her almost-fifty-year-old legs churned her closer to Salome's house.

Mama turned as Maxwell Joe rounded the corner, almost bumping into Delfine. She shot a quick glance at Waylon. The frown on her brow deepened. Delfine, huffing and bent over with Maxwell Joe's arm around her, staggered into view. She looked up at Salome standing on the porch.

"Celeste . . . she . . ." Delfine took in three deep breaths. "She tell me, Salome, you've got to come the quick." She straightened up. "It's His Grace and . . ." The cook spotted Margaret's buggy. "Oh, *mon Dieu*." She tapped at her chest.

Waylon reached the porch steps just as his mama hurried to Delfine.

"What is it you're sayin?" Mama grabbed the woman's shoulders.

Delfine peered around Salome at the half-closed front door. Waylon watched the green of a dress dissolve into the darkness.

"His Grace, he have the spells of the shaking. Lady Bertha, she spread out like . . . You hurry yourself up to the Big House fast, Salome. Lord Hardin, he no at the house. Lady Elvera, the mind of the woman, it leave her for the sure this time. She wave the knife in the faces of the one and all. Salome, you come *fais vite*." Delfine turned back toward the house, her feet moving her at a dead run.

"Knife? You say knife?" Salome turned toward Waylon. "I wants that there horse. Maxwell Joe, can I ride behind you?"

"Mama, I'll take you up to the Big House." Waylon started toward the horse.

"No." His mother shouted an order. "Maxwell Joe's gonna take me."

"But he doesn't know how to ride. Not well, at least. Why can't—"

"'Cause you needs to get in the house and stay with . . ." She headed toward the animal, Maxwell Joe right behind her. "She don't need to get hooked into nothin' like this. You keep Lady Margaret here, and safe."

Maxwell Joe mounted with a little help from Waylon. Together, the men lifted and pushed Salome onto the horse and seated her behind the carpenter. She circled her arms around his waist.

"No more than a trot, now." Waylon put the reins in Maxwell Joe's hands and headed him up the path. Waylon turned back to his mother's house. There, in the doorway, stood Lady Margaret Hardin Slocum.

"Lady Margaret." Waylon put a hand to an imaginary cap as he stepped through the front door. "I'm sorry it's taken me so long to . . ." *Oh, Lord, what's the right word?* "To acknowledge your wedding and the arrival of your two sons." Waylon glanced down at the two blue-iris-painted china teacups sitting on his mother's round table, a half-eaten biscuit beside them.

Margaret stood near one of the drawn window shades. Mama never usually drew her blinds in the daytime.

"Is there something I can help you with, Lady Margaret? If you'd like, I'd be delighted to teach your boys about the timber business. I know they're young . . ." Waylon wasn't a chattering kind of man, but something had to fill this awkward silence.

"Those boys are Slocum children." Margaret took one step deeper into the gloom. "No need for them to learn anything about Hardin timber."

Waylon shook his head. He understood. "Salome is a remarkable woman, Lady Margaret." He pointed to a teacup. "Won't you sit back down?"

In the gloom, he watched her shake her head no.

"Salome has three children." Waylon picked up the half-filled cup and added more hot water from the dainty teapot Lord Hardin had supplied. He walked over to Margaret. "No matter how they came into this world, she loves each and every one of her children." He held out the cup. "As I'm sure you're aware, my mother has no husband. Never has had."

Margaret took the cup. "Not the legal kind, anyway."

Waylon offered a low grunt. "You know my mother's father was the overseer here—in the old days." He searched Margaret's face for an acknowledgment that did not come. "A brute of a man. Forced her into all sorts of hurting things. He . . ."

The cup rattled in Margaret's hand as she turned sideways to him. "Yes, Salome explained that to me."

Waylon tapped the tabletop between them. "My mother told me that her mother didn't want anything to do with her newborn because of what that Irishman did to her."

Margaret looked into the cup. "Salome's mother did not want her firstborn because of the father?"

"She felt a child should only come out of love. If not, that child would pay the price of its evil father."

As Margaret lifted the cup to her lips, her eyes stayed on the wallpaper behind Waylon's right shoulder.

"And Mama felt the same about her own firstborn." Waylon waited while the surprise registered on his sister's face.

"Salome's firstborn?" Margaret looked pale.

"But she changed her mind. After about the first two minutes, Mama said she couldn't help herself. She'd do anything in this world for that new baby." Waylon waited. "And she did."

Margaret took a deep sip and rolled the tea around in her cheeks before she swallowed. "But Salome and her children . . . the father of Salome's children did not force himself on her. He was not an evil man."

Walking over to the front window, Waylon lifted the blind. "Lady Margaret, in many ways I am glad you were shielded from so much wrongdoing in this world. But the fact is, colored—men or women—don't really have full say on how we're going to live our lives. Not here in the South."

Margaret nodded like she'd heard this story before. Waylon reached around her and raised the second shade.

"No, my mother wasn't forced, not in the way I hear other women have been." He looked at the rug with the cabbage-rose pattern on Salome's scrubbed pine floor. "But Mama couldn't really say no to a powerful man, now could she?"

Margaret made her way back to Salome's settee and lowered herself onto it. She glanced up at Waylon. "There's a difference between my father and scoundrels like Sylvester Morse. Lord Hardin is a very refined man. And, as coarse and unlettered as he is, even Jebediah shows consideration for me." She pushed the biscuit aside.

Waylon settled himself across from Margaret in his mother's rocker. He saw the girl who had grudgingly come to him for the correct answers whenever the tutor stepped out of the room. Now here she was—in need of more correct answers. "All I'm saying, Lady Margaret, is that no matter who the father, or what evil that man did to the mother, the blame is not on the child. Again, I'd be honored to take your boys on my rounds to the timberland."

Looking across the space at him, Margaret gave a slow nod. "Morris and Junior are two truly unfortunate children. You see, it's not just their fathers who are unsuitable; so is their mother."

"Unsuitable? Is Jebediah making unreasonable demands on you?" Waylon disliked the man, but he'd never considered him a villain on the scale of Sylvester Morse.

"Jebediah?" Margaret placed the cup on the glass-topped table in front of the settee. "No, but the man is so unlettered and unmannered, I cringe whenever I see him." Her shoulders shook as she grimaced.

"Ignorance is neither a crime nor a sin, Margaret. It's just a lack of knowledge. Jebediah Slocum is most surely clumsy and annoying, and maybe a hair backward, but none of those things have been visited upon his son, as far as I can see."

"When I look at Junior, I see the face of a man I was forced to marry. A man I do not love. Yet he looks at me and I know he'd like nothing better than to have me in his bed more than what I allow him." Margaret looked at Waylon, not a sign of embarrassment in her face.

His poor sister had gone through misery, indeed. "Then Slocum is not unkind to you?"

"Unkind?" A dry laugh came out of her mouth. "Just the opposite. When we do accidentally run into one another at Hardin House, the man bumbles and stutters almost like he hopes I'll change myself into his real wife." She shook her head. "Waylon, you may take the boys, but God forgive me because I can't. I don't want either of them to know who you are. I don't want them to know that you're my brother and their uncle." Her hand went to her mouth. "Never."

Waylon leaned forward. "Margaret, when your mind finally gets used to being a colored girl, you'll find that if one of us is lucky enough to get a better life, those of us who aren't will go to our graves protecting that secret." He held out his arms.

Margaret reached out an arm toward the man who was her brother. Then the sobs came.

CHAPTER
TWENTY-TWO

Salome pushed Maxwell Joe half off the horse even before the animal came to a halt near the kitchen porch, with its two galvanized washtubs stacked just inside the screen door.

"Oh, praise all the saints and Mother Mary, too." Delfine crossed herself as she leaned against the side of the house. "Salome"—her breath came in spurts—"you must go up the stair. Lady Elvera, she . . . that woman . . . she 'bout to kill them all."

Maxwell Joe reached up and swung Salome to the ground in one smooth motion.

"Come. Come. Come." Delfine stamped her foot.

"What in tarnation?" Salome rushed to Delfine. "Where's Lord Hardin?"

"Not here. Not here." Delfine clutched at the fabric of the dress over her heart.

Salome turned to Maxwell Joe. "Git on back to the house. Lord Henry don't want you nowhere around me when I'm up here at the Big House."

Maxwell Joe, his straw hat tipped forward, shook his head slow. "I'm waitin' 'round to find out what's what."

"No! I don't know what kind of commotion is goin' on upstairs, but I sure don't need you to worsen up matters." She hurried to the back door. "Please, Maxwell Joe. I need you to keep Waylon and Margaret out of harm's way." She swept through the kitchen door held open by Delfine.

As soon as she stepped into the foyer, Salome heard the ruckus. Thank goodness no other servants were about this morning. She headed for the back stairs as shouts and curses traveled down the grand staircase.

"Look at her! Look at her!" Elvera said. "Oh my heavens and all the stars."

Salome grabbed the handrail and rushed up the back steps. Lady Elvera? What could have set off James's wife? The woman rarely left her bedroom. Hardly ever said more than two words at a time. Doc Henderson called it the melancholy. His Grace said his wife hated Arkansas and everything about it. Declared the whole state dowdy and dull. Said the Union County gentry were nothing more than jumped-up country bumpkins. Elvera was a third cousin of these Hardins, twice removed. Lord Hardin said it had been an arranged marriage. Cousins marrying cousins. Lord.

"Oh, my glory, Yo' Grace. Please, ma'am, stop waving that there knife ever' which way," Celeste said, squealing.

God in All His Glories. There was indeed a knife. Salome bore down on the banister handrail and took the back stairs two at a time. What was that low moaning? It sounded like a rabbit caught in a trap. She mounted the last step. Oh, oh. Now screaming and cursing filled the upstairs hallway. Salome raced toward the sounds—forward and to the right, just two doors down from the front hallway and the grand staircase. Across the way from Lord Henry's room. The sound, that awful commotion, came straight from the room of James, His Grace, duke of Maryland. Salome grabbed the doorknob, twisted it, and put her weight against the wood. She stumbled into the room.

"Jesus! God! Noah, Moses, and John the Baptist!" Salome's breath was ragged. Her knees wobbled, and she had to steady herself against the wall.

"Salome. Salome." Celeste, sore hip and all, jumped up and down. "Please tell Lady Elvera I gots to get outta here."

"No. No. Don't leave me. Not alone with her." Lady Bertha's muffled voice called out from somewhere in the bedroom. "Salome, in the name of God, get this man off me."

Salome's jaw felt unhinged as her mouth gaped open. Her eyes stared but couldn't sort out what to do with all the pictures blasting at her. To the right of the bed, cowering against the wall, shivered Celeste, looking for all the world as though the Grim Reaper had called her name. At the head of the bed, on the left, hovered Her Grace, Elvera, holding a jackrabbit-skinning knife. Lying in the bed was—oh, Jesus— what was that? A man. James, the back of him naked from head to toe, sprawled on top of someone. Salome counted four white legs. *Jesus have mercy.* Two of those legs were spread far apart and tied with strips of white sheeting to the bottom of the four-poster. Salome ordered her eyes to travel from James's bare behind to his head. Four white arms. One of James's dangled almost off the bed. The other lay halfway under him and on top of . . . *No, God deliver us.* It was those other two white arms that made Salome hang on to the wall lest she slide to the carpeted floor. Like the strung-out white legs, the two arms were spread wide and tied to the bedposts. *Jesus, help us all.*

Elvera yanked at something near the top of the bed. Hair. She pulled a handful of hair from beneath the stretched-out body of His Grace.

"Lady Berth . . . ?" The words croaked out of Salome's mouth.

"Yes, this is the slut. The Whore of Babylon. The Harlot of Eden. May she turn to salt like Lot's evil wife. This here is Delilah!" The knife in Lady Elvera's hand blurred silver as it slashed through a brown-red mass streaked with gray. Her Grace held up a cut-off, eighteen-inch hank of hair. Locks that had just been shorn from the head of Lady Bertha Hardin.

"Salome! Salome!" Bertha screamed. "Help me. In the name of God, get this woman away from me, and this man off me. He's dead!"

"You've harmed my husband, you slut. Whore! Harlot!"

"Celeste!" Lady Bertha screamed. "Untie me. Get me away from this crazy woman."

Celeste took a hesitant step forward and turned a scared face toward the door, back to Elvera, and finally over to Lady Bertha. With the speed of slow-thawing molasses, she moved toward the tie holding Bertha's left arm stretched taut. Before Salome could blink, Elvera reached across the bed and sliced the knife across Celeste's forearm.

"Aaahhh, Jesus!" Celeste grabbed her forearm. Blood dripped over Lord James's back, onto the sheets, and down to the floor. "She done killed me."

Pushing away from the wall, Salome stepped forward. "Lady Elvera. Celeste needs to get Delfine to tend to her. You done . . . I seen it was a accident but she . . ."

"Accident? I will 'accident' any of you who dares try to free this woman—this Whore of Babylon, this inhabitant of Sodom and Gomor—"

"Yes'm, yes'm, I understand." Salome took in a deep breath. "You right upset, but Lady Bertha, she ain't said how she got in this fix."

Elvera turned on Salome as she threw the shorn-off hair to the floor. "Oh, this whore made it perfectly clear why she's spread out like a sow about to be gutted. Playing a game, she said. She and James . . . my husband . . ." Elvera's voice rose as she swung back to the two in the bed. "Look at what this wanton slut has done to my husband. He passed out after this temptress from Hell seduced him." She swung the back of her hand against Bertha's face, the knife barely missing the woman's eye.

"Oh, my God. She's gonna blind me, then kill me. Untie me. Please, someone, in the name of God, untie me."

Elvera grabbed another handful of hair and swept the knife close to Bertha's scalp, right in front. She pulled hard as Lady Bertha yelped. Her Grace whacked off another patch.

Bertha's screams must have filled the entire house.

"Yo' Grace, ma'am"—Salome's heart pounded—"I can sho see Lady Bertha done you a great wrong. She got no business layin' under yo' husband like this, but Lady Elvera, if you don't mind, I'd like to see to His Grace. He ain't lookin' so good for a drinkin' man. I thinks he needs some attention." Salome felt urine start a trickle down her leg. She squeezed tight.

"Oh?" Elvera looked down at James. She shook him. "I suppose . . ."

"Yes'm. Lord Henry gonna take it hard iffen his brother took sick and ain't none of us helpin' him."

"Lord Henry." Elvera's eyes seemed like those of a madwoman—like Salome's mother when she couldn't tell the real from the nightmare. "I want Henry to see his wife just like this. The slut. The Whore of Bab—"

"Yes'm to all them things. Lord Henry should see what done happened to his brother. Don't you think we oughta settle him comfortable-like on the floor first?" Salome took a step closer to Elvera. She avoided the bedpost and the white cloth strung from it to Bertha's leg. With a slow hand she reached for the bed coverlet and let it fall to the floor. "If you stand down yonder by the foot of the bed, me and Celeste can help His Grace to this here pallet. Celeste, fetch me a pillow for His Grace's head."

"I'm bleedin' to death over here. I can't fetch nothin'."

Putting a tiny smile on her face, Salome aimed a glare at Celeste. "Ain't neither one of us gonna disturb Lady Bertha. We jest gonna lay His Grace comfy-like on the pallet. Now you climb on that side of the bed and push, whilst I pulls. After that, you needs to get downstairs and get some camphor to bring His Grace back around. Lord Henry bound to appreciate that."

Salome slid slowly past Elvera, who took two steps toward the foot of the bed, knife still in hand. Her Grace dug the flat of the knife into Lady Bertha's trussed-up big toe. Bertha stretched her foot hard against the tying cloth. Salome put one knee on the mattress while she braced her other foot on the floor. She looked down at the half-turned face of James, duke of Maryland, simultaneously shielding Lady Bertha's face from Elvera with her back.

One open blue eye, the clammy touch of the man's skin. Salome had never touched a dead body before, but she had no doubt one was now under her hands. She pulled while Celeste pushed. Salome half dropped, half lowered the naked body of James Hardin onto its back. After a quick look at what passed for his manhood—the stubby little thing he'd once tried, and failed, to put into her—she closed his eyes.

Elvera grabbed a corner of the coverlet and threw it across His Grace's lower body.

"Celeste needs to get to Delfine for that camphor." Salome rose to her feet. "Get on now with you."

Clutching her bleeding arm, Celeste backed out of the room. "Delfine. Delfine." The maid's screams followed her all the way down the back stairway into the kitchen.

"Look at the slut." Lady Elvera's face frowned into a raisin. "Stretched out at all four corners." She leaned over the woman. "Naked as the day you were born." She aimed the point of the knife blade at Bertha's right breast. "Did you use them to entice my husband, you hussy?"

"Elvera, I didn't do nothin' wrong. Cut me loose. It was just a game James liked me to play. He tied me up. He liked to see me like this. Mostly, he just looked. He couldn't . . . he wasn't able to . . . you must know."

"No more of your lies about my husband." Elvera broke the skin with the blade and drew a thin half circle around Bertha's right nipple. Two drops of blood bubbled up.

"God help me! Jesus, save me!" Bertha's face fell to purple. "She's gonna cut me to pieces."

"You low-down whore, you got no right to call upon God and Jesus. Neither one will help a trollop like you. Worse than Mary Magdalene. I want Henry to see you just as you are. Naked for all the world to see. Naked, but missing a tit or two. I know you, you whore. You'll get to Hell and use those things to suckle the Devil to avoid your righteous punishment." Elvera adjusted the knife in her hand. "I'm going to cut them off."

"Aahhh!" Lady Bertha's scream might have reached passersby on the main road—a good third-mile distant.

Salome trickled pee onto her bloomers. She jammed her body between Lady Bertha and Elvera. "Lord Henry gonna wanna see her strung out like this. That's fo' sure. I ain't never seen no bigger disgrace in all my life." She licked her dry lips. "But if there's to be any hurtin', I'm thinkin' it's the husband what gots the right to do it. Lady Elvera, let's just us wait 'til Lord Henry come back. Fact of the business, why don't we throw a sheet over Lady Bertha? Refined ladies like you don't need to see no other woman buck naked." Salome squeezed to stop more pee from running down her legs.

"Where is Henry, anyway?" Elvera settled herself in the chair next to the bureau. "And where is Celeste with that camphor? James looks peaked."

Salome pulled the crumpled sheet from the foot of the bed. She tossed it over Lady Bertha. "They'll both be here directly. Yo' Grace, since Lady Bertha probably gonna get a good beatin' once her husband do get here, why don't you sing her some hymns?" Salome eased to the side of the bed and picked a spot where she could sit beside Bertha and avoid looking at the very dead body of James Hardin.

"A good beating? That's all? That harlot should be paraded naked out to the front yard and burned at the stake for the witch she is."

"Then it's a hymn she be needin', Lady Bertha. Bible say even the biggest sinner needs a hymn to lead them to the Forever After. 'Specially if they goin' to Hell.'"

"A hymn? Of course. I've been told I have a beautiful singing voice." She smiled. "I believe I'll start with 'Amazing Grace.'" Still clutching the knife, Lady Elvera sat back in her chair, closed her eyes, and broke into her first stanza. "I once was lost, but now I'm found . . ."

Lady Bertha groaned.

Salome sent a sidelong glance to her mistress along with a quick shake of the head. She reached out to Bertha's side and gave her a quick pat while addressing Lady Elvera. "Yo' voice sho is beautiful, Yo' Grace. I believe I'm gonna pray hard fo' Lady Bertha's soul while you keep on singin'. Sound sweeter with the eyes closed."

"Marvelous." Elvera, her lids still lowered, trilled as she went through three more stanzas. "Amaaazing Grace, how sweet the sound . . ."

Salome eyed the ties holding Bertha. Should she chance it? She kept patting Bertha's side while she debated. Lady Elvera squeaked out the last tortured note, smiled, and opened her eyes.

"Yo' Grace, that beautiful voice of your'n makes me want to hear mo'. I gots me a hankerin' to hear 'Swing Low, Sweet Chariot.' You know that one, ma'am?"

"Swing looow, sweet chariot, comin' for to carry me home." Her eyelids drifted downward once more.

Salome shifted her weight toward the head of the bed. As she eased an arm upward, she heard shouts from downstairs. The door burst open.

"What in the name of God?" Henry Hardin stood there, the door open behind him. "Bertha? He looked at her sheet-covered figure. "Elvera? Salo . . . ?"

Elvera opened her eyes and jumped to her feet. In two strides she was at the foot of the bed. Mouth twisted into a grin, she yanked the sheet off of Bertha. "Look. Look upon that sight of sin and degradation for yourself. Your wife's a whore. Tied up like she was a four-masted ship. Stretched out with my poor James, sick as he is, laying all on top of her. I declare I . . ."

Henry's eyes swept the room, taking it all in. They rested on Salome.

"His Grace took sick." Salome rose from the bed and nodded toward the floor.

Henry moved to the edge of the bed. "Merciful saints." He dropped to his knees beside his brother. "James. James? Oh, my God." He crossed himself and rested his forehead on his hand.

"Henry," Bertha whispered, "cut me loose before she . . ."

Lord Hardin looked up at his wife as though seeing her for the first time. "What . . . how did this happen? And what the hell are you doing trussed up like that?"

"She's the Devil's plaything. That's what she is. Cleopatra and Delilah and Bathsheba, all rolled into one." Elvera reached out a hand toward Henry. She still clutched the knife. "Here. I was going to cut them off, but you can do the job."

"Cut . . . them off?" He rose to his feet.

"Henry, please. Lord God, nooo." Lady Bertha's screeching started anew.

"How did she get like this?" Henry looked down at James. "Did he . . . ?"

"Said it was a game, suh." Salome kept her eyes on the knife as Her Grace aimed the blade at Bertha's chest. "Said His Grace liked playactin' and . . ."

"Henry. Please. Please." Bertha sent frantic looks toward Elvera. "You're the one who threw me at James. This was his idea. Not mine. I'm not to be blamed."

Elvera rested the knife just below Bertha's left breast.

"Aaah. She's gonna do it!" Bertha struggled to roll away as the weapon pricked her skin.

Elvera moved. The knife slashed a curve under Bertha's breast deep enough to draw a slim line of blood. Henry grabbed his sister-in-law's wrist.

"I'll discipline my own wife."

"No. You'll go too easy on her. She'll enchant you just like she did James. She's the Devil's minion. You must be stern. Teach her a lesson. Take God's vengeance against her. Parade her naked in the front yard. Put her in the stocks. Then burn her at the stake."

Salome laid a quiet hand on Henry's sleeve. She forced a little smile on her lips as though speaking pleasantries to Her Grace. "Lady Elvera taken hard by what done happened to her husband. Her mind a little upset right now. Might do her good if she could go to her room and have Delfine give her some sleeping drafts."

Henry kept his grip on his sister-in-law's knife hand. "Elvera, you're right. Bertha has given herself over to sin, but this is neither the time nor place for you to deal with it. Let me take you to your room. Give you a good cup of tea. I'll think of a fitting punishment for my wife." He moved an arm to one of her shoulders while he kept a tight grip on the other. He eased the woman toward the door.

"Salome. Please, I beg you, cut me loose."

Lord Hardin spun around. "You leave her just as she is 'til I get back." He maneuvered Elvera into the hallway.

Rushing to the door, Salome slammed it shut.

"Salome, oh please, in the name of God, help me. I'm sorry what I did to Margaret. All of it. I'm powerful sorry. I swear, I'll make it up to her. To you." Racking sounds shook Lady Bertha's body.

"You gonna be all right." Salome dipped the drying cloth into the water basin. She leaned over Bertha. "These here cuts ain't nothin'. Ain't even gonna leave a scar. And yo' hair, it gonna grow back befo' you know it. Her Grace jest addled in the head over seein' her husband like . . ." She dabbed at the slashes.

"Henry. It's Henry who's gonna punish me."

"Oh no, ma'am. I don't reckon Lord Hardin gonna do you much harm."

"He doesn't like to be crossed. He's beaten me a time or two. Even if it was him who threw me to James, he's gonna take it out on me." The shrieking started again.

"Hush, hush, Lady Bertha. I'm gonna talk up fo' you. Lord Hardin jest upset 'bout his brother."

Bertha shook her head. "No. He's gonna keep me like this." More wailing.

"Lady Bertha"—Salome pulled the sheet up to the woman's chin—"forgive me fo' askin', but iffen I knows, maybe I could help Lord Hardin understand how this . . . this . . ." She straightened up and pointed to the sheet.

"Elvera's right 'bout one thing. I've been livin' in Hell ever since Margaret . . . what happened to that child. I riled him, you see. Henry. My husband doesn't like to be riled. He whipped me good and threw me out of the bedroom. Gave me to James."

Should Salome let the mistress of the manor know she'd already heard this story? Pretty hard not to know where Lady Bertha laid her head every night with the second floor crowded with lady's maids all day long and part of the evening. She kept her silence.

"He treated me like a woman."

"Lord Hardin?" Salome frowned as she sat back on the edge of the bed.

Bertha shook her head. "James." She turned to Salome. "You know how good it feels to have a man look at you like he wants you? Henry hasn't wanted me since our wedding night. James did."

Should she say yes'm or no'm? Salome simply patted the sheet.

"The way he looked at me. He wanted me. Course, he couldn't actually do nothin' 'bout it, but he sure wanted to. That's how this happened." She flicked her chin toward the sheet. "James was sick, you know. Couldn't act like a man. Not much there, really. Couldn't get much of a rise out of himself. That's why we played the game." She turned to Salome, a smile on her face.

"Game, ma'am?" Salome steeled herself.

"He said if he could tie me up to the four-poster it might exci . . . you know, get a little bit of a rise out of him. Most times, it did. Oh, not so's he could go through with anything, but enough to make him happy. And it sure made me happy. I don't care anythin' 'bout that stuff men like to do to us women, but the way James looked at me when I was trussed up . . . Oh, Lord, that felt good. The way he moved his tongue around my . . . Salome, I felt like a woman for the first time in my life." She closed her eyes. "I'm gonna miss him somethin' terrible."

"Uh-huh." Salome felt her face flush. What kind of feeling was Lady Bertha talking about? "What done happened, 'zactly?"

Bertha blinked back a fresh set of tears. "He'd just climbed on top of me like usual, then he started movin' around on my body. You know, jerkin' up and down, goin' all around. His arm shot out and he got hold of my tit. I thought he was gettin' a good rise on, but then his arm flew out to the side, and his face, it looked all white-like. He started moanin' and groanin'. I thought somethin' might be wrong so I started hollerin' for Celeste. That's when she came in."

"Lady Elvera?" A bitter turnip taste filled Salome's mouth.

"She started cussin' and callin' me names right away. I begged her to help James, who was humpin' and bumpin' all over me. If she couldn't help him, then cut me loose so's I could help the poor man. Then she picked up that knife. I was sure she was gonna turn me loose, but all she did was threaten me." Bertha let out a wail. "And cut off my hair. Oh, Jesus." A fresh round of tears. "Salome, I been tryin' to do right by Margaret these last four years. Now please, help me get away from Henry. I know that man. He doesn't like to be crossed. The least he's gonna do is beat me with his belt. In front of everybody. Help me and I'll go to my grave helpin' Margaret."

"Lady Bertha, I don't need you makin' no last-minute promises like that. I'm gonna help you all I can 'cause it's the right thing to do."

The door eased open and Henry stepped inside the room, a gold cross in his hands. He walked over to James and lowered himself to one knee. He crossed himself. *"Per istam sanctam . . ."*

Salome stared down at the figure, then up at Bertha. "Them words." She lowered her voice: "What he sayin'?"

More tears rolled down Bertha's cheeks. "They're secret Catholic, you know. All the Hardins are."

". . . indulgeat tibi Dominus quidquid . . ."

"But you and Lord Hardin, y'all goes to Lisbon Baptist Church."

Bertha nodded. "Nobody's supposed to know the Hardins are Catholic. Something about the third duke gettin' his head chopped off way back when. They've had to hide their religion ever since. Keep it secret."

"Any more secrets you care to tell, Bertha?" Henry rose to his feet, the cross still in his hand, its gold chain dangling from his fingers. He turned to Salome. "I trust you will keep a secret better than my wife. Yes, more than one of my family was beheaded back in England. Several of them by our very own cousin. The queen hated Catholics. Hunted us down. Sent us to the Tower."

Salome shook her head. The ways of the Hardins never did make any sense to her. Lady this and Lord that. Folk in England so long ago, so far away. How could any of them matter in America today? She moved over to the bedpost holding Bertha's left leg and reached for the wrapping holding the woman.

"Let her be." Henry raised his voice: "Bertha here is good at spilling secrets." He leaned over his wife. "I'm going to allow you the opportunity to practice the art of remaining silent. In fact, you're going to be a lesson in silence. I'm going to bring in all the servants—the women—to watch you stay quiet. Say one word and I'll keep you trussed up like this until . . . well, I'm not sure when I'll free you." He straightened up.

"Henry, please, please, please . . ."

"No mo', Lady Hardin. Stop yo' beggin'." Salome turned to Henry. "Don't the Bible say not to trade one ugly fo' the next? The Good Book say do unto others the way you wanna be done. Don't nary one of us want to be treated like this." She leaned across the bed. "This here business was betwixt Lady Hardin and His Grace. This was their game—for they eyes only. Nobody else's. Even iffen she done wrong, don't no woman want to see another female shamed like this. Folk laughin' and pointin'. Pinchin' at her body. It make me sick to my stomach." She nodded as she straightened. "I knows you a good man, Lord Hardin. You don't have no real ugly in you." She held his eyes. "Turn this woman loose."

"My, my. You've got quite the mouth on you, Salome. Mind it doesn't get you in trouble." He glanced down at his brother. "Oh, untie the stupid woman and get her out of my sight."

Salome unknotted the first tie. Lady Bertha drew her knee inward while Salome moved to the top of the bed and freed Bertha's left arm. Lady Hardin covered her breasts.

"I suppose I should thank you, Bertha. After all"—Henry looked down at her—"James and I never did get along. He was always the son nothing was expected of. By birthright, he inherited everything without having to lift a finger. I resented him." Henry worked his lips as one hand swept over his eyes. "But he was my brother." He watched Salome release the tie holding Bertha's right leg. "Thanks to you, I know James died in whatever passed for happiness for him. I suppose that's worth letting you go."

"There." Salome unknotted the last bit of cloth.

Bertha groaned as she rolled to her side and slid, more than scooted, to the floor.

"Get some clothes on her. Doc Henderson will be here any minute. I sent Waylon to get him and to stop by the telegraph office."

"Telegraph office? Waylon?" Salome paused, her hand on the chifforobe door. What of Maxwell Joe? "You find Waylon at the house?"

"I heard Waylon talking to Celeste when I called down for a woman to tend to Elvera." Henry shot her a curious look. "I sent him to Lisbon. To get word back to the family in Maryland. I'm sending James home for burial. He'll be happy there, if the man can be happy anywhere. Elvera will go with him, of course. There are doctors there who can help with Elvera's particular kind of . . . melancholy."

Salome sucked in a breath. "Lady Bertha, ma'am, where yo' bloomers and chemise?" She peered into the open chifforobe.

"No. No." The keening started again. "Bath, I've got to have me a bath."

"Yes'm." Salome pulled out a pale blue robe.

"Ahh, ahh." Bertha sat on the floor, her legs drawn to her chest, her arms wrapped tight around them, her chin resting on her knees. She moaned as she rocked.

"It's gonna be all right, Lady Bertha. That woman, she gonna be gone soon. Put this here wrapper on and I'll take you over to the bathin' room fo' a good wash-off."

"No!" Henry boomed. "Dr. Henderson, the undertaker, Waylon, and probably Mrs. Henderson will all be here in a few minutes. I don't want them seeing Bertha in this state. Lady Margaret's downstairs, and Maxwell Joe will be back with the wagon to take the body off to the funeral home in a minute or two. I want Bertha out of here." He turned to Salome. "By the way, I found Maxwell Joe at the house when I first arrived. What's he doing here?"

"Maxwell Joe? Yes, suh, he brung me up here on Waylon's hoss when Delfine come fo' me, but I sent him straight back to my house to be with Waylon and Lady Margaret."

Henry walked toward Salome, his face losing the hard lines that held him these last thirty minutes. He reached for her arm. "Sorry." He stroked her back as he helped her to her feet. She looked into those blue eyes. Today, she'd taken way more chances with this man than was good for her. She turned to Lady Bertha and guided the weeping woman to her feet. "Yes, suh. Soon as you tell me it's safe, I'll bring her back up here."

"Up here?" Bertha pulled the belt tight around the wrapper now covering her body. "Sleep here? In this room? Where James just died?" She turned a trembling face to her husband. "Don't make me do it, Henry. I can't come upstairs again."

Salome patted the woman's back. Here she was, giving comfort to a woman who'd shown her and her daughter very little of that commodity all these years. "It be all right, Lady Bertha. Once you all freshened up, we jest go on over to yo' old bedroom."

"My bedroom? Oh no, Salome." Lord Henry wrinkled his nose. "That won't do. I'll allow Bertha to have Elvera's room in about a week, but my so-called wife is not welcome in my bed."

"But where she gonna sleep 'til that time?" Salome bit down on her lower lip. She hadn't meant to tempt the fates one more time.

"I really don't care." Henry raised his voice: "Maybe Delfine will have her. Now get her out of my sight. I want time alone with my brother."

No need wasting more words on the man. Salome bustled her charge into the hallway, aiming the two of them toward the back stairs.

"Closer this way, Salome." Lady Bertha took two steps down from the landing and onto the grand staircase.

"Uh, Lady Berth . . . ?" Salome had never gone up or down the front stairway in all her life.

"Salome, hurry please. I've got to get the smell of James . . . of death off me before I go crazy. Get me to Delfine's tub and put some clothes on me before Henry up and changes his mind."

Salome looked up and down the hallway. Not a servant in sight. She held tight around Lady Hardin's waist and took her first steps down the grand staircase only to be greeted by Lady Margaret coming up.

Her daughter said not a word as she stopped midway on the stairs. She looked up at her two mothers. Salome read the girl's face: disgust mixed with triumph.

"Margaret," Lady Bertha called out as she made her way down, step by step, until she stood one stair above the girl, "I want to tell you . . . to let you know those words I said four years back, I didn't mean none of that. It was just the trials Henry put on me."

Lady Margaret took her sweet time canvassing Lady Bertha head to foot. "What's happened to you? You look as though you just got out from under some ruffian of a man. Could that have been Uncle James?"

Lord, Salome was going to have a time straightening out her daughter. "His Grace took sick, Lady Margaret."

"Too much excitement, I'd say." Margaret turned to Lady Bertha. "Lord Hardin said you disgraced yourself with his brother," she said, her voice dripping snake venom. Her lips turned into more of a sneer than a smirk to Salome's eyes.

If Salome could have trained her girl up from childhood, she'd know better than to gloat over another woman's misfortune. Any woman—no matter the color—never knew when her own humiliating time might come. "Lady Margaret, ma'am, beggin' yo' pardon . . ."

"Margaret, I know I haven't done right by you." Lady Bertha shook so hard, Salome feared the woman might topple to the next stair. "But it was a hard burden Henry put on me." Bertha clutched the wrapper tight with one hand while she reached with the other for Margaret's shoulder. "I'm needin' a place to sleep 'til next week when Elvera . . . when she moves back to Maryland."

"I'm sorry? You need a place to sleep? You've been sleeping with Aunt Elvera's husband these past four years, haven't you? Why not continue to sleep in that room?"

"Lady Margaret, she ain't wantin' to go back to that there place where . . . where . . ." If only Lord Hardin had allowed Salome some say in how their girl was raised. "His Grace, he done passed on."

"So, what of it?" Margaret looked as though she were about to spit. "My mother"—she made the word sound like she had a mouthful of vinegar—"didn't mind committing adultery with her husband's brother in that very same bed. When Sylvester Mor . . . did what he did to me, I didn't want it. Yet it was me she condemned to damnation even though I fought that man with all that I had." Margaret's lip quivered.

"Oh, child, I was wrong." Lady Bertha started her wailing again. "I know you fought him off as best you could. Margaret, can you find it in your heart to forgive me?"

A smile that looked like it pained the corners of her mouth moved across Margaret's face. "I'll forgive you the same way you forgave me." She moved around Bertha and Salome. "Now, if you'll excuse me."

Bertha grabbed her arm. "I need a place to sleep. Your father won't allow me in his bed. I'm to beg the servants for a place to lay my head. Please allow me to sleep in the room with your boys. I won't be no bother."

"With Junior and Morris?" She shook her head. "Lady Bertha, you want to sleep in the room with my children? Two children I never would have birthed except for your unkindness to me?"

Lady Bertha's chest heaved. "The Good Lord knows Sylvester Morse ought to be horsewhipped for what he done, but that marriage your father arranged for you, that may be hard, but it was the best thing."

"Best thing? Best for me to spend each and every long night with the likes of an uneducated oaf like Jebediah Slocum? No, thank you, Lady Bertha."

"Margaret, please call me Mother Dear—the Hardin way."

Margaret advanced up one stair. "Mother Dear, is it? After twenty-five years, that's what you want me to call you? Well, Lady Bertha—as you stand here on the grand stairway of Hardin House wearing nothing but a wrapper—I want you to know my children already have a governess. Would you have me throw her out of bed so a trollop like you might take her place? I think not."

"Lady Margaret, ma'am, Lady Bertha, she needin' yo' help."

"Salome, I can see that." Margaret looked down at Bertha's bare feet. "Mother Dear must have been quite a sight when you walked in. My father didn't say what he found when he saw his wife in Uncle James's room, but judging from his face, it must have been scandalous." She moved up one more step and looked down on Bertha. "Tell me, Lady Bertha, what I'm already thinking. Was it not your idea to remove every stitch of your clothing for Uncle James and, might I say, perform the acts of an adulteress with him, night after night? And now that my father has forbidden you to enter your old bedroom, why should I let a hussy, and what was that word you called me four years ago—*whore*—stay in the room with two innocent children?"

Salome felt Bertha sag as her knees crumpled beneath her. She stared up at her daughter. "I don't reckon no woman alive wants to be nekkid in front of folks she ain't invited to see her thataway. Lord Hardin zactin' his punishment on her, all right. Makin' Lady Bertha use the servants' bathin' tub. Makin' her sleep any ole place. Makin' her walk 'round the house wearin' next to nothin'. I ain't sayin' she don't deserve all of it fo' the way she treated you. I am sayin' you gots better in you than hate. It's you, Lady Margaret, what'll be feelin' mo' pain than Lady Bertha ever will. Hate make you old, gray, and dried-up way befo' yo' time. Worse, it make you so bitter, yo' heart shrink, leavin' no room fo' nobody to get in there."

Margaret scowled at Salome. "My heart will shrink, you say? Salome, my heart is already dead." She walked up two more stairs. "Bring a cot—one with broken springs and a lumpy mattress—into the boys' room. Mother Dear can sleep there until Aunt Elvera leaves and takes that loathsome man's body with her."

CHAPTER
TWENTY-THREE

The straight ladder-backed chair Sylvester Morse pointed to looked as though it would hurt Henry's back. Without glancing at his daughter's rapist, he shook his head, walked across the lawyer's office, and lowered himself into the burgundy leather armchair. What could Morse want? Thankfully, the rascal had not troubled the Hardins. He hadn't even afforded them the courtesy of a condolence note following the death of James six years ago.

Morse, sitting in his own swivel leather chair behind his big but bare oak desk, frowned. "Won't you move up closer, Henry?" He glanced at the closed walnut door. "Don't want to have to shout across the room." He laid on that lopsided grin again. "This bein' personal business and all."

Henry adjusted himself in his chair and glanced at the portrait of Jefferson Davis on the wall behind Sylvester's head. Personal business, indeed. Nothing could be more personal than this man with his daughter. "Sylvester, I am seventy-five years old—much too advanced in years to sit in a chair like that. Now . . ." He paused just long enough to allow Sylvester time to process that his first-name-only insult had not gone over Henry's head. "Why have you commanded me—Lord Hardin—to your office?"

"Well, the party tells me with two years to prepare, I'll be just about ready."

"Indeed." Henry let out his I'm-yet-to-be-convinced tone.

"Absolutely." Morse beamed. "I've done quite well. I've gotten more money for the schools. Tightened up the local segregation laws here in Union County—thank God for that '96 Supreme Court separate-but-equal decision." The man pursed his lips as he gave Henry a long, hard stare.

A twitch of pain in Henry's left shoulder swept his mind away from this bothersome creature for a second. But Henry Hardin was no novice at the blackmailing ways of Sylvester Morse. He stared back.

Morse cleared his throat. "But there are two problems."

These past ten years, Sylvester Morse had never ceased to annoy Henry. Even had he not attacked his daughter, Henry would have disliked the man. "This campaign you're about to mount for the 1912 state elections—the one the Arkansas Democratic Party says you'll be just about ready for in two years—how much will it cost me?"

"Now, now, Hardin. No need to sound so petulant. I'm runnin' for secretary of state. But to run a winnin' campaign the boys tell me I'll need at least fifty thousand." He sucked in his cheeks. "And a solution to two problems."

What was that saying—give a man enough rope and he'll hang himself? Henry put his oft-practiced patience into place.

"As I was sayin', I've added quite a bit to the education budget in Union County. But as you know, the colored tried to put up a fuss about me takin' money from their schools to give to our children." Sylvester turned his chair to face Henry.

"So I've heard." The shoulder twitch moved down to his elbow.

"By the by, I hear your own colored college man—I believe he calls himself Waylon Hardin—got himself married to a gal from Alabama."

Henry nodded.

"A schoolteacher, I understand."

"So she is."

"Just had a baby, I believe. That goin' to keep the wench home and out of politickin'? Most unbecomin' for a married woman to go out rilin' up folks unnecessarily, don't you think?"

"Mr. Morse, you appear fascinated with the goings-on at Hardin House." Henry steeled himself for the upcoming unpleasantness.

"As stiff-necked as ever, Lord Hardin? I should have known I could not speak reason to you." Morse slammed a hand on the desk. "Look, I need fifty thousand dollars to run this campaign along with your prom-ise to keep Waylon and his schoolteacher woman out of the education business. That woman's been goin' all around the county stirrin' up the coloreds about gettin' a 'fair share' of the education budget. Somethin' about havin' enough books for all their students. Our colored are get-tin' a fair share, as far as I'm concerned. How much education can a colored handle, anyway? About six years is more than enough schoolin' for them, don't you think?"

"What I think does not appear to be the issue." Henry rubbed his arm. "What do you want of me other than fifty thousand dol-lars?" Henry, an expert at these negotiations with both Morse and the Slocums, did a quick calculation. Sylvester always padded his requests by double and a half.

Morse leaned forward, elbows on the desk. He shot one look at the still-shut door. "Nobody faults you for havin' a roll with a colored wench. Nothin' wrong with producin' a few pickaninnies, either. But there sure as hell is somethin' wrong when one of those pickaninnies forgets his place. Now, you stop your nigger son's woman from actin' up or—"

Henry shook his head. "Mr. Morse, I assure you, I have no idea of what you speak. But I am sure that twenty thousand dollars will give you a great start on your campaign."

"I'm serious, Hardin. I intend to be secretary of state. To do that, I've got to show the party I can handle the coloreds. Your boy's woman is puttin' roadblocks in my way. Now, you get her under control or I can't be responsible for what might happen."

Henry's left arm throbbed. "What might happen? Sylvester, do I hear a threat in there?"

"Never from me, but there has been talk. The night riders aren't happy with the actions of an outside agitator like that Alabama nigger woman livin' on the Hardin estate." He leaned back in his chair. "I strongly advise you, Lord Hardin, to corral that gal of yours. Accidents have been known to happen."

"I suggest no accidents occur to any Hardin employee, anywhere, ever, if it's fifteen thousand you're seeking."

"Thirty thousand might work except for that other little thing—our second problem." Sylvester put on that disgusting smirk again.

Waylon and Tom-Tom popped into Henry's head more and more often these days. No, he wouldn't give the man the satisfaction of seeing the worry on his face. So far those night-riding dunderheads had dared not disturb anything Hardin, but still . . .

"It's the classes for Saidie Belle, you see."

"Umm." What could he do to save Waylon? Emerald Hardin was a firebrand, though Henry had cautioned her.

A flicker of annoyance crossed Sylvester's face. "To succeed in this campaign, I need to keep the colored in their place, and I need a properly educated woman by my side. One who knows which fork is which, and one who can tell a demitasse from a teacup."

"What?" Henry pulled himself out of his musings. "Was it not you who rushed yourself into a speedy marriage with Saidie Belle Brown? As

I recall, your first daughter was born six—or was it five?—months after the wedding, though as a gentleman, I would never count the months."

Sylvester reddened. "Enough of the past. You know good and well Saidie lacks what you, Lord Hardin, call polish."

"I'm sure your wife will do her best to serve at your side."

"That's just it. Saidie and her shopkeeper's-daughter upbringin' makes her fade a little too much into the background. She's not trained to stand at any gentleman's side. I need sparkle and dazzle in a woman to capture the voters. I've considered sendin' Saidie off to a secret finishin' school to learn how to stand, sit, walk, and talk like a lady, but upon further consideration, I realized there's not enough time to finish Saidie Belle Brown Morse. I need a woman already polished. A woman who shines quality wherever she is."

"A woman of quality? In case you haven't noticed, Sylvester, quality or no, women are not allowed to vote, despite their protest marches."

"Now, Lord Hardin, you know as well as me, the voters I need to attract are the big-money men. And, voters or not, it is their womenfolk who influence them." Morse rocked forward again. "I believe you and I know who was my first choice for wife. Except for that little matter standin' in our path, your lovely daughter would have made a perfect First Lady, don't you agree?"

Henry's breath caught in his chest. He steadied himself before rising to his feet. "Sir, I wish you well with your campaign. Over the next two years, I will supply five thousand dollars into your election fund every six months. If your wife requires polish, I suggest you withdraw the money from those deposits and hire a tutor." He headed toward the door.

"Only twenty thousand?" Sylvester raised his voice. "I don't believe you quite understand. You are lord of the manor in name only, Henry Hardin. This is now my game, and I am serious when I say Margaret would have made the perfect political wife in so many ways. At my side during my swearin'-in. Dancin' in my arms at the inaugural ball. And that's where I intend to have her."

Henry reached the desk in three strides, swung around the edge, grabbed the leather armrests, and tipped Sylvester's chair backward. "Sir, you speak sacrilege. If I ever hear my daughter's name on your filthy lips again, I'll . . ." Something akin to a saw zigzagged across his chest. He clung to the armrests.

Sylvester, his knees higher than his head in his chair, looked up at Henry. "You'll do what, old man? Enough of your showboatin', Hardin. Now let me go so I can tell you how this campaign is really goin' to play out. And, yes, it does involve the beguilin' Margaret."

Perspiration beaded across Henry's forehead. His hands clenched and unclenched on the armrests. As he straightened, his arms dropped to his sides.

Sylvester stood, grabbed Henry, and swung him around to the chair.

"Morse, I'll not . . . hear . . . another wor . . ." Henry had not enough breath to finish.

"Oh, you'll hear more than another word. You're goin' to hear all I have to say about your lovely daughter. Margaret Hardin has both the polish and the name I need. And as much as I disliked her arrogance durin' our courtin' days, that haughtiness plays well on voters hopin' to better themselves. She looks like she belongs at the top. Every Democratic voter in Arkansas holds secret hopes that, one day, he can rise to the top like the Hardins."

Henry's grimace came both from Sylvester's slimy words and the pain growing in his chest.

"Saidie will be on my arm for now, but I'll park her someplace as soon as provident. It is your Margaret who will be the real draw at all the galas the party will throw for me. She will be there as your daughter—showin' the world that Union County's richest and most influential citizen is a staunch supporter of my cause against the coloreds."

Sylvester let out a laugh. "Quite funny, don't you think, old man? Your colored daughter forced to stand against her own kind? But if Margaret does exactly as instructed, no one else will ever be in on our little joke."

Henry glowered at Morse. His head was full of curses against the man, but his breath lay stuck in his chest. "Instructions?" He managed only the one word.

"Dress her in her usual finery. She carries elegance well. With all eyes on her, Margaret will attend ladies' teas, luncheons, symphony fund-raisers, anyplace where society women congregate. Even shop-keepers' wives will envy and admire your daughter's style, enough to press their husbands to vote for me."

"Out of my way." The pain subsided in Henry's chest, and air rushed in. "And how will you explain the presence of another woman at these events? Don't tell me others won't notice your wife has been replaced."

"What others will notice is that the white daughter of Union County's most illustrious inhabitant, Lord Henry, is lendin' Hardin support to a worthy campaign."

Henry turned to the door. "Sir, your plan is preposterous. Not only is my girl a respectable married woman, for excellent reasons she cannot bear the sight of you."

"Oh, she'll bear more than the sight of me. Margaret will smile when I enter a room. And when I ask, she will dance every waltz with me—Saidie is lucky to know even the Texas two-step. As for Margaret's poor excuse of a husband—Jebediah Slocum—he can sit with Saidie. That will dampen down any talk of scandal."

Enough of this man's rantings. Henry headed for the door.

"I suggest you strongly urge Margaret to comply," Morse called out from the center of the room. "As she's learned, the consequences of opposin' me are dire. Henry, you're aware that Saidie and I have only daughters. I'm feelin' partial to a son. Perhaps on one of our campaign swings Margaret might bring her oldest boy—Morris is his name, isn't it? I'd like to meet the boy with a name so like my own."

Henry grabbed the doorknob to steady himself. "That boy, sir," he said, his voice hoarse, "is a Slocum." He pulled the door open only to have Sylvester hurry across the room and slam it shut. In the commotion, Henry jammed a shoulder into the wall.

"Please tell Margaret I will forgo the pleasure of meetin' her oldest boy only if she agrees to spend a night or two with me on the campaign trail—mappin' out strategy and such—whenever I want." The man's breath, smelling of this morning's grits and ham, brushed Henry's neck. "You know, Henry, I did find her quite pleasurable that Fourth of July, ten years back. All that pretend squealin', squirmin', and protestin' like she didn't want it. Most satisfying."

More perspiration beaded on Henry's forehead. He longed to grab Morse by the collar and throttle the man, but the pain in his arm, joined by a tightness in his chest, rendered him unable to even utter a single sound.

"Nothing for you to worry about. We'll be very discreet, of course. I'll muffle her cries with somethin' stuffed in her mouth." Morse leaned close to Henry's ear. "Quite a body on that girl of yours. I look forward to exploring each and every one of those curves many, many times over. Now, good day." He opened the door, laid a hand on Henry's back, and pushed.

Maxwell Joe held open the car door of Henry's brand-new, 1910 black Model T Ford. Henry, seated on the plush backseat, looked over at the carpenter he'd temporarily converted to chauffeur until a proper one could arrive from Baltimore. He needed to deal with another lout in his daughter's life, but his ordeal with Sylvester Morse a few moments before had left him drained. And then, there was this troublesome pain in his arm that stayed with him more than it went.

"Suh?" Maxwell Joe peered into the backseat. "This here be Mr. Jacob Slocum's place. You gettin' out?"

"And Jebediah's here as I asked?" Henry saw the Hardin House horse and buggy on loan to his son-in-law parked in Jacob Slocum's driveway.

He took a little time to catch his breath, then held out a hand. Maxwell Joe helped him out of the car just as his eldest grandson sped around the corner of the gray clapboard two-story house that Henry's money had bought and paid for.

"Morris," Henry called out as the boy flashed inside the front door, ignoring him. "Jebediah Jr.!" He made his way up the front steps, across the porch, and to the front door.

"What are those boys doing out of school? Where's Tessie?"

"Right here, Lord Hardin, suh." As usual at the Slocums' house, Tessie, there with her charges, Jebediah and Morris, looked wary.

Henry searched the room. No sign of the tutor he'd hired for his grandsons, but there, sprawled on the settee, was Jebediah. Jacob Slocum sat in the rocker. Mrs. Slocum, wearing an apron over her shapeless sack of a dress, walked out of the kitchen, her arms white with flour. Her eyes darted around her front room, where only company was allowed to gather. The poor woman looked as though she was checking to make sure every doily on the back of each and every chair was properly starched.

"What are these children doing away from their classroom?" Henry stood in the center of the floor awaiting an invitation to sit that he doubted would come. With Maxwell Joe's help, he lowered himself into the stiff-backed, tufted armchair. "Well?" He turned to Jebediah.

"Pa wants me to take 'em out to the cotton fields. We got hands workin' there."

"Time for them boys to learn how to train up workers—'specially colored," Jacob Slocum piped up. "Give a nigger a mile and he'll take two if you don't stay on 'em." Jacob shifted the wad of tobacco in his mouth.

"Is that so?" Henry nodded for Maxwell Joe to wait in the kitchen.

Jacob's wife, head bowed, turned back to the kitchen.

"Woman!" The fury Jacob flung at his wife caught Henry unawares. "You tryin' to tell me that you're okay with a nig . . . colored in your kitchen? That I'm the kinda man allows colored inside his house?"

Shaking consumed Mrs. Slocum, strong enough for Henry to see across the room. The woman looked as though the hangman were coming straight for her.

A little smile played across Jacob Slocum's face. "I'll tend to your behind later."

Maxwell Joe stopped still and looked toward Lord Hardin. Henry gestured him outside.

Enough of the Slocums and their evil ways. Henry turned to his son-in-law. "Jebediah, you and I have had this discussion before. My grandsons are to be educated at Hardin House by a private tutor until they are old enough to attend the new high school. Both those boys are destined for college." Henry put as much conviction into his voice as he could muster. From what he'd seen so far, Junior especially would never see the inside of a college classroom, and every day Morris was showing more and more signs of his no-good father.

"Margaret don't care much how these boys is raised as long as I keep them out of her hair."

Henry turned from Jebediah. "Jacob, you and your missus head into the kitchen and close the door. Tessie, round up the children and take them to the car. Tell Maxwell Joe I said to keep them there."

As the others dispersed, Henry's son-in-law stretched out even more on the settee. "Ain't no need for us to do no more talkin', Henry. Like I said, Margaret turned both of them boys over to me. I ain't complainin'. I'm doin' my wife a favor."

That his son-in-law was putting on a show of bravado wouldn't have gotten past a six-year-old. Henry moved to the edge of the uncomfortable chair. "Jebediah, it has come to my attention that my daughter's behavior toward her children might be attributable to you."

"Attrib . . . what?" Jebediah scrunched himself more upright on the settee.

"Are you putting too many demands on my daughter? The medical doctors say oftentimes women may not interact with—pay attention to—their children because they fear having more."

"Ain't that what she had Mattie Lou for? Stoppin' babies from comin'?"

"Mattie Lou's been dead these past six months. Another stroke, I'm afraid."

"I know she was livin' with that preacher boy son of hers." Jebediah shook his head. "Margaret tried to use that to keep me from one of my husband visits . . ." He wrinkled his nose. "Said she was grievin' for one of her old servants."

Face reddening, Henry cleared his throat. "That's what I'm saying. I think it best if you stop having . . . visits with my daughter. At least until Margaret is feeling better. Perhaps a year."

"A year?" Jebediah straightened on the settee. "Henry, you bein' her papa and all, you don't see her like other men." He planted his feet on the floor. "My wife's a good-lookin' woman. And when a man sees a woman built like her, he can't help himself. Hell, Henry, I'm her husband, and I got my rights."

Henry unclenched his fists when he realized his palms burned. If Jebediah uttered one more *Henry*, Lord Hardin couldn't hold himself responsible. "Mr. Slocum, I believe your rights stop at the sickroom door. If, God forbid, the worst happens and my girl is no more, well then . . ." Henry gazed around the room, his arms spread wide. "It's a good thing your mother enjoys cooking. I trust she's talented at it. A good white cook can command two dollars a week in a well-to-do home. But unfortunately, the best cooks happen to be colored. And my Delfine, with her French cooking, commands twelve dollars a month."

Jebediah gave Henry a what-is-he-getting-at look.

Time to make this simple. Henry leaned forward and pasted on his most serious face. "Can your mother roast a decent pheasant? Can she julienne potatoes? How about her pork cassoulet? And then, of course, there's your father. I don't know what sort of work he could find if his income suddenly evaporated—went away. And where would any of you live when this spacious house is no longer in your family's hands?"

Finally, this awful day offered a moment of levity. The look on Jebediah Slocum's face as he sorted out Henry's meaning—he and his would be out of house and home—almost made up for the pain still battling in Henry's arm and chest.

"You sayin' you would cut us off? Us knowin' what we know? And them boys. If folks know 'bout that first one . . . well, then."

"The boys will remain at Hardin House, of course. With their grandfather. As for people knowing what they think they know, I doubt the good citizens of Union County will listen to gossip from a fired overseer."

"Fired overseer?" Jebediah pursed his lips. "Look, I know I ain't got the schoolin' like you and Margaret, but I've been doin' right by your girl. A whole lot of people know why you had me marry her." He looked at the floor while he nodded. "I'm keepin' up my end of the bargain even when you three—you, Lady Bertha, and Margaret—treat me worse than the dumbest field hand in the back forty." He lifted his eyes to Henry. "Right after I gave her Junior—so's folks would quit their tongues from waggin'—Margaret put me on the most goddamn bed rations any husband ever had to deal with: my birthday, my choice of Christmas or New Year's, Valentine's Day, and if she was wantin' somethin' from me, one other day—never no more than four times a

year. Fact is, no other man would put up with such foolishness." He
held Henry's gaze. "I ain't so stupid that I don't know Margaret had a
hard time with that lawyer fella, Sylvester Morse. He was rough with
her. I ain't never been rough with your daughter, and I follow that damn
schedule without too much out-loud complainin'. But if you want me
to give up even that, I'm not likin' it."

Henry stifled a groan. "A schedule? From what I understand, you've
scheduled yourself with one or two colored girls around here every
Saturday night."

Jebediah stiffened his shoulders and glared at Henry. "Ain't touched
no colored woman on Hardin property. I take my business elsewhere,
and I ain't never had me a white woman, not since I married Margaret."
He narrowed his eyes. "What would you have me do while I'm waitin'
for my wife to come around? Henry, I'm thirty-three years old. I'm
gonna have me a woman one way or t'other. I'll thank you not to
bother me or mine with talk about my ma workin' as a cook in somebody's kitchen. You got no business firin' me when I'm protectin' your
daughter."

Henry dropped his gaze. He wished no further discussion with this
annoying boy. "Give Margaret a rest for another six to nine months and
you'll hear nothing further from me."

Jebediah nodded. "Ain't gonna be easy. Some mornin's I catch her
comin' out of her room wearin' nothin' but her wrapper. In summer-
time, that wrapper's mighty thin. If the sun comes through the hall
winda just right, I can almost see straight through to her . . ."

"That will do, Jebediah." Henry stood and headed for the door.
"I'm taking the boys back to their classroom." Henry grabbed on to the
door frame as a sharp pain claimed his chest.

"Maxwell Joe. I need you."

CHAPTER TWENTY-FOUR

"Emerald, set yo'self down. I got this pot of greens. You jest tend the baby." Salome lifted the lid on her collards, poked a fork into her frying chicken, and sniffed at the biscuits baking in her oven. She would have used her toes to check on more of the cooking pots if necessary. Waylon's new wife might be pretty and smart, but she sure was no cook. To allow her in the kitchen on Sunday morning was to let yourself in for a night of bellyaches.

"Mama Salome, you just show me how to fix those collards, and I'll cook them next time. For Waylon." Emerald bounced baby Freddie in her arms. The baby's blue eyes darted around his grandmother's front room. "I suppose Thomas's fiancée already knows how to cook."

Salome followed her grandson's eyes as he lifted a chubby arm toward her new cookstove complete with its warming drawer and a place for the ashes. Almost as fine as the one in the Big House. She heard little Freddie gurgle as his cheeks dimpled into a smile. Even a babe as young as him could appreciate the pale yellow color Salome had especially asked for. She chucked the baby under the chin, walked past her wooden worktable, and took a quick peek into her oven. The biscuits were browning nicely. "I knows you a college girl and everythin', but seem funny to me yo' mama didn't teach you how to cook."

Emerald shrugged. "My folks just wanted me to study hard and do well in school."

"So's you could end up being a schoolteacher woman." Salome wiped her hands down her apron. She still hadn't quite forgiven Waylon for sneaking off to Alabama and marrying the preacher's daughter without a by-your-leave to her or Lord Hardin. Henry wasn't happy about it, either. Salome walked into her new dining room and checked the table settings.

"My mother was a teacher, too, you know. Went to school up in Nashville. Fisk."

"I hear tell." Salome counted her place settings. Five, and one plate set aside in case Henry decided to drop by. Salome glanced at her daughter-in-law. High-yellow skin, green eyes, fair-to-middlin' straight hair. No wonder, with two white grandfathers.

Salome walked to her front room, looked down at her round coffee table, and spotted a stack of papers. "Emerald, they's somethin' I got to talk to you 'bout."

"Yes, ma'am."

"Are them more pamphlets you gonna be handin' out?" She pointed to the coffee table.

"I thought I'd ask Thomas's fiancée if she'd be interested. The baby is keeping me busy. What with tutoring students and caring for Waylon and Freddie, I don't really have time to visit all those colored churches in Union County. I can't do a decent job until next year." She jiggled the child. "But I'm determined to get our kids the education they deserve. Do you think she'd be interested in filling in for me until Freddie gets up to some size?"

Salome breathed in relief. Henry had threatened all kinds of bad things to stop Emerald from parading up and down the county with her pamphlets about equal education. It had been Waylon who'd finally talked his wife into tutoring instead of politicking.

"I believe Tom-Tom call his girl Ladora. I don't know what-all Waylon knows 'bout her. This be the first time any of us, 'ceptin' Tom-Tom, be meetin' her."

"Mama Salome, I'm so sorry we didn't have a big, fancy wedding in Arkansas, but my mother was so set on having the very same thing in Alabama. Waylon and I didn't want to choose between you two, so we compromised. We got married with just a few people in attendance."

"In Alabama. Seem like to me, y'all could have invited the groom's mother."

Emerald cocked her head. "And the groom's father?"

Salome sent her daughter-in-law a sharp look. She, more than most, should know folk didn't talk about their white fathers in polite company.

The rattling of the buggy brought Salome's eyes to her front yard. Waylon sat in front with Maxwell Joe. Salome peered out her curtained window as Tom-Tom stepped from the backseat followed by a curvy, brown-skinned girl with a head of press-and-curl hair piled into a pompadour. Another good-looking daughter-in-law.

Salome held open the front door. Tom-Tom bounded up the steps first.

"Mama, this is Ladora Peterson. From Camden."

"Uh-huh." Salome swung the door wide. "Come on in. I'm 'bout to set dinner on the table."

Salome busied herself with last-minute preparations while the young ones got acquainted. She'd badgered Lord Hardin as much as he would tolerate about the whys of Tom-Tom marrying so young. Her baby wasn't but twenty-five. All Henry had answered was that he wanted everybody settled. The sooner, the better.

Salome caught a glimpse of a man's outline before she heard the tap on her kitchen door.

"Maxwell Joe, let me fix you a plate." She grabbed two chicken thighs.

"No, Salome. No, thank you, that is . . . I gots . . ." A peculiar look crossed the carpenter's face. "I gots places to go, and I don't reckon Lord Henry gonna be comin' down here, after all. He up at the Big House with Lady Bertha." Maxwell Joe's right cheek twitched. He stepped just inside the kitchen door. "Salome, I be wantin' you to know somethin' . . . in case things . . . troubles come. I wants you to know you the finest woman I ever knowed. I done what's right." His eyes bored into her like he was saying his last good-byes. He turned and walked away.

What on earth? Salome carried the bowl of collards in one hand and the chicken platter in the other. She set them both down on her lace-covered dining room table.

"My, that looks good, Miz Salome." The girl called Ladora smiled up at her from a dining room chair.

"Ladora was just telling me that she does cook." Emerald looked to the corner of the dining room where she'd placed Freddie in his sleeping basket. "She keeps house for her father since her mother passed on. Ladora's eighteen, and her father told her it was time for her to get married."

"Well, ain't you found out a lot in a little bit of time." Salome cocked an eye at Emerald.

Ladora dropped her head. "He—my pa—he's marryin' again. The widow Boyd." She looked up. "She don't really fancy me stayin' at the house after they gets hitched. Says I'd be one woman too many in the kitchen."

And Tom-Tom, son of Union County's richest man, was quite a catch. This girl, as good-looking as she was, could she make a proper wife for Tom-Tom? Didn't sound like she'd gotten much more schoolin' than Salome—third grade. While Salome's youngest hadn't gone to

Tuskegee, he had attended that colored preachers' school—Philander Smith College—and could deliver a mighty fine Sunday sermon full of Israel history and everything.

"Ladora, if it's all right with you, after dinner I'd like to talk 'bout where this here weddin' gonna take place. But right now, y'all eat up." With a motherless bride and her don't-care father, Salome could lay out all the wedding plans she wanted.

Baby Freddie let out a squall just as Waylon finished his second helping of Salome's berry cobbler. The timing was just right. Emerald left off her questioning of Ladora and went to tend her son. Ladora, already clearing the table after the meal, looked relieved. Salome, stuffed from her own cooking, headed to her front room and took a seat. She aimed her chair so she could get a good view of her kitchen. Now was the time to see what this Ladora girl was all about. Emerald had already made her lack of housekeeping talents known. Salome didn't want to chance the same mistake twice. After watching Waylon and Tom-Tom step outside for their after-dinner smokes, Salome took her time peering at Ladora scrubbing and cleaning the kitchen to Salome's standards while Emerald played with the baby.

"Mama Salome, care to hold him?" Emerald knew just how to get to Salome. She handed over baby Freddie.

"Miz Salome?" Ladora peered around the kitchen door. "I done washed up all yo' pots and pans, but I'm scared to touch yo' good dishes, they bein' so fine and all. Got hand-painted roses on 'em."

"Don't you fret none, Ladora. I'll be gettin' to those dishes directly." Salome jiggled Freddie in the air. As she cooed at the child, she heard her front door burst open. "Waylon! Tom-Tom! I tole y'all 'bout bustin' into my house like they was a fire." She aimed a glare in their direction.

"You best come on up to the Big House, Miz Salome." Maxwell Joe's apprentice, Danny-boy, stood in her front door, cap in hand. "They's been a accident."

Waylon and Tom-Tom bounded in, pushing Danny-boy into the center of the front room. Both her sons wore worried frowns.

Salome clutched the baby to her chest. "Margaret?" Her heart pounded.

"No'm, ain't none of Lady Margaret. Maxwell Joe, he . . ."

"Oh, my God in Heaven, no!" She moved to her feet, baby Freddie slipping to her stomach. "Not Maxwell Joe!" Not the man she'd give her heart to if he ever asked!

Emerald caught her son before he slid to the floor.

Danny-boy held up a hand, his head shaking left and right. "No, ma'am, ain't none of Maxwell Joe, but him and me, we the ones what found him. Look like the buggy done broke an axle. Funny though how it ran all the way 'most to the creek. He must have fell headfirst into the creek 'cause he sho done drowned."

Waylon reached her side first, then Tom-Tom. Ladora rushed over with a glass of water while Emerald gathered up a fan.

"Who this happen to?" Salome clamped her eyes shut. Henry. She'd known the man so long. He'd been in her bed since she was seventeen years old. Now she was about to turn forty-nine. Lord, she hadn't wanted that man—but how was she supposed to get along without him?

"Lord Hardin, he sent me and Maxwell Joe to town to fetch some hams."

The tears started, then the moaning.

"Hams?" Waylon burst out as he held his mother close. "On a Sunday?"

"Yeah, I'm thinkin' it kind of strange, too." Danny-boy frowned. "But, Lord Hardin, he say he need them hams, so me and Maxwell Joe hitched up the wagon and went on our way up to Lisbon. We got 'bout halfway there when we saw one wheel and a big rut in the grass." Danny-boy shook his head. "Funny how that wagon first went up the hill, then came crashin' down. Landed a good twenty yards from the creek."

"May God have mercy on his soul." Tom-Tom circled his arms around his mother and brother. Salome heard Emerald take in short breaths.

Danny-boy slapped his cap at his knees. He lowered his voice. "Mr. Sylvester Morse is who it was."

Sylvester Mor . . . ? Had she heard right? The little breeze stirred up by Emerald's fan helped settle her mind enough to allow her ears to work better. Salome broke free of her boys' arms. She reached for the glass held by a wide-eyed Ladora. "Mr. Sylvester, he done . . ." Her mind came back to her. "Where all did y'all say this happen?" Her words croaked in her throat. "Whereabouts by the creek?"

"That place you can't see too good from the road. Maxwell Joe said we had to turn right around and go back and tell Lord Hardin what done happened befo' we tell the sheriff. Lord Hardin, he say he knew that place. When he told Lady Margaret what done happened, she went all pale-like. Tessie had to put her to bed. Come to think of it, Tessie looked kind of funny herself. Fact is, Tessie said she knew that there place from a long time ago. Fourth of July, I believe she say. Ten years back."

"Y'all, help me up. I gots to get to Margaret. She be needin' her mo . . . maid."

Waylon grabbed one arm, Tom-Tom the other. They pulled her to her feet.

"Oh, my Lord. The sheriff? Where's Maxwell Joe?" Salome's heart threatened to break out of her chest.

"Oh, the sheriff, he done come. Him and the deputy pulled po' Mr. Morse out of the water. Sheriff say look like he been dead since last night."

"Last night?" Waylon and Tom-Tom said together.

"That's what the sheriff be thinkin'." Danny-boy dropped his voice. "Say it look like Mr. Morse been doin' some heavy drinkin'. Me and Maxwell Joe, we found two whisky bottles empty—one in the buggy, the other on a tree branch what looked like a seat."

Salome gulped the water and shook her head.

"Get Mama some medicinal spirits. Lord Hardin keeps brandy in the dining room safe," Tom-Tom called out.

Ladora rushed to the mahogany breakfront and pulled out the bottle and some glasses.

"Was this Mr. Morse a drinking man?" Emerald swept up a folding cloth for Freddie's changing.

Danny-boy nodded. "That ain't all." He looked from Salome to Ladora to Emerald as she headed to the bedroom with the baby. "I don't like to say in front of ladies."

"You don't like to say what?" Salome took a slug of Henry's spirits and coughed. "Would you get on with the tellin', Danny-boy?"

"Yes'm, Miz Salome. Sheriff reckon Mr. Morse done had him a night of carousing 'cause he had somethin' else in the buggy 'sides that brandy." Danny-boy clamped his lips shut.

"Boy, you want me to hit you with this whisky glass? You get on with the talkin'." Salome glared.

"It was ladies' . . . things."

"Ladies' things?" Tom-Tom looked over at Ladora. "Why don't you help Emerald with the baby?"

"Uhh." The girl looked confused but gave a slow nod. "If that's what you wantin', Tom-Tom." She followed Emerald into the bedroom.

"Now they gone, you tell it to me." Salome tried to shuffle the pictures of that awful July Fourth out of her head.

"Ladies' bloomers. And a chemise. No corset."

"What?" Waylon boomed.

"They was all on the ground by the buggy. Wasn't no woman with Mr. Sylvester when we found him, but Sheriff say them drawers looked like the kind white women livin' down there by the railroad station puts on. Buys them at that sto' that sells only to white folks. Sheriff gonna go down there tomorra and see what white woman missin' her drawers."

Tom-Tom walked to the bedroom door and pulled it shut.

"They's mo'."

Salome took another gulp.

Danny-boy held a hand to his mouth and turned his face from Salome. "Mr. Morse, he was buck nekkid in that water. Wasn't nary a stitch on 'im. Sheriff done found Mr. Sylvester's clothes all cattywampus across the grass. Sheriff figure he took the woman there fo' . . . y'all know . . . when that buggy axle broke and tossed them both out on the ground." He looked at Salome. "Anyhows, they took off they clothes and directly, Mr. Morse, he must have just plumb walked into the creek and passed out. The woman got scared, left her drawers, and lit out back to shanty town. That's what the sheriff believe."

"I've got to get to the Big House." Salome handed off the glass and moved to the front door. She stepped off the porch and headed to the buggy. A breeze kicked up. Would she need her shawl? Best to take it. Salome turned back toward the house. She heard Danny-boy's voice lingering outside.

"Ain't none of y'all know the worst part. I was fudgin' the truth 'cause of Miz Salome."

"Fudging the truth?" Tom-Tom asked.

Salome pressed herself against the side of the house.

"Weren't gonna say all of it in front of her. Some things ain't fittin' fo' ladies' ears."

Waylon said, "Say what you have to say."

"When me and Maxwell Joe first come up on Mr. Morse, they was a rope hangin' from the tree. Not but a little bit of a piece, but . . ."

Salome sucked in a breath. Oh, Lord God. What had Maxwell Joe done? Whatever it was, he'd done it for Margaret and her.

"A rope?" Waylon asked.

"Like I was sayin', jest a piece of one. All tore up on the end. Then, I took me a good look at Mr. Sylvester's ankles. Looked to me like they had rope burns on 'em."

Salome jammed a hand to her chest.

"Lord, have mercy," Tom-Tom intoned, practicing his new preacher ways. "Are you trying to say the man was hung?"

"Looked like he was hung upside down. By his ankles."

Oh, Jesus. Salome steadied herself against the clapboards of her house.

"Maxwell Joe, he think Mr. Sylvester and some white gal was playin' some sort of game—maybe takin' turns hangin' upside down. Since the man was nekkid as a jaybird—with him hangin' upside down, his midpart in touchin' distance—y'all can figure what was goin' on when it was Mr. Sylvester's turn. If a regular-size woman stood up tall, her mouth would be right level with his . . ."

"What did the sheriff say?" Waylon sounded worried.

"Oh, we ain't tole him 'bout none of that. After we found Mr. Sylvester the way we done, we went on back to Lord Hardin. He say it would be a big disgrace to the Morse family—they son runnin' fo' secretary of state, and all—if such a thing was found out."

Salome held a hand to her throat. She tried to coax the tightness holding it to let go.

"Lord Hardin, he figured that gal got mad or scared and left the man hangin' there, upside down. Lord Hardin, he think Mr. Sylvester might of hung there fo' hours, clawin' at hisself, tryin' to get loose of that rope. Him there swingin' to and fro', hollerin' fo' help that ain't never come. I tole Lord Hardin, he probably right, 'cause me and Maxwell Joe done found throw-up on the ground beneath that rope."

Henry! Salome's heart thumped so loud it almost drowned out Danny-boy.

"Lord Hardin, he figure when Mr. Sylvester finally swung hisself loose, he bounced on his head. That, and bein' light-headed after all them hours squealin' fo' all he's worth, he ain't knowed who or where he was. Tumbled in the creek and passed out. That's it."

"And the sheriff?" Tom-Tom asked.

"I tole you. He don't know nothin' 'bout no rope 'cause Maxwell Joe, he done cut it down."

"But the rope burns on the ankles?" Another question from Tom-Tom.

"Lord Hardin, he tole me to make it look like a coon scratched the man's backside up good. Took me a pointy rock and that's what I done. Lord Hardin say it'd be a mercy fo' the family."

Salome felt her head go woozy. Henry. Lord Hardin always told her the Good Lord would make things right for their daughter. Never mind the shawl. She held on to the porch pillar and made her way down the steps. Her knees wobbled, but she stumbled over to the buggy just as Danny-boy and her sons stepped outside.

"Let me help you up, Miz Salome. Lord Hardin, he wantin' you and the boys up at the Big House. I'll drive you. Waylon and Tom-Tom can bring the women." Danny-boy climbed aboard, clicked to the horse, and headed up the path.

CHAPTER TWENTY-FIVE

The pain felt like a vise squeezing his chest. Somewhere, sitting by his bed, was Salome. He knew she was there though neither his eyes nor his hands had the strength to hold her. Downstairs, in the great hall, his ears picked up the faint tick-tock of the grandfather clock, its beats coming closer and closer together. Henry had sent Maxwell Joe to town thirty minutes back to fetch Dr. Henderson. He loaned the carpenter a horse since the road to Lisbon wouldn't be cleared of buggy debris until morning. Even so, it would be too late. Sylvester Morse was no more. Henry would have thanked God that his daughter's tormentor had been sent straight to Hell, but it had not been God who'd taken that man, evil personified, off the face of this earth two days before.

Henry closed his eyes as another pain claimed him. Breaths came harder and harder. It wouldn't be God Henry would greet within this hour. He'd be shaking hands with the Devil. No matter. Margaret had been avenged and Salome's mind put to rest. Salome. A clamp so strong his rib bones felt melded together grabbed at his chest. The gaslights in his room dimmed and pitched him into total darkness.

"Lord Henry, suh. I knows what done happened." Salome's breath fell like a soft zephyr breeze into his awakening ears. "Fo' Margaret. Suh, won't you open yo' eyes so's I can thank you proper?"

Open his eyes. Yes. He wanted to do just that but lead weights held them shut.

"Please, Lord Hardin." Salome's voice played more musically than he remembered.

A burst of air filled his lungs, and the lights brightened. The smell of Salome—warm buttermilk biscuits, sun-drenched linens, sandalwood oozing off her skin though she never wore perfume—surrounded him. "Come to bed." Had he spoken aloud?

Salome leaned in close, the side of her face brushing his lips. "Suh, you wants me to come to bed? Now? Lord Hardin, this here's yo' bed. I ain't never been in it."

"Come. Bed. Now." Each word cost him so much.

Air filled his lungs, and the weights over his eyes fell away. He watched Salome stand and fumble with the top button of her dress.

"No. Clothes on. So you'll . . . know." Henry closed his eyes, waiting for more air to fight its way past the pain.

"You wants me in the bed with my clothes on?"

Should he form the word *yes* and waste the precious breath God was so rightfully taking from him with the tick of every second of the clock? There was no air left to tell her. He wanted her in his bed with her clothes on so she would know that for a very long time now, she had been so much more than a bed playmate to him. Henry looked into her face. But how could she know? How had he treated her these thirty-two years? No air to speak. He nodded. A flash of worry ran across Salome's face and stayed. He watched her pull back the coverlet. She eased herself to the edge of the bed and reached down toward her shoes.

First a whiff, then a puff, then slow drips like January maple sap squeezing through a narrow tube. Air. "Bed. Now."

"Um?"

Where the strength came from, Henry couldn't say, but he threw back the sheet. Salome nodded and slid in beside him—one shoe unlaced, the other off.

"Lord Hardin, I knows it ain't supposed to be Christian to wish harm to another, but I be thankin' you fo' what you done fo' Margaret. It be justice, and it will ease her mind." She laid a hand on the side of his face. "God in Heaven know what's right and what's wrong, not us. But, iffen you think you need it—and I don't reckon you do—ain't never too late to ask His fo'giveness."

"Salome." Her name took almost his last batch of air. "You and me at first . . ." How many ticks of the clock until more drops of air fed through the tube? "I think . . . just another good-looking colored wench . . . bed."

He watched her suck in her lips while he waited for the next breeze to lift his chest.

"You chose me fo' some reason, Henry. I ain't never rightly knew why. Ain't never been much good in bed."

"You, Salome . . . you give me . . . all you are . . . all you have. To me. I . . ." God knew he was in no position to bargain, but if the Good Lord would grant him one, maybe two more minutes with her, he would gladly pay his dues to the Devil for James, Bertha, and even Sylvester Morse.

"Henry!" Salome lifted up on one elbow, her face staring into his own. Her eyes showed panic. How long had his chest failed to move?

His mouth hurt as he tried to carve out a smile for her. "Always . . . from you to me . . . loyalty. I give you . . . nothing. Salome . . ." One more drip of air, please Lord. Just enough to breathe sound into five words. Just five. He needed no explanation for the Devil. Henry Hardin, the late duke of Union County, was guilty as charged—adultery, selfishness, false pride, murder. Eternal fire would be his punishment. So be it. Salome and Margaret were worth all the hellfire and pitchforks Satan could muster. The weights dropped back over Henry's eyes. Chains bound his chest. One more breath. God, just one more. "Salome, I always loved you."

CHAPTER
TWENTY-SIX

Black bunting swagged over the grand staircase. Papa's portraits in the foyer and the library all draped in black. Hardin House, indeed the whole county, plunged into the deepest mourning for Lord Henry Hardin, descendant of English aristocrats, and the duke of Union County. Margaret took the last steps down the grand staircase, her black taffeta mourning dress swirling about her ankles. She headed for the library, her arms carrying a vase of flowers—the heads of the deep red roses angled downward, the vase tied with a black velvet bow. All for Papa. Margaret shook her head as she turned toward her father's library. The tears that had never fully left her these last seven days flooded back. At least the funeral was over and Lady Bertha had played her part well.

The dowager Lady Hardin hadn't cried, but she had looked mournful. Salome held up well in the church section set aside for the colored household staff during the service, but she had collapsed at the grave site. Waylon, Tom-Tom, and that new agitator wife of Waylon's had quickly carried her back to her own house. As for herself, Margaret still couldn't believe her father was gone. Now she was truly all alone in this world. All alone with a secret that had to be kept. Margaret turned the knob on the library door and stepped inside.

"Jebediah?" She stared at her husband. "What are you doing in here?"

He stood behind Papa's desk, pulling at the drawer her father always kept locked. "Margaret, now that your pa's gone, leavin' you without a man to do the business of this here farm, I reckon it's time for me to step up. I'm lookin' for the key to your pa's filing cabinets."

"Step up? The key? Jebediah, what are you talking about?" She turned to face Tessie. And a man holding her by the arm. "Tessie! What are you doing in here, and who is this gentle . . ." Margaret surveyed the stained overalls, the shirt with a pocket hanging loose of its stitching, the scuffed shoes, the straggly beard. "This man?"

Tessie stood in front of the shelves holding Papa's oldest volumes, in a far corner of the room. The servant's eyes darted between Jebediah and the stranger. "Lady Margaret, ma'am, this here man . . ." She took a step toward Margaret. "He grabbed ahold of me."

"Grabbed ahold of you?" Margaret whirled around to Jebediah, water sloshing from the vase in her hands. "Who is this man, and what is he doing in my father's library?" She set the flowers on a side table.

Jiggling the brass handle of the locked drawer, Jebediah nodded toward the stranger. "Oh, that's just Gopher. Gopher Dennis. My best friend."

"Your best friend? You've never mentioned him before. What's he"—Margaret glowered at the oaf—"doing with my maid?"

"Pleased to meet you, ma'am." The man stuck out a grimy hand. "I was just havin' me a bit of fun with the gal." He jabbed a thumb toward Tessie. "Didn't know no ladies was about or I'da held myself 'til later."

"I want you out of here." Margaret folded her arms at her waist. "As for you, Jebediah, what do you mean bringing a man like this into my father's house?"

"Margaret, I know you're mournin' your pa. It's natural that you're upset. But Gopher didn't mean no harm against Tessie. He just wanted to have a few words with her. Orderin' up lunch is all." Jebediah never was good at lying.

Margaret pointed a finger at the interloper. "Out."

With a quick nod toward Margaret, Gopher started to rush from the room, bobbing his thank yous.

"You, too." She kept her arms crossed as she glared at Jebediah.

"Hold on, Gopher. You hold on now, too, Margaret. Gopher can be of some help to me when it comes to runnin' this farm. I can't know everything about a place this size." Jebediah looked down at the Aubusson carpet. "Gopher's got experience in such things, and I'd rather not have my pa involved."

Margaret shook her head, wondering if her ears had plugged. "Running Hardin Acres? You? Jebediah, you don't know how to run a farm."

Her husband reached down to the lower desk drawer. "That's why I'm lookin' for them keys. So's I can get me a head start on what's what."

"What's what? Jebediah, what makes you think you'll be in charge of my father's affairs?"

He settled his eyes on her in a way that made Margaret shudder. "I'm your husband."

Her husband? Yes, but in name only.

"That will readin's gonna be tomorrow, but that ain't gonna make much never mind. I reckon your pa's divided things up between you and your ma."

"Lady Bertha?" How dare this buffoon not give Lady Hardin her title. Margaret scowled. She'd given little thought to Papa's will.

"Lady Bertha." Jebediah nodded. "I'm not knowin' who she's gonna get to handle her part of the inheritance, but you've got a husband to guide you through your'n." He looked at Margaret as though she should understand his gibberish.

Jebediah tapped the closed drawer and walked around the front of the desk, leaning against its edge. Margaret took a step back.

"You're a married woman, Margaret. Law says it falls on the husband to manage his wife's affairs. Women not havin' no head for business."

"Law?" What was Jebediah saying?

He called out to Gopher Dennis, who rested both dirt-speckled hands on the back of Papa's damask couch. "Ain't that what you told me, Gopher?"

"I just got back from Texas, ma'am . . . Wildcattin'. Oil, you know. That's what Texas law says." He ran a hand along the top of the couch. "Husband's the head of the household in all things. Hell, all law says 'bout the same thing. What's your'n is sure 'nough your husband's."

Margaret's heart thumped. Papa had never included her in his business or legal doings. She knew very little of Arkansas law. "I'll ask Mr. Richardson tomorrow after he reads the will."

Jebediah turned to his friend. "Step outside a minute, will you, Gopher? I've got to talk to my wife."

Gopher Dennis moved past Margaret, then stopped with one foot in the hall. "Sure 'nough, I'll just go and make sure Tessie gets my lunch order right." His grin—more of a smirk—showed a missing eyetooth.

"You'll do no such thing. You will—"

Gopher Dennis closed the library door in her face.

"Margaret," Jebediah said, "I want you to know, I'm gonna come on you slow. I'm thinkin' you didn't have no good time with Sylvester Morse."

Her head throbbed. *Sylvester?* "Come on slow?" She'd never been good at riddles and hated when her old tutor posed his teachings in riddle form. She headed for the overstuffed chair nearest Papa's desk even though Jebediah was standing no more than five feet away. It couldn't be helped. Margaret had to sit.

"I know you and I ain't had a regular kind of marriage like other folks, but now that your pa's gone, we can start fresh."

Her head jerked up so hard, she heard the crack in her neck. "A fresh start?" She raised her voice. "Jebediah, I really don't know what it is you're trying to say about Hardin Acres, about marriage, about anything."

"Now that I am to run all this"—he leaned toward her—"it's time I start actin' like a real husband to you. Now, don't you fret. I'm gonna give you some time to get used to the idea of havin' me in your bed every night. I won't be movin' in until after the will's read."

The library door swung open. "What's all this commotion in here?" Lady Bertha stormed inside. "And who in the name of the Good Lord is that ruffian stomping around my house callin' for Tessie?" Lady Bertha scanned the room, and her glare landed first on Jebediah, then on Margaret. "What's this one doin' in my husband's library?"

Margaret looked at her mother. Maybe Lady Bertha could make sense of Jebediah's babbling. "He wants to come into my be . . ." She couldn't get the word out.

"What is wrong with you?" Lady Bertha advanced on Jebediah. "What have you done to my daughter? And what in tarnation are you doin' in this room? You know you're not allowed in here unless you're invited." Lady Bertha looked mad enough to pick up the paperweight from Papa's desk and smash Jebediah with it.

Jebediah pushed away from the desk. He wasn't a tall man, but even still, he towered over Mama. "That's just it, Ma Hardin, I ain't where I'm not invited. May your husband rest in peace, but he's gone to meet his maker, ain't he? I'm here lookin' for the key to the cabinet."

"Key to the cabinet? Jebediah Slocum, you've got no business with my husband's files."

"Ma'am, I'm afraid I've got all the business in the world. It's my wife what's gonna inherit half of all this." Jebediah spread his arms. "I'm Margaret's husband. Law says a husband's got last say over what the wife does with the money."

Lady Bertha slapped her hands onto her hips so hard the sound registered like a clap. "I've never heard of such foolishness in all my life. Jebediah Slocum, you know as well as me, you're nobody's real husband."

Jebediah nodded. "Yes, ma'am, I reckon I know the truth of that. All three of y'all—you, Lord Hardin, and Margaret—tried to pass off Morris as my boy. Never mind how I was feelin'." He turned to Margaret. "Wasn't no need to do all that. You could of tole me the truth. If you'd promised me just a little bit of friendly, I might have married you anyway. Even with you bein' a n—"

"Don't you go doin' us no favors, Jebediah Slocum. I know as well as you that my husband paid you and your no-good father a fortune to do your part." Walking over to the door, she opened it. "Now, Mr. Slocum, I'll thank you to get out of my house." She jerked her head toward the hall where Gopher Dennis had disappeared. "And take that thing with you."

Jebediah gave his head a slow shake. "Ain't quite gonna work like that, Miz Hardin. I've got myself some legal rights." He walked over to Margaret. "And you're one of 'em. I'll give you two more nights if you want—to get used to the idea." Before he moved into the hallway, Jebediah turned to Lady Bertha. "I'm gonna be needin' all them keys. I'd hate to go for the sheriff to make you turn 'em over." He stepped through the door.

Lady Bertha closed the door and turned to Margaret. "I don't know what this man's goin' on about, but I do know your papa was a clever man." She lowered herself to the armrest of Margaret's chair and ran a hand over Margaret's pomaded hair. "He'd never take a chance that Hardin Acres might fall into the hands of somethin' like that."

"You . . ." She looked into Lady's Bertha's face, trying to meet her eyes. "You called me your . . . daughter."

Lady Bertha licked her lips.

"You told Jebediah I was your daughter."

"Who do you think you are if not my daughter?" Lady Bertha laid soothing strokes against Margaret's cheeks as she stared at the drooping roses on the nearby table. "Oh, I'm not sayin' there wasn't many a day I wanted nothin' to do with you, but that feelin' didn't lay on you. You were a sweet, sweet baby." Lady Bertha stared at the flowers. "This was all 'bout Henry not loving me."

"I know what Papa did to you and I'm sorry he thought it necessary because of me." She couldn't stop the tremble in her voice. "But, Bertha, you were so mean to me for so long, I . . ."

Lady Bertha stared at the pattern in the rug. "I'm sayin' I know what I done." She looked up at Margaret. "I done wrong by you. I laid Henry's blame on you. He didn't allow me to put it anywhere else."

"The things you said. The things you did." Margaret pushed Bertha's hand away. "Now you want to make amends?"

"Time is movin' on for us all. I understand your forgivin' me might never come, but can you hear me out? That would mean the world to me."

Margaret spotted a corner of Papa's desk and settled her eyes on it. She nodded, neither a no nor a yes.

"You didn't have nothin' to do with none of it. No, this was about Henry hatin' me for not givin' him the babies he wanted so bad. 'Bout him lovin' another woman." Lady Bertha's voice trembled. "None of that had anythin' to do with you."

Margaret turned her head slowly toward her father's wife. "Another woman? Lady Bertha, are you saying my father actually loved her? Salome?"

Bertha folded her hands in her lap. "I know it seemed like I was hard on you, but I was really bein' hard on myself. I couldn't satisfy my husband. She could." Lower lip quivering, Lady Bertha held her breath for more than three ticks of the clock. "Yes. He loved her. Salome." The woman's eyes glistened. "I took all my mad and hurt against Henry out on you. But your papa did one good thing for me." A small smile tried to make its way across her lips. "Salome may have been the woman Henry gave his heart to, and she may have given birth to you, but you were my little girl. He gave you to me to raise, not to her." She picked up Margaret's hands. "I know I don't deserve it, but if you could find it in your heart to call me Mother Dear, it would do my soul ever so good."

"Your little girl? How am I supposed to believe that?" Margaret shook her head.

"Maybe it's myself I'm hatin' for my ugly-actin' ways. I don't know why I'm thinkin' it, but I do know if I let go of all those old feelin's, it's goin' to be a burden off my soul." She rested a hand on Margaret's arm. "If forgivin's not in your heart, Margaret, I can understand that. It's taken me all these years to feel what's in my heart. And I'm thinkin' I do love you."

CHAPTER
TWENTY-SEVEN

"Lady Margaret." Tessie tapped on the bedroom door. "Lady Bertha say come on down. It time. Lawyer Richardson, he waitin' in the liberry."

Sitting at her dressing table, Margaret laid down the powder puff and moved to the chair she'd slid under the knob of her bedroom door last night, just in case. But Jebediah hadn't taken the bother. She pushed the cushioned chair aside, undid the door latch, and followed Tessie down the back stairs.

"Uhh, Lady Margaret, they's some people there . . . well . . . you'll see." Tessie pointed to the open library door.

Puzzled, Margaret kept her eyes on Tessie as she stepped inside the doorway. No wonder the servant was hesitant. Even thinking about going back into that room where the boorish Gopher Dennis had accosted her brought unease.

"Thank you for joining us, Lady Margaret. You're the last person to arrive." Richardson, the balding lawyer, sat behind Papa's desk, a sheaf of papers spread in front of him. "Are you quite all right, Mrs. Slocum?" Richardson leaned forward and squinted at her face. "You do look pale."

Margaret started to lift a hand to her cheek, thought better of it, and nodded. "Yes, I'm quite fine."

"Then close the door, please, and we can begin." Richardson pointed to a chair next to Lady Bertha.

"Most everyone named in the will, or their representative, is in this room right now. I can commence with the important disbursements and read the particulars later, if you'd prefer." Richardson peered over his glasses at the group of nodding heads. Waylon, Tom-Tom, Lady Bertha, Jebediah. The servants. Then Margaret joined the others in the room.

"All right. Let us begin."

The room, already quiet, felt more silent than prayer hour at church.

"This is the last will and testament of Henry Hardin, born in Maryland, residing at the time of his death—September fourteenth, nineteen hundred and ten—in Union County, Arkansas. This here is a legal and binding document."

"I reckon we already know most of that." Jebediah kept his head bowed.

Margaret gasped.

Lawyer Richardson sighed. "Lord Hardin left money to a number of his favorite charities here in Arkansas and in Maryland, along with a generous bequest to Lisbon Baptist Church." He looked at Pastor Brown. "And the Archdiocese of Arkansas."

"The who? That sounds like the Catholics to me." Jebediah's head jerked up. "He gave money to idol worshipers?"

Margaret looked straight ahead.

Richardson gave a look of disbelief as he let out a second sigh. "Shall we continue?"

"Let's do," Lady Bertha spoke up.

"Lord Hardin left a thousand dollars a year—each—for the rest of their lives to Delfine and Celeste. Tessie and Georgia are to receive five hundred a year for life, each."

"Praise Jesus," Celeste called out.

"Mon Dieu." Delfine's muffled voice carried tears.

"And, Salome . . ." Richardson kept his eyes on the sheet of paper before him.

Margaret heard Bertha suck in a breath. She looked across the room at Salome's two boys—her brothers. So that was why they were here. To support grief-ridden Salome, who hadn't left her room in a week. Both boys appeared chiseled from stone.

"Salome gets five thousand dollars a year for the rest of her life."

"What the hell?" Jebediah's face blanched. He scanned the room before turning back to Richardson. "I heard tell of takin' care of your colored wench, but not like this."

"May I continue, Lady Bertha?"

"Please do." Lady Bertha reached an arm across the distance toward Margaret.

"That's it for the servants. There are, of course, the usual small bequests for the butcher, the baker, and such. Would you care to have me read those now?"

Henry's wife shook her head. "I think I'm ready to hear what Henry's done."

"Very well. Lady Bertha, Lord Hardin has allowed you to remain at Hardin House for the rest of your natural life. He has given your care, feeding, clothing, all your expenses, over to the discretion of your daughter—Margaret Hardin Slocum. She will be in complete charge of your finances."

Jebediah turned a full-face grin toward Lady Bertha. He mouthed what looked like *Where's the keys?* to his mother-in-law.

Margaret stroked her mother's freckled hand. Too many years of bitterness. She gently squeezed Bertha's fingers. "I'll take good care of you, Mother Dear."

"Lord Hardin has seen fit to divide his holdings in a bit of an unusual way." Richardson ran a hand over the top of his head. "As he had requested, I followed through with a thorough research of the law, lookin' for any possible loopholes or evasions that might undo his last wishes. I found none. His bequests are all quite legal and bindin'. Even in Arkansas."

"When does my wife get her money?" Jebediah's voice was low but insistent.

"Mr. Slocum"—Mr. Richardson looked as though he wished he had a horsewhip handy—"Lord Hardin has given this house to his daughter, Margaret Hardin Slocum, along with one-third of his remaining estate."

Jebediah began to smile, then his eyes hooded. "What you mean, one-third of his estate? How much is that?"

Richardson looked toward the ceiling—plainly calling on the Deity. "Three people will inherit the bulk of Lord Hardin's estate—thus, one third."

Jebediah settled back in his chair. "Uhm?" He stretched out his fingers. "Margaret gets one of them three parts. I get the next part, but Lady Bertha . . ." He turned to his mother-in-law and frowned. "You just said she don't get nothin'. So who's getting that last part?"

Richardson removed his glasses and tapped them on the desk. "Sir, are you Mr. Jebediah Slocum, the husband of Margaret Hardin Slocum?"

Jebediah grinned, his angled front tooth plain to see. "I am that."

"Then Lord Hardin has written a special section of his will just for you."

"I waited me a long time for him to say his sorrys."

"Arkansas law allows a husband to manage his wife's affairs in inherited money unless that husband is specifically excluded from his wife's estate by her benefactor."

Jebediah grimaced as he leaned forward in his chair. "What's that excluded and benefactor thing got to do with me?"

"You, sir, have been left four thousand dollars a year for every year you remain married to Margaret Hardin. If she decides to terminate the marriage through"—Richardson wrinkled his nose—"divorce, you are to receive nothing. In addition, you have been excluded from any and all management of the bequeathed property gifted to Lady Margaret."

"I . . . I don't understand." Jebediah shook his head.

"You've been cut off, you fool," Lady Bertha spoke up. "You've been given less than Salome and that, only if you follow Margaret's rules." She glared at the man. "Now do you understand?"

"No. I don't understan' nothin' 'bout this three parts business. If Margaret gets a part and you and me don't get nothin', then who gets the other two parts?"

Lawyer Richardson picked up a sheet of paper. "'I, Henry Hardin, also known as the duke of Union County, and being of sound mind and body, hereby bequeath to Waylon Hardin one-third of all my assets including his exclusive use of, and all profits from, the timberlands. He is to use part of his inheritance to support his mother, Salome, the rest of her natural life.'"

"Me?" Waylon's voice boomed out from the corner of the room. "My fa . . . Lord Hardin's left something for me?" He stepped away from the concealing draperies and joined his mother. "I was told to come here this morning, but . . . I thought maybe a small memento, the paperweight on his desk, a small photograph . . . I never thought, never dreamed . . . Me? Lord Hardin . . . he's left me . . . ?"

"One-third of all his assets. A fortune." Richardson peered over to a corner of the room. "There's more." Richardson cleared his throat. "'I pass on to Waylon Hardin the exclusive use of the title I assumed since my arrival in Arkansas. He may style himself as Lord Waylon, duke of Union County.'"

"I'll be damned!" Jebediah jumped to his feet and stomped around his chair.

"Sit down, Mr. Slocum, there's more." Richardson adjusted the spectacle wire behind his right ear. "'I leave one-third of all my assets, including exclusive use of, and total profits from, the agricultural fields, to Thomas Hardin—known as Tom-Tom. He, too, is to support his mother, Salome, from these proceeds. Deeds shall be executed to convey proper title to the above-named three persons—Margaret Hardin Slocum, Waylon Hardin, and Thomas Hardin.'"

"I'll be double damned. Waylon and Tom-Tom? Named in a will? I ain't never, ever, heard tell of coloreds inheritin' that kind of money!" Jebediah's face went the color of communion grape juice.

"Now you have, Mr. Slocum. Now you have." Mr. Richardson settled back into Papa's leather chair.

"I'm protestin'. Such a thing can't be legal in Arkansas." Jebediah stalked to the desk.

"You wish to contest Henry Hardin's last will and testament?" Richardson peered over his glasses at Jebediah.

"Damn right, I do."

"Fine, as long as you understand that by doing so, your four-thousand-dollar-a-year inheritance will be cut down to a thousand." He fumbled through the papers on Papa's desk. Richardson picked up a sheet as he tapped his spectacles back in place. "'Anyone contesting the terms of this will—specifically, Jebediah Slocum—shall have his or her benefits reduced by seventy-five percent.'"

"Huh?" Jebediah sputtered.

"Settle down, Jebediah." Lady Bertha stroked the bodice of her dress. "You act right and do exactly as my daughter tells you, and you just might be able to keep that four thousand dollars you get each and every year."

"This here can't be right." Jebediah turned to Margaret. "You knew 'bout this all along, didn't you?"

Richardson cleared his throat. "If you wish to contest the terms of the will, I can give you the appropriate forms." He held out two sheets of paper. "Otherwise, I need to speak privately with the three main beneficiaries." Waggling papers in the air, he looked around the room.

Lady Bertha was the first to stand. "Jebediah, what's your poison?"

Jebediah shot Margaret one final glare as he stalked out of the room just ahead of the others, Tessie bringing up the rear. "This ain't over."

"Now, Margaret, Waylon, and Thomas, will one of you lock that door?" Richardson pointed to the library entrance. "Now that Jebediah is safely out of earshot . . . Lord Hardin has left specific instructions just for you three."

Margaret always wondered how Salome's boys carried the Hardin name. Salome had merely snatched the Hardin name away from its rightful owners to use as her own. The woman who gave birth to Margaret had really been an O'Brien—after the Irish overseer. Now Margaret understood the full truth of it. In death, Papa had acknowledged his two sons as his own body children in a way he couldn't in life. Waylon scooted his chair in front of Papa's desk so that he and Tom-Tom sat on either side of her.

"As I've just explained"—Richardson removed his glasses—"Lord Hardin saw fit to divide his land into three equal sections."

"Yes." Tom-Tom nodded.

"Thomas and Margaret, I'm not sure if you know how extensive those land holdings are." He turned to Waylon. "I suspect you do."

Waylon pursed his lips. "After I returned from Tuskegee, Lord Hardin asked me to look after his property, so yes, I do have some idea. A stretch of land a little over six miles wide and one mile deep."

"That's correct." Richardson's fingers strummed the desktop. "And those holdings have been divided into three equal parts as I explained at the reading. You will each receive the exact same number of hectares. Two—"

"Hectares?" Margaret said. Why hadn't she studied as hard with their tutor as Waylon had?

"A real estate measurement, my dear. In layman's terms, you will receive land approximately two miles long and one mile deep, along with mineral rights"—he turned to Waylon—"as will you and Thomas."

Thomas shook his head. "I can't believe . . . Lord Hardin . . . I was never his favorite. Why would he be so generous to me?"

Richardson looked in Tom-Tom's direction. "Lord Hardin never discussed his reasons with me." He shook his head. "But there are complications." He turned to Margaret. "Mrs. Slocum, you are married to Jebediah. Lord Hardin did express concern about your husband's ability to . . . uh . . . manage your investments."

"Investments?" Waylon got the word out first, but she and Tom-Tom weren't far behind.

"Yes, that is one of the complications. You will remember from the reading of the will that Waylon has inherited the profits from timberland, and Thomas, those from the agricultural pursuits. Both self-sustaining resources. You will both be quite wealthy for a long, long time."

"And Lady Margaret?" Waylon frowned.

"Ah, yes. She has inherited Hardin House and all the expenses that go along with it. However, her source of income will not come from timber or agriculture, but rather from investments made over the years by Lord Hardin. Mostly in stocks and bonds. In New York."

"Stocks and bonds? New York?" Margaret heard her voice rise. "I know nothing about such things."

"Precisely. That's why Lord Hardin has prepared this addendum to the will. Lady Margaret, if you will agree, your father wished to contract with Waylon to manage your investments. He feared if they were not handled properly—or were left to your husband—you would soon be bankrupt. If you allow Waylon to do the job, then you will retain an income equal to that of the other two heirs."

Margaret sat back in her chair. "What sorts of investments?"

"Lord Hardin has chosen wisely. Railroads, Standard Oil, utilities—a highly profitable portfolio. You should do just fine under proper management."

Margaret glanced over at her brother. Her financial future, indeed the future of Hardin House, now rested in the hands of the boy she'd tormented as her natural-born inferior all through their school years. "What did you say about mineral rights?"

"Ah, yes. That is the second possible complication." Richardson fumbled with his glasses. "As I said, I believe I've closed every loophole, but there is always the possibility—though slim—that someone will find a way around the various rights inherent to this property."

"Would those be the mineral rights?" Waylon leaned forward.

Richardson shook his head. "Yes, but I wouldn't put too much stock in those. Ever since the California and Alaska gold strikes, and the silver strike in Nevada, every purchaser of land has sought to include mineral rights in their deeds. Lord Hardin secured such rights for all his properties and as such, they will be passed on to you." He pulled out a handkerchief and wiped his glasses. "Under Arkansas law, each deeded property is layered with rights. Mineral rights are just one of them. There is also the right to water."

"You mean the creek that runs through Hardin Acres?" Tom-Tom lifted his chin.

Richard replaced his glasses. "The very same. Mineral rights have a slim chance of ever amounting to anything. Striking gold in Arkansas is about as likely as traveling to the moon. Water rights are far more important." He turned first to Margaret, then to each of her brothers. "All three of you will need to be vigilant to protect your water rights. Water is essential in farm country." He shook his head. "Unscrupulous men have been known to take devious—indeed, deadly—actions to obtain water rights from careless owners."

"Steal them, you mean," Waylon said with a nod.

"And kill for them." Richardson's face reddened as he looked at Margaret. He must have realized he had misspoken. "Again, I believe I've constructed airtight deeds to protect all your rights—especially water—but I caution all three of you, be ever observant. Especially you, Waylon, and you, Thomas. Water rights in the hands of . . ." He cleared his throat. "That is to say, some of our good citizens might have a problem with Negras holdin' such important rights."

Margaret sucked in her lips as she laid a hand on the desk. "Where's the pen? If my father thought it best, I'm quite prepared to have Waylon look after my water interest as well as all the rest." She looked up to see the hint of a smile flicker across her brother's face.

CHAPTER TWENTY-EIGHT

The stink of slow-cooking chitlins drew Salome out of her latest cat-nap. She flicked open her eyes to see the newly risen sun through her windows. A good hour past dawn, she reckoned, and time to get up for good. She eased her feet off her soft feather mattress and down to the blue-bordered rug on her bedroom floor. Time to check yet again on the pots she'd set to the fire last night.

Knock. Knock. Now, who on earth could be at her front door at seven o'clock on New Year's Day? Salome grabbed her robe, slipped it over her rosebud-print flannel nightdress, walked down the stairs, sniffed the chitlins mingling with the ham hocks and the black-eyed peas, and hesitated at her kitchen door. All three of her simmering pots needed a stir—especially her greens.

Knock. Knock. Louder this time. She'd go straight back to her kitchen as soon as she opened the door. Who had the nerve to come calling before decent folk were up and about? Her curtains were still drawn so she couldn't peek through the window to get a look at her early-morning visitor. She reached her door.

"Who's standin' outside my house so early in the mornin'?"

Knock. Knock. Knock.

Salome pulled open the door and smiled. "Lord, if that ain't you, Maxwell Joe."

Her guest, clean-shaven for so early an hour, stood there grinning at her. "Now, I could turn myself around and head on off to some other woman's house if it's not good luck you be wantin', Miz Salome." He turned sideways to her like he was about to go.

The laugh rising out of her belly felt good. She reached out a hand and grabbed Maxwell Joe's coat sleeve. "You better cross this threshold if you know what's good fo' you."

He pulled back, his head in a mock shake. "I don't know, Miz Salome. The old folks tell me if the first visitor to yo' house on New Year's Day is a man, then nothing but good luck gonna follow you all year long." He made a show of trying to walk off her front porch. "What you gonna give me if I steps across yo' threshold and brings you luck fo' this brand-new year of nineteen hundred and thirteen?"

Salome released the man and opened her door wider. She said nothing as the smell of chitlins, greens, black-eyed peas, and the sweet potato pie she'd baked yesterday rushed into the chill air of a Union County January first. She didn't need to.

"All right, all right." Maxwell Joe stepped across her threshold. "Can't no man resist Miz Salome's cookin'."

"You know you got me outta bed with yo' early-mornin' shenanigans. Come on into the kitchen and I'll make you a pot of coffee."

"Can I get me a sample of yo' greens whilst you at it?" He walked behind her. "Eatin' greens on New Year's Day means money's a'comin'."

"I reckon it do." Salome still had a hard time remembering that money was no longer a bother for her. How many dollars did Waylon say she had in the bank in Little Rock? (Her son didn't trust the banker in Lisbon.) Ten, twelve thousand, was it?

Maxwell Joe pulled up a chair at the kitchen table and sat. Salome gave the pots a stir, went to her newfangled sink with its water pump, and filled the coffeepot.

"It's the black-eyed peas I'm fancyin' most, I reckon." Maxwell Joe smoothed out a wrinkle in his jacket.

Salome put the coffee beans she'd ground just yesterday into the coffeepot and set it on her one empty burner. She took herself a good look at Maxwell Joe. The man sure was spiffy for this early in the morning.

"Well, Maxwell Joe, you get back here fo' dinner at one, and you can eat yo' fill of everythin'. Everythin' but the chitlins is done, seems like." She turned off the stove eyes.

"Greens is fo' money. Black-eyed peas fo' luck." He moved to his feet, his mouth working like words had stuck in his throat.

Salome frowned.

"Miz Salome, ma'am . . ."

She stared at him. "What you wantin', Maxwell Joe?"

"I'm wantin' to say . . . it's luck I'll be needin'."

Salome cocked her head. "Maxwell Joe, you tryin' to get ahold of my New Year's Day dinner fo' yo' breakfast?"

He reached her before she could blink. His hands gripped her shoulders; his face, just inches from her own, looked down at her.

"I knows, Miz Salome. It's been over two years. Fo'give me if I'm rushin' you or anythin'."

His breath was awfully sweet for a just-woke-up man, and what on earth was Maxwell Joe doing smelling like bay rum aftershave? She laid her hands on his waist. "What is it, Maxwell Joe? Somethin' amiss? What is it you know?"

He took a step back, but he kept his hands on her shoulders. "I knows you ain't wanted it, but it jest normal that after so many years, well . . . you'd miss the man."

Breaking Maxwell Joe's hold, Salome took a step backward. Henry. The carpenter was talking about Henry Hardin, dead since 1910. But why?

Maxwell Joe's face creased in worry. "I ain't sayin' it right, Miz Salome. I jest wants you to know I understands 'bout . . . 'bout you and Lord Hardin."

Salome raised her voice. "You understands about me and Lord Hardin? What is it you thinkin' you understand, Maxwell Joe?"

"Yo' feelin's." He held up a quick hand. "No, ma'am, I ain't sayin' you was wantin' it. Wantin' him. Not none of it. It's jest that . . ."

Salome clutched at her stomach. Oh Lord, her belly hurt. "You right." The pain in her stomach raced up to her eyes and loosened tears she thought had dried up two years ago. "Oh Lord, Glory, Maxwell Joe, what is it you thinkin'?" Though she wished to, her eyes refused to let her look in the carpenter's face. She stared at a button on his jacket sleeve instead. "I didn't want that man—Henry Hardin—nowhere near me in the beginnin', but I got used to him. And . . . and . . ." Her throat tightened with all the salt from her tears dripping into it.

Maxwell Joe slipped his arms around her before she could take another step.

"Miz Salome, you ain't got to tell me nothin' 'bout yo' feelin's fo' the man. A colored woman in a white man's bed ain't got no real choice in how her feelin's go." He hugged her to his chest. "I don't need to know if you think you favored him or no."

"Favored him?" Salome's words were muffled by Maxwell Joe's shoulder. "You thinkin' I favored Henry Hardin? I reckon it's time you know 'bout my feelin's fo' that man." She pressed her cheek against his arm. "It be true. I had me feelin's fo' him, all right. 'Specially in them later years when Henry was so good to Margaret, to Waylon, to Tom-Tom." She swallowed. "And to me." She pushed far enough away to see into Maxwell Joe's face. "But I ain't got me no real word to tell you what them feelin's was. They falls somewhere between *obey* and *cherish* with *tolerate* in the middle." She shook her head. "But I gots me no stumblin' over the word I feels fo' you."

Maxwell Joe stared into her eyes so hard, she was sure she could see right into the deepest part of the man's soul.

"*Love*. That's my word fo' you. Been my word fo' thirty years."

It looked like Maxwell Joe stopped breathing for the passing of a minute. Then his cheek muscles twitched. His arms moved out from his body and wrapped themselves around her so tight she worried he was about to squeeze the life out of her.

"Lord, Jesus. Praise God." He moved her to arm's length. "Salome, ever since I first stepped foot on Hardin Acres and saw you walkin' down the path to yo' little house, I knowed never, ever, anywhere in this world was there ever gonna be another woman like you. Not fo' me." He jerked her to his chest. "Salome, girl"—his breath hotter even than the warmth of her kitchen, brushed the top of her head—"I love you more'n I love all the angels put together, more'n I love . . ." Letting her go, he took a quick step backward. "I liked to forget." He reached into his jacket pocket and pulled out a small cardboard box. He dropped to his knees on her kitchen floor.

"Maxwell Joe, what you doin' down there?" Her heart thumped.

Shifting his weight, he raised up on one knee. He worked the lid off the cardboard box. His hand fumbled at something inside. Maxwell Joe pinched a thing between his fingers. He held the object in front of her—something slender and silver, topped with a white pearl. Maxwell Joe held out a ring.

"I knows this here ring ain't much of nothin' compared to what you can get fo' yo'self these days, but it would please me powerful much, Miz Salome, if you was to take this here ring my daddy give to my mama when they was finally able to get hitched legal-like."

Salome straightened, put her hands on her hips, and laid on a pretend frown. "Maxwell Joe, stop goin' on 'bout how the ring come about, and tell me why it is you wavin' that thing around my kitchen with yo' hand shakin' so?"

Maxwell Joe's face took on the look of a man struck with the galloping consumption. Salome wanted to laugh, to shout, but she knew she had to hold herself back.

"Oh, Miz Salome, I'm more than fifty years old, and I ain't never done this befo'." Which shook most, his hand or his voice? "Miz Salome, please, would you consider, would you think on, would you ponder, would you . . ."

"Maxwell Joe!" She couldn't help it: a little giggle escaped.

He shook his head more than a chicken having its neck wrung. "Ma'am, Salome, would you . . . could you . . . I'd like it a powerful lot if you would . . . marry me."

"After all that time it took fo' you to get out them words, I 'spects I'm too old to be anybody's wife."

Maxwell Joe looked like he just spotted a hatchet swinging in his direction.

"Yes!" Salome grabbed his wrist. "Now get yo'self on up from there and put that thing on my finger."

Salome couldn't tell if the sounds coming out of her brand-new fiancé were laughs or cries, but the man climbed to his feet, grabbed her finger, and jammed the ring on it, acting for all the world like he'd forgotten the fine touch needed for making his best carpentry. Maxwell Joe pulled her into another of his chest-squeezing hugs.

He rocked her in his arms for what felt like two minutes before he turned her loose. He kept one eye cocked.

"Miz Sal . . . Salome, I am mighty sorry I caught you so early in the mornin'." He wrinkled his nose. "'Pear to me you could be in need of a bath in that fancy new indo' bathroom of your'n." He tugged at the belt on her wrapper.

"Ooh?" Salome sniffed her underarm. She started to reach for his hand and then dropped her arms to her sides. "Oh. Bath." She nodded.

Maxwell Joe opened her wrapper, grunted, raised his hands to her shoulders, and slid the garment to the floor. He frowned as he looked at her neck-to-ankle flannel winter nightie. One hand reached for the buttons in the front. Salome held her breath as he undid one, two, three, four—down to her chest. His hands slid to her knees and gathered up yards of flannel. He worked the gown past her thighs, beyond her hips, to her chest, and over her head. She was fifty-two years old. No more the young girl's tight body that had thrilled Henry Hardin. Her breasts had been full and round twins back then. The size and shape hadn't changed all that much; they just sat a bit lower these days. But Salome could see none of that reflected in the eyes of Maxwell Joe. His breath came quick and warm as he squeezed one breast, then the other. One hand ran down her belly while the other stroked the roundness of her backside. She smiled. Her husband-to-be lifted her naked body into his arms and headed up her stairs.

CHAPTER
TWENTY-NINE

Waylon stood on his veranda, squinting at the sky. That was definitely a patch of blue, and the last thunderclap had been over an hour ago. He turned toward the big picture window fronting his entry hall. Havoc was breaking loose inside. The birthday boy, Freddie, ran between the tables Maxwell Joe had dragged into the entry just as the drops of April rain turned serious. And now, here were twenty children, their parents, grandparents, uncles, and aunts, all congregating in his foyer, helping Waylon's eldest celebrate his twelfth birthday.

"Waylon—'scuse me, I meant to say *Lord Hardin*." Maxwell Joe chuckled as he stepped from around the corner. He turned toward Waylon. "Eleven years since the first Lord Hardin passed, and I still ain't got used to callin' you by yo' right title."

"I guess you're Papa to me these days. And all that old stuff—Lord this and Lady that—means nothing to me." Something thumped inside the house. "I'll tell you what does mean something. All that commotion going on inside my own front door, what with Freddie's birthday party."

"Oh, yo' name mean plenty to the colored folk in Union County. They proud as punch one of our own got hisself such nice doin's." Maxwell Joe grinned. "Can't quite git myself to believe little Freddie twelve years old already. Seem like he jest born yesterday."

"Well, yesterday was nineteen aught nine. This is Arkansas's year of our Lord, nineteen hundred and twenty-one." Waylon took a step toward his front door. Nothing as grand and pretentious as Hardin House, but his own twelve-room, two-story, colonnaded structure was substantial enough to house his growing family of six along with three of his five servants. He looked back at his stepfather. "I won't have a house at all if I can't move that mob outside."

"Give that back!" Morehouse, Tom-Tom's nine-year-old, screamed out to the sound of feet running up, down, and around stairs.

"No! It's mine." Waylon's daughter, Joe-Annie, accompanied her protest with a smack to a china bowl, sending it crashing to the checkerboard marble floor.

"See what I mean?" Waylon turned back to Maxwell Joe.

The front door opened and Salome, worry scrunching down on her forehead, stepped outside. She pulled her shawl around her as she closed the door. "Waylon, you gonna have to take hold of that daughter of your'n. I can get ahold of yo' other young'uns and straighten them out quick, but that Joe-Annie, she's a pistol."

"Mama, she's just high-spirited." Like her grandmother.

Salome didn't look like she was having any of it. She turned back to Maxwell Joe and pointed a finger. "Well, Grandpa, ain't you gonna talk some sense into her?"

"He hit me!" The wail of somebody's child burst out onto the veranda.

"I did not! That was her." Joe-Annie's rising voice carried disgust.

"Yes, she did," Morehouse called out. "I saw the whole thing. Mama, aren't you going to do something?"

The door burst open and Joe-Annie careened onto the veranda. Within seconds the girl spotted her savior. She ran straight to Maxwell Joe.

"Grandpa Joe, I didn't do it. I didn't do it." Joe-Annie knew just how to play her grandfather.

Waylon wanted to plant his hands over his ears as Ladora stormed out of the house. Tom-Tom's wife stopped almost as soon as she spotted her in-laws. Sometimes Waylon wondered if there was a trick that made some men good at this fathering business. His own father, Lord Hardin, certainly didn't have the knack, at least not for him, while childless Maxwell Joe was a natural.

Ladora clenched and unclenched her hands over and over. Tom-Tom's wife was pretty enough, though her maiden figure had broadened considerably with the births of two children these past twelve years. "Miz Salome, ma'am, I can't do nothin' with that granddaughter of your'n . . . Morehouse, he say he saw her—"

"Grandpa Joe"—Joe-Annie knew just when to start her defense— "tell Aunt Ladora I never hit Alexander, and I didn't take Morehouse's toy gun, either."

Ever since Joe-Annie turned two and first trotted out that blazing smile and irrepressible charm, Waylon knew he had a battle on his hands to control his incorrigible girl. Here she was, ten, his golden-skinned daughter with the oversize green eyes and cascading curls—far less kinky than Lady Margaret's—and she already possessed all the earmarks of a real beauty, and a father's nightmare. Maxwell Joe was putty in her hands.

Salome raised her voice as she walked to the edge of the veranda and watched Joe-Annie wrap her arms around her grandfather. "Let me have that girl. You much too soft on this one jest 'cause Waylon done named her after you. Could be the truth she done somethin' wrong in there jest now."

Maxwell Joe unwrapped Joe-Annie's arms, bent down, and peered into her face. How did this child learn to make those guilty-as-sin eyes look so innocent? Waylon shook his head. Too bad acting was not a respectable job for the daughter and granddaughter of a duke of Union County, because this girl was a natural.

"Could it be, sugar pie"—Maxwell Joe laid his big hands across Joe-Annie's shoulders—"that Morehouse's toy gun done fell on the flo' and you jest happen to pick it up lessen you stumble over it by accident, like?"

Joe-Annie nodded her head. "Almost like that, Grandpa Joe." She put the perfect quiver into her voice.

"And that other chile jest happen to run into yo' arm when you swung around quick-like?"

Waylon watched his girl squeeze out a tear as she made her bottom lip tremble. She gave her head a slow nod.

"Seein' this here was done jest by accident, why don't you go on and give Morehouse back his toy gun? Because you sech a big girl, I'm thinkin' it wouldn't hurt you none to tell that there little boy, Alexander, you is sorry he ran smack-dab into yo' fist. That be all right with you?"

As quickly as the two fake tears rolled down her face, Joe-Annie summoned the sun. She reached up, kissed Maxwell Joe on the cheek, then headed upstairs only to be met by the considerable figure of Salome. Waylon stepped back. He held the back of his hand to his mouth. He had grown to love these exchanges between two of the strong-willed women in his life.

"Ain't I taught you wrong from right, girl?" Salome blocked her granddaughter's path.

Now the green eyes opened wide as Joe-Annie leaned forward and brought out her best pretend-whisper. "Grandma, you just said *ain't*. Mama says we're not supposed to use that word."

Waylon watched his mother's mouth open for a second. She made a quick half step backward. That was all it took. Joe-Annie zoomed around Salome, rushed past him, bumped into Ladora, and burst into the entry hall.

"I'm sorry, everybody. Let's eat cake." Joe-Annie's voice drowned in the shouts and claps coming from inside.

Salome folded her arms and turned her full wrath on Maxwell Joe. "Now what you got to say fo' yo'self? You tryin' to raise a chile to tell fibs to her elders?"

Waylon kept his smile to himself. Poor Maxwell Joe—caught between a rock and Salome. If the man knew what was good for him, he'd find a way to slip out from between the two.

"Let me git on 'round to the back. I'm gonna see if y'all's new cook gonna allow me to use her pantry fo' these young'uns to play in." Maxwell Joe scampered almost to the corner of the house. "Old folks can go into the front and back parlors." He disappeared around the corner. "Mo' rain a'comin'."

Waylon glanced at the sky. The gathering clouds threatened thunder. Just what he needed. Thunder, lightning, and screaming children. Waylon rubbed the right side of his head.

"Lord Waylon, suh. Somebody round back to see y'all." Mae Ollie, one of Waylon's downstairs maids, stood at the front door.

"Who?"

Lady Margaret, Mae Ollie mouthed.

Waylon made his way down the front steps and around to the back door. He knew his sister had to keep her visits to his house more or less a secret from her husband. Jebediah didn't object when Waylon and Margaret met in Mr. Richardson's law office once a month to go over her portfolio, but his grumbling had increased over the years every time Waylon showed up on the front lawn of Hardin House—white and black never crossed each another's thresholds—to collect his nephews,

Morris and Junior, for their learning rounds. Not that Morris had ever shown the slightest interest in learning anything about the timber business. The boy reflected the attitude of his white grandfather, Jacob Slocum. What was a colored man doing holding all the strings to his white mother's fortune? Waylon and Margaret talked many a time about her children. She was determined neither would ever know about their colored blood.

"Margaret?" He looked at his sister standing next to his back door. "Is something wrong?"

She shook her head. "Not a thing." She glanced over her shoulder as she took out her hat pin and adjusted the bonnet covering her frizzy but still light-colored hair. At forty-two, Margaret showed very few strands of gray. "I just wanted to wish Freddie a happy birthday and give him this." She held out a box wrapped in blue and tied with navy-blue ribbon. She leaned in close. "It's Papa's paperweight. I think Freddie's old enough now to appreciate a legacy from his Hardin grandfather."

"Freddie's old enough, you say? He's twelve. Morris just turned twenty and Junior, nineteen. What about their legacy from their grandmother?"

"Oh, don't start that again, Waylon. You know I can't say a word about Salome."

"And why not? Jebediah's under control. If he lays a hand on you, he knows you'll head for the divorce courts. Then, he's out on his as . . . ear."

Margaret sucked in her lips. "Oh, he hasn't laid a hand on me. He knows better, but he does keep hinting at . . . that he knows about me." She stared at the grass surrounding Waylon's back door. "It's his father. Jacob Slocum keeps spreading the talk." She glanced up. "He's been poisoning those children against me."

"Junior doesn't act at all poisoned."

Margaret nodded. "I'm glad I took your advice and sent him up north to school. He'll graduate from Yale in a few years." His sister looked into the distance. "After that, I don't know."

Waylon watched a squirrel climb a tree as the clouds overhead darkened. He did know. Junior—Jebediah's only body child—was the most unlikely Slocum of all. Though Margaret had as little to do with his rearing as she had with Morris, somehow Junior turned his back on Jacob Slocum's colored-hating ways. Escape to the North had been the boy's answer to all that was Jacob Slocum and Union County. "I'll make sure Freddie sends a thank-you note."

His sister turned to leave. "Boys are not big on writing notes, I've noticed."

Waylon heard the sound of a motorcar churning along his road. He looked up. Morris Slocum, a straw hat set at a peculiar angle on his head, sat behind the wheel. Morris—son of a white rapist—was the real worry. Not Junior.

"Uh-huh. I thought I'd find you here." The engine shuddered as he turned off the ignition.

"Have you followed me in that new car?" Margaret turned a reproachful face to her son.

"No, Mother Dear, I ain't been followin' you. I come to talk to Waylon here." Morris opened the car door. "Has it come to your attention that I had to beg you, practically on my knees, to get this Model T?" He stepped out of the Ford. "Waylon, here, the man who's supposed to be watchin' your investments. So, how come he's the one with a brand-new Lincoln Model L, and I'm reduced to driving a Ford?"

"Morris, I've asked you not to use the word *ain't*. It sounds so uneducated."

"Talk proper like you and"—he sneered at Waylon—"him? Well, I'd rather talk like Pa and Grandpa—respectable white Southerners—and not like some upcountry, prissy Maryland dandy . . . or like coloreds who forget their place in this world."

"Your grandfather was the duke of Union County, I'll remind you." Margaret looked more annoyed than she sounded.

"So how come we don't own all his duke property?" Morris leaned back against the dusty black Ford. "I keep askin' myself, *What's a thing like that doin' with any part of my grandpa's holdings?* And why is he allowed to call himself the duke of anything? I'm my grandfather's blood descendant." He glared at Waylon.

Waylon hoped that little twitch in his sister's cheek went unnoticed.

"I've explained all that. That title's not real or anything. Papa just decided to give it to Waylon as a reward for his loyalty. It means nothing."

"Is that right, Ma? Why do you always take up for this colored? Makin' me trail him around learning about a business that will do me no good? What do I care about timber? All those profits go to him—a colored."

Margaret refitted her hat, jabbing in the three-inch pin. "If you know how one business works, you can transfer that knowledge to another."

"And if I do learn, will I be the one put in charge of our family investments instead of him?"

"I begged you to go to college, Morris. Your brother listened."

"My brother." Morris spit a pretend stream of tobacco juice on the ground. "Junior's never acted like a real Slocum. He's weak." He grimaced. "Ma, Pa will thank you to get on home. It's a good thing my father's not a beatin' man, but if I was you, I wouldn't try his patience. Grandpa Slocum taught me how to treat a woman. Tried to teach Pa, too, but he and Junior are two peas in a pod. Can't tell them a thing."

"Morris," Margaret said with a scowl, "I think it best you get back to the house."

Morris folded his arms across his chest. "Grandpa Slocum told me stories about how he brought Grandma to heel when they first got married. *Got to get to them on day one,* he says. Every time Grandma did the least little thing wrong, he whacked her. Started with a slap. If she was still slow to understand, then he tanned her behind with his hand. If she kicked up too much of a fuss—especially if she went blabbing to her ma about being mistreated—he really lit into her. Whomped her good with his thickest leather strop."

Waylon watched his sister cringe. "Morris . . ." He took a step forward. "I'm not sure this is a tale for a lady's ears."

"Oh, no? My Slocum family stories ain't as fancy in the telling as the Hardins'?"

Waylon shook his head. Morris had never been an easy child—petulant, argumentative—almost a carbon copy of the grandfather who had pretty much raised him. But one look at his sister warned Waylon to hold his tongue.

"Grandpa Slocum makes me pay heed to his words. Says I'll get married someday and I'll need to let the woman know up front the price she's going to pay for disobeying her lawful husband."

Margaret looked at the dust on her shoes.

Her son pasted a half smile on his face. "Ma, I'm thinking you ought to be grateful Pa doesn't take after his father. On the other hand, it's never too late for Pa to heed Grandpa's words. I suggest you get in your buggy and get on home just in case Pa finally gets fed up with you and your hifalutin airs." Young Slocum stepped back into the Ford and turned on the engine. "Tell Tessie to have Cook fry up a chicken dinner for me. Don't know when I'll be back. I'm off to the diggings. Gopher says he's close."

Hifalutin airs, was it? Waylon held his tongue in check. If anyone took on hifalutin airs, it was his sister's child by that monster, Sylvester Morse. "Margaret . . ." Waylon looked at her as Morris drove off. "You sure you're all right with Jebediah? Why don't you divorce the man?"

"You think I don't want to? I can't. Jebediah says he'll tell the children about me being . . . you know."

"Your husband's bluffing. Jebediah doesn't know for sure. He's like his father—threatening to stir up all that old gossip."

"Waylon, I can't take that chance. If Jebediah does talk . . . having my boys find out about themselves that way . . . it would be devastating. Especially for Morris. If he discovers he's not only colored but also the child of rape, I don't think he's strong enough to understand."

Waylon helped his sister into her buggy. He wanted so much to relieve her worry, but how? She would never willingly allow herself to be known as anything other than a white woman. He watched the horse trot up the road back to Hardin House just as the April clouds dropped their wet load.

CHAPTER THIRTY

"What are you doing in here?" Margaret opened the door to her bed-room. Jebediah stood at the foot of her four-poster. "Where's Tessie?" What was her husband doing in her room? First, that unpleasant encounter with Morris this afternoon—in front of Waylon—and now her husband entering her bedroom. The man knew to keep to his own quarters across the hall.

"Where is Tessie ever? Fixin' to tattle on me 'bout ever' little thing." Jebediah made no sign of moving.

"I thought you were going out to that dry digging with your no-account friend, Gopher?" She stared at him from the doorway.

Jebediah frowned. "Gopher ain't no-account. He thinks he's got hisself a hot one this time. Says it fits all them criteria things he learned about when he was wildcattin' out in Texas."

"Oil, oil, oil. That's all I've been hearing coming out of your mouth ever since your lowlife friend came back from Houston."

Jebediah shook his head. "Gopher ain't no lowlife, neither. He says it's all right, even normal-like, to have five, six, ten, fifteen dry diggin's before the big one comes in."

"And who's supposed to pay for all these dry wells?"

Her husband worked his mouth. "I took my full four thousand from this year's pay and gave it to Gopher." He studied the pattern on the carpet.

"You did what?" She stepped inside the bedroom.

"Margaret, you boss me around like I was one of your colored maids. Like I got no sense when it comes to money. Well, I ain't your slave. No, I don't have your book learnin', but I ain't stupid. I'm due that money ever' year. Fair and square."

"Fair and square?" A pain stabbed at her belly. What possessed her to open that topic?

Jebediah sent her a quizzical look. "Margaret, I've kept my part of your pa's deal these twenty-one years." He straightened his shoulders. "I married you, didn't I? Took that silly business our fathers worked out. Neither one of them asked me a damn thing. My pa just said I had to marry you, or he'd give both me and Ma a lickin' we'd never forget." His face pinched as his eyes clouded with a faraway look. "Hinted like he might kill her this time. I went to New Orleans to save my ma even though I knew all about you." His eyes drifted over her frame, head to toe. "Just like most everybody else in Union County. At the end of the business, my pa made a pile, and yours got to keep all your lies secret."

"I don't wish to talk about any of that." Margaret's heart picked up a pace. Jebediah had been hinting more and more about her these past months. Was it a bluff? "You know nothing." She turned to leave.

He took two steps toward her. "Well, maybe it's time we did. Talk about it, I mean. You questionin' me about what I do with the money that's rightfully mine. Your pa put it in his will. I get four thousand a year. All I have to do is stay married to you." He pursed his lips. "And keep your stories quiet." He shook his head. "I don't know which one is the biggest lie—you already carryin' another man's baby when you married me or . . ."

Margaret shut the bedroom door. She stood with both hands clutching the doorknob at her back. "Jebediah, I said I don't want to talk about any of that. And keep your voice down." Calm. She had to let him see he couldn't rile her into an extra bed visit. That had to be what he was after. Her stomach in turmoil, she shrugged, doing her best to appear nonchalant. "Of course, you're right. The money is yours. I just wanted to say you'll get no more from me when that well turns up dry."

He shook his head. "That's just it, Margaret. I don't get much of nothin' from you as it is. Way it is now, you give me three, four times a year—Christmas Night, Good Friday, my birthday—and dependin' on how you're feelin', maybe one other day of your choice." Jebediah shook his head. "I done my part with you and those children for twenty-one years now. From where I'm standin', it ain't asking too much to expect you to put a little bit of effort into actin' like a real wife. You can't say I'm not doin' my part—keepin' my mouth shut about Morris all these years and takin' you on as my wife, even though you're . . ."

Margaret couldn't help it. The shudder raked her body. "Jebediah! Tell me you're not . . . sharing vicious lies with the likes of . . . of Gopher Dennis?"

Her husband sighed as he shook his head. "Not yet, I ain't, but you got to know Gopher's guessin' the truth pretty good. Margaret, no good you keep on callin' the truth a lie. Everybody in Union County knows who your mama is."

"Uhh." Margaret's eyes scanned the ceiling, the walls, and the floor of her bedroom, searching for a quick response. "Gopher." She gave her head a quick shake. "It's Gopher. The rumors. That's why I don't think it's a good idea for you to hang around that man, not to mention sinking all your money into his wildcatting schemes."

"What rumors?" Jebediah tilted his head as he closed the distance between them.

"I've heard bits and pieces." She took in a breath. Please, let him not put voice to that other business. "That Gopher might be . . . could be running with the night ride . . ." She couldn't get the words out.

"Oh, is that all? Margaret, women don't need to know who is and who ain't ridin' with the Klan."

She stared at her husband. "Are you saying it's true? That Gopher does ride with the Ku Klux Kl . . . ?"

Jebediah nodded. "Nothin' much wrong with the Klan. They keep uppity coloreds in their place." A little grin wreathed his face as he quieted his words. "Nothin' to worry about here at Hardin House. The only uppity coloreds we got around here are Salome's boys—Waylon and Tom-Tom. And that's your pa's doin', what with all the land he left them in his will." The grin turned into a smile. "Margaret, I know those two boys are the sons of your favorite maid, Salome, but why are you worried about them? You know 'bout some more uppity coloreds?"

She couldn't let him see how hard her chest heaved. She struggled to hold her breath, but Margaret felt her face redden.

He moved to within a foot of her. "You know, you're forty-two years old now. White women your age don't look nothin' like you. Got faces lookin' like shirts balled up and stuffed in a drawer for ten years. Wrinkles aplenty. Tits hangin' almost to their bellies. Behinds wide and flat as a barn door." He shook his head. "Gopher may or may not run with the Klan." He laid a hand on her waist. "With you not lookin' exactly like a white woman, what better cover for a man keepin' a secret about a colored woman passin' herself off as his white wife than for him to hide out with the Klan?"

"Oh, Jesus, Lord!" The words flew out of her mouth before her mind could pull them back. She tried to jerk away, but the closed door blocked her.

"Now, Margaret, let's us have that little talk about me spendin' a little more time in your bedroom." His hand slid under her left breast. "I ain't gonna say yea or nay to Gopher about his suspicions of you.

If I want a woman in my bed—white or colored—that's my business. None of his." His hand moved over her breast as he pressed her back against the door. "I can keep that secret, but those boys, now—your children—are a different story. They got a right to know about their mama being touched by the tar brush and . . . well, Morris, he needs to know about his real father."

Margaret's head banged against the door. "No! No!" If only she could hold her breathing steady. "Jebediah, what are you talking about? I'm not . . . you mustn't think . . . you shouldn't believe . . ." Her words stumbled. "And even if I were, you're not to say a word about . . . about that."

He reached to the top of her head and plucked out the hairpins holding her unruly hair in place, one by one. "Now, while I kind of fancy it, white women don't have frizzy hair like yours." His cheek brushed an outcropping of pouf above her right ear. "What's it to be, Margaret? You and me talkin' about me comin' to your bedroom more often or"—he pressed his body against hers—"me havin' a word or two with Junior and Morris about their grandma Salome?"

"Jebediah, no . . ."

"Pa! Pa! Hallelujah, glory, it came in! Goddamn it to hell, it came in!" Morris Slocum's whoops rushed up the grand staircase of Hardin House, down the hall, and straight into his mother's shocked ears.

"Pa, you upstairs?" Margaret recognized the sound of her twenty-year-old's feet slapping against the stair treads.

Jebediah pushed her aside as he opened the door and rushed into the hallway. She caught her breath, stuck two hairpins back in place, and dusted off the top of her frock where his hand had rested. She scrambled into the hallway, keeping two paces from her husband, and peered over the banister as her son climbed the steps two at a time.

"Morris? What you goin' on about, boy?" Jebediah called down.

"The well! The goddamn Smackover oil well. The one you put your money into, Pa. It just blew." He surmounted the staircase, leaving a

299

trail of oily black footprints on the carpeted treads. He laid a hand on the newel post, plowed down the hall, and bear-hugged Jebediah. "Gopher said to get there quick."

"Smackover?" Margaret frowned as her reprimand to her son for his salty language scooted out of her head. "Gopher Dennis actually drilled into an oil gusher? Where in Smackover?"

"Come on, Ma. Grab your shawl. The Ford's outside. We'll be there lickety-split. This strike will even impress the grand Lady Margaret Hardin Slocum."

Margaret didn't feel so grand sitting in the backseat of her son's Model T as it careened across places where there was no road. She braced herself against the seat in front of her. The Arkansas moon, only a quarter full on this spring evening, made it hard to see anything inside or outside the Ford. She squinted at Morris's bobbing head as he turned the car this way and that. Something about her son looked different. Morris's hands were covered in goo. It was more than that. He smelled worse than cooking grease used thirty times over. The car hit an ugly bump and jostled her against the back passenger door. She caught another quick glimpse of her boy's hands gripping the wheel. Black and sticky. She leaned against the car door. She twisted to look out the side window.

"Where are we going?" Her last word ended in a squeal as Morris ran the Ford over something solid.

"Smackover," Morris called out between yells.

Margaret wasn't sure which man was loudest—her son or her pretend husband. They said little to each another, but the shouts, yells, curses, and whoops filled in where words were supposed to be.

"Where in Smackover? You know that's all Hardin land. Has been for over fifty years."

The right front wheel of the Ford dropped into some sort of hole. Margaret raised her voice to combat the din. "In our family . . . oops . . . ever since 1867, when my father moved here from Maryland, this has been . . . Hardin land."

She heard the freight train roar way before Morris shifted gears and raced the car into the source of the cacophony.

"God in Heaven." Margaret clamped a hand over her nose and mouth to block out the stench. The car screeched to a halt, throwing her headfirst against the back of the front seat. She didn't hear the motor click off before the two front doors flew open and Morris and Jebediah leapt out. A smell more pungent than a decaying hog carcass burned her eyes, throat, and nose. Margaret righted herself.

"Hot damn! Hot damn!" A black man—no, a white man covered in black crude—jumped at least a three-foot distance straight into Jebediah's arms. Both men, hugging each another, fell to the ground out of Margaret's line of sight. She fumbled with the handle on the door just as Morris ran off toward another man drenched in black.

"Shit! Shit! Shit! We did it!" The two embraced. "We did it! Hot damn, we did it!"

Margaret got the door open. A huge black plume splattered the night-gray sky. She looked up. Was it about to touch Heaven? Morris got to his feet, tugging the other man with him. The two weaved out of sight.

"Oh, goddamn. Oh, goddamn." The man wrestling in that pool of goo on the ground with Jebediah sounded like his best friend, Gopher Dennis, six months back from Texas.

All around her, men ran in circles kicking up thick sludge. Others rolled in the slop. Some scooped handfuls of the most awful-smelling goop Margaret had ever encountered and smeared their faces and hair as though it were the most precious confection on earth. Ten, twelve, maybe fifteen men jumped on one another's backs or dropped to their knees and lifted their arms to the heavens, while others sat spread-eagled in something as thick as pitch. A tree here, a piece of old fence there—all covered in the same sticky mass—smelling of the Devil's tar. She'd never seen such a sight in all her days. Wait. Yes she had.

"Jebediah." Margaret took a step and her leather shoes sank into thick-as-molasses globs. "Where, exactly, is this well?"

"Hey, Jeb." A man with a maniacal laugh climbed off the ground and pulled Jebediah up with him. "That there your missus? The hifalu-tin one? Her pa called himself some kind of a duke?" The man swiped oil off his lips. "Still won't allow you in her bed more'n once a month?"

Oil soiled her hem and stockings. "Gopher Dennis, I don't believe I welcome your comments. I'm speaking to my husband." She coughed as the stench snatched at her breath.

Gopher turned to Jebediah, who was smearing even more oil over his face. "You're a rich man, now. I'm thinkin' much richer than this fancy piece." He jabbed an oil-soaked finger at Margaret, and in a slightly lower voice he said, "Now you can do what you want with her." He cackled as he started back toward the gusher. "Have her six ways from Sunday any time you get good and ready."

"If that well is where I think it is, Gopher Dennis, you and Jebediah may not be as rich as you think," Margaret called out over the noise.

"Margaret"—Jebediah's angled teeth shone through the grime on his face—"be happy for both of us. You and me."

"Who gave you permission to drill on this land?" She rushed past her husband, oil splattering the skirt and bodice of her new dress.

Dennis stopped and turned. She wasn't sure, but that might have been a question she read underneath all that oil on his face.

"This here's your land, if you gonna get picky 'bout it, Mrs. Slocum, but the oil diggin's was all paid for by your husband. I done it all up legal like I learnt in Texas. You, me, and Jebediah, we're gonna split the profits. I get half for the findin' and the drillin'. You two get half for the backin' money, and you . . ." He took a step toward her. "Why you askin'?"

Margaret whirled toward her husband. "Jebediah, don't you recognize that stand of trees? Look at that fence post. Underneath all that oil, you're going to find an old rock with words scratched on it. Something special from the Cherokee nation when they lived in this part of Arkansas. Papa showed it to me when I was nine." Her breath came in short spurts.

"What are you talkin' about?" Jebediah turned in the direction of the gusher.

"Hold on." Gopher Dennis walked closer. "Cherokee? Why's she goin' on 'bout a bunch of dead Injuns?"

Margaret ignored the wildcatter. "Jebediah, don't you see? When you make your rounds of our property, you must have spotted the boundaries—mine, Tom-Tom's, and Waylon's."

Her husband wiped a hand over his face, leaving a streak of white.

"If I'm right, a part of that well does sit on my land, but the other, maybe more than half, sits . . ."

"Sits where, woman?" Gopher Dennis rushed up and clamped his oil-encrusted hand on her shoulder.

"Hold on, Gopher." Jebediah reached them in three strides. He pulled his friend away. "I do the disciplinin' of my own wife." He turned to her. "Margaret, what is it you're sayin'?"

"Tom-Tom." She shuddered from the lingering touch of Gopher Dennis's hand.

"Tom-Tom what?"

"Most of that well could be on his land." She pointed a finger at the gusher. "Under all that oil is the Cherokee rock—the boundary between my land and my bro . . . Tom-Tom's." She peered first at Jebediah, then at Gopher.

The beginnings of understanding flashed on Jebediah's face.

"That's where his property begins—the boundary between my third and Tom-Tom's third." A blob of oil flying through the evening sky landed on her right cheek.

Gopher looked first at her, then at Jebediah. "What's all this *third* blabber? Jeb tole me you own the mineral rights to this here." He waved an arm around. "I been spottin' out this piece of property for a good while now. Goddamn it to Hell, looks like oil underneath this ground for near six mile in all directions." He turned to where Margaret had just pointed. "Includin' that."

"Well, that piece of property"—she nodded to the west—"belongs to Thomas Hardin. He's the one who'll be rich."

"Tom-Tom? I know 'bout that one. He's one of them uppity coloreds." Gopher worked his mouth as though he wanted to bring up a wad of chewing tobacco. He stopped and stared at Margaret. "Now I'm seein' it clear." He lowered his head but kept his eyes aimed straight at her. "It'll come a day in Hell when the Devil's shiverin' from the cold before I allow a half nigger to get his hands on this kind of money."

Despite the lingering warmth of the April evening, Margaret felt a chill. Surely, Gopher Dennis—a man with the manners of a garter snake and the education of a plow mule—couldn't have heard those ugly rumors. The county gentry was much too refined to share their gossip with the white trash likes of Gopher Dennis. The wildcatter couldn't possibly be privy to those awful stories. Struggling to keep her face composed, Margaret turned to Jebediah, who stood staring at her. Her eyebrows dared not arch. Her lips best not twitch. How could he? How could the man, well paid to play her husband, share those awful stories about Margaret? A cramp grabbed Margaret's stomach and refused to release it.

Gopher waved an oil-covered arm at her, his eyes glistening even in the quarter-moon. "Jeb, if what this wench is blitherin' on about is so, me and you gotta fix this."

Margaret stood frozen in the hustle, heat, blaring noise, and overpowering stink of the oil field. She felt the bile rise to her throat. She held herself steady. *Don't let this oaf see one sign he's hit truth.* She lifted her chin and let out her most haughty grunt.

"Morris. Drive me home. I'll not stand here and be insulted by this . . . this . . ."

With his burly arms Gopher Dennis yanked her to his chest. He pressed his chin against hers. Her neck angled in pain.

"I know who you really are, you so-called Lady Margaret. You ain't nothin' but a nigger-bitch pretendin' to be white."

The smell of sulfur rising from Hell mingled with the gall collecting in her throat. She couldn't breathe. She wriggled her hands against the man's chest and managed to turn her face. "Jebe . . . ," she croaked out, but too late. Gopher spun her around, laid a rough hand against the back of her neck, and tipped her body upside down. Sky and ground traded places. Her feet flailed in the air. A pool of oil rushed up to greet her grasping hands. Landing on her side, she thudded into the cesspool, oil splashing all around her. Her body sank into the muck, her face caked with thick crude. Margaret twisted to grab air, but large hands pushing down on her back held her fast.

"Nnn . . ." She gurgled for breath as she squirmed to free herself. No use. Crude lodged in her nose, eyes, and ears.

"Hey." A voice floated above her. Jebediah? "Get your hands off her. I tole you I do my own disciplinin'. Friend or no friend, don't you never put a hand on my wife again."

Margaret's ears were plugged, but strands of sound drifted in through the goo.

"She ain't fit for nothin' 'cept to gap her legs for any white man comes along."

The holding hands slammed into her even harder. Oh, God. She fought through the battlefield of oil, trying to stretch her arms to the back of her head. Can't reach. Air disappearing. Chest paining.

Thwack! A sound somewhere far above whispered into her ears. Then in the quickness of a blink, the viselike hands lifted off her. Free. Now, to push to her hands and knees—get to her feet. But her legs scuffled to find purchase on the slippery ground. Her hands slid forward, then sideways in the sludge. No good. She fell chestfirst into the pool of oil. Her shoulders ached. Then something—arms, hands—grabbed her by the shoulders and jerked her upward. Night air, warm but flecked with oil, rushed at her face and squeezed its way into her mouth and nose. She strangled out a cough, but her throat clogged. She clawed at her face, clearing first her nose, then her mouth. Blurry figures faded in and out of sight. Who was standing next to her? Jebediah. Her knees buckled. She tumbled into her husband's arms.

"Jeb, you best get all them Hardin half-breeds in order, or there's gonna be Hell to pay." She heard the voice of Gopher Dennis, but couldn't make out his form.

"I know what to do better'n you, Gopher." Jebediah's tight grip kept her upright. "Keep your hands off Margaret." He turned her away from the oilman and walked her back to the Ford, then bent his face close to her right ear. "I ain't gonna allow nobody to manhandle you, but, Margaret, you gonna listen to reason. 'Cause if you don't, it ain't just your secret that'll come out to all Union County."

The taste of oil thickened her tongue. She heaved.

Jebediah pulled a blob of oil out of her hair—hair that had lost all semblance of the straightening her maid had carefully arranged that morning. "You gotta know oil changes everything. This here's 1921, and folks don't take it too hard anymore if a white man gives his secret colored family a piece of land like your pa did all three of you. Ain't polite to speak out loud about such private doin's, though."

Margaret's legs slid against each another as she staggered toward the car. Her oily clothes weighed her down. She clung to Jebediah.

"But when that piece of colored property come up with oil, like just now, all that toleratin' of a man's colored family gonna go out the winda. Ain't no white man, woman, or child in all this county gonna sit back and see coloreds get filthy rich while they got to break their own white backs grubbin' for food."

The shaking started in her shoulders. Was it from what Gopher had just done to her, or was it from her husband's words?

"And if one of them wildcatters know for sure that you're one of them half-coloreds, they'll bring you down. And, God help me, Junior and Morris, too."

Now her entire body shuddered in time to the pumping well.

"Even harder 'cause you tried to fool 'em." He opened the car door, one hand at her elbow. "Margaret, you've spent twenty-one years payin' me no mind, treatin' me like a freckle-faced field hand in the back forty." He helped her into the backseat. "That's gonna stop right now. I don't want you talkin' to Salome 'bout none of this. You, Waylon, or Tom-Tom do or say one thing that rubs white folks the wrong way or take one wrong step, there's gonna be Hell aplenty to pay."

CHAPTER
THIRTY-ONE

Salome sat in her floral-print easy chair with the two-day-old Union County colored newspaper spread out before her.

Friday, May 19, 1922
MORE SMACKOVER WELLS BROUGHT IN

She glanced at her Bible lying open on her side table. "Maxwell Joe, this here ain't gonna end right. They gots our family business all over this here front page. Don't they know white folks—some of 'em—can read, too?"

"Not no colored newspaper, they don't." Maxwell Joe yawned awake as he shifted his position on the blue davenport stationed across the room from Salome's chair.

"But it says right here where these oil strikes is. On Hardin land. If white folks find out the truth 'bout that first well bein' mostly on my boy's land, Lord knows what's gonna happen."

Maxwell Joe grunted himself to sitting, his eyes fixed on the cabbage-rose pattern on the dark blue rug Salome put so much store by.

"What is it you ain't tellin' me, Maxwell Joe?" She peered at her kitchen door, making sure it was closed. Ladora had offered to make the dinner this Sunday.

Her husband fixed his eyes on the newspaper in her lap. "Dannyboy had to pick up a bale of fencin' last night. Had to pass 'round the back of the Lisbon Baptist Church house."

"Uh-huh?" Why did Salome feel the need to reach for the Good Book?

Maxwell sucked in his lips. "He heard him some talkin'."

"What kind of talkin'?" Salome folded the newspaper.

"D-boy quick-stepped his way past a winda. He saw himself a pile of robes layin' across a table." Maxwell kept his head down. "And a cross."

"Well, of course he did. Lisbon Baptist is a church." She traded the newspaper for her Bible.

"A white church, but that ain't all that was white inside that buildin'."

Salome opened the Bible without looking at which chapter or verse showed up. Ladora poked her head out of the kitchen. "Everythin' all right in here, Miz Salome, Papa Maxwell Joe?"

"Jest fine." Salome pulled up a smile from somewhere. "That stewin' chicken smells just 'bout ready to come out of the oven. You better git on back in there and start yo' gravy."

"Yes'm. It's jest that I was wonderin' if Tom-Tom and Waylon done come in off the front porch yet. I wants to time the dinner jest right fo' them."

"They'll come on in when I say. Now you git back in that kitchen." Salome kept the smile in place until she heard Ladora slamming pots and pans behind the closed kitchen door. "Now what you sayin'?" She turned back to her husband.

"Them robes was white. Had hoods attached to 'em. Eye holes cut out . . ."

"Jesus, Lord. When was the last time the Klan rode?"

"'Bout five year back, and that was 'cause of a fuss over a colored buying hisself a new Ford motorcar."

Salome put both hands over her open Bible. "What's this fuss over?" *Please, Lord, don't let it be what I'm thinking.*

Maxwell Joe had come over from the davenport and now pulled a chair close to hers and laid his hands over hers. "Gopher Dennis was there."

Salome sucked in a breath. "And . . . ?"

"Jacob Slocum."

She dropped her head to her chest. "Oh no, Lord. Where the father go, so do the son!" She heard her own voice reach for the ceiling.

"Weren't there. No Jebediah, least not that D-boy could see. Plenty others, though. Sheriff, that white preacher, that big-bellied fella that runs that little mercantile on Brush Street, that red-faced automobile-fixin' man, a couple of deputies." He wiggled his fingers. "'Bout ten of 'em altogether."

"What was they wantin'?" Her heart told her the answer long before Maxwell Joe could fix his mouth to speak.

"Papers."

Her fingers flicked at the Bible pages.

"Deed papers. Gopher Dennis was tellin' the others to git ready jest in case. He said he wasn't expectin' no trouble, but it could be that one or two 'uppity niggers' might need a little convincin'."

"They ain't ridin' tonight?" Salome held her breath.

"D-boy couldn't linger none, but it looked to him like them fellas was in the plannin' jest-in-case stages." Maxwell shook his head. "No. They ain't ridin' tonight, 'cause Gopher Dennis said he gonna try somethin' else first."

Salome stroked the Bible pages just as her front door opened.

Waylon and Tom-Tom stopped inside her front room. "Mama, are you expecting company? There's a car coming up the road. Looks like it belongs to Gopher Dennis."

Oh, Lord Jesus. Salome dug her fingers into Maxwell Joe's wrists.

Her husband shook her loose and stood. "I don't reckon I'm needed here." He turned toward the little room next to the kitchen pantry. To the door he always kept locked. The room where his stack of guns lay. "Could be Mr. Dennis comin' here fo' a nice social call on colored folks." He looked first at Tom-Tom, then at Waylon. "Might be some oil business." He pulled a key from his pocket.

"What time you say Emerald be over here with the chil'ren?" Salome's heart pounded.

Waylon glanced at the grandfather clock standing in the far corner of her front room behind her davenport. "Said she'd be back from the pony rides about two—another fifty minutes or so." He shot a quick look at his brother.

Tom-Tom, dressed in his Sunday preacher suit, walked over to his mother and kissed Salome's forehead. "Mama, put your trust in the Lord. This will all work out." He took the matching chair opposite her and pulled out the Bible he always carried. Waylon sat on the davenport.

The knock on the front door came just as Ladora dropped something heavy in the kitchen. Maxwell sucked in his lips. Salome looked from one of her sons to the other. There was no sound except Ladora's scrambling.

"I know you're to home, Waylon. I see your car." Jebediah Slocum, dressed in a seersucker suit that looked like it had been cut just for him, pushed open Salome's always-unlocked front door. He stepped into the front room. "Salome, I figured you'd enjoy a nice Sunday visit with Lady Margaret."

Salome sat unmoving. "Margaret? You brung Lady Margaret to see me?"

"And a friend."

Her daughter followed Jebediah inside.

"Lady Margaret, I'm pleased to see you?" Salome's voice edged up as a white man she'd never seen stepped through her front door, pushing Margaret aside. Salome rose to her feet.

"Smells good in here." The stranger—his new suit might have been made for him, too, but no tailor on God's green earth could make a garment that would look good on this squat, barrel-chested man. "Afternoon, auntie."

"Mr. Slocum, suh." Salome had already waited the two seconds needed for one of her menfolk to speak up. "Thank you fo' bringin' Lady Margaret fo' a visit." She struggled to put on her innocent face in front of Jebediah. "But who might this be?"

"Mr. Dennis, to you. Mr. Gopher Dennis, and I know who you are." The stranger stared at Salome before waving an arm around the room. "Fact of the business, I know who each and ever' one of you is."

"Can I help you with something?" Waylon carried more than a hint of wariness in his voice as he laid his hands on Salome's shoulders and eased her back to her easy chair.

"Which one are you, Thomas or Waylon?" The man called Gopher reached into his suit jacket.

Salome's heart thumped out of time with the click she heard coming from the little room where Maxwell Joe had disappeared.

Waylon pasted on a smile. "Dinner's about to be served, true enough. Of course, we'd be happy to serve you, too . . . if only we'd known you were coming. Perhaps, next time, Mr. . . . did you say Dennis?"

Gopher Dennis, standing with one foot on Salome's cabbage-rose rug, the other on her pine-wood floor, frowned as he pulled out a sheaf of folded papers from his jacket. He turned to Jebediah. "Well, ain't he a proper-talkin' nig . . . colored." The man looked around, but his eyes did not linger on the door to the little room. His gaze landed on Tom-Tom and his white-collared church shirt. "Preacher man, which one are you?"

Tom-Tom fingered his cross. "I am the Reverend Thomas Hardin, wishing God's blessings on you this Sunday afternoon."

Mr. Dennis blinked. "Well, that's all well and good, Reverend. I got somethin' for you." He tapped the sheaf of papers against his free hand.

Salome heard the faint creak of a door opening to her left.

"Mr. Dennis." Margaret, her face flushed, stepped in front of the Gopher fellow. "Sunday is a day of rest, not one for doing business."

Smirking, Mr. Dennis squared to face Margaret. "Is that right, Mrs. Slocum? Accordin' to Jebediah here, you don't do no business for him any day of the week."

Salome shook off Waylon's hands, moved to her feet, and walked to Margaret before she knew how she got there. She glared over her daughter's shoulder at Dennis before her right mind could warn her off.

"Hold on there, Gopher." Jebediah shouldered his way between Margaret and Gopher Dennis. "I know we got important discussin's with these here folks, but most of that business comes from me and Margaret." He looked over to Salome. "We just want to have a word or two with these boys."

"I hear me some voices out here?" Ladora stood framed in the kitchen door.

Salome won the battle to keep her voice steady. "Thanks to you fo' cookin' Sunday dinner. I can serve myself." She turned to her youngest, praying her daughter-in-law would take the hint and get herself out of harm's way. "Tom-Tom, why don't you see Ladora home. She lookin' plum wore-out."

"Hold on there, auntie." Gopher Dennis glared. "I said I got business with a Thomas Hardin." He turned to Waylon. "And this one, too. Wore-out or no, ain't nobody goin' home just yet."

Tom-Tom rose to his feet and went to stand in front of Ladora.

Jebediah tapped Gopher Dennis on the shoulder and nodded toward the front door. "Let me and Margaret have a talk with these folks first."

"This here's my business, too, Jebediah. It's me what brought in that well."

"I ain't denyin' it was half you." Jebediah nodded to the open front door. "This here ain't gonna take long." He turned first to Tom-Tom, then to Waylon. "These boys gonna see reason right quick-like."

Dennis made a face. "I'll wait out here."

"Tom-Tom and Waylon, this here's gonna be simple." Jebediah nodded toward Margaret, who still held her place in the center of the room. "I come to say my sorrys. Me and Gopher ain't meant no harm with the drillin' of that first Smackover well. Thought for sure it was settin' square on Margaret's land. Made a mistake. Seems like a little corner might've been on your side."

"Almost two-thirds." Waylon kept his hands on Salome's shoulders.

Did Salome catch a flash of sun reflecting off something black coming from the little room?

"I ain't never been good with this third business." Jebediah turned to Tom-Tom. "You ain't got no reason to fret. My new oil company's gonna see to it you get your rightful share."

"How much is a 'rightful share'?" Waylon put in.

Jebediah made a face like he was trying to run numbers in his head. "That well's pumpin' 'bout five to seven thousand dollars' worth of oil a month."

"My God in Heaven." Ladora's eyes opened wide. "Each and ever' month on God's calendar?"

"But that's just it." Jebediah laid a sorrowful look on his face as he turned to Ladora. "That money's good, sure 'nough. The oil people reckon that well might pump twenty, thirty years." He looked down at the rug, this time like he was trying to memorize his ABCs, then lifted his face. "What with expenses and all taken out, well, what's left, it don't amount to much of nothin'."

Ladora frowned in confusion.

"Mr. Jebediah, suh, what might them 'spenses be?" Salome glanced at her daughter, who looked like she was suffering a bout of the croup.

"Oil rigs and crews. Takes a lot to bring in a well." Jebediah glanced over at Margaret. "But that's where I'm willin' to help y'all. Gopher, he got lots of his own riggin'. Brung it straight from Texas." Jebediah put out a smile that showed his angled eyetooth. "Tom-Tom, I can help you out. Gopher's already gonna let you keep eight, maybe even nine hundred of your share of that seven thousand dollars each and ever' month." He reached out a hand for Margaret. "I know how much all y'all mean to my wife. I want to keep her happy."

Salome shot a quick look at her girl. True enough, Jebediah had been easing up on her girl these past few years. Still, Margaret looked anything but happy.

"Mr. Slocum," Waylon broke in, "did I hear you say Tom-Tom's well is pumping oil but not enough to pay expenses?"

"That's right."

Salome read her son's face. Not only had Waylon failed to say *suh*, but a white man might take his question as uppity. She spoke up. "And 'cause you's a good man, suh, you gonna give my Tom-Tom some money ever' month?"

Jebediah nodded.

"Then, what is them papers in Mr. Gopher's hand?" Salome cut in before Waylon could say anything.

"You wanna know 'bout papers?" Gopher Dennis stormed through the front door. He slapped three sheets down on Salome's dining room table, almost knocking one of her china plates to the floor. "This here's a fair deal to keep everybody in Union County happy." He turned to Tom-Tom. "Boy, you sign."

Waylon jumped to his feet and pointed to the documents. "What are those?"

Dennis whirled around. "Jebediah, I told you not to do no nego-tiatin' with coloreds. Now, you"—Mr. Dennis pointed to Tom-Tom—"put your *X* right here."

Waylon and Tom-Tom reached the table at about the same time.

"This one's a deed," Tom-Tom announced. "And so is this."

Salome felt a chill race down her back.

"You want me to sign my land over to you?" Tom-Tom tilted his head as he faced Gopher Dennis. "Why on earth would I do a thing like that when you've trespassed on my land? That's my oil you're pulling up. My money you're spending."

Salome held her breathing as steady as she could. Tom-Tom had always been her quiet child. Waylon had been the one who spoke his mind when holding his tongue was the best way to go. Tom-Tom always took his sweet time looking at a thing before he spoke his piece. Not this day.

Gopher Dennis's face turned the color of two-day-old raspberries. "Look, nigger boy, I ain't got no time for this. We can do this the easy way or the hard way. It's Jebediah who's givin' you any choice at all. I ain't for givin' you none. Sign the damn paper and you gonna get two hundred dollars a month as long as that well's pumpin'. That's more'n 'nough money for colored."

"And if my brother refuses?" Waylon crossed his arms over his chest.

"Oh, Waylon, I ain't got to you yet. But I'll tell you all this much." Gopher Dennis did a slow turn toward Margaret, his face as ugly as a toad's. "That one, she's as black as the ace of spades. If you all don't want everybody in Arkansas knowin' she ain't fit to be nothin' but somebody's housemaid, then you better put your *X* right there." He jabbed a finger at the paper.

Margaret's eyes snapped shut like a raccoon trap. Her body swayed against Jebediah.

Salome reached down to pick up her Bible from the floor where it had fallen. *Lord, where was that story of Job?*

Waylon took in a deep breath. "Mr. Dennis"—he turned to Jebediah—"and Mr. Slocum, I can't speak for my brother, but I'll thank you both to leave my mother's house." He looked at Margaret.

"I don't need anybody speaking for me," Tom-Tom said and advanced toward Gopher Dennis. "I'll give you my decision in a few days."

"Don't no nigger tell me when to come and go."

Out of the corner of her eye, Salome watched the door to the little room open an inch. Something black eased between door and door-jamb. Salome watched Jebediah's eyes sidle toward the door.

"My wife likes bein' Lady Margaret. Now she's gonna have more money than she knows how to hang on to. I'm willin' to see that y'all have money, too. That's why, Waylon, I'm leanin' toward lettin' you keep your power of control over Margaret's investments. All you and Tom-Tom got to do is share a bit of your land with Mr. Dennis."

Gopher Dennis slammed a fist on the table. "I tole you, Jebediah, stop negotiatin' with coloreds." He pointed a finger at Waylon, then at Tom-Tom. "Sign them goddamn papers or else."

Though it was a sunny Sunday, the room turned dark. Salome's head felt woozy. Ladora slapped a glass of water into Salome's hand.

Margaret's gaze ran from scared to mad as she looked at the wildcatting man. "Mr. Dennis, I beg your indulgence. Since the two of you are partners and it is partially my land you're drilling on, please allow my husband two more days, and I'm sure he can help Salome's family see the benefit to us all." She swallowed. "Without any trouble."

"What makes you think Jebediah's gonna listen to the likes of you now that he don't have to?"

Salome fastened her eyes on her daughter. Margaret had never been a girl with a whole lot of gumption about her—Lady Bertha saw to that. But now her face took on a hardening Salome didn't know the girl possessed.

"Trouble in an oil field as big as this Smackover strike can bring unwanted attention from the newspapers." She flicked her tongue over her upper lip. "You know how harsh these Yankee newspaper writers can be against us Southerners. Could bring on an investigation."

"Hmm." Gopher scrunched his face like thinking was a trial for him.

"We all must do what's best. You'll see." Margaret, her face looking close to a ghost's, snuggled against Jebediah. She turned to her husband. "We'll all get something we want out of this."

Jebediah looked confused.

Salome turned her back on Margaret and headed for her chair. Was her daughter playing a game as old as Jezebel with that husband of hers? Lord, Jesus, was it going to work? A woman selling her body—even to her husband—didn't work out well most times.

Gopher ran his eyes over Margaret, letting them linger over her breasts before he turned them to Jebediah. "Hell, I guess I can't begrudge you a good time or two." He leveled a forefinger at Salome's son-in-law. "You'd better make sure she gives you a damn good ride, 'cause if them papers ain't signed by Tuesday night, I fancy me and my friends havin' ourselves a ride and bonfire one of these evenin's." He walked through the front door. Jebediah grabbed Margaret's wrist and steered her after the man, but not before Salome's girl looked at the door of the little room. Just in time to see that black metal thing disappear.

Salome couldn't stop the quiver in her lip. Yes, she'd made Margaret promise to look after her brothers, but had she asked too much? Her baby girl—just another colored woman at a white man's mercy.

CHAPTER THIRTY-TWO

"Uncle Tom-Tom, talk Papa into buying me an ice cream." Joe-Annie, again. Cajoling her father's brother under the unseasonably warm May sun. The child slid a finger under the round collar of her dress. She frowned, then yanked at the slender black tie decorating the front of her bodice.

Waylon suppressed a smile. Hollywood motion picture star Mary Pickford had nothing on his daughter.

"Even though you know colored are only served at the back door of the ice cream parlor?" Freddie, trying to talk sense into his younger sister, aimed for the shade cast by the row of brick buildings lining this side of the street. Sweat beaded the boy's brow.

Waylon sent a sympathetic look toward his son. Long trousers—the downside of being over twelve.

Waylon and Tom-Tom, approaching the narrow bridge over the creek in the center of Lisbon, walked two steps ahead of Waylon's dawdling daughter and his patient son. He gave a quick glance at the briefcase in his hand—his counteroffer on the oil land drawn up all nice and legal to stall Gopher Dennis. Stall him until he and Tom-Tom could finalize part two of their plan. Yes, the padlock was still secured. The deadline imposed by Gopher Dennis was now. Nonsense, but best to be wary. Mama had spent the past day and a half wiping away tears, pushing away plates of barely touched food. *Nothing but hot air,* Waylon decreed. Yes, the Klan liked to play at scaring colored people, but there hadn't been a cross burning in this part of Union County for five years. Still, Salome hadn't been soothed.

"Uncle Tom-Tom." Joe-Annie's wheedling broke through Waylon's thoughts.

"Honey, why don't you ask Cook to make you some ice cream once you get back to your place?" Tom-Tom the preacher still believed it possible to reason with a hardheaded, ten-year-old girl.

His brother was just as adamant as Waylon. They would not be blackmailed. Arkansas wasn't the only place their passing sister could live as a white woman. There was also Chicago, New York, Boston. But not New Orleans. She might be suspected of being an octoroon there. No, it was the North that beckoned. The brothers agreed to set her up in style somewhere far away from Jebediah.

"Papa, just this once, can't I have some ice cream from a store? I know you say Hardins don't go to anybody's back door if we can help it." She skipped up to him. "Well, I can't help it." She wiped a hand across her honey-colored brow. "I'm burning up with heat. I need something to cool me down."

Waylon turned to his brother. The white-owned ice cream parlor stood just two blocks east. On the building's other side, he glimpsed the upper story of the Mount Moriah Masonic Lodge, the old structure's wood frame in glaring contrast to the new sign displaying a giant cone. They were fast approaching the ice cream parlor's street. "What about you, Freddie? You can't help wanting ice cream from a shop that takes colored money but makes us go to the back door where they throw the cones at us?"

Freddie nodded his head yes, then shook it no, then went back to nodding as he frowned at his father.

"Oh, Papa." Joe-Annie, as usual, jumped ahead of Freddie. "It's just ice cream and it's only one time. I know white folks act stupid sometimes."

Tom-Tom laughed while Waylon struggled to keep his chuckle inside. "Look, I'll take the degradation over this child's whining." Tom-Tom grabbed Joe-Annie's hand.

No, neither brother could be blackmailed. Mr. Richardson had just assured them, not ten minutes ago in his office, that the land survey was accurate. Two-thirds of that pumping oil well in Smackover sat on the land of Thomas Hardin.

"Take them. Take them." Waylon lifted his arms in defeat. "The bank's just across the bridge. I'll stick these papers back in the safety deposit box, and that will be that. I should be no more than fifteen minutes." He looked up and down the street at passersby—a mixture of colored and white—going about their workaday business.

Tom-Tom surveyed the path. "To set your mind at ease, brother, not a white sheet in sight. I'll walk the children there, we'll grab a couple of cones, and we'll make our way to the colored side of town and that phaeton-style car of yours, Waylon."

"That's ten whole blocks, Uncle Tom-Tom! Why can't we park the phaeton closer to Mr. Richardson's office?" Joe-Annie put on that defiant look again.

"Don't be stupid, Joe-Annie. You know perfectly well why not. It's green and easy to spot." Freddie the peacemaker took after his uncle more than Waylon.

"You're the stupid one. You do everything the white folks say. If you ask me, I'd—"

Tom-Tom let out one of his patient smiles. "Joe-Annie, remember what you learned in Sunday school?"

"Uhm." Waylon's daughter looked as though Sunday school was the farthest thing from her mind.

"Joe-Annie"—as usual, Tom-Tom was determined to deliver the Word—"when does God work His miracles?"

"In His own time." Joe-Annie sounded as though God's time had better come within the next ten minutes or she was having none of it.

Tom-Tom grabbed Joe-Annie's hand. "We've brought enough attention to ourselves as it is. Now let's get that ice cream." The trio made their way across the street, stopping just before they reached the other side to let a white man and his woman pass. Tom-Tom, holding back Joe-Annie from racing in front of the couple, tipped his hat with his free hand. Freddie laid a hand on the bill of his cap.

A three-year-old Model T chugged past the threesome and onto the narrow stretch of road crossing the creek. Waylon scanned the path ahead. No white folks walking toward him. If there had been, he'd have to step off the sidewalk and onto the roadway, chancing passing cars and their sometimes-erratic drivers. Butted up close to the right of the sidewalk, a four-foot-high brick wall rose and beyond that a twelve-foot drop to the rolling waters below. No place to step aside—but never mind, crossing the bridge would take no longer than a minute.

Waylon looked down at the leather case he carried and smiled. He, Tom-Tom, and Richardson had plotted out a strategy to stay way ahead of Gopher Dennis. A Pennsylvania oil exploration company would be in Arkansas setting up test equipment by the end of September. Waylon put a foot on the bridge and looked over at the muddy water. Low at this time of year with a few sharp-edged rocks showing. A familiar purring sound played in his ear. Waylon turned to look. Sure enough, a red phaeton pushed along not forty yards behind him. Funny, the machine seemed to be barely moving. Should he chance a smile? He knew not to raise a hand in greeting.

"Nigger." Gopher Dennis's head poked out of the passenger-side front window. "You gonna sign them papers?" The car puttered along at not quite a quarter mile an hour.

Waylon stopped still. Gopher Dennis?

That the wildcatter wanted him to sign over his property was obvious, but what was the man doing yelling out his demand on a public street in broad daylight?

The phaeton moved closer. Where was it now? Thirty yards behind him? Where was it heading at its slow-as-molasses speed?

"You a smart-assed nigger, ain't you? Went to see that nigger-lovin' lawyer, didn't you? Well, I'm here to tell you, white folks don't like to see niggers get ahead of themselves."

Now the car, already at a slow crawl, was twenty-five yards from him. Waylon glimpsed Gopher Dennis, but who was at the wheel?

Gopher turned to the driver. "Go!"

The tiger's purr revved up. A grin that looked like the smile of the Devil crossed Gopher's face.

Waylon's heart jumped as the phaeton aimed its headlamps straight at him. The briefcase clutched in his hands, he broke into a dead run. The tiger's sound rose a notch. Sweat beaded on Waylon's forehead, his breath spurted out of his mouth, his legs churned. How close? The engine noise threatened deafness. Dare he chance it? Take the time to look back? Yes. The automobile, fifteen yards away, took dead aim. Oh, Jesus! Run faster. Legs cramping. Heart thumping. There. On the right, the brick wall. Twelve feet straight down to the creek.

Behind him, the motor gunned. The sound moving closer. Where to go? The ledge? Jump to the top? No. Too narrow. No more than three bricks wide. What to do? A slash of red caught the corner of his eye.

"Get that nigger!" Gopher Dennis screamed as the motorcar barreled down.

Waylon flattened himself against the brick wall as the phaeton climbed onto the sidewalk. God in Heaven! Crooked teeth flashed in

Dennis's mouth. The phaeton missed Waylon's legs by an inch. His chest hurt as the driver—Good God Almighty, it was Morris Slocum—backed up, rammed the gearbox twice, swiveled the front tires, and took fresh aim at him. Waylon steeled himself. He clutched the case to his chest with one hand and readied his left. Here came the phaeton again.

"I tole you to sign, nigger." Gopher Dennis stuck an arm out the window. "Today."

Waylon grabbed the man just above the elbow and hoisted himself onto the running board—left foot first. Jesus—his right leg scraped against the bricks. Waylon felt his body swing wide and almost topple over the low wall. His right leg flailed in the air. He plastered his body against the side of the car. His breath caught in his throat, but both feet planted themselves solidly on the phaeton's running board. He clung to Dennis's arm as the car swerved from one side of the bridgeway to the next, barely missing a mule and wagon plodding in the opposite direction. Waylon held his face and body tight against the side of the car, the case stuck between his chest and the car. Two colored men strolling across the street stopped and pointed. The car swerved right. A portly white woman and a beanpole of a man jumped back as the right front tire nearly skimmed them.

"Turn me loose, nigger." Dennis Slocum clawed at Waylon's death grip.

Waylon spotted the just-poured-last-month concrete sidewalk in front of the bank. He had to chance it. He clutched his case, spotted a tiny area of grass by the old oak tree, and threw himself at it. He heard a thud explode in his brain along with the sound of a tiger roaring off to chase new prey.

"Next time, nigger!"

Night blotted out the sun.

"Lord Hardin! Lord Hardin!" A dark brown face, one he knew only vaguely as a man who brought his timber from distant Camden to the Hardin sawmill for the cutting once a year.

"Out of the way!" Tom-Tom's voice. Then his face gazed down at him. "Jesus, spare my brother." Tom-Tom's worried-looking eyes, joined by a screaming Freddie and a crying Joe-Annie, greeted him.

"Papa! Papa!"

"Get up, Papa." Joe-Annie reached down to grab his arm. "Please get up!"

Pain racked his shoulders. Waylon eased his right leg out of some peculiar angle. It throbbed but didn't feel broken. He stretched out his left. Good. Both arms and legs seemed to be in working order. He still held on to the briefcase and his important papers. He steadied his gaze on his brother and children.

"Papa's just had a little motorcar accident." Waylon's voice still worked. And his thinking. "It was scary, but no bones broken." He managed a chuckle. "What did I tell you children about looking both ways?"

Tom-Tom, aided by two other colored men, reached down to move him to his feet. Pains stabbed Waylon's back, but he kept his misery to himself. He put on a smile. No need to further upset the children. The children? Joe-Annie. Freddie. How frightened they must be. He turned to Tom-Tom, his face away. He mouthed, "Gopher Dennis and . . . Morris Slocum."

CHAPTER
THIRTY-THREE

Salome dipped the pen into the inkwell as she hunched over her writing table set in the corner of her living room. *Margaret. Waylon doing alright. How is you?* She bore down hard on the fountain pen. The nib bent. She hadn't seen Margaret in days. Nor had the servants at Hardin House. All they knew was that Mrs. Slocum was in her bedroom. With Jebediah. Lord, help her girl.

Maxwell Joe stepped off the bottom stair. "Havin' me a time keepin' that boy in the bed."

"A losing time." Waylon stood at the head of the stairs, a bathrobe knotted over his summer drawers. "A little bump on the head and a few bruises do not require me to stay in bed for two entire days."

A bump on the head, was it? Salome clamped her lips together to keep from calling out. Bless Waylon. Her boy was trying his best not to unsettle his mama. Didn't he know she'd been unsettled—how she'd fretted over him—all his life? At least he held on to the banister as he walked down Salome's stairs. He stationed himself at the foot of the staircase.

"Besides, Tom-Tom just pulled up. Caught a look at him out of the bedroom window."

"Waylon, why don't you and Tom-Tom . . ." Why didn't they what? Salome's head hurt from struggling to sort out a plan to save all her children. Her eyes swept over Waylon, then she turned back to her writing desk. She couldn't have her boy see the worry in her, nor the plans she was trying to sort out in her head to save her family.

A quick tap, but before she could say *Come in*, Tom-Tom swept into her front room. He turned to Maxwell Joe. "What's the word?"

"What word?" Salome frowned at her two boys. Lord, not more bad news? Her fingers played with the edge of the writing paper.

Waylon walked off the last step and nodded to his brother. "Mama, this is nothing for you to fret over."

"Not fret over?" Her voice rose. They—all three of her menfolk— were keeping something from her. She could feel it in that secret place every mother held. "Gopher Dennis tried to flatten you with his motorcar two days back." She turned to her husband. "Maxwell Joe, he don't tell me nothin', but I knows Danny-boy got him some fresh word." She'd said too much, but what was done was done.

Maxwell Joe rubbed her shoulders. "I ain't keepin' nothin' from you, Salome. D-boy do have some news, but he ain't heard it with his own ears. Might be no truth to it."

Salome shook off her husband's hands. "I don't care who he heard it from. What is they sayin'?"

"Mama, you're getting yourself into a state." Tom-Tom turned to Waylon as his brother eased himself onto her sofa. "We've got it under control. The Lord's shown me a way."

"Under control? The Lord showed you?" Salome slammed a fist against her writing table.

"I know the Good Lord, He be tryin', but you ain't got nothin' under control, not with the Klan fixin' to ride."

"Well, that's jest it, you see." Maxwell Joe reached out his hands toward Salome then pulled them back. "D-boy's cousin's wife is washerwoman fo' the Smackover sheriff."

"The sheriff's in the Klan!" Salome shouted. Couldn't any of her menfolk see how bad off things were? How much they needed her?

"Mama," Waylon spoke up, "listen."

Salome felt her heart thump in her chest. Didn't her men understand? She had to do more than listen. She read their faces. Waylon believing he could put this mess right all by himself; Tom-Tom knowing in his heart of hearts that Jesus would save them; and Maxwell Joe. His face showed the most. He'd do what had to be done—even if it meant the loss of his own life.

"Lisbon sheriff the one's in the Klan." Maxwell Joe nodded to Waylon. "Smackover sheriff standin' on his back porch talkin' to two of his deputies. Arzalea—she the washerwoman—she jest steps away puttin' the sheriff's dirty drawers and such in her wash bag to take home when she hears what they sayin'."

Salome squeezed the front of her dress.

Maxwell Joe jutted his jaw. "Sheriff ain't got but three deputies. Workin' hard to get some mo'. Seems since the oil strike, a whole lot of them wildcatters been floodin' into Smackover. Actin' up bad. Hard drinkin'. Street fightin' with knives and fists. Not to mention all them loose women showin' off their . . . wares. Hard bunch to control. Arzalea, she said she heard one of the deputies bring up the name of Gopher Dennis. Sheriff said he ain't had no time fo' that kind of mess right now. Can't be battlin' them wildcatters and the coloreds at the same time. Maybe later."

"Arzalea sho she heard them words?" Salome looked at all her menfolk, but her eyes rested longest on Maxwell Joe. Were they telling her what was so, or was it their way to keep her quiet? "I'm prayin' to the

Good Lord it's the God's truth, but the Smackover sheriff ain't the Lisbon sheriff, now, is he? Gopher Dennis in thick with that Lisbon white man."

All three of them—Maxwell Joe and her boys—clucked their tongues at her like her weak woman's heart would give way if she knew the real truth. Enough of her men and their pigheadedness, making plans without her. Salome had to find word about her Margaret. Every time her mind took to pictures of Margaret lying in bed next to Jebediah, having done to her what she didn't want, Salome's belly riled up. Now, where had she put that other fountain pen?

CHAPTER THIRTY-FOUR

Jebediah rolled off her for the second time that night. Margaret turned to the clock on her bureau. Two fifteen in the morning. Would her husband want another round like he had last night, and the three before that?

"Maggie." Jebediah, still breathing hard, broke up the name he'd taken to calling her into two long, sighing syllables. Like he'd done each and every time he'd finished his business, he gave her a kiss. Right now, he picked up her hand and brushed his lips over her fingers. "You ain't got no idea how good you feel to me." He lolled his head toward her side of the pillow. "Even if it was a long time in comin'. Now that I got you where you oughta be, I can take my time with you."

Jebediah had surprised her even though he'd wasted no time getting her into bed right after they left Salome's Sunday night. As she walked the path back to Hardin House, her head filled with plans to turn herself into a wanton woman—however that worked—she struggled to ready herself for Jebediah's usual ramming bed ways. But, that's not what she got. Instead of her husband pounding and pawing at her, Jebediah took his sweet time. Why, every now and again he'd even slow himself down to search her face. What he was looking for, he never said.

"Jebediah." She laid a hand over his arm. She'd learned after round two on Sunday that her husband relished her touch. She'd use that knowledge. "Did Gopher agree with your new plan? Give Tom-Tom a thousand dollars a month for the next six months? Then, once he'd gained his trust, have him sign over the oil rights, but only for that one well?" Margaret ran her hand down her husband's arm. She wanted no more murder attempts like the one last Tuesday on her brother. She had to do this right. When Salome told her about Waylon's accident, she knew she could afford no mistakes.

Jebediah let out a low grunt as he flicked her breast with one hand. He shook his head against the pillow. "Gopher ain't goin' for that plan. Said he don't like no negotiatin'. I tole him it was best to keep his patience. Don't nobody want no trouble."

Margaret felt her heart kick up a beat, but she kept her voice soft: "No. No trouble." Rolling over to her side, she pushed her breast against Jebediah's side. This had to work. "Waylon had an accident a couple of days back. Does Gopher know about that?"

Jebediah rubbed a shoulder against her chest. "Brakes went out on him. He said that won't happen again."

"Oh?"

Her husband shook his head. "Too much rough stuff goin' on in Smackover, what with all the new folks comin' into town. But that don't mean those two niggers can do as they please." He turned toward her. "I'm tellin' you, Maggie, you'd better get them brothers of yours in line."

She scooted her body into his. "Jebediah, tell Gopher he won't have to worry about a thing." She rested her arm on his belly. "Of course, he may have to wait a little. You know how stubborn Waylon is." Tracing a small circle across his chest, she counted to fifty in her head. Now. "Is it true what I heard about the Smackover sheriff?"

"Hmm?"

"He doesn't have enough deputies to patrol the oil fields and the town, too. Not with all the newcomers. He's asked all the good citizens of Smackover to help him out by reporting any trouble." She rested her hand just below his belly button, her little finger stretched down. "You know. Keep order. Do you suppose you could remind Gopher of that?"

He stroked her arm. "Oh, that tellin' business. Gopher says he don't much fancy this tattlin' on one another's business. Seems like a woman worker at that bank in Lisbon saw his phaeton go out of control the other day, just missin' Waylon. That busybody up and tole the sheriff."

"But Gopher will get his brakes fixed, won't he?" Her hand slipped lower. "So there'll be no more accidents."

Jebediah pulled her hand down to his manhood. "Hush up all this talk about accidents." He raised himself on an elbow, one hand squeezing her breast. "What you goin' on 'bout accidents for?" He looked into her face as he climbed on top of her. "I'm thinkin' you finally gettin' the hang of this wife business."

Margaret closed her eyes. Let her husband think she was delighting in his touch. She needed time to think. Wiggle here, wiggle there, while she let him do what he wanted.

"Lord have mercy!" Jebediah called out his pleasure—his third this night. He fell back onto the bed. "Maggie, gal, you're gettin' better and better." He poked an elbow into her ribs as his breath came out in pants. "Glad as hell . . . I ain't Gopher . . . and that yella-headed wife of his. I want a woman I can teach stuff to, not one who got her learnin' from twenty, thirty other men. Before I come along."

"Gopher's wife?"

"Yep. Oh, I liked to forget." Jebediah let out a sigh. "Gopher was fussin' 'bout that new wife of his. Oh, he don't say she's spread her legs for every wildcatter from Texas to Louisiana. But he did tell me she's too rough around the edges for the wives of the business folks Gopher's dealin' with these days. She needs some schoolin'." He turned to Margaret.

"I tole him there was nobody better'n you to school her on all that manners stuff." He laughed. "I guess I did get me some good luck with you, after all. A woman with manners and big titties, too."

Margaret hoped her husband didn't notice her cringe. She'd do her best to keep her promise to Salome—she was in the man's bed, wasn't she?—but sometimes Jebediah's words made her sick to her stomach. "You told Gopher I'd help his wife?"

"I figure you do him a favor, and he'll do one back for you. Buy you some time is all." He stretched out both arms. "I been thinkin', Maggie, 'bout teachin' you somethin' new." His grin looked more like a leer. "You catchin' on so quick and all. Next time, I want you on the floor."

"Rose Linda, why are you rushing me?" Margaret, sitting at her bedroom dressing table, glared at Gopher Dennis's wife. The tall, big-boned woman acted more like Margaret's jailer than her pupil, if anyone cared to ask Margaret's opinion.

"We got to be on the seven fifteen to Memphis." The woman's Texas twang grated on Margaret's nerves, as did everything else about Rose Linda Dennis.

"That's a good hour from now. Since my husband's given me a car and chauffeur, it'll only take thirty minutes to get to El Dorado and the Missouri Pacific railway station. "Where's Tessie? I need her to finish my hair."

Rose Linda shook her head. "I told you I don't know how many times, your husband gave Tessie the day off. That's why I'm here to help you get yourself ready this morning."

Margaret frowned. "Look, Mrs. Dennis, I don't mind—"

"Rose Linda." The woman managed a smile on her sun-drenched face. Texas white women didn't seem to mind when their skin color resembled the color of a mulatto. "Our husbands are partners, so's you and me can be the best of friends. You can call me Rose Linda."

"As I was saying, I don't mind helping you out with a few lessons, Mrs. Dennis." It had already been two weeks and the *ain'ts* kept flowing out of the woman's mouth like rain during a summer squall. "I really don't see this sudden need to jump on a train for a four-hour ride into Tennessee just to pick up some dresses and shoes for you. My Lord, by the time we get back, it'll be eight o'clock at night!"

"Lady Slocum—I mean to say, Margaret—you know if you don't put some polish on me, Gopher's likely to divorce me."

Margaret picked up her brush. She'd have to do her own hair. "I don't believe a man will divorce his wife just because she doesn't know which fork to use at dinner or wears clothes too revealing." She looked into her mirror at Rose Linda's almost-on-the-shoulder blouse. The top of the woman's breasts mounded out of the garment. Clearly, Mrs. Dennis wasn't wearing one of those new binders to strap them down.

Rose Linda, her bosoms bouncing, said, "He will. He will. Margaret, you know as well as me Gopher weren't rich when he married me back in Houston." Was that a shimmy Rose Linda just did, her breasts wobbling this way and that? "I used to be a dancer in a . . . a men's club. You know the kind of place—where the wildcatters come to let off some steam on the days they ain't workin'?"

No, Margaret did not know the kind of place wildcatting men frequented, thank God. As she braided her hair, she kept an eye on the woman's reflection.

Rose Linda prattled on. "But now that he's got his own wells a'pumpin', he said he'll quit me if I don't learn how to walk, talk, look, and act like a lady. He said he's got to have him a woman he can show off to the wives of them new businessmen friends of his. That's why he said you was the perfect one to give me some polish."

Margaret's ears threatened to shut down. The sound of the woman's voice grated on Margaret's nerves. The sooner she got on that train and picked up whatever overblown floozy dresses Gopher had ordered for his wife, the sooner she'd get back home. And, hopefully, be finished with Rose Linda Dennis. Margaret bit down on her lip. She twisted her braid in place. How selfish. She'd given her promise to Salome. *Keep danger away from your brothers. Protect her boys.* Lying next to Jebediah without a stitch on would be her great sacrifice. But compared to the hours spent with this Texas cowgirl, Jebediah riding her two, three times every night was a New Year's Eve ball.

"Lady Margaret, ma'am." Georgia tapped on Margaret's open bedroom door. "The Ford car's all ready to take us to the railroad station."

Margaret slipped in the last hairpin and put on her traveling hat. She stood and followed Rose Linda out of the room.

CHAPTER
THIRTY-FIVE

"Emerald, have you seen my . . . oh, there it is." Waylon plucked his scarf from the middle drawer of his carved mahogany bedroom bureau—a perfect match to the bed's intricately worked head- and foot-boards. Weather should be warm enough at the end of September in Philadelphia, but better safe than sorry.

He heard the grandfather clock bong in his foyer. The quarter hour struck. He still had an hour to get to the El Dorado train station and Tom-Tom. He folded the scarf in thirds and poked it into a corner of his valise. One step closer to thwarting Gopher Dennis. Waylon sighed as he ran a hand across his forehead. Sweat. Late September might be iffy in Pennsylvania, but there was no doubt the temperature still scorched in Arkansas. What had he read about that new invention of Willis Carrier? Called the contraption an air conditioner. Declared it could keep an entire house cool even in August, but the machine was not only big in size but in price.

"Old Pete just brought the wagon around," Emerald called up the stairway, taking away his welcome distraction. "Are you sure you want to ride in that old buggy? The Ford's much faster."

Waylon hoisted his valise and headed toward his broad staircase. "Nope. I want as few people as possible to know Tom-Tom and I are leaving town. On a northbound train, yet."

"But it's not like you're driving that showy phaeton."

He started down the steps. "No, Emerald, the horse and buggy is safer. That's why I'm not wearing my best clothes to the station. The better to blend in. Old Pete can just drop me off a block from the place, and I'll walk the rest. Meet up with Tom-Tom, and the two of us will slip aboard that train. We'll be in Philadelphia by this time tomorrow night. Sunday. Put on our good suits. Take care of oil business. Be back in four days' time."

Emerald put on her worried face. He moved off the last step, grabbed his wife around the waist, and spun her around.

"Then the rigging gets set up with no help or hindrance from either Dennis or Slocum. Then you and I, we're going to be filthy rich."

"We're already rich." She squeezed him around the neck. "Not sure filthy rich with oil money is the safest way to go."

He set her down. It wasn't like Emerald to show so much fret.

"And I'm not sure parking our own drilling equipment under the nose of Gopher Dennis is the right way to go so soon after"—she swallowed—"what happened to you on that bridge."

He kissed his wife on the lips. "My dear, you do worry too much." He held her at arm's length. "I haven't forgotten Gopher tried to scare me, but if there's one thing I've learned from Lord Hardin, it's you've got to fight strength with strength."

She searched his eyes before she spoke. "Gopher Dennis isn't after a white man."

"No, but—"

The front door flung open. "Mama! Papa! Come quick!" Freddie waved an arm as he scurried back outside. "Joe-Annie! A.C. told her not to ride so far ahead but . . ." His voice melted into the sound of his running feet.

Waylon rushed out the front door. He heard Emerald scrambling behind him. "What? What about Joe-Annie?" he called out to Freddie, who seemed to be moving in the direction of the horse paddock.

His son rounded a corner. Waylon raced after him. In the distance, he spotted the white fences holding in those horses being trained by his head groomer, A.C. But Freddie ran past the paddock. Waylon heard Emerald pant as she struggled to keep up. Waylon squinted after the scampering figure of his son. Three hundred yards distant he watched Freddie stop abruptly and grab the reins of the gelding grazing on the open patch.

"Hurry up, Pa. A.C. says you're to take Firefly here. I'll saddle Bitsy for Mama."

Waylon, gulping in air, stopped his run beside Freddie. "Why . . . where am I going on Firefly?"

Freddie jumped up and down, his slender arms waving toward the path leading to the springhouse. "Hurry, Papa. A.C. says you've got to see it."

"See what, Freddie?" Emerald grabbed her son by the shoulders.

Whatever it was, Waylon couldn't wait. He mounted the brindle horse, turned the animal's head, and trotted down the path, Emerald screaming after him. He steered the animal over a fallen branch. A few more turns, and he'd be at the old springhouse. What on earth could have happened to Joe-Annie? She knew better than to play in that falling-apart structure.

Waylon dug his heels into Firefly's sides. There. The last stand of trees.

"A.C.? Wha . . ." Waylon first spotted Joe-Annie. The groom stood in front of his daughter as though he was shielding her from something.

Waylon let his eyes follow the direction where his child frantically fought to look. His gaze went past Chameleon, Joe-Annie's horse, to the trunk of the stunted tree, and then toward the ramshackle building. The springhouse was already out of use when he'd inherited the property from Lord Hardin. The need for a building to cool foodstuffs by a stream had passed when his father installed electricity.

"God in Heaven!" Waylon jerked hard on Firefly's reins.

The animal snorted and came to a stop, pitching Waylon forward.

"I'm tryin' to keep this chile from seein'," A.C. called over his shoulder. "I done tole this girl over and over again not to get to ridin' this here hoss too far ahead of me, but she ain't listened."

A.C.'s voice floated in and out of Waylon's ears. But it wasn't his ears that held him transfixed in the saddle.

"Papa," Joe-Annie, still wrestling with A.C., called out. "You can smell it in the air. There was a fire last night. A whole wall of the springhouse is gone."

The hard trot of a horse reached Waylon's ears. Emerald called his name as she fast approached. He turned to watch her. Freddie sat behind her in the saddle, his hands encircling her waist.

"Oh, Lord. What? When?" Emerald turned toward the pile of wood littering the ground around the fallen wall.

"I ain't heard nor seen nothin', Lady Emerald."

Joe-Annie broke free and ran toward her parents. "Mama, Papa—it's a cross. A big cross. And it's black around the edges. Do you think it set the springhouse on fire?"

Waylon slid off the horse and pulled Joe-Annie to him. He stared at the framing of the old wall. "Yes, my girl, you do see a cross but not a very big one." He cupped his daughter's face in his hands. His breath stuck in his lungs. "I want you and Freddie to go back to the house. It looks like we've had ourselves some vandals last night." He tried and failed to bring up a chuckle.

Pushing back from him, Joe-Annie shook her head so hard, her pigtails slapped at her face.

"Not vandals, Papa." She lowered her voice. "The Ku Klux Klan."

Waylon pulled up his best half smile. "No. Joe-Annie, Freddie, look there. See how small that cross is? Not even four feet high. The Klan's crosses are almost twice as tall." He found that little laugh. "This is the work of a few wild young bucks playing an early Halloween prank on us." He turned to Emerald, hoping she could read the pretense on his face. He called over his shoulder. "You children get on home with your mama. A.C. and I will start the cleanup."

Emerald held her eyes on Waylon, but she spoke to the groomer. "A.C., take the children to the house."

A.C. looked first at Emerald then at Waylon. The man nodded to Lady Hardin, reached for Chameleon's bridle, and headed toward the children.

Emerald waited just until the group rode out of sight. She turned to her husband, her brow knotting and unknotting. "This is the work of the Klan. Their second warning. There won't be a third."

Waylon reached her in three strides. He rested his chin on the top of her head. "Emerald, my love, you're right. This is a serious thing, but the tale I told the children wasn't a complete lie." He turned her toward the damaged springhouse. "See? That building must be close to a hundred years old. It wouldn't take much of a spark to light up the whole nighttime sky with its blaze. Yet this was a very small fire." He let her go and pointed to the cross. "The wood is barely singed. Those old boards on the springhouse more fell to the ground than burned." He shook his head. "The Klan may hide their faces but never their calling cards. Any fires they set, they want their handiwork seen for miles around."

Emerald opened her mouth but said nothing.

"See this?" Waylon ran a hand over the cross. "Nobody even took the time to paint the thing white. The Klan wouldn't be so careless. This was a hurry-up job, more bluff than anything. Like the phaeton the other day, designed to scare me, maybe even break a few bones, but not kill. This was the work of thugs, of Gopher Dennis. Not the Klan."

The morning sun shining behind Emerald's head made her face appear like an angel's. "Waylon, I know there was a time you and Salome considered me reckless because I campaigned for decent books and supplies for our colored schools."

"Emerald, I never tried to stop you from caring about our kids, only to caution you."

A ray of smoke-laden morning sun caught her hair. "That's exactly what I want for you. Caution. Waylon, this is not about a woman passing out new schoolbooks and crayons to children. This is about a colored man sitting on oil land worth millions of dollars. I know you believe you know all about the ways of white men in Union County." She shook that light-colored hair of hers. "But you don't. Your father protected you with his wealth and power. Allowed you to believe you were not only as good as any white man, but better by miles. You're the duke of Union County. Oh, my husband, to show what you know to be true is so very dangerous in the South."

"Emerald"—it was the dread he read in her eyes that most unnerved him—"I do understand."

"Not enough. I know far more than you about the evil white men can inflict on us. You believe because this cross stands only four feet tall, this was not a serious attempt on our lives." Her head moved in a slow arc, right to left. "I saw the aftermath of a lynching. When I was twelve. A white farmer and four of his sons killed a colored boy no more than twenty. His crime? He stole a ham for Christmas dinner. The farmer and his boys wore no sheets. They burned no crosses, but they left that young man four days dead, hanging from a tree."

"Oh, my darling. I'm so sorry." He wrapped his arms around her. "I do understand Gopher Dennis wishes me no love. But the man is no match for the last will and testament of Lord Henry Hardin. Emerald, if I'm dead, I can't sign deeds. Dennis needs me alive to sign those papers."

He rubbed his cheek against her hair. "I'll have Maxwell Joe, D-boy, maybe a few of the others come here while I head to the station."

"Four days' time and you'll be back from Philadelphia?" A tremor he was sure she wanted to hide edged Emerald's voice.

Waylon shook his head. "I'm going to the train station to tell Tom-Tom I can't travel with him this morning. He'll have to go to Philadelphia alone. I'll join him tomorrow once I've got you and the children secured." He kissed her forehead. "I wouldn't have you worry like this for the world."

"Waylon, be on the alert. Your father is no longer here to buffer you. Even if Margaret were so inclined, she's no match against her husband or Gopher Dennis. Whether he wears a sheet or not, Dennis is a night rider to his soul. Promise me you'll take care. If a boy can die over a ham, what do you think will happen to you over oil?"

"I'll be even more careful than I normally am, but I still believe this is more scare tactic than anything." He led her to Bitsy and helped her mount.

No, he'd not witnessed a lynching, but growing up as a white man's other family had taken its toll. He was not as oblivious to danger as his wife supposed. Emerald was wrong: Lord Hardin hadn't meant to, but the late duke had trained him to be forever wary. Money held its own power. Wealth, combined with caution, would buy him protection and insulate him and his family against the Klan. Even in Union County.

CHAPTER
THIRTY-SIX

In this heat Margaret longed for the days of ladies' fans—even at this early-morning hour. But in September 1922, very few ladies fluttered the delicate creations outside of church. No wonder she felt more warm than usual, what with all the pacing Rose Linda was doing up and down the train platform. The woman, wearing cowboy boots, an ankle-slapping skirt, a gingham top with the first three buttons undone, and a kerchief looped around her neck, was acting like a giant, twittering hummingbird.

"What time did you say it was?" Rose Linda stopped long enough to throw the same question at Margaret she'd asked four minutes ago.

Margaret pointed to the big round clock with the brass numbers standing near the door of the train depot. "It's five past seven."

A smile suddenly flickered across Mrs. Dennis's lips. "Train'll be here any minute. Let's walk this way." The woman brushed past Margaret and headed up the tracks toward the colored waiting room.

"What on earth?" Margaret scowled. "We've got another ten minutes. Where are you going?"

Rose Linda turned quickly and beckoned Margaret to follow.

Margaret peered around the Texas woman's back. "We can wait right here. This is where we board. You're heading toward the back of the train where the color . . . Oh, who is that?" Margaret tilted her head.

There he stood, dressed in a workman's everyday clothes so unlike his own. Tom-Tom? What was he doing at the train depot? She rushed toward her brother. Odd. Rose Linda seemed to be of the same mind, or did she? Mrs. Dennis pulled up abruptly about ten feet from Tom-Tom and busied herself with the colored train porter. Rose Linda looked almost like she expected to see Tom-Tom at the station, but why?

"Tom-Tom, what are you doing here?"

Her brother's stare equaled her own. "Marg . . . Lady Margaret? What . . . you . . . I . . ." He sounded even more flustered than Margaret felt surprised.

"Salome told me nothing about you taking a train trip." She peered at her brother's workman's getup. Judging by that shirt and those overalls, and ignoring his finely chiseled good looks, he might have been one of those field hands who'd opted to leave the South forever. Those men tossed everything they owned into little cardboard suitcases and hopped a train heading anywhere north. "And why are you dressed like that?"

Tom-Tom swiveled right and left as though he were trying to avoid someone or something. "Have you seen Waylon?"

"Waylon?" The train whistle and the chug-chug of the steam engine drowned out her voice.

"Tom-Tom." Waylon's voice rose above the noise from the fast-approaching New York City–bound train—its cowcatcher leading the way.

Margaret turned toward Waylon just as he jogged past Rose Linda. Did the woman's face light up? Surely Rose Dennis didn't know Waylon.

Waylon halted in front of her. "Margaret? What are you doing here?" He sounded winded.

"Here comes the train. What kept you?" Tom-Tom picked up his valise as the steam churning from the train's engine covered the waiting passengers.

"Can't go." Waylon panted. "Something happened at the farm. Nothing serious but big enough for me to pay it some mind."

"You're not coming?" Tom-Tom stood flat-footed, his mouth agape.

"Tomorrow." Waylon leaned close. "I'll take tomorrow's train to Philadelphia. Explain then."

"All aboard. Memphis, Cincinnati, Philadelphia, New York City, and all points in between." The white conductor stood on the platform, his step stool placed on the ground. "All aboard."

"But . . . but, Waylon, Tom-Tom? What are you two do—?"

"Margaret. Let's get on the train." Rose Linda came at a run through the hiss of steam. She grabbed Margaret by the arm. "White folks get on down here."

"Let go of me! Those men are my—"

Rose Linda's tug threatened to dislocate Margaret's shoulder. What an annoying woman. Margaret struggled to free herself, but Rose Linda wrestled her toward the whites-only car and up the retractable steps.

Inside the train car, Margaret jerked her arm free, stumbled down the aisle, and scooted into her train seat. She turned to the window. Tom-Tom must have boarded. She spotted Waylon waving as he backed away from the now-moving train. Rose Linda plopped down beside her, sighing as she stretched out her long legs. She had to tower over her husband by a good four inches. Mrs. Dennis seemed extremely pleased with herself. The train picked up speed.

"Excuse me." Margaret turned to Rose Linda, who gave her a lop-sided smile but didn't move. "I'd like to get out."

"Out? No, no, Margaret. Ain't no need for all that. You just set back and enjoy the ride to Memphis."

Margaret stared at the woman. "I said I want to get out."

"Whatever for?"

"Those men on the platform. I know them. They worked for my family for years." Margaret glared at Mrs. Dennis. Why should she have to explain anything to this uncouth woman?

Rose Linda folded her arms and closed her eyes. "Them men looked colored to me. You can't be seen with them."

Margaret bumped Rose Linda with her leg. "Only one of those men boarded the train."

"What?" Rose Linda jerked herself upright. A flash of worry splashed across her face and stayed. "What do you mean—only one of 'em got on the train? Both of 'em was sposed to be on here."

Margaret blinked. Something was amiss. "Are you going to move and let me out or am I going to have to call the conductor?"

Rose Dennis turned a face that looked threatening toward Margaret. "You ain't callin' nobody. My husband wants you to sit tight 'til we get to Memphis." She sucked her lips in and out.

Did Margaret hear her issue a *damn* under her breath? And, why on God's good earth did Gopher Dennis care if she sat tight or not? What was Tom-Tom doing on this train? "Conductor," she called out, raising her voice.

Rose Linda punched Margaret in the shoulder, sending her slamming into her train seat. "Gopher won't like it if you go wanderin' around."

"Yes, ma'am?" The conductor peered over at Margaret. "Somethin' I can help you with, ma'am?" He sent a disdainful look down the front of Rose Linda's much-too-open blouse.

Margaret leaned forward and put on her most beguiling smile. "The facilities," she whispered, "could you please show me where they are?"

"Of course, madam." He stepped aside.

An unmoving Rose Linda stared straight ahead. The conductor frowned as he lowered his gaze at Mrs. Dennis with her stringy hair and clothes no respectable woman would ever wear.

"If you don't mind." The conductor sneered in Rose's direction. "Please allow the lady"—he let the word hang in the air—"to pass."

The look on Rose Linda's face as she turned to Margaret said one thing: given the chance, Mrs. Dennis would clearly throttle Margaret within an inch of her life. But the woman grudgingly swung her legs to the side. Margaret slipped past but not quick enough to avoid the foot Rose Linda placed in her path.

With the conductor looking on, Margaret turned to Mrs. Dennis. "No need to hold my seat. If there's a vacant one up ahead, I believe I'll take it." She put on her sweetest smile for her savior conductor as she hurried down the aisle.

"There's facilities at the end of this car, but two cars up ahead, you'll find a room for ladies to lie down if they get taken by the vapors."

"Thank you so much." She struggled with the heavy door separating her car from the next.

The conductor slid it back. "Mind your step at that gap." He pointed to the space between the cars.

Margaret laid a hand on his arm. Oh, my. She spotted the rail bed below the empty space between the cars and the short iron railings. It would not be that difficult to tumble over the railing and fall onto the tracks. Worse yet, slip between the cars. She landed her high-heeled shoe with care as she wrestled open the door to the next train car. Margaret made her way up the aisle of the swaying train, her mind jumbling with thoughts of Tom-Tom, Rose Linda, Waylon, and Gopher Dennis. Her stomach, usually quite settled, acted up. She laid her hand on the backs of the seats as she made her way toward the next door.

"Ma'am, may I help you?" A second conductor looked at her.

"The lavatory," she mouthed.

"That's just fine, ma'am, but don't go too far. The car after the next one is for colored. I don't reckon you'll want to go in there unless"—he took inventory of Margaret—"you got maids and such travelin' with you. They can't come see you in the whites-only car, but you're welcome to check on them." He smiled.

Margaret nodded and picked her careful way across the connecting vestibule. With the train door open, the clank-clanking of metal against metal deafened. The train felt as though it had reached a high speed—maybe even fifty miles an hour. She held on tight as she made her way up the final whites-only car. She'd slip into the colored section and find Tom . . . wait, there he was. The train swerved around a curve and she spotted her brother, his arm pushing against the door of the last of the colored-only train cars. Was that a piece of paper in his hand? He didn't act as though he'd seen her. Margaret hurried her feet, but the moving train forced her back two steps. She recovered her balance and headed toward the connecting door just as Tom-Tom opened the last door on the colored side and stepped into the space between the cars. What was he doing? He knew he couldn't enter the whites-only car. Was he trying to reach her? Why? She watched her brother wave his arms as though he were talking to someone just out of her line of sight. The train straightened. Margaret took three more steps before she halted to regain her balance. She stared ahead. What was Tom-Tom saying? He held his hands in the air. Wait. Another pair of hands reached out for his shoulders.

"Tom-Tom?" She tried to hurry.

The sound of the train drowned out any cries her brother may have made. Margaret clutched the seat back as she stared through the moving train's glass door. It most definitely looked like her brother was engaged in a wrestling match with someone. The train lurched. Margaret almost landed in the lap of a seated male passenger.

"Sorry." She bobbed her apologies as she struggled to get her feet under her.

She looked straight ahead. *Oh, my Lord.* The other man's back—covered in a light-blue seersucker jacket. Not Tom-Tom's. She caught a glimpse of one of her brother's arms. Was he being pushed against the side rail? The train's whistle blew loud as the railway car swerved around a bend. Margaret's feet tangled, and she dropped to the floor.

"Oh, are you hurt?" A woman in a proper traveling suit reached down.

"Uhh." Her ankle felt sprained. "I'm not sure. I think—"

The connecting door flew open. "Conductor! Conductor! There's been a terrible accident! A colored boy just fell off the train."

Two fellow passengers knelt beside Margaret. Questions swirled in her ears. Voices—some surprised, some shocked, others horrified—all riddled with questions. Her ears failed her, but not her eyes. All she could do was stare. There, his arms spreading open the connecting doors, his blue seersucker suit torn in three places, stood her son. Morris Slocum.

CHAPTER
THIRTY-SEVEN

Salome could see them surrounding her. She watched their lips move and their wet eyes carry worry for her. She pretty much knew where she was. A big strapping man called Maxwell Joe had led her to a bench of some sort on the grassy lawn just outside a white building. Underneath a tree. Someone must have sat her down for she felt her body held upright by something. She saw men and women flapping fans at her. She supposed they thought she must have been overly warm. But they didn't know she couldn't tell hot from cold. She could hear voices, each and every word, but the trouble Salome had was in matching the voices to the mouths of those worried faces.

"Lord Jesus, when's the last time she said a word, Maxwell Joe?" A man's voice.

"When Waylon"—a voice that carried tears—"first come to the house with the news, she hit the flo', and when we brung her around, she ain't said a word."

"That's been fo' days, Maxwell Joe."

"Where's Waylon?" A woman's voice, but to which of those female faces did it belong?"

"Inside." The voice barely got out the word. "With the coffin. My husband hasn't left his brother's side since . . ." The voice was swallowed in tears.

Salome cocked her head. That last voice had a hint of the familiar to it, but for the life of her, she couldn't match the sound to a face.

"Shouldn't Miz Ladora be here by now?" Another female voice. "Ain't the service sposed to start at 'leven?"

"It be all right. A.C., he gone to fetch Miz Hardin and the chil'ren. In the Ford. Car mighta broke down." Another strange man.

"Miz Salome, ma'am, sip on this." A brown face looked down at her, holding a glass full of what looked like lemonade.

Salome stared at the woman's lips. They moved, sure enough, but their movement didn't match the clamoring sound in her ears.

"Lord, help her. She takin' it awful hard."

"I hear tell the coffin got to be closed. Him bein' run over by the train and all. They say his head jest 'bout—"

"Hush up. She can hear you in there."

"Naw. Old folks say when they like that they don't know nothin' goin' on 'round them."

"Maxwell Joe, where Freddie?" Another man's voice. "Emerald, where the other chil'ren?"

"She left the little ones back at the house. Said it was too hard on 'em. Joe-Annie, she say she had to stay the night with Ladora to look after her cousins." Did this last voice belong to someone called Maxwell Joe?

A little twinge in her chest prodded at Salome. Maxwell Joe. She must know him. The sound of his name felt pleasing on her ears. The voices kept talking around her, the faces moving in and out from where her eyes could see.

Fresh voices—a man and a woman, but far away—shrieking, and all the faces turned away from Salome.

"A.C., Ladora, what y'all two hollerin' 'bout?"

"Jesus, help us!" said the woman, her voice pitched higher than a screech owl's. "Waylon, Emerald, Ms. Salome, weren't nothin' I could do." More shrieks to the high heavens poured out of the woman's mouth.

Salome blinked. Children screamed. Whose children? Did she have children? Once she imagined she might have. Were they boys or girls?

"What done happened?" That sounded like the Maxwell Joe person.

Salome ran a hand down her shoulder. Hadn't there been a comforting arm there a moment ago?

"Joe-Annie was helpin' me in the kitchen when . . . when . . ." More screeches from the woman folks called Ladora.

"Ladora"—another woman's voice—"where's . . . I see your boys . . . but . . . where is . . . ?"

"What's all the commotion?" A man stepped outside of a building with a cross on its roof. Oh yes, that must be a church. "What's happened, Ladora?"

"Waylon, Waylon"—the other woman's hollering got even louder—"is she with you?"

"Emerald, Waylon, I gots to tell y'all." The Ladora woman sounded like she'd just danced with the Devil. "They come in quick . . . framed in my front do'. Fo' of 'em. White mens and they had rags tied 'round they faces. They . . ."

"What are you talking about, Ladora? What men? Where's Joe-Annie? Where's my daughter?"

"She . . . they done took her." Wails that hurt Salome's ears clawed at the sky.

"Who they done took? Joe-Annie Hardin? God and Jesus, too. White mens? Lord, Glory." So many voices called out at the same time,

Salome figured they must be singing a choir hymn. "In the name of Jesus."

"What are you saying? What are you saying?" The Emerald woman again. "Joe-Annie, my baby, my baby!" A scream that Jesus Himself must have heard reached the heavens.

"Who were these men?" The Waylon man's voice carried the sound of brass on the coldest January day. "Did they say anything?"

"They say . . . they say you is hardheaded. That even Tom-Tom ain't given you 'nough of a message. They say I has to give you a fresh message." The woman named Ladora's heavy swallow reached Salome's ears. "They tell me you better sign them deed papers if you don't want nothin' bad to . . . to happen to Joe-Annie."

A banshee couldn't hold nothing against the sound coming from the woman called Emerald.

"Maxwell Joe, take Emerald and Mama out of here. Ladora, who were these men?"

A chill surprised Salome as it ran down her back.

"They had masks on they faces, but I knows me the eyes of Mr. Morris Slocum when I sees 'em." The Ladora woman's voice settled into certainty. "And ain't no two ways 'bout the talk of Mr. Gopher Dennis."

CHAPTER THIRTY-EIGHT

"Emerald, I've come to talk to Waylon." Margaret stood just inside the foyer of her brother's house. Even now, a week after the funeral, black bunting twisted around the banisters and hung over the painting of Tom-Tom. A black wreath decorated every interior door.

The hollow-eyed woman, dressed in head-to-toe black, looked Margaret over before her head did a slow bob. "You've come to tell me where Joe-Annie is?"

"You know I don't know, Emerald. I just left Salome. Maxwell Joe's got her eating a little bit these days."

Emerald's shoulders slumped. "But she's still in that other world." The woman walked toward her front parlor. "I'm not sure if coming out of it would be a blessing or a curse. What with Tom-Tom and now Joe . . ." Her voice dissolved into sobs.

Margaret skimmed a hand down the front of her dark gray dress. She followed Emerald's slow steps inside the house. She was certain that was disapproval stamped across the face of her brother's wife. But even Emerald must understand Margaret could not slip into the attire of full mourning—not for a man who had ostensibly been her father's servant. "How is Waylon?"

Emerald whirled around in the center of her foyer.

"How is he? How do you think he is? His brother's been murdered, his daughter kidnapped." Emerald clamped her hand to her face. "He blames himself, and I'm waiting for the other shoe to drop."

Ever since Margaret found out the truth about herself some twenty or so years back, she knew she'd forever be in a world by herself. Neither fully colored, nor fully white. Different from Waylon and, God bless him, Tom-Tom. Even with the same parents, the tan that dusted their skin made them forever colored. This afternoon it was easy to see that Emerald blamed the white half of Margaret for Tom-Tom's death.

"What do you want?" Emerald shook her head as she reached for the call bell. "I'll order tea. You'll drink, then leave. I don't believe Waylon wants to see you."

She took in a deep breath. "He certainly won't when I tell him what I know." Margaret followed Emerald into the parlor and closed the heavy walnut doors behind her.

Emerald's eyes widened, then narrowed. "Of course. You're the other shoe. Has Jebediah sent you here to give us his final terms so that we can have our daughter back?"

The cabbage-rose pattern decorating the ice-blue carpet in Waylon's front room caught Margaret's eye. "I told my husband what I saw, but Jebediah doubts it's true." She walked to the center of the room and the still-standing Emerald. "But I've put two and two together."

"I'm delighted, Margaret, that you can do math, but I for one doubt you will come up with four if it benefits your colored kin. To you, we dark Hardins will always register five. Even Joe-Annie." Emerald folded her arms across her chest. "I'm not Salome or Waylon." She leaned toward Margaret and whispered, "I don't trust you."

The door to the parlor opened. "I thought I heard voices." Waylon, his hair uncombed and his top shirt button undone, stood with his hands on the door lever. "Margaret?"

She rushed to her brother and laced her arms around him for the first time since she was six. Back then, before she died, Lady Bertha punished her for hugging a servant. "Waylon, it's just so awful." She held him tight, but his arms were slow to encircle her.

"Oh, I see." Emerald's voice dripped chill. "First, you want to play the doting sister, then you deliver Gopher Dennis's next warning."

Waylon pushed Margaret away, scanning her face, his eyes hooded, his look grim. "Do you know something of Joe-Annie?"

Margaret bit down on her lip as she shook her head.

"Now I understand. You were high-and-mighty to me as a child. Lording it over me. Never letting me forget you were the daughter of a duke, while I was merely the son of a lowly colored house servant." Waylon shook his head. "Is Emerald right? Are you Jebediah's emissary?"

A tap on the doorjamb brought Waylon's housemaid to the parlor. She set a silver platter with tea and cakes on a table and bobbed her way from the room.

"Here's your tea, Margaret." Emerald walked to Waylon and grabbed his arm. "Drink it quickly. Then Hester will show you out."

"Wait." Waylon eased away. "Margaret hasn't betrayed us, Emerald. I . . . I find it difficult to believe that of her. If she has brought news from Jebediah, it comes out of worry for Joe-Annie's safety."

"Safety?" Emerald wrinkled her nose. "The only safety she's concerned about is holding her own in a white world where she doesn't belong."

A trembling started at Margaret's knees and traveled up to her jaw. "Waylon. When I tell you what I suspect to be the truth, you will hate me even more than Emerald does."

"Margaret," Emerald snapped, "I do not give you the courtesy of hate. I merely don't trust you."

Waylon steered his wife to a chair and pointed to another for his sister. "Let's sit. My wife may have temporarily forgotten the code we have in this family. That Margaret was raised as a white child was none of her doing, or our mother's. That is the world chosen for her by our father, and I am honor-bound to respect it." He sat on the stuffed arm of Emerald's chair and leaned toward his sister.

"Whatever you have to tell me cannot be a quarter as bad as what I've done to my own brother and daughter." Waylon wiped a hand over his eyes. "I allowed him to get on that train by himself. I wasn't there with him, to help him. If I had been . . . you see, it was me—my failure." Waylon's face shone ghostly pale. "I killed him."

Margaret jumped from her chair, brushing the tea table. She fell to her knees in front of Waylon. "No. You did not kill Tom-Tom. If you'd been there, I'm"—her throat tightened—"I'm afraid I would have lost you both." Margaret stared at the floor. Her lips trembled. "I saw the entire thing."

"You what?" Emerald scooted forward. "You never said a word."

Waylon's eyes widened. He stood and helped Margaret to her feet and led her back to her seat.

"Tell me what you saw." He poured her a cup of tea, steam smelling of chamomile wafting into the room.

"You watched me board. Did you wonder why I was on a train heading north? With Mrs. Gopher Dennis?"

"That trashy thing out of Texas?" Emerald frowned. "Is she a part of your plot, too?"

"Emerald," Waylon cautioned as he turned to Margaret. "Why were you on that train?"

"Because of a plan I'm positive Gopher hatched." Margaret shook her head. "A plot I think he had against"—her throat went dry—"against you and Tom-Tom." She reached for her teacup and took a sip. "Jebediah and I had reached a deal. That Sunday . . . at Salome's . . ." Her face flushed. "He . . . Jebediah . . . would keep Gopher away from the Hardins—make him stop pressing to have all the oil land signed over immediately—if I would allow him back into my . . ." She flushed. "It's not important what I had to do for Jebediah. The point is, Gopher promised to hold off on doing anything rash for a couple of weeks if I agreed to train his wife in manners and etiquette."

"Manners and etiquette?" Emerald leaned over the arm of her chair. "What on earth does a trollop from Texas need with such training?"

Margaret shook her head so hard a loose hairpin jabbed at her scalp. "I was told it was to impress the wives of his new business partners. Rose Linda Dennis is almost illiterate. She has the manners of a brood sow. I gave her daily lessons on how to speak, how to sit, how to walk." Margaret shook her head. "Not that any of it worked."

"Uh-huh." Waylon sounded impatient as he walked back to his wife.

"Oh, Waylon." The tears puddled in Margaret's eyes, and the teacup shivered in her hands. "I thought it odd Gopher wanted me to accompany Rose Linda on a train trip all the way to Memphis just to pick up some new frocks for his wife."

"And where was Jebediah in all this?" Emerald settled back into the chair, her arms crossed over her chest.

"In Camden. Sent on some silly errand by Gopher Dennis. Now I know that must have been part of the plan—to get Jebediah out of the way so Rose Linda could trick me into getting on that train." She shook her head. "Jebediah knew nothing of all this, I'm sure."

"And what is it Waylon and I are supposed to be sure of?" Emerald kept a frowning face directed at her.

Margaret sipped the hot tea, the soothing chamomile bathing her tongue. "I'm positive Rose Linda knew all about her husband's scheme. She maneuvered me onto that train. Tried to hold me prisoner in my seat." She wet her lips. "I think I was supposed to be bait—a lure for you both. I'm convinced Tom-Tom was trying to get to me to tell me something when . . ." Not even another sip of tea could loosen her tight throat.

Waylon shook his head. "I'm afraid I'm not following. Lure me and Tom-Tom into what? Who, besides close family, even knew we were going to Philadelphia? We didn't tell Mama. We knew she'd forbid such a trip."

"I've racked my brain over that one." Margaret refilled her teacup. "Where did you buy the tickets?"

"I didn't. I had Maxwell Joe buy one, and A.C. the other. Both in Lisbon." Waylon's face paled.

Margaret looked up, her hand still on the teapot handle. "The ticket master in Lisbon is Jacob Slocum's cousin."

"My God!" The sound burst out of Waylon.

Hand shaking, Margaret lifted her cup. "I know that Rose Linda wanted you and Tom-Tom to see me get on that train. I remember her speaking to a colored porter on the platform. I think, maybe, she may have slipped the porter a piece of paper. Perhaps a note."

"A note." Emerald grabbed Waylon's hand. "Saying what?"

"I don't know. I do know when I told Rose Linda only Tom-Tom had boarded, she looked stricken. That's when I knew something was terribly wrong. I managed to escape from Rose Linda. I was on my way to find Tom-Tom in the colored car when . . . when I saw him heading toward the whites-only section, a slip of white notepaper in his hand. Why chance breaking the law if he wasn't trying to reach me?"

"Reach you for what?" Waylon walked over to her.

"Waylon, I know you blame yourself for not being on that train. But if you had been, I'm afraid you both might have been pushed overboard." She set the cup on the table, rattling it against the saucer. "You see, I saw the argument. Rather, I saw the tussling, and I don't know how many other of Gopher's men might have been on that train."

"What tussling?" Waylon's breath came in quick spurts. "What other men?"

"I could see Tom-Tom—not all of him, mind you, but his face and arms—through the train door window. I saw into the space between the cars, and our brother was not alone."

"In the name of God, woman, who was there with Tom-Tom?" Waylon raised his voice.

Margaret shook her head and the hairpin tumbled to her lap. "I couldn't get a look at the man's face, just his arms. Covered by a blue suit. Then the train swerved. I fell. I saw no more . . . not until a man opened the door. He screamed that a colored man had just fallen off the train."

"Who was that man?" Emerald's voice blended with Waylon's. "Who, in God's name, did you see?"

The words felt like knives slashing out of her throat. "Morris. My son."

CHAPTER
THIRTY-NINE

Margaret looked over her shoulder as she made her way down the path. The servants had long known she visited Salome's house, but of course, they never acknowledged those visits aloud. But today was different. Salome's house was empty. Waylon had spirited his mother to his own home, along with Maxwell Joe. Margaret sucked in her lip as the outline of the two-story building appeared in the distance. Salome still remained silent. The woman stared for endless hours at the wallpaper in Waylon's guest room, uttering not a word to her family. Not even to Maxwell Joe. But it wasn't her mother who worried Margaret this afternoon. It was her brother.

Margaret glanced around one last time before she slipped through Salome's kitchen door. No one had seen her enter. She peeked through the doorway into Salome's front room. There stood Waylon, waiting as she'd asked. Her heart picked up speed. "Thank you for coming," she managed to say as she latched the door behind her. "I know how Emerald feels about me."

"Margaret, I've got to get Joe-Annie back, and you're going to help by telling Morris the truth about everything." Waylon, grim faced, standing between his mother's favorite chair and her chintz sofa, wasted no time.

She trembled. "Surely that's not necessary. I didn't exactly see what happened."

"But something did happen. And you saw no other person in that train vestibule except your brother and your son."

Would he give her an ounce of pity? She'd lost a brother, too. She glanced down at the rug on her mother's polished floor. "I know what I saw and what I didn't see." Margaret gazed up. "Yes, Morris was in the vestibule tussling with Tom-Tom, but I don't believe my son had anything to do with our brother's fall from that train." Margaret frowned. "Why would he do such a thing?"

"Have you asked him?"

"Of course. He swears he knows nothing about the accident. He happened to step into the vestibule just as Tom-Tom slipped from the car."

Waylon pursed his lips as he scanned her. "Margaret, you saw enough of the fight between those two to know better than that."

She rushed to Waylon and grabbed his coat sleeve. "He's my son."

Waylon, his eyes the color of oil-field steel, looked down at her. "And Joe-Annie's my daughter."

"What do you want me to do?" Her shoulders sagged.

He cast a sidelong glance as though weighing and measuring her. "We've got to get Joe-Annie back, and Tom-Tom must be avenged. We Hardins cannot allow any of our own to be kidnapped and murdered with impunity . . . even by each other."

Margaret shook her head so hard her neck hurt. "Not murdered. I won't believe you could think such a thing about Morris. Yes, he's spoiled. Wants his own way, but he would never—not deliberately—kill anyone, let alone one of his grandfather's servants."

Waylon's chin jutted. "That is what your son believes, isn't it, Margaret? That Tom-Tom was just another of his grandfather's house servants, albeit a favored one. One who got too uppity. Prime for a smacking down." Waylon chewed his upper lip. "That's precisely why Morris must be told the truth. He didn't kill an uppity Negro, he killed his own uncle."

"You can't believe your own words." She searched her brother's face. "Waylon, Morris is my child. He wouldn't—he couldn't—do such an awful thing to Tom-Tom whether he knew he was his uncle or not."

"Are you sure? Yes, Morris is your son, but he's also Sylvester's." Muscles twitched on the right side of Waylon's face.

The tightness clutching Margaret's throat trapped her breath. "Waylon . . ." The name came out on a thin reed of air. How could her brother say such a thing to her?

A flush of redness appeared and disappeared on Waylon's face. "When Gopher Dennis ran me down with that phaeton, who do you suppose was at the wheel? Your son."

Waylon stared in defiance. "It's time you told Morris the God's truth. He was born a colored man, and he will die a colored man. And now he's kidnapped his own cousin."

"I can make things right." The words scratched her throat as she fumbled for the back of Salome's sofa to steady her trembling. "Let me talk to Jebediah. I can get him to hold Gopher Dennis at bay. Just until I can straighten out this misunderstanding about Morris." If it *was* a misunderstanding. "No one could wish to harm Joe-Annie. She's just a child."

Waylon closed the distance between them, until they were standing within two feet of each other. "You're asking me to put my faith in a killer and a kidnapper? I'll give you this much. Whatever Morris did, you can bet Gopher Dennis orchestrated it. That fool of a man wants all our oil land—that's just about every square inch of dirt the three of us own. Neither you nor your so-called husband can hold back a cretin like Dennis."

Her head wobbled between a yes and a no.

A raw laugh came out of Waylon's throat. "Oh, I see. It's your own land you want to save. Not mine. Not Tom-Tom's." A snort more than a sigh passed his lips. "That job should be relatively easy for you, Margaret. You may hate the task, but all you need do is not upset Jebediah, and all those lovely oil wells will keep pumping cash into your bank account. But for Ladora, for Tom-Tom's kids, for me and mine, we'll not have those options. We will be left with nothing." He slowly shook his head. "Margaret, I cannot allow one of Salome's children to prosper at the expense of the others. Not even you. Our father did not want that."

"I don't want that. Please, Waylon. I know you're the duke of Union County, but I'm Henry Hardin's child, too. I want to carry out his legacy as much as you do." She clasped her hands. "Don't fault Morris for all the troubles. You may not trust Jebediah, but give me time, and I promise he will be helpful to us. He's been listening to me more and more. We will get Joe-Annie back. I'll make up something for him to tell Gopher—to buy time."

"And what makes you think Dennis gives a hound's tooth what Jebediah has to say? Gopher Dennis believes that he's God Almighty. That he can take anything he damn well pleases from colored, Jebediah or no Jebediah."

Her head felt fuzzy. She headed to Salome's kitchen. Water. That would clear her thinking. "Waylon, I haven't worked out every detail just yet, but I know if you give me time, I can get Jebediah to hold Gopher back." She bit down on her lip. "I only know if you protest too much, more harm will come to us." She turned just inside the doorway. "To all of Salome's children."

"All of Salome's children, is it? Mama's convinced you're one of us—a true Hardin."

Waylon walked toward her. "I'm not so sure. Your son killed our brother. Of that I am certain. Call it an accident if it makes you feel better, but, Margaret, that deed cannot go unpunished."

She took a step backward. "He's my child! Blame me, not Morris. I did a terrible job of raising him. That's why he's so rotten. Old Jacob Slocum had far more influence over Morris than anyone. Punish me."

"Oh no, sister dear, you may not take the easy way out. If Mama's right, and you are to be trusted, then you have a responsibility to this family. No half measures. And your first priority is to tell Morris the truth about himself. That's the first step in getting Joe-Annie back."

"All right, I'll do just that!" The words burst out of her mouth. "But you've got to give me time to prepare him for the truth. I know you'll hate me all the more for saying it, but moving from white to black is no easy thing. It's like . . . it's like having all your clothes ripped off and being paraded naked in front of the world." Her hand went to her mouth. She read the growing thunder on her brother's face. "Waylon, you know Morris is not strong enough for that. Not just yet."

"What I know is that despite my nephew's white skin and blue eyes, the law says he's as black as the blackest colored man in all of Union County. Work whatever wiles you can manage with Jebediah, but in one week, if I can last that long"—Waylon gritted his teeth—"I want you to engineer a meeting at the Big House between me and Gopher Dennis. Your task? Have Jebediah carry word to Dennis that he is to come to the meeting alone—none of his wildcatting goons with him. And find out what tricks Gopher's got up his sleeve. Can you do that?"

Her heart thumped. "You ask a lot. I don't know if I can get Jebediah to act as a stool pigeon—to deliver a message, yes—but to tattle on his best friend . . . I don't know." She frowned.

"Margaret, are you or are you not Salome's daughter?"

Her knees felt weak as she made her way to the kitchen sink. She pumped herself a glass of water. "You will spare Morris?" She drained half the glass. "I want the best for all of us. Joe-Annie, you, Salome,

Tom-Tom, and Mor . . ." She clutched the water glass as she turned to Waylon.

"Now is the time to decide, Margaret. Who are you? Can you act as a colored woman with a family to protect, or will you sell out your darker kin to remain a pretend white woman?"

"How dare you say such a thing to me?" The tears broke free. "Ever since I found out that Salome was my mother, I've tried to help all of you."

"To help all of us? How benevolent of you, Lady Slocum. Spoken like a true white mistress of the manor." He shook his head. "Margaret, it's not me you've got to convince of your trustworthiness, it's yourself. Arrange a meeting in one week's time on my terms. Then I'll know where your loyalties lie." Her brother turned and walked to the front door.

She had never felt such coldness from Waylon, not even when she'd laid her childhood taunts on him for being the maid's son.

The gravel on the path leading from their mother's front door crunched under Waylon's feet as he marched away. He called out over his shoulder. "In one week's time we'll know not only your truth, but Morris's fate." He didn't look back.

"Way . . ." The cry drowned in her throat. Margaret gripped tight to Salome's door frame, her knees shaking. Tom-Tom. Waylon. Morris. Salome. Gopher. Jebediah.

God help her. Her fingers lost their grip. She slid to her knees.

CHAPTER FORTY

The good-looking older man laid a pretty quilt across Salome's body. Lots of colors—blues, greens, a smidge of tan, and just a touch of red. And those patterns—swirls and curlicues, what the old folks called storytelling—all hand stitched. *Wonder who made a keepsake like that.* But look at the man. Why was worry spread across a face as well put together as his?

"It ain't often we gits a cold snap this deep in the year." He tilted his head so close she could just about count the whiskers. "Let's keep you nice and warm."

Warm? Had she been cold?

He straightened his back and frowned. His lips sucked in and out like he was pondering something mighty. "Salome, I don't rightly . . . I mean to say I can't rightly understand what you . . . uh." He looked deep into her eyes.

Why was this stranger staring so hard at her? And had he called her Salome? Was that her name? The man took in a deep breath like a big rock had just been lifted off his shoulders.

He laid a hand on the top of the winter quilt tucked under her chin. "Salome, you knows I loves you more'n anything. You knows I'd turn the world upside down if it could show me how to stop pain comin' on you." His finger traced teeny-tiny stitches making up the North Star on the quilt. "But the Good Lord ain't seen fit to make that happen jest yet." He looked into her eyes. "Salome, I gots to say words that gonna be hard fo' yo' ears to take in, but they's words that needs to be said."

Was there something about this man who was talking these serious things at her? Maybe if she squinted her eye she could get a better look at him.

"You knows me good and well. I am and always was Maxwell Joe . . . the man who's gonna love you even after Heaven Time calls."

"Max . . . ?"

"Yo' husband. And it's been jest 'bout two weeks since . . . since . . . since Tom-Tom done passed on to Glory."

Now his eyes laid hard into her.

Tom-Tom? Why did those sounds hurt her heart so?

"Salome, I knows they ain't no pain like a mama feels when her baby passes on to the Great Beyond befo' herself. Ain't no need of me lyin', sayin' I knows how you feel. I don't. I can't. But"—he laid both hands across the quilt covering her shoulders—"I can tell you this: I'm gonna try ever'thin' I knows to make things right by yo' son Tom-Tom . . . and by you."

"Tom-Tom?" Now the man's eyes wouldn't turn her own loose. "What . . . what you sayin'?"

"Tom-Tom up in Heaven now, and he wants me to tell you it ain't time fo' you to come join him jest yet. He say yo' time's comin', but it ain't now. He say you gots to come back to the land of the livin' 'cause you still gots the Lord's work to do."

"Maxwell Joe?" The man wavered in and out of her sight like a windstorm got ahold of him. "You be my husband, and Tom-Tom, he be . . . he be . . . ?" Lord Jesus, the sound pounding her ears felt worse than a hurricane ten times over. She looked up at the man—her husband.

"Maxwell Joe . . . Tom-Tom . . . my . . . son?" The grin spreading across the face of Maxwell Joe made his eyes look like they were dancing. "Tom-Tom, he talk to you? I needs to know what . . ."

"I knows what you needs, Salome." He pulled off his overalls and his plaid shirt. He folded back the quilt. Maxwell Joe, the man she loved, climbed into the bed beside her.

He eased his body next to hers. Lord, the warmth coming off the man felt like God doing His everlasting best to breathe life into her. Touch him—that's what she needed. Feel the strength of the man under her fingertips. She reached out a hand and stroked his shoulders and said her hallelujahs as her fingers played down the muscles of his carpenter's arms. Strong. That was him. That was her Maxwell Joe. If Tom-Tom wanted her to come back this way, it was him, her husband, who had to lead the way. His warmth, his strength, she had to have them. "Maxwell Joe, I wants you to . . . I . . . needs you to . . ." She reached for his undershirt, his long johns. "I ain't gonna keep on breathin' if you don't hold me tighter'n . . ."

"I ain't let you walk this long beside me to let you go now."

He slipped off her nightdress, the one she'd had on since last evening. Her nighttime drawers, too. She lifted her arm toward his side and gentled him toward her, helped him roll on top, cradled his body between her stretched-open legs. Oh, God, and Jesus, too. His strength, his warmth—healing medicine to her. *Can't live without it.* The feel of his heart, his belly touching hers. Lord, give her more. His manhood. She reached down and stoked his strength. She guided his warmth. She let her eyes drift closed as Maxwell Joe pumped the joy of living back into her.

CHAPTER FORTY-ONE

Margaret, standing in the middle of her bedroom, stretched her arms around her back. Her shoulders wrenched as she pushed hooks into the eyes of her new brassiere. Drat. How she hated the newfangled contraption. As if a corset wasn't bad enough, now this bit of lace and straps wrapped too tight around her rib cage and crushed the breath almost out of her body. But for all its torture, the thing failed to fully encase her breasts. Never mind, she wouldn't suffer its torments for long. Jebediah did so love unhooking the garment and slipping it off her shoulders. With three days to go before Waylon's dreadful deadline, she had no other choice. She had to enlist her husband to buy time. Time to figure a way out of telling Morris the truth. She picked up the matching panties. Disgraceful things they were. Pink and studded with rosebuds. She shimmied into them. How ridiculous she must look to all but Jebediah. She fastened the pink silk wrapper around her waist just as she heard her husband's footfalls on the hall floor. She watched the doorknob twist and door open.

"Uhh." Jebediah stepped into the carpeted room, stopped, and stared. "You gettin' ready for bed so early?"

"It's almost nine. You've been at the oil fields all this time?" She had to do this right. If she could just hold Waylon off for a few extra days, hours even. Time to think of something . . . she'd come up with a plan to change his mind. Joe-Annie would suffer no harm. That feisty girl might even think of her sojourn with Morris as a bit of an adventure.

Jebediah shook his head. "Only 'til dark. Me and Gopher had some business to tend to."

Margaret ran a hand down the front of her dressing gown, leaving a small show of skin. "I've been thinking—worrying, really—about Gopher and any thoughts he might have about Tom-Tom's land." She loosened her hair from its bun and shook her head. "Ladora's in charge now." She didn't mean it to happen, but her breath stuck in her throat. If she could gain advance knowledge about Gopher, she could trade that to Waylon—make him back off his demand for truth-telling.

"Ladora? Oh, Tom-Tom's widda. Best for her to up and sell while she can."

Margaret's heart quickened, but she held her gaze toward Jebediah. "What can you mean? What does Gopher plan?" She opened the top of the dressing gown another inch, the bulge of her breasts exposed.

"What does Gopher plan?" Jebediah walked up and surveyed her chest. "Maggie, what is it you're tryin' for here?" He reached for the tie at her waist, spreading open her dressing gown. "I ain't seen this one before. New?"

"Oh, I've had it a while."

"I reckon you expect me to take this thing off you." He traced a finger around the top edge of her brassiere. "And these, too." He slipped two fingers under the waistband of her underpants. Jebediah raised his hands and stepped back. "Maggie, I ain't quite the idiot chile you take me for. I know better'n you I ain't in your league, but no man likes bein' played for a fool. Why don't you tell me straight up why you're standin' in front of me half-naked? What do you want?"

Time to let the dressing gown slide to the floor. "You. Jebediah, I want you."

He shook his head. "No, Maggie. Wantin' me ain't it. When you and me made our agreement—we would please one another for a price—both of us knew what we was bargainin' for. Now tell me what you really want."

The flush started in her cheeks and plummeted to her throat. She looked at Jebediah. His face reflected the look of a man weary of patience.

"Jebediah . . . it's Morris." Desperation overwhelmed her. One last try. She pushed the right strap off her shoulder. "I'm sorry. I didn't mean to . . . it's just that I'm desperate about my son."

Her husband frowned. "Morris? What's he got to do with you tryin' to vamp me into tellin' you somethin' 'bout Gopher?"

She jerked. Vamp? "Gopher?" She struggled to make her brain work. "Not Gopher. This is about Morris. On the train. I saw him fighting with Tom-Tom, then Tom-Tom fell." She stared into Jebediah's eyes. "I know it had to be an accident, but Wa—" No, she couldn't involve Waylon. Couldn't mention Joe-Annie. Not yet. Suppose Jebediah went back to Gopher with her suspicions?

"You told me you ain't seen Morris push that colored, and Morris says he ain't done it. Jest natural that Waylon gonna fault Morris." He cocked his head. "That what's frettin' you?"

"Uhh." She stared at him. Jebediah was holding back.

He tilted his head and gave her a long look. "No, that ain't it. You put on all this getup for somethin' big." He shook his head. "What's your brother plannin'?"

"Nothing." Her head throbbed. If she could only buy herself a little more time beyond Waylon's deadline. Just three days beyond Waylon's deadline.

"Fine. If it's nothin', and all you want is to give me a good toss in bed, well, I can take that." He unbuttoned the top of his trousers. "Get your clothes off and get in there, then." He nodded toward the French-blue comforter covering their brass bed, the window facing the front yard closed against the unexpected chill.

"Jebediah?" Oh, Lord, no. Did he expect her to give her body and receive nothing in exchange?

Reaching her in two steps, Jebediah wrapped his hands behind her and unhooked the brassiere. He stepped back, leaving the garment hanging from one of her shoulders. "Well? What's keepin' you? Take the thing off and get in the bed."

"No. I mean yes, but . . . but it's Waylon's demanding . . ." Her tongue twisted as her brain struggled to buy time. "That . . . Waylon wants me to tell Morris the truth about himself. He thinks it's a first step to getting Joe-Annie back. About . . . about him being . . . you know."

Jebediah's eyebrows arched.

She spotted his hesitation and leaned in even closer to him. The brassiere dropped to the floor. "Please, oh please, Jebediah, I need to hold Waylon off for a little while. Just until I can talk to Morris. Tell him to send Joe-Annie home right now. That'll satisfy Waylon. For now. Buy me time. Find out about what really happened in that train vestibule. With all this oil business, everybody's on edge. Waylon. Gopher. You. Me." She took in a breath. "Can you help?"

Jebediah gave a noncommittal tilt of the head as he surveyed her bare breasts. "Uh-huh. You needin' me to speak to Gopher—to help you with your brother. And you thinkin' rollin' around with me in that bed like a New Orleans whore gonna make me talk against Gopher."

"Against Gopher? No, that's not what I mean." She covered her chest.

"Yes, it is." He flung her arms away and pushed her panties to her knees. "Maggie, in case you thinkin' I done forgot 'bout how you lorded it over me all these years, I ain't. How you treated me like poor white trash. Well, that hurt ain't never, ever, gonna go away. And you bein' a colored woman, too."

"Colored?" Margaret's heart pounded. "Jebediah, let's not go through all that again."

"I ain't the one tryin' to pull another fast one. Maggie, truth be told, I kinda fancy your colored woman body. Get your drawers off." He stared at the pink rosebuds. "I told you, give me what I want when I want it, and I'll do what I think's right by you." He pushed her panties to her ankles, grabbed her arms, and stepped her out of the garment. "Now does that help your understandin'?"

Margaret nodded, but she didn't feel her yes.

"That's a good thing. Now get in the bed."

She made her way toward the brass headboard, laid one knee on the sheet-covered mattress. Margaret settled herself on her back, her hands folded over her belly. Jebediah sat on the edge of the bed. He leaned over her, his breath hot on her ear.

"Gopher's already after your family. You're thinkin' he's gonna go after you, too." His hand squeezed first one breast then the other. "Use what he knows 'bout you to get to that brother of your'n. He ain't gonna hurt that little gal, but he sure will use her to get what he wants."

Her quick intake of breath filled her ears.

"That's why you got yo'self laid out for me. Hopin' I'll tell you somethin' 'bout Gopher. Somethin' to pass on to Waylon. Somethin' that will help the colored bastard."

"No. Yes. No. It's Morris." Words pushed between her lips as she scooted away from her husband's touch. "I've got to hold off Waylon."

"Helping Morris through Waylon. By giving me your body, is it? Well, that ain't gonna do it no more. I'm gonna save you the trouble of playactin', Maggie. You want to know what Gopher's thinkin' so's you can tell Waylon? Well, I'll tell you. He ain't thinkin' much of me. I'm married to a colored woman, and that ain't settin' well with Gopher. He wants me to divorce you. Says it's God's sin for a white man to be married to a colored. He says I got to marry me a real white woman." He searched her face.

What could he see? A face drained of all color?

"Gopher says he don't see nothin' wrong with me keepin' you on the side if I want. Lock you in a bedroom. Naked most of the time. Give you a good whuppin' every two or three days just because. Fuck you hard. That's what Gopher says."

Margaret felt the top of her head threaten to float away. Her mouth opened, but her throat closed. She could find no words, and if they did appear in her head, she had no breath to push them out. Jebediah watched her body tremble.

"Gopher says it shouldn't take too much time. He got his own colored woman trained in two months. Says it might take six months of me takin' turns whuppin' and fuckin' before you understand your real place in this world." He nodded. "That what you wanted to hear?"

Her head wobbled. "Jebediah, I . . ."

"You ain't likin' the sound of my words?" He released her breast. "Well, I ain't prettifyin' my talk just fo' you."

She crossed her hands over her chest. Jebediah shoved them to her sides, held them tight like he meant business.

"There's many things I am, Maggie, and you ain't never bothered to find out which one's what. Well, one of the things I ain't is a welcher. You and me made a bargain. You do what I want when I want it, and I'll keep my part. You can stop yo' pretendin'." He released her.

Margaret sucked in a breath. "I . . . it's Salome. She won't survive if something happens to her last son or to Joe-Annie. But if Waylon tells Morris before I can prepare him . . . then . . . then anything might happen."

"Somethin's gonna happen to Waylon, all right, if he butts up against Gopher. That brother of yours is too uppity. You can get naked all night and half the day tryin' to make me do your biddin', but if he don't change his ways, Waylon and his gonna come to grief."

She blinked at her husband.

"Maggie, you've always took me for slow-witted. Well, I can see your thinkin' as clear as I can see you spread out buck naked in front of me right here and now." A hard stare aimed its way at her. "Waylon wants a meetin' with Gopher, don't he? With Gopher comin' alone I reckon." He cocked his head. "Well, Maggie, that ain't gonna happen."

A new wave of fear gripped her. "But if I can't arrange it, Waylon's going to make me tell Morris about . . .'"

He looked at her, his head cocked. "When's this here meetin' sposed to come about?"

"Three days from now."

"Here's the way this here thing's gonna go, Maggie. You wantin' to drag out the tellin' time to Morris ain't gonna work. Waylon's gonna get his way with Morris, but at a price."

"No. No. Waylon will kill my son if he doesn't tell him about Joe-Annie . . . and because of Tom-Tom." She looked up at her husband.

Jebediah pulled the sheet to her waist. "You wantin' to use your body to get three extra days to tell what shoulda been told years ago. You gonna tell Morris the God's honest truth. Tomorra."

Margaret dislodged the sheet as she sat up. "But Morris will hate me." She shook her head so hard her curled frizz slapped at her cheeks.

"God's truth, can't nobody take that kind of news good. But, as for hatin' you, that'll pass in time."

"He'll have to leave Union County. Be on his own. He's not strong enough."

"He is or he ain't. Either way, he's got to be told, and your brother's gonna pay a price for the knowin'.'"

"No. No. I don't think—"

"Ain't no use of you thinkin' it ain't gonna be, 'cause I say it is. Here's what you gonna do. Invite Waylon here to face Morris. I'll be standin' next to you both to keep the boy from harm. I know Gopher's gonna offer Tom-Tom's widda woman twenty, thirty thousand to make her sign. I can tell her that."

"Ladora won't go for that. Waylon won't let her."

"Waylon can get that money up to seventy-five, but he's gotta make her sign. Your job is to convince your brother to take this deal. And stop vampin' me."

Margaret reached for the sheet and pulled it to her chest.

"Ladora signin' gonna hold Gopher fo' a week or so. Give Waylon time to understand he won't get that gal back 'til he come to his senses. I'll tell you this, Maggie, whatever happens, them two stubborn fools can't go toe-to-toe over no oil land." He stood and walked to the doorway. He laid a hand on the doorknob. "If they do, your brother's gonna lose."

"Where are you going?"

Jebediah inclined his head. "Across the hall. To my old room. Remember, no more pretendin'. Me and you got a bargain."

CHAPTER FORTY-TWO

Waylon snapped open the LeMat, his father's—and his grandfather's—antique revolver. Used by Confederate officers in the Civil War. A beautiful weapon. It would work just fine as a backup. He tapped at his waistband. A Beretta 1922. New. His business gun. He lifted one foot over the opposite ankle. And, of course, the Star Model would work, too. He looked over at Maxwell Joe standing in the back parlor. Salome's husband preferred an old-fashioned shotgun, but Waylon told him a pistol would be necessary if he continued to insist on going with him to Margaret's house for the meeting with Dennis. Now all that was left was settling the women, and he would be ready.

He spotted his wife coming down the staircase. "Emerald, has Doc Jackson given Mama the sleeping draft yet?"

His wife lifted a finger to her lips as she left the last step. "Yes. And he had a time getting her to swallow it."

"I ain't right sure this is the thing to do." Maxwell Joe turned toward the stairs. "Emerald, Salome don't fancy bein' kept in the dark. Pumpin' her full of sleepin' drafts is gonna set her off."

Emerald looked over at Maxwell Joe. "Can you think of a better way to keep her safe? You know as well as I she'd never leave if she knew the truth."

"I reckon I know that better'n anybody." Maxwell Joe snapped open the shotgun. "Joe-Annie's the reason why I'm lettin' you try this jacked-up mess. I'm here to tell y'all, Salome ain't gonna find it in herself to fo'give none of the three of us once she comes to and find herself hauled off to Little Rock in the back of some strange fella's Ford. She's wantin' to be here to help her granddaughter."

There was something in the way Maxwell Joe spat out his words that told Waylon his stepfather was trying his best to convince himself there would be survivors enough to warrant Salome's wrath. But right now he had to go over the plan one more time in his head: get the women and children out of Union County, then confront Gopher Dennis. Lull the wildcatter into a false sense of victory, then when the man least expected it . . . He faced Maxwell Joe. "I told you, you don't have to come with me tonight. That way, Mama won't blame you if things don't go as planned."

"That be the next thing." Maxwell Joe inserted two shells. "I ain't certain this be the right way to go 'bout takin' care of business. You playin' this deal mighty close to the vest with that Gopher man."

Emerald gave her head a hard shake. "It's foolhardy to play with the Klan at all. Waylon, you're making everything so much worse. To put your trust in a jumped-up white woman is more than foolish. Margaret will do just about anything to keep her place in their world. Even risking our daughter." She turned toward the sound of a ringing telephone.

Waylon frowned at his wife as he made his way to the black phone on the wall in the foyer. He lifted the receiver. "Hello?"

"Waylon, is that you?" Margaret's voice came over the private line he'd installed a year ago.

"Yes. Has Jebediah been able to do what he was told—keep Gopher away until after I get there? I need to be at your place by three with Gopher arriving no earlier than seven."

"They're still in the oil fields. Gopher's marking out the new boundaries." His sister sounded worried—as well she should.

"Good, let him mark all the boundaries he pleases. Just make sure Jebediah keeps him away until I can deal with Morris." Waylon checked his wristwatch. He'd soon know if his wife was right—whether or not his sister could be trusted. "I assume you've already told Morris what he needs to know. Remember, your niece's safety depends on it." He placed the phone back on its hook.

Maxwell Joe slipped in the shotgun shells as the grandfather clock played two on its Westminster chimes.

"You're making a mistake." Emerald stood with her hands folded across her chest.

Waylon went back to the LeMat. He'd heard it all before from his wife. How she was right. How he had miscalculated. How Tom-Tom had paid the price . . . and now Joe-Annie. But they were mistakes he would not repeat. Waylon ran a hand along the revolver. If a life had to be forfeited tonight, it would be only his own.

"Hmph." Maxwell Joe grumped at the back of the hall.

"Ignore me if you wish, but it's foolhardy to put so much trust in her." Emerald's face wore a frown.

Waylon laid the LeMat aside. "Ignore you? How could I ignore you? You called it right about Gopher Dennis. I was wrong, and it cost my brother everything." Waylon moved toward his wife. "That's why I've got to get this thing right this time."

"At the risk of Joe-Annie's life and your own? Over oil?" She dug her fingers into his arms. "Waylon, we're comfortable enough. Rich, even.

We don't need more money." She sucked in her lower lip. "What we need is safety. At least as much as we can get in the white man's world."

He placed his hands on her shoulders. "If it were that simple, I would gladly sign away our mineral rights, but you know as well as I, Gopher Dennis won't be satisfied until he reduces us to sharecroppers."

Emerald bit down on her lower lip. "At least we'd all be alive."

Did he see tears forming in her eyes?

"Waylon, I'm not afraid. You know I believe in standing up for what's right, but you're standing up for money at the risk of our daughter's life." Her hands balled into fists.

"How could you think such a thing? This isn't about money."

"No?" Emerald arched those carefully manicured eyebrows. "It sure feels like it. And why? We've got more money than any colored in all of Union County." Her eyes drifted from his waistband to his pant leg. "How many guns are you taking with you? Two, three?" She looked toward Maxwell Joe. "Four? And, don't tell me this is all for Tom-Tom." She leveled her gaze at Waylon. "I know you believe your father's white friends won't put on Klan robes and ride against you, his colored son"—she looked into his eyes—"but rile Gopher any more, and he will do harm to Joe-Annie . . . and get the full Klan after us."

Waylon shook his head slowly. Emerald was right again. Indeed, the Klan would ride against any colored man, woman, or child who overstepped their place. But she was wrong about not harboring fear. She was frightened, all right. For him. "In a way, this is about oil." He waited while her head nodded emphatically. "But that's not the all of it. I regret with everything in me that I didn't recognize Dennis for the killer he is." He tried to pull her to him, but she pushed away. "You say I'm drawing a line in the dirt over oil. That we already have enough money. For colored folk, you mean. Real money should belong only to white men."

The hazel in Emerald's eyes sparked. "That's not what I said. I just want you to pick your battles carefully. Oil isn't worth this fight."

"My daughter's life is . . . and my father's legacy is." He waited for his words to register.

She blinked once, twice.

"Give a man like Gopher Dennis even an inch of land to which he is not entitled, and he will strip us—any Negro—bare." Waylon kept his voice soft but certain.

"Isn't that your plan?" Now she scanned his face. "Give him that inch? Walk that line? So you'll offer him a compromise. Keep the peace in Smackover. Remind him that any kind of ruckus—especially one involving the Klan—will scare away Northern investors. Gopher Dennis takes your compromise—releases our daughter—and we all live happily ever after. Isn't that your pipe dream, Waylon?"

"Emerald, that's not what—"

"What you talkin' 'bout a compromise?" The voice floated down the staircase.

"Mama!" Waylon spotted Salome holding the banister, walking down the stairs, her step certain.

"Salome, the medicine Dr. Jackson gave you, didn't you take it?" Emerald looked up at her mother-in-law.

"Spit it out as soon as y'all turned yo' backs."

"Honey. Sugar pie. What you doin' outta bed?" Maxwell Joe rushed up the stairs.

"Don't you *honey, sugar pie* me, Maxwell Joe." She snatched her arm away from his reaching grasp. "You jest as bad as these two. Tryin' to knock me out so's y'all three can carry out some foggy-headed plan to get back Joe-Annie."

"Mama Salome, ma'am, let me help you back to your bed." Emerald headed up the staircase.

"You stay right where you is, missy. I ain't goin' to no bed."

"But, Mama, you need your rest." Waylon looked up at Salome, now halfway down the staircase.

"Waylon, Emerald, y'all stop lookin' at me like I'm the addlepated one. I know"—her voice wavered—"I know my baby's done gone to Heaven. It done took me some time to get used to my Tom-Tom setting down next to Jesus instead of me, but now that I knows he's settled in good, I'm feelin' glorified." She made her way down two more steps. "And, Waylon, I know, sure as Sunday come ever' week, you workin' on some plan to avenge yo' brother and get our girl back."

Three more steps. "Well, I ain't havin' you work on no damn plan without me."

"Mama!" Waylon had never heard his mother utter a curse word in all his life.

"I knows what you feelin' 'bout losin' yo' brother. Ain't no pain greater than grievin' one you loves. And I knows you rightly scared for Joe-Annie."

"Then, help me, Mama. Go with Emerald. To Little Rock."

Four more stairs. "Where the chil'ren?"

"With Ladora. Her two, my Freddie. All safe."

"Where?"

Waylon stared at the polished mahogany wood that was his entry floor. How much to tell her?

Salome, her hand on the newel post, stepped off the staircase. "Where? And why is it you ain't answerin' me?"

"Mama, Ladora's gone to her family."

"Camden?" Salome aimed her most punishing scowl at him.

"Little Rock."

"Little Rock?" His mother raised her voice and said, "Ain't none of Ladora's kin livin' there 'cept a cousin two times removed." She narrowed her eyes. "And where is it you three fixin' to send me?"

"Emerald will be with you." Waylon felt a quick burst of hope.

"Tell her the truth of it." Emerald's face looked chiseled out of marble. "This fight of Waylon's is all about making the Hardin family the richest coloreds in the whole of America. And to do it, he's trusting Margaret."

"Margaret?" Salome let go of the newel post.

"My wife has most of the story right." Salome didn't need the details. "I'm meeting Gopher Dennis at Margaret's house. He's bringing papers for me to sign. Margaret says it's for the mineral rights to both our properties—mine and Tom-Tom's. And half the surface rights for the timber." He looked down at a leather pouch on the hall console table. "I've had Lawyer Richardson draw up my own set of papers. The two of us—me and Dennis—are going to come to an agreement."

"And what do yo' papers say?" Salome lowered herself into the second of the entryway chairs.

"I can't give away what my father entrusted to me. It's up to me to guard his legacy for Tom-Tom's children, for my Freddie and Joe-Annie."

Salome nodded. "And, Maxwell Joe, you thinkin' totin' a gun to stick in Gopher Dennis's white face is the way to go?"

"That wouldn't be my call, Salome, but yo' son is bound and determined this is the way to go." He turned to Waylon. "I'm reckonin' he's the leader of this here family, now. If he thinks he done worked it out"—Maxwell Joe moved his mouth like it held a cud of tobacco—"I reckon I ain't got much choosin' other than to follow him." He leveled his eyes at Salome. "You'd have it some other way?"

Mama squinted as Emerald rushed toward her. Emerald knelt at her mother-in-law's feet. "Waylon's trusting Margaret to set up that lowlife husband of hers to listen to Waylon's proposal. She told Waylon that Jebediah was on board." Emerald planted her hands on Salome's knees. "But suppose it's all a lie. Once Waylon gets there, both Gopher and Jebediah will pull guns on him and make him sign anyway."

Salome nodded again. "Emerald, is you tellin' me everythin' hangs on Margaret bein' strong fo' her real family?"

"Yes!" Emerald's response came out on a shout. "There's no way she's going to give up what she has just to help us." She gave Waylon a quick glance. "Look at Tom-Tom."

Pain stabbed at Waylon's chest, but the pain on his mother's face made his own agony feel like nothing.

Salome grabbed her daughter-in-law's hands in her own. "Here's what me and you gonna do." She turned from Maxwell Joe to Waylon. "Ain't gonna be no Little Rock for neither one of us. We gonna stay right here. Waitin'." She turned back to Emerald. "Waiting fo' our men-folk to come back home to us."

Emerald frowned in confusion. "Mama Salome?"

Salome nodded her head for almost a quarter tick of the clock. "Waitin' fo' Waylon and Maxwell Joe to walk back through that do'. Tonight. Don't matter none what papers is signed or not signed, they both gonna walk right through that there front do'." She squeezed Emerald's wrists. "'Cause ain't nothin' on God's green earth, His Heaven, or the Devil's Hell gonna convince me that my girl gonna turn her back on her family. Margaret ain't 'bout to betray her brother."

Waylon had never been a praying man like his brother, Tom-Tom, but now, the words jumped into his head.

CHAPTER
FORTY-THREE

"Mr. Slocum, beggin' your pardon, suh." Tessie's tap on the bedroom door brought Margaret out of her fitful nap. "Mr. Morris, he just come back to the house."

"Tessie?" Was her maid a part of the turmoil rumbling in her belly that kept her just on the edge of a decent sleep? She laid a hand across her forehead: warm with a dull throbbing right behind her eyebrows. Was she getting sick? She pulled up the coverlet she'd laid over her body.

"Hmm? Tessie?" Her husband's voice. Where was Jebediah? Oh yes, working on some papers at the desk across from the fireplace.

Margaret opened her eyes as Tessie cracked open the door.

"I ain't rightly sure it's my place to say, but . . ."

"Speak up, Tessie." Jebediah stirred.

"Well, Mr. Slocum, suh, you told me to tell you jest as soon as Mr. Morris stepped foot into the house. Well, I'm doin' that."

"Spit out the rest, Tessie." Jebediah never had been a man to show patience with the colored servants.

"Ain't all that much to spit out, Mr. Jebediah. That is to say, Mr. Morris got back to the house, but he ain't come in through the front do'. Naw, suh. He made his way in through the kitchen. Made the mind-yo'-own-business sign to me and told Cook to send Waylon Hardin to the woodshed when he show up." Tessie peeked her head around the barely opened door. "I ain't knowed Lord, uhh, Waylon Hardin was expected. Is there somethin' I'm sposed to be doin' fo' him?"

"What? Waylon here?" Margaret struggled to sit up.

Jebediah strode over to the door. "Tessie, don't say nothin' to Mr. Morris 'bout me knowin' he's in the woodshed."

"Whateva you says, suh." Tessie took her sweet time closing the door.

"Get on up, Margaret." He walked to the four-poster, kicking at a pillow that had fallen to the floor.

Get up? No, not yet. She needed more time. "My dress." She straightened her skirt that had hiked above her knees in her sleep. "It's all wrinkled from my nap. I need to change." Panic steamed from her belly to her chest. Help. She had to find help. Her eyes darted around the room. They rested on the highboy—all eight drawers stacked one atop another. What was she looking for? There could be no answer in sixteen brass drawer pulls.

"You don't need to change no dress to talk to your own son."

A flutter hit her chest as she reached for the coverlet she'd thrown over her legs.

"You heard Tessie. Waylon's on his way here. To talk to Morris about Tom-Tom and Joe-Annie. Oh, Jebediah, I haven't told Morris anything. Waylon said I had to tell him or . . ." Margaret clamped her eyes shut. Was she ever going to have the strength to tell her boy such a thing? "I can't believe he'd hurt Joe-Annie. What am I going to do?"

"Waylon's due here at six." Jebediah looked at the clock on the fireplace mantelpiece. "Ain't but half past four right now." He walked over to the bed, grabbed the dressing gown, and tossed it to the floor. "Get up."

The flutter kicked up two or three notches. Margaret's lip trembled as she got to her knees on the bed. "Jebediah, you didn't . . . you don't know where Joe-Annie is, do you?"

"What I know is that's enough of your foolishness." He grabbed her by the arm and headed toward the door.

"My shoes, my shoes." She pulled against him.

Jebediah shoved her into the hallway, retrieved her caramel-colored daytime shoes, and guided her down the staircase, through the foyer, into the kitchen, out the back door, and down the path to the woodshed before he dropped her shoes to the ground.

She scrambled into her shoes but had no chance to buckle the straps. "Why does Morris want to meet Waylon in the woodshed?"

"I hate to think." Jebediah stopped at the shed door. The latch was undone. "Morris, you in there? I'm comin' in to talk."

The door creaked open. Morris scowled when he set eyes on Jebediah, but his face resembled a crinkled prune when he spotted his mother. "What are you two doing here? Go back to the house and have your dinner."

He tried to close the door, but Jebediah blocked it with his body and pushed the opening wider. Margaret stepped inside the darkened building.

"What you doin' sittin' here in the blackness? Break your neck over these piles of kindlin' wood on the floor." Jebediah flicked on the new electric light he'd just installed. "We come to talk to you."

"Talk to me? Why in the world would I want to talk to you two?"

"Morris, where's Joe-Annie Hardin? Was you on that train when Tom-Tom fell off?" Jebediah had his back to the door, the only way in and out of the windowless woodshed. "Ain't no time to pussyfoot around the pigpen. Morris, where's that little gal?"

"How am I supposed to know? As for the train, Pa, you know good and well I was." He glared at Margaret. "What's she been saying?"

"I saw you." The shaking started in her hands and soon traveled to her shoulders. "On the train. You were with Tom-Tom when he . . . when it happened. Did you . . . please tell me it wasn't you who pushed my . . . him?"

"What is it with you two? We're talking oil here. You know as well as me that neither of those coloreds—Waylon or Tom-Tom—is really entitled to that land."

"My father left it to them!" Margaret shouted at the child she'd been forced to bear for Sylvester. "Tell me about Joe-Annie. Where is she? If you know, you've got to send her home. Now!"

Morris shook his head. "Mama, you're much too sentimental with these coloreds. But let's not forget—they are coloreds. Now I don't mind them having some money to feed their families, but those two—especially Waylon—live like royalty. The duke of Union County, indeed. If I believed in such nonsense, I should be the duke, not him." He looked at Margaret. "The way you're carrying on, Mother Dear—going to Tom-Tom's funeral, fawning over Lord Hardin's whore—folks are beginning to think you're a nigger-lover."

It was the smacking sound of her open palm against her son's cheek that first settled in her head.

Jebediah moved up beside her. Morris rubbed his cheek.

Her son lowered his voice. "I'll make myself even more clear, Mother Dear. My grandfather's nigger whore—Salome—had much too much influence over the man. He signed that ridiculous will because she was flaunting her colored woman's ways in front of him." Morris stroked his silver belt buckle. He turned to Jebediah. "What kind of a man are you? You let your wife keep you out of your own bedroom just about all the time I was growing up. Grandpa Slocum was right. He always said you were too soft on her. She needed a good hiding, he'd say, for acting stuck-up. And if it was up to him, he'd do more than that to her."

"Morris." Jebediah shook his head. "Don't you say no more."

"Salome!" The name propelled itself out of Margaret's mouth. She felt the shock waves of the sound explode in the air and bounce off the walls.

"That's the whore of whom I speak." Morris put a silly half smile on his face. "I didn't know her when she was young, of course, but in her day, I imagine—"

"Shut your filthy mouth! She's my mother!" The sound hurtled from her throat. "And your grandmother!"

Words were supposed to disappear right after they were formed. Not these. They bounced around the woodshed from wall to wall, from floor to ceiling, gathering strength with each reverberation. Something tight wrapped around Margaret's chest. She couldn't breathe. She couldn't move. All she could do was hear and see. She could not turn her head away from her son's mouth.

The smile stayed solid on Morris's face for maybe the count of three, then his upper lip on the right side twitched, accompanied by eyes that stared wider than any owl Margaret had ever seen.

The words she prayed she'd never have to give voice to clogged up her head. She looked to Jebediah, a fresh plea in her eyes.

"Maggie, best you finish what you just started."

"Jeb . . ." She felt the tears forming behind her eyes.

Her husband shook his head.

"Mother?" A paleness the color of parchment crept into Morris's face.

Margaret winced. Her hands clenched so tight her nails dug into her palms. "Lord . . . Lord Henry Hardin . . . he . . . that man was my natural father."

A look that confirmed his mother had lost her mind layered itself on her son's face. "Mother, I know Henry Hardin was your father. And Grandmother Bertha was your mother."

Her head wobbled itself into a shake. "Bertha Hardin never gave birth to a living child."

"What? Of course Grandmother gave birth to a living child. You're here, aren't you?"

"A woman named . . . Mattie Lou"—the words came weakly— "helped by another named Georgia, pulled me out of . . . Sal . . ." The name stuck. "Out of Salome forty-three years ago. Lord Henry Hardin was in the room holding Salome's hand when I was born."

One blink. A pause. Two more blinks. A stare. Then three, four, five, and more blinks.

"Unn. Unn." Her son's throat must have closed. He swung his head from her to Jebediah and back again. He opened his mouth, tried to get out a sound, and failed. He ran a hand down his throat and tried again. "Don't . . . don't be absurd," he managed. "Have you never seen yourself in a mirror? You're white."

Margaret laid a hand on her hair. "Am I? Madame C. J. Walker's hair pomade for colored women, with a little heat, does wonders at turning kinky hair into marcelled waves." She sucked in her lips. "My father took a desperate chance. He passed me off as his white child."

The move came in slow motion. Her son's face turned the white of a cotton boll. His hand moved like molasses to his belly. He bent over and let out two good dry heaves before Jebediah reached him.

Her husband led Morris to a pile of wood and sat him down.

"Why do you let your wife tell such lies?" One more heave, and this time Morris brought up bits of his noontime dinner.

Jebediah stood over him. "Morris, I know you ain't never set high store by me. Ain't you ever wondered how come a country boy like me come up on a quality lady like your mother—daughter of the duke of Union County?"

Morris swept the back of his hand across his mouth.

"Don't!" Margaret shouted. "Not that, Jebediah. I've done what you've asked."

"It's you what asked for my help with Gopher."

"Gopher? Gopher Dennis? What . . . what's he got to do with . . ." The boy's voice wavered.

"It's truth-tellin' time 'bout Tom-Tom and Joe-Annie." Jebediah helped Morris to his feet. "Boy, you might think otherwise, but it don't give me no pleasure to tell you these words. My pa, your beloved Grandpa Slocum, found out something about your ma."

"Found out? About Mother Dear?"

Jebediah nodded. "The God's truth. My pa made a deal with Lord Henry to keep that secret safe—his secret 'bout Margaret."

"There's no need to go on, Jebediah." Margaret ran to her husband and grabbed his arm. "Please, please!"

Morris, one hand tracing circles around his belly, looked from Margaret to Jebediah. "Why is she carrying on so? I think she has taken leave of her senses. Both of you have."

"Morris, you ever asked yo'self how an overseer like Jacob Slocum come up on that fine house you halfway grew up in? Overseers can't usually 'ford nothin' more'n three or four rooms—and that don't include no indoor plumbin'. Your grandpa had hisself a full six rooms, not countin' that bathroom of his."

"Grandpa's house? What secret? How you came to marry Mother? What are you trying to tell me, Pa?"

Margaret's knees buckled. She grabbed at Jebediah's shirt and missed. Margaret fell to the ground. "No. No. No." Her hands climbed up his legs.

"It was the Fourth of July, I'm told." Jebediah reached down and pulled her to her feet. "Yo' mama was twenty-one. Ain't that right, Maggie?"

Wails came out of her mouth.

"Goddamn it! One of you tell me what's going on. First you ask me to believe some colored woman is . . . then you go on acting like . . . like I don't know what. How am I supposed to believe any of this?"

"Oh, you can mark my words. Salome's the one who gave birth to Margaret. Your mother's a colored woman."

"God Almighty. She can't be black. If she's colored, that means I'm . . ." Morris held his hand under the electric light in the shed.

Margaret wobbled her way to her boy. She reached out to gather him to her.

"Get off me, you black bitch!" His backhand sent her sprawling against Jebediah.

Margaret stumbled to the floor, one leg caught by a splintered piece of kindling, and her silk stockings ripped. She watched Jebediah whirl toward Morris. He grabbed her son by his collar and slammed him hard against the wall.

"You ain't learned much of nothin' from me and you learned plenty of wrong stuff from my pa. But here's one lesson you oughta learn good. You ain't to never, ever, lay a beatin' hand on your ma ever again or I'll beat the livin' tar outta you."

Morris struggled to break Jebediah's hold.

"You askin' for the truth, well here 'tis: you're a colored man and ain't no two ways 'bout that. Get used to it."

Margaret climbed to her feet, her heart pounding.

Morris clamped his hands over Jebediah's. "You're trying to frighten me because you want me to tell you about Tom-Tom. How do you expect me to believe even you would marry a colored woman? Such an abomination isn't legal."

"You're not listening, boy." Jebediah pressed a forearm into Morris's chest. "That was the secret your grandpa held. Your mama come up in the family way, and . . ."

Margaret leaned back against a waist-high cord of wood, her fingers clutching at her cheeks.

"Family way? You mean Mother and you . . ." Morris broke free. "And her pretending she was purer than the driven snow. Always preaching the respectable Hardin way at me."

The tears ran in rivulets down her face.

Jebediah stepped back and tugged his shirt into place. "Driven snow ain't got nothin' to do with it but, uh-huh, yo' mama ain't knowed nothin' 'bout a man 'til that day."

"You got a nigger pregnant and then married her? That makes no kind of sense."

"She was with child when I married her, right enough, but it weren't none of mine."

Margaret leaned against the stack of wood. Morris's figure mixed with the memory of Sylvester leering at her blurred in and out of her teary vision.

"None . . . none of yours? But . . ." Her son's eyes moved from anger to disbelief to growing shock. "But I thought I was Mother's first child?"

"You was."

Margaret splayed her fingers over her face, but she caught sight of her son's furrowed forehead, his eyes blinking to make his ears believe the words he'd just heard. Jebediah stood wide-legged, his arms folded over his chest, his face sending Margaret a message: all was lost. There was nothing more she could do.

"Your mama was took against her will by another man. He's the one what got her in the family way. Weren't none of me."

"But . . . but you're my father. Grandpa Slocum's my . . ."

"Your grandpa Slocum was paid well enough to make you believe that lie." The bitterness of her husband's words slammed into Margaret even as she knelt down and rubbed her forehead against her knees. "Paid well because Henry Hardin had to find hisself a husband quick for his daughter—her bein' in the family way, and all." Jebediah looked down at Margaret. "And I was that man."

Morris held out his open palm to Jebediah. "Wait. Wait. Are you telling me my mother—a colored woman—laid with some man, got herself pregnant, and my two grandfathers arranged some kind of a shotgun wedding?"

"That's most of the God's truth, Morris." Jebediah reached down and pulled Margaret to her feet.

"But I don't reckon your mama had much of a good time with Sylvester layin' on her."

Her son stared at her as though she were a visiting stranger. "Then that makes me a bastard, and you a whore."

"Morris, please. I beg you, I didn't want . . ." Margaret leaned into Jebediah.

"No need for you to beg, Maggie. I don't reckon you wanted Sylvester Morse to come into you like he done." Jebediah slipped a hand around her shoulder. "And I know, sure as hell, you didn't want to marry me."

"Pa . . . did you say Sylvester Morse? Not old Judge Morse's son—the one who died in some kind of a funny accident?" Even more color drained from Morris's face. He shook his head as though all the new thoughts rolling around his mind were marbles escaped from their circle. "He was my father?"

Jebediah left Margaret's side and walked back to Morris. "It's his seed you carry, but I'm your pa. I'm the one raised you as my own. Right alongside Junior. That's what you need to know."

"What I need to know?" Morse pointed to his mother. "I need to know a hell of a lot more than that. First you tell me that woman's colored. Having the nerve to pass herself off as something she can never be." He shook his head as he leveled a glare at Margaret. "How many men did you lay with before you got yourself a white one?"

The move came up so fast that Margaret felt the swish of air before she heard the resounding punch in the gut Jebediah threw into Morris. "I told you, Morris, what's done is done." He pounded two more blows into Morris's belly, slamming him into the wall.

"You know what you need to know. Now we got business to talk over before Waylon Hardin gets over here." Jebediah, his mouth set in a grim line, stepped away from Morris.

Margaret took two steps toward her son before Jebediah caught her arm.

"Ain't gonna be no more of that. Maggie, you're through tryin' to protect this boy. Morris, it's past time you come to know who you really are. You're a colored man, and you're always gonna be one. Now it's best to tell your mama what you done to Tom-Tom and where you put Waylon's girl."

"Tom-Tom? You've just told me I'm a white man's bastard by his colored slu . . . woman. No one, do you two hear me"—Morris's voice carried loud enough to be heard by the highway a quarter mile up the road—"can ever find out I'm . . ." Color flamed back into Morris's cheeks. "Jesus, I'm ruined!" He turned pleading eyes first to Margaret, then to Jebediah. "And you want me to talk about Tom-Tom and Joe-Annie Hardin?"

Jebediah brushed a wood chip off the sleeve of his striped shirt. "Well, Morris, the way I sees it, you can either be a nigger boy or a white man for the rest of your life. Your mama kept the secret for twenty-one years. Me, too, but lessen I hear the truth come out of you, that secret just might slip past my lips. Now, tell your mama where that gal is and what's what with Tom-Tom."

The sobs came again shaking Margaret's body. "Just tell me, please, you didn't do anything to Tom-Tom. In the name of the Lord, he's your uncle, and Joe-Annie's your cousin!"

Morris's eyes darted from one parent to the other. The look of panic sparked out of his eyes.

"Gopher Dennis."

"Gopher?" Jebediah scowled.

Morris nodded. "Gopher said we had to talk some sense into the Hardin boys. Said he'd found out they were both heading north. To Philadelphia. He didn't know why for sure, but he thought it might have something to do with the oil business."

Margaret clenched her hands. "But how did he find out about the train? Even I didn't know my brothers were supposed to be on that train."

Morris nodded. "Gopher set all that up. Once he got word from the stationmaster about Waylon buyin' tickets heading north, he knew he had to stop the Hardin boys. That's when he gave Rose Linda her orders. It was her job to get Mother Dear on that train."

"That woman was like a jailhouse guard." Margaret shuddered at the memory.

"She was supposed to be. Her job was to get you to the El Dorado train station so Waylon and Tom-Tom could catch a quick glimpse of you. You weren't supposed to talk to them. When you weren't looking, Rose Linda slipped a note to the conductor to give to Tom-Tom."

"A note? What kind of a note?" Margaret stared at her son.

"Telling Tom-Tom to meet you in the vestibule between the colored and white train cars. That you had something for him. Gopher just said for me to scare Tom-Tom. Make him agree to sign. Then he'd go back and convince his brother. All I had to do was wait there in the vestibule until Waylon walked up—all ready to give in."

"Umm." Jebediah didn't look convinced. "What was your mama supposed to be doin' all this time?"

"Mama? Mother Dear was never supposed to be in that vestibule. It was Rose Linda's job to keep her in her seat. I was the one to meet Tom-Tom in the vestibule. With a deed for him to sign."

A burst of heat rose up in Margaret's chest. "I saw the two of you wrestling between the train cars. You pushed To . . ." Her lips trembled.

"I did no such thing." Morris shook his head. "It was an accident. You've got to believe me."

"Well, then, what did happen?" Jebediah looked impatient.

"I had a gun."

"Good Jesus." Jebediah frowned. "Gopher told you to tote a gun?"

Margaret covered her mouth.

"Mother, I've told you the truth. I was on that train just to scare Tom-Tom. Gopher said if I scared the preacher into signing, giving Slocum-Dennis Oil most of the land, the whole thing would go easier with Waylon. He was the tougher brother. Harder to convince."

Margaret shook her head. "You pulled a gun on my brother? How could you? You knew he was your grandfather's other family. Even without knowing about me. That makes him your uncle whether or not you knew we shared the same mother."

"What did Gopher promise you?" Jebediah acted as though he were having none of it.

"Nothing." Morris turned his back to Margaret and whirled toward Jebediah. She could not read her son's face. But she watched Jebediah lower his gaze to Morris.

"Well, maybe Gopher did say I'd be the one in charge of Mother Dear's properties once Waylon and Tom-Tom signed over the deeds." Morris shook his head. "But Tom-Tom was tougher than I thought. I showed him the deed. And the gun." He looked up. "That's when he grabbed for the pistol. The train swung around a curve right at that moment, and Tom-Tom just slipped out from between the cars before I could snatch him back." Morris turned from Jebediah to Margaret and back again. "It was an accident."

"And Joe-Annie? What you done with that child?" Jebediah glared. "And I suggest you let the truth come out of your mouth." He glanced over at Margaret. "Yo' mama half believes I had somethin' to do with takin' that colored gal."

Margaret's heart pounded. "Morris?" Her voice sounded unnaturally high even in her own ears.

Her son looked from one to the other parent. His eyes widened. "Gopher's not wrong in this, you know. Mother Dear, now I know why you feel the way you do about the Hardins, but . . . but Gopher . . . he . . ."

Jebediah grabbed Morris around the shoulders and shook him—his pomaded hair loosening.

"I ain't had nothin' to do with takin' that gal. Now you tell yo' mama the goddamn truth."

Margaret shuddered.

"Gopher doesn't trust you." Morris's voice trembled in time to Jebediah's shaking him. "Not all the way. He thinks you might want to cut him out of his fair share of the oil. Because you're Mother's husband, and the law favors you in handling her property. Even I could get cut out of the profits. I had to help him, you see."

She stared at her son. "I would never do that to you, Morris. You must know that."

"Joe-Annie?" Jebediah tightened his grip.

"Gopher said he had to scare Waylon. We didn't plan on killing Tom-Tom, just scaring him enough to sign. Gopher said that would convince Waylon, but it didn't. That's why he said we had to take Joe-Annie. For good measure."

"Good measure? Where's the girl now?" Jebediah stopped shaking Morris.

"In an old slave cabin. In the woods. In Smackover. With Rose Linda."

"Rose Linda?" Margaret pulled Jebediah away from her son. "The woman's a monster. How are we going to tell Waylon all this so he doesn't kill Morris?"

Jebediah pulled out his pocket watch again. "Quarter to six. Waylon be here in fifteen minutes. Maggie, this ain't lookin' good. You've done your part of the bargain with that colored brother of your'n. Now I reckon it's up to you to talk sense into your brother." Jebediah stepped outside the woodshed. "Gopher ain't gonna have it no other way."

CHAPTER FORTY-FOUR

"What time it be?" Maxwell Joe, shrouded by five loblolly trees that stood at the back of Hardin House, stroked the barrel of the shotgun.

Waylon, pocket watch already in hand, answered, "Five minutes to six. It's time for me to head over to the woodshed." He looked at the lights brightening the rear of Hardin House. "Funny. When we first came up, I didn't see a light in the dining room. I thought Morris said his folks would be having dinner when I arrived."

"Ain't you cuttin' it a mite close? You don't reckon this here's a trap, do you?"

Of course this could be a trap, but what else could he do with Joe-Annie's life on the line?

"A trap that can't be sprung until I've signed those papers." Waylon looked at Maxwell Joe. "You're clear on what to do?"

"I ain't to give no details to Salome even if she's dead set on knowin' ever'thin'. On that, you is right, Waylon."

"Let's pray Mama never finds out I'm testing Margaret." Child against child. Even if Salome couldn't understand, Waylon knew he'd made the best choice.

"Uh-huh. By usin' that boy of her'n." Maxwell Joe gave Waylon a questioning look. "Waylon, I knows you thinkin' they ain't no other way, but you takin' yo'self a mighty chance. How you know Mr. Morris ain't gonna play a setup on you? Get you to come over to the woodshed, then have that good-fo'-nothin' wildcatter and his friends jump you and make you sign over ever'thin'? And then not get Joe-Annie ba—" Maxwell Joe's words got swallowed in his throat.

"How do I know?" The laugh coming out of Waylon's mouth contained no mirth. "Because I know Morris Slocum. A chip off the old block of his conniving father." Waylon nodded. "Make no mistake, Maxwell Joe, Gopher Dennis and his lowlife thugs will be lying in wait, but even a thickhead like that buffoon will know I'll never sign without Joe-Annie's safe return."

"Gopher will show at eight, you says. You be thinkin' that give you 'nough time to get rid of Morris?"

Maxwell Joe looked around before he sighted down the barrel of his shotgun.

"I'm not inclined to kill Margaret's son . . . unless he refuses to cooperate. Morris isn't exactly what you'd call filled with bravery. He'll take me to my daughter, all right. The trick is in the timing."

"So you say. Waylon, I'm here to stand beside you if shootin' commences, but I gots to tell you I can't let no mo' worries fall on yo' mama. She might commiserate with Lady Margaret if her boy come up with a broken leg or sech, but she can't take no mo' deaths."

"Maxwell Joe, I don't want to cause Mama any more misery. It's not going to come to that. Morris is nothing but a coward, and if Margaret's done her duty, her boy will be more than willing to help out his Hardin family."

"The colored Hardins, you mean. That news gonna take that young'un powerful hard. Waylon, I tole you I ain't all the way sho this is the way to go to get our girl back, but one thing I do know is Morris Slocum gonna be in for a mighty big shock."

"If"—Waylon gazed into the distance—"my sister's done her job. Let's go over the plan again."

"I don't need to go over no plan again. I knows how to make a killin' look like it was an accident if it come to that. Po' Mr. Dennis got hisself into a fuss with some of them roughnecks he got workin' on the oil rigs. Damn shame them fellas shot themselves up, one t'other."

"I'm just hoping he doesn't bring more than two goons with him." Waylon checked his pocket watch again. "Just make sure you get any bodies away from Hardin House."

"Waylon, I ain't had me no trouble fixin' things jest right with Sylvester Morse, now has I?"

"Time to go." Waylon headed toward the woodshed, the sound of Maxwell Joe's scurrying feet falling across the grass behind the loblolly trees.

He squinted. Was that a gleam of light he detected filtering around the edges of the woodshed door? Waylon knew every step, every foot, every square inch of this place—his childhood home. He circled around the shed and came up to the front door. Waylon flattened himself against the wall. He reached into his pocket. His fingers closed around the handle of the Beretta.

Now to see if Margaret had kept her word. If Morris knew the truth, Waylon bet the boy would agree to anything to keep his secret. "Mr. Morris Slocum, are you in there?" Waylon kept his voice low but insistent.

The door creaked open. "Waylon?"

Waylon startled. That was not the voice of Morris Slocum, though it was familiar.

Through the sliver of an opening at the back of the door, he spotted the profile of a man—a white man.

"Waylon, if that's you, come on in here."

Jebediah Slocum. Waylon pulled the gun from his pocket and held it at the ready. Had father and son teamed up?

"Morris is supposed to be here alone." Waylon lifted his voice, hoping Maxwell Joe could catch that something was amiss. "He knows I want no company."

"Waylon?" His sister's voice.

The door flung open wide, smashing Waylon on the forehead. He swallowed his grunt.

"Where are you? Get inside. Gopher's coming." The dim outline of Margaret stood in the doorway.

At eight o'clock. It was just six. Had the betrayal started already? Jebediah stepped through the door, his arms reaching for Waylon. Waylon met Jebediah with a Beretta pressed into his chest.

Jebediah lifted his hands. "Whoa! Ain't no need for that." He called over his shoulder in a low voice: "Margaret."

His sister stepped outside the shed. "Morris is inside." Her eyes were red, matching the flush of her cheeks, her hair disheveled. "He knows." Her voice broke.

"You told him everything?" Waylon stared at Margaret. He shook his head as he pushed the gun deeper into Jebediah's belly.

"Everything."

"Did he tell you where . . ." No, not out here in the open. Especially with Jebediah right in front of him ready to run off to Gopher Dennis at the first opportunity.

"Waylon, you're supposed to be the smart one of Henry Hardin's bastards. Didn't you just hear your sister tell you Gopher's on his way up here?" Jebediah lifted his arms. "Now it don't make me no never mind if you and Gopher have a shoot-out right here and now. Any good white lawyer gonna see that Margaret gets them deeds. And what she gets,

I get. Best all around if you just git on in this shed and talk to Morris instead of pushin' that gun into me."

Waylon kept his eyes on Jebediah. "Who's here besides you and Jebediah?"

His sister rushed to his side and laid a hand on his gun arm. "Just Morris."

"Move," Waylon said as he jammed the weapon into Jebediah's ribs. Margaret held the door open enough for him to see the interior. Morris looked stricken. At last, a sign. Maybe Margaret had delivered on her promise.

"If you'll take that gun off me, I'll do just that." Was that a smile on Jebediah's face?

Waylon shot a quick glance to the wooded area where Maxwell Joe hid. He hoped his stepfather had caught the action.

"Here he is," Margaret called out as Waylon marched Jebediah into the woodshed.

Waylon latched the door, shoved Jebediah hard to the floor, and rushed Morris. He slammed the butt of his gun against the side of the man's face. Morris's scream was loud—too loud. Margaret was upon Waylon a second later. She clamped both hands over his gun hand.

"No. No, Waylon. He said he didn't do it—not on purpose—it was an accident. Yes, there was a gun and a tussle, but the train hit . . ."

Morris, on his knees, rocked to and fro, a hand over the welt rising on his left cheek. Waylon pushed Margaret aside. He watched her stumble into Jebediah's arms.

Waylon grabbed Morris's collar and yanked him to his feet. "Where's my daughter? Tell me everything or you're a dead man."

The trembling body and frantic eyes only partially convinced Waylon of the truth of his nephew's account of the events on the train. But the time had to be nearing six thirty.

"What's Gopher planning for tonight?"

"Tonight?" Morris still trembled.

"I know killing you could bring grief to Salome, but only because it will upset Margaret. But that's the chance I have to take. Now tell me, and tell me straight, how many other men are coming with Gopher tonight?"

Morris's eyes bucked. "Men? Just me."

Probably a lie, but Waylon had no more time to waste. Retrieve Joe-Annie safe and sound. Send her to Salome with Maxwell Joe, get back to the woodshed just before eight. Confront Gopher Dennis. Pray Maxwell Joe could make it back to Hardin House in time—just in case. In less than an hour and forty-five minutes.

Waylon pushed open the woodshed door. "Out, all of you." His biggest problem: he had to drag the three of them—the lamebrained Jebediah, the treacherous Morris, and his sister, who'd sell her soul to remain a white woman—with him back to the woodshed meeting with Gopher Dennis.

When Waylon first stepped into the kitchen of the old cabin a short while later and saw the chicken bones, remnants of buttered mashed potatoes, and the beets his daughter disliked littered across a cracked plate, his feet refused to move until his head had decoded the entire scene.

Joe-Annie looked up and showed her what-took-you-so-long face. "Beets! That woman made me eat beets." Joe-Annie pointed an accusing finger at Rose Linda Dennis, who appeared frazzled to her last nerve. "I want some ice cream when I get home."

He'd grabbed the child into his arms and hadn't released her these last three, four, maybe five minutes.

"Papa, you can let go now." Joe-Annie patted his head as though he were Chameleon.

"Never." He squeezed her all the tighter.

"Besides, I want to give that man a good kick in the shins." She glared at Morris. "He took me out of Aunt Ladora's house in my pajamas! I've been in my pajamas for one week. That awful woman wouldn't let me go back to Aunt Ladora's to get my funeral dress. Did my cousins get to the church for Uncle Tom-Tom?" The child crinkled her nose in outrage.

"Them's questions yo' grandpa gonna answer all the way back to yo' grandma's house."

Maxwell Joe looked over Joe-Annie's head at Waylon, his eyes showing his urgency.

"Honey, never mind your pajamas. I'm going to buy you eight new dresses—one for every day of the week and two for Sunday."

"I don't need two dresses on Sunday. Just make sure"—Joe-Annie sent a withering glare toward Rose Linda—"she doesn't get any new dresses." Joe-Annie walked over to Margaret. "Do you know you have a naughty son? All right with you if I kick him in the shins even if he is a grown-up?"

Margaret bent down to her niece. "You can kick him in the shins all you want—tomorrow. Right now, you've got to get home to your mother and grandmother. They've missed you. And you want that ice cream."

"Well"—Joe-Annie cocked her head—"maybe just one little kick now and—"

Maxwell Joe grabbed Joe-Annie's hand and whisked her out the door.

Letting out a breath, Waylon pulled out his pocket watch. An hour and fifteen more minutes.

The drive back in the Ford with Maxwell Joe at the wheel took no more than ten minutes. He motioned Jebediah and Margaret out of the car. "Maxwell Joe, take the car around the back of the shed. Not much of a path for driving, but you'll not be noticed."

Waylon waited until the taillights flickered their last along the little-used path.

"Get in, you two." Waylon waved Margaret and Jebediah inside the woodshed. "I want you both to sit down in that far corner." With Morris and Rose Linda rendered barefoot, undressed to their underwear, and tied up tight back in the cabin, all Waylon could do now was pray and wait.

"Sit in the corner? That ain't gonna paint no good picture for Gopher. Me and Maggie squattin' like we was prisoners. Gopher gonna figure out you holdin' a gun on us."

Margaret turned in the middle of the shed floor and faced Waylon. "He's right. If Gopher feels threatened, he'll just make the terms of the deed all the more harsh." His sister glanced around the shed and spotted a shovel. "If . . . if Gopher refuses to negotiate, I'll help you, but you've got to listen to us first."

The thought of Lady Margaret wielding a shovel against the side of Gopher Dennis's head threatened to bring a smile to Waylon's lips. But he tapped at the Beretta in his waistband. He felt the steel of the other weapon tucked in his sock. He stared at Margaret. Dare he trust her offer of help? Even a little bit?

"Waylon, you always did think of yourself as sittin' mighty high. Too high for a colored." Jebediah leaned against the back wall, his knees bent. "I'll sit myself down if that's what you wantin', but that's a bone-headed move if you was to be askin' me."

Seventy minutes. Could be less. That's all he had. Now was not the time to trade insults with Jebediah Slocum.

Margaret turned to her husband. "What would you do?"

"You ain't the one need to be askin' me that question, Maggie. That needs to come from your brother."

"All right. All right." Anything to shut up Jebediah. "What do you have in mind?"

"Whatever it is you got in your head ain't gonna work with Gopher. He told you often 'nough he don't believe in no negotiatin' with colored."

"Jebediah, you're telling me nothing I don't already know." Waylon deliberately called Jebediah by his first name.

"All right, keep on bein' stiff-necked and see where it gets you." Jebediah slid to his haunches. "Iffen I was you, I would settle my mind into acceptin' you ain't gonna get what you want. You gonna have to sign them papers one way or t'other."

"You forget, Gopher's bait is gone. I've got Joe-Annie."

"For now." Jebediah followed Waylon with his eyes.

Waylon tapped at his pocket watch. "What do you suggest?"

"Like I said, you ain't gonna like it 'cause you got to give the bet-ter part of your oil land over to Slocum-Dennis Oil. That ain't what Maggie's wantin', but that's the only way to keep you coloreds from hangin' from a tree. It don't do me no good if folks find out Maggie's a colored woman. Gopher thinks he knows, but all he really knows is gossip. To keep him from stirrin' the pot, you gonna have to make him a sweet deal."

"How sweet?"

"Maggie"—Jebediah turned to Margaret—"you asked me 'bout that land I bought over in Ouachita County, near Camden. I bought it 'cause if Gopher gets to hirin' detectives and whatnot to find out 'bout you, then I have some place to go." He clasped his hands over his knees. "Iffen I was you, Waylon, I'd get me and mine clean out of Union County. I'll let you take that land off my hands for next to nothin'."

"You'd be safe there," Margaret said, her excited voice rising.

Waylon put a finger to his lips. He listened for sounds outside the door.

"Safe? With our land stolen from us? I don't believe I can do such a thing." Waylon shook his head.

"Let me talk to Gopher. You sign most of your land over and get Tom-Tom's woman to do the same, and you'll get to keep a little somethin'. Most of all, you get to keep you and your'n still breathin'.'"

"You want me to give Gopher Dennis that which he has absolutely no right to?"

"Waylon, please listen." Margaret turned to her husband. "Jebediah, do you think you could talk Gopher into letting Waylon and Ladora keep some of their oil land if I were in charge of administering it?"

Jebediah cocked his head. "If I'm in charge of it. Maybe. But what Gopher's most likely to agree to is for your colored folks to get a piece of money every month from the oil."

"A piece of money is not enough." Waylon pulled out the Beretta.

Margaret grabbed the barrel and shook her head. "Waylon, this is Arkansas in 1922. It's the same as Arkansas in 1822. It's never going to change." She dropped to her knees. "Please. Please. I can't bear it if anything happens to you or Joe-Annie or Salome . . . any of my family." The tears came. "Please listen to Jebediah."

"Your brother's got the thinkin' of a mule. No need of you pleadin'. He's gonna do the wrong thing no matter how many times right is pointed out to him." Jebediah eased himself to his feet. "You keep on runnin' your mouth 'bout the land your pa left you—the Hardin legacy. What you ain't got sense 'nough to see is you already got what your pa wanted you to have more'n anything."

Waylon shook his head. "What did my father want me to have more than anything?"

"Your name."

"My name?"

"You're duke of Union County. I can't say I really understand all that old English stuff, but I know that's what Old Man Hardin wanted for you. And I know that's what he set great store by." Jebediah ran his tongue over his teeth. "Duke this one, duke that one—all the way back six, seven hundred years. Meant more to that old man than anything. He ain't given that title to Margaret. She ain't nobody's duchess. Morris don't have it and never will. Just you. And you get to pass it on to your boy, Freddie. Not mine. Not Junior. My boy's a good boy. Smart, too. But he ain't never gonna be a duke even if it *is* all pretend."

"Morris, you in there?" A hard knock, then two soft ones. Gopher Dennis's whisper poured through the thick door.

"It's me," Jebediah called out. "I got me Margaret in here. Give her a minute to get her dress back on." He turned to Waylon and mouthed, "You're the one meant ever'thin' to Lord Hardin."

"Finish your business with her, then open this door. Where's Morris? He watchin' you give his mama that whuppin' she's been askin' for?"

"Five mo' minutes, Gopher." Jebediah looked at the still-latched door. He slipped a finger to his lips.

Duke of Union County. Henry Hardin had worn that make-believe title as though it were the greatest honor in the world, and the late duke had passed it on to him. Next would be Freddie. What was that old book Lord Hardin insisted Waylon memorize? *Brook's Peerage?*

That was it. All the dukes of Norwalk back to the fourteenth century. Jebediah's words did hold the ring of truth. That book had been more dear to Henry Hardin than the Good Book.

They spoke in hushed tones. "He trusted me with his title. And his honor," Waylon whispered.

"You always gonna be the duke as long as you live. And it ain't like you gonna be dirt-poor, neither. You ain't gonna have much in the way of oil money that's for sure, but money ain't ever'thin'. From what I'm seein', there's men around Gopher that won't stop at nothin'—not hurtin' a man, nor a woman, nor even a child—to get control of that oil land. Won't take nothin' to wipe you all off the face of the earth in six months' time."

Waylon's mouth felt dry. Jebediah—coarse, ignorant Jebediah Slocum—knew the truth. "So it's come down to this. Oil or my family."

"I reckon you thinkin' a lot of this here is wrong. I ain't sayin' I see it like you do—God made the white man to rule over the colored—but I can tell you're wishin' it weren't so."

"Jebediah, you finished with that woman yet?" Gopher rattled the knob.

"Gopher's standin' outside that door waitin' with papers in his hand. You can keep your name and pass it down forevermore, or you can tear up them papers. Just so's you know that if you do rip 'em up, won't be no more duke of Union County. Never. No matter how you play it, Waylon, oil gonna win."

Waylon walked to the door, undid the latch, spotted two wildcatters flanking the new oil baron, rifles in the crooks of their arms. "Come on in, Mr. Dennis, let's talk business."

CHAPTER
FORTY-FIVE

Where were the clouds? The rain? Wasn't it supposed to rain at funerals—especially one for your mother? Not today. September 14, 1942. Not a cloud in the blue Arkansas sky. A little breeze just to keep everyone comfortable in the 78-degree weather. But then, this wasn't really the funeral part—that had happened an hour ago in Camden. This was the burial. In Smackover.

"Waylon?" Margaret walked up to him carrying something covered in brown paper. "I know there's no sense in asking if you're all right. None of us are. Good to see you and Emerald back in Union County. We don't get together as often as we should."

A weak smile played across Waylon's face. "Yes, we're all scattered about. Ladora and the kids in Little Rock. It's hard to keep track sometimes." He looked down at the bronze casket with the worked ivy vines on both sides. Mama. Salome. "You put her between Lord Hardin and Maxwell Joe. She'd like that."

"I think that's what Mama would have wanted—lying between two men who loved her so."

That little breeze blew, and his sister's frizzy hair brushed back a little from the side of her face. Why hadn't he seen it before? Margaret Slocum was a white-skinned version of their mother—the shape of the nose, that oval face. And his sister's hair was almost as white as Salome's when she passed five days ago. Why shouldn't it be? Margaret was sixty-three.

"Papa." Joe-Annie, arm in arm with Emerald, picked her way through the grassy area that was the Hardin family cemetery. "For Grandma." She held three red carnations. She kissed each bloom, one by one, and let them slip through her fingers and into the still-open grave. She turned to Margaret.

"Thank you, Mrs. Slocum, for allowing my grandmother to be buried on Hardin land. I know it means a lot to her."

"Aunt Margaret. You're to call me Aunt Margaret when we're in private." She smiled at Joe-Annie. "You're my niece and a Hardin, and all the Hardins are entitled to be buried here." She smiled, just a little. "At least you were a Hardin until you married a Clay."

Joe-Annie wiped at an eye with her white hanky. "I'll always remember Uncle Tom-Tom and Aunt Ladora." Her pink-lipsticked lips trembled. "But they're buried together at Uncle's little church in Lisbon, not on Hardin land."

"That's what Tom-Tom would have wanted." Waylon still felt that unalterable surge for justice—a signal from his brother—whenever he thought of Tom-Tom.

Margaret, misty eyed, forced a smile. "Joe-Annie, tell me about that husband of yours now that he's joined the military."

"Grandma approved, you know. She really liked William." Joe-Annie twisted her handkerchief.

"Salome took to him right away." Emerald turned a face sporting a mock frown toward Joe-Annie. "Unfortunately, I can't say the same about myself. It took me a while to get used to the idea. Your father and I sent you up north to school. The next thing we know, you've eloped with a college boy from St. Louis." Emerald clutched the lilies she carried to her chest. "Bless Salome. I'm so grateful the Good Lord took her without a day of sickness. She told me good-night Monday, and Tuesday morning she was no more." Emerald scattered the lilies over the casket.

Waylon laid his arm around Emerald's shoulders. "She'd been pining for Maxwell Joe these past seven months. It was like she didn't want to be here after she lost him."

Margaret dabbed at her eyes. "I know I should have visited more often. But what with my lumbago . . . Still, if Salome had shown someone she wasn't feeling up to snuff, I would have found a way to be with her." She turned to Joe-Annie. "Did your husband ever see Mama more than that one time? I never met the man." Margaret shook her head. "Is it the Navy he's joined?"

Waylon gathered his sister into his embrace. "Will Clay doesn't like the South. Only came down to Camden once to show off our first granddaughter, Salome Eyota." He looked down at the coffin. "Mama loved all of her brood. She approved of Joe-Annie's choice even when Emerald and I were throwing fits."

"I did not throw a fit. I was merely disappointed that my daughter didn't choose to have a proper wedding." Emerald caught Margaret's eye. "You know, a long white dress, flowers, a church. Instead, she ran off to City Hall." She winked at Waylon. "Just like the two of us."

Margaret broke away, a wistful look on her face. "Oh, here come Jebediah and Freddie now." She called out to her nephew: "You look very handsome in that uniform. Did Mama get a chance to see you all decked out?"

Freddie, in his army uniform, smiled.

"Salome telephoned. Not as much as I would have liked." Margaret let out a little chuckle. "You know how much she hated to use that *telephone contraption,* as she called it."

Waylon tapped at his son's shoulder. "Refused to have one in her house. She made Maxwell Joe bring her over to my house whenever she felt there was no way out of it and she had to use the thing." Waylon returned his sister's grin. The memory was sweet.

"I remember." Freddie nodded.

Margaret brushed away a tear. "But, Freddie, she wanted to talk . . . about you. She told me she was both proud and worried after you were drafted."

"What's this I hear tell 'bout you lettin' Joe-Annie go off to California?" Jebediah walked up.

He stuck out a hand to Waylon.

"Good to see you back on Hardin property."

Waylon scanned the acres—land he barely recognized. Had it been twenty years? Though he saw Margaret three or four times a year—and Jebediah even less—he couldn't bear to look at the loss, a legacy that should have been shared by all of Henry Hardin's children. "You've made quite a few changes." He took Jebediah's hand.

"Had to put up a stout fence 'round most of the land surroundin' the house."

"Why's that?" Even if he tried, Waylon couldn't miss the barbed wire and armed guards standing near the thirty or so oil wells he saw pumping as he drove up a newly paved road to Hardin House.

"Unwelcome visitors," Margaret answered. "But you know Jebediah and I moved to Little Rock about twelve years ago. Too many curiosity seekers coming to Smackover to see where the great oil strike occurred."

"Anyone living in the old house now?" Emerald rubbed Waylon's back.

Margaret hesitated and her face flushed. She glanced awkwardly down at the grave. Jebediah looked first at Waylon, then the others.

His gaze settled back on Joe-Annie. "So, what are you doin' runnin' off to California?"

Waylon watched his sister as she shot a *Be careful* glance at her husband.

"No, Mr. Slocum, I'm not running off anywhere." Joe-Annie looked at her brother. "When my husband finishes his basic training at Great Lakes, he'll be transferred to California." She sucked in her lips. "He'll be put aboard a ship and sent to the South Pacific. I want to be as close to him as possible when he comes back."

Freddie gave his sister a quick hug. "I'll be stationed in New Jersey with my wife and my boy, Henry. Once I'm shipped to Europe, my family's going to join Joe-Annie in San Francisco."

"Henry's eleven already, if you can believe how fast time flies." Emerald turned to Joe-Annie. "Go on, tell the rest."

"Aunt Margaret." Joe-Annie took in a big breath. "Mama wants me to confess. I'm taking a job."

"A jo . . . ?" Margaret laid a hand over her heart. "My word."

Joe-Annie bubbled. "I read in the newspaper that the shipyards out in California are desperate for workers. Women workers. I'm going to be a . . ." She turned a sheepish grin to Waylon.

"A riveter." He laughed. "My daughter, Lady Joe-Annie Hardin Clay—college graduate and a trained teacher—is going to build ships in Richmond, California, while her mother and I take care of the two girls back home."

Margaret looked stunned.

Emerald laid a hand over her arm while she grabbed Joe-Annie with the other. "If you don't mind, Margaret, can we go up to the old house? You know, I've never been inside. Maybe Joe-Annie can explain herself better there." She stared down at the coffin as workmen shoveled in the first pile of dirt. "I don't want Mama Salome to hear the story of a married woman working outside the home when she doesn't have to."

Jebediah turned to follow. Waylon laid a hand on his back.

"A word, Jebediah. Who's living in Hardin House?"

Jebediah waited until the women were out of earshot. "Morris. Off and on, but he ain't there now."

Waylon cocked his head as more dirt rained down on Salome's casket.

Jebediah worked his mouth before he turned to look Waylon in the eye. "He's a drunk. Margaret says Morris is just like her uncle James. Sixteen years back we had to put him in the sanitarium for the first time. The best money could buy. After a year or two in there, the doctors told us he was good as new. We brought him home—back here to Hardin House. He lasted six months, then we had to send him back. Keeps happenin' over and over."

"What sets him off?" Freddie asked. He knew every detail of the Morris Slocum story.

Jebediah looked from Freddie to Waylon. He kept his eyes on Waylon. "A hauntin'. Oh, Morris, he don't call it that. He just says he can't sleep at night because . . . of the visitations. Says that's why he drinks."

Waylon looked over at Freddie, a questioning look on his son's face. Waylon knew what was coming next.

"Tom-Tom." Jebediah's mouth set into a thin line. "Wearin' minister robes and holdin' a gold cross. Sometimes sayin' Catholic things in a foreign tongue."

"My uncle Tom-Tom? Are you saying this Morris person sees my father's brother though the man's been dead twenty years?"

"All the time, to hear Morris tell it. Won't leave him alone. Stands there dressed in black, showin' this gold cross, first the front and then the back, and talkin' in a funny language. Morris says Tom-Tom's busy condemnin' him to the worst part of Hell."

"A funny language?" Waylon remembered the many Latin lessons he'd drilled into Tom-Tom at the little schoolroom Henry Hardin built at Salome's house. Once, when Waylon was about twelve or thirteen,

Henry ordered him always to be generous to the Catholic Church even though Waylon was a Baptist. When Waylon plucked up his courage enough to ask why, Lord Hardin said it was a duty all Hardins had a responsibility to discharge. At the time, Waylon had understood none of it. He turned to Jebediah. "Catholic things?"

"Morris says ain't no two ways 'bout it. Tom-Tom comes to him, night after night, sometimes even in the day, holdin' that cross, but callin' it a crucifix, and sayin' Catholic things. Morris says there ain't 'nough alcohol in the world to make that apparition go away, but he keeps on tryin'. Doctors don't hold out much hope for him. Liver's shot."

"Grandma used to say the Lord works in mysterious ways." Freddie spread his hands.

"The wonders of the Lord are many," Waylon said, recalling one of his brother's favorite sayings. "Your boy. Where is Junior?"

"New York City. Couldn't wait to get away from this place. Been gone fifteen years. Workin' for Dennis Oil. Last time he come home was three years back."

"And he's not here for Salome." Waylon tried to keep the criticism out of his voice.

"He called his ma. Margaret told him to do what he thought best."
Waylon nodded. "Hmm. New York City and Dennis Oil."

"I remember Junior." Freddie squinted. "Let me see if I've got this straight. Grandma Salome told me her father was an Irishman." Freddie turned to Jebediah. "Even with three generations of white men in his line—you, his grandfather, and his great-grandfather—Junior's still a colored man. I don't suppose he's told anyone at Dennis Oil that little detail? I wonder how long Gopher Dennis would keep him in the employ of Dennis Oil if another white man found out what Gopher knows."

"Freddie!" Waylon cautioned. "You've been in the North too long. You know we respect family members who choose to pass."

Jebediah shook his head. "Oh, Gopher, he thinks he knows what's what with Margaret, that's for sure, but he likes to keep his hand on a person's neck. He figure if he just hints a bit, then Junior will do his bidding. He don't know Junior. Best for me and Maggie that way. You, too. Gopher keeps Junior, and me and Margaret get a little bit of inside information on Dennis Oil doin's. Otherwise, Gopher just sends us a check every month and nothing else."

"If Junior wants to pass, I'll not be the cousin standing in his way, but is the information he's privy to at Dennis Oil going to make things right for my branch of the family?" Freddie sent an accusatory look toward Jebediah.

Waylon raised his voice. "This is not the time nor place, Freddie."

"Papa, there's never going to be a right time or a correct place if we wait for someone else to set them. We've got to be the ones to pick our own time and place."

Jebediah straightened the lapels of his black funeral coat as the last shovels of soil covered the casket. "The country's at war. Needs a lot of oil. A lot of money comin' into Dennis Oil 'bout now. More'n the last twenty years. If Dennis Oil didn't stop at nothin' in '22 to grab that oil—Tom-Tom, Joe-Annie, your own pa—you don't want to imagine what they gonna do with all this war oil at stake." He shook his head. "I don't reckon it's wise for you, Freddie, to call that time and place right now."

"Maybe not, but this war can't last forever, and God willing, I will survive. I'm going to make sure that time and place is called one day. If not by me, then by my boy, Henry."

"Waylon." Margaret stepped quickly down the path from the main house, holding out the brown package. "I almost forgot to give you this." She laughed. "Here."

He frowned as he took the parcel from his sister, untied the string, and removed the brown wrapper. He looked down at a book with cracked edges. *"American Descendants of the Dukes of Norwalk."* He sent a quizzical glance to his sister.

She smiled as she pointed. "It's for you. Open it."

Waylon turned the pages. Even after fifty years, the paper felt the same. Smelled the same. There were the opening two pages listing the English dukes—all the old names he'd memorized: Henry I, Duke of Norwalk, 1302; Henry II, Duke of Norwalk, 1423; James III, 1501; Frederick III, executed by the swordsman, Tower of London, 1629.

"Not there." Margaret sounded impatient. She turned the page. "Here."

Waylon stared at a page he'd never seen before. There, in the center of the book, the Hardin family pages listing the births and deaths in the Hardin line going back to the beginning of their American exile. She flipped nine, ten more pages and there it was—their father's name, Henry Hardin—the third in the line. In Lord Hardin's own hand came Margaret's name; then his—Waylon Frederick, born November 3, 1882; and finally, Tom-Tom's—Thomas Hardin. "What's this?" Waylon flipped a page and stared at the next entry. Frederick Hardin, born 1909 in Smackover, Arkansas. "Who wrote . . . ?" He recognized his sister's hand.

"Here." Margaret held out one of those new fountain pens. "You're to write down the name of your grandson."

Waylon passed the book to Freddie. "You're going to be the care-taker of this now—the book and our name."

Freddie took the pen offered by Margaret. He shook his head. "I'll come back from this war. I'll bide my time." He looked up at Jebediah. "If not me, then Henry, if not him, then his son, even his grandson, but one day justice will be done for all those who've gone before. I owe it to Uncle Tom-Tom, Grandpa Maxwell Joe, Salome, Grandma's driven-out-of-her-mind mother, Eyota. We will have our legacy and our land back."

Freddie flattened the page, removed the cap from the fountain pen, and took his time spelling out the name of his son. Henry IV. Born 1931 in Camden, Arkansas. Duke of Union County.

ACKNOWLEDGMENTS

No writer can get his or her novel before the eyes of the public without standing on the strong shoulders of a horde of other people. To all of them, I owe a deep debt of gratitude. Thank you, Alex, Anne, Bruce, David, and Risa, for your dogged determination that I stay true to the craft of writing. To you, Jodi Warshaw, senior acquisitions editor at Amazon Publishing, a multitude of thanks for seeing what I saw in *The Daughter of Union County*. Kelli Martin and Amara Holstein of Lake Union Publishing, your support has been invaluable. Thanks to the California Writers Club—Berkeley Branch, for your constant reminders of the joys of being a writer. My family and friends—Hank, Doug, Lidia, Andrew, Tootsie, Rozelle, Juanda, Gilles—I know I can depend upon you to draw much-needed strength. Most of all, I offer thanks to three generations of my husband's family. Your immeasurable sacrifices in the struggle to correct an injustice laid down the inspiration for the writing of *The Daughter of Union County*. Thank you all.

ABOUT THE AUTHOR

Francine Thomas Howard is the author of *Page from a Tennessee Journal* and *Paris Noire*. Exploring the multicultural legacy of African-descended people throughout the diaspora, her stories reflect her own African, European, and Native American heritage. Originally from Illinois, Howard earned a BA in occupational therapy from San José State and an MPA from the University of San Francisco. She left a rewarding career in pediatric occupational therapy to pursue another love, writing. Desiring to preserve the remarkable oral histories of her family tree, she began writing down those stories with little thought to publication. That all changed when she turned a family secret about her grandmother and grandfathers into *Page from a Tennessee Journal*. Howard submitted the novel to the Amazon Breakthrough Novel Award contest. Weeks after the contest ended, Howard was contacted by Amazon Publishing. She resides with her family in the San Francisco Bay Area.